"*Lazybones* isn't your formulaic murder mystery . . . Deft touches with character and humor help set it apart from the crowd."
Detroit Free Press

"It's difficult enough to write even one exceptional thriller, but when you consistently turn out engrossing tales, you have one exceptional storytelling talent. Mark Billingham has that kind of talent, as his third thriller shows. With *Lazybones* following *Scaredy Cat* and *Sleepyhead*, Billingham has won the trifecta and readers have scored big."
Denver Rocky Mountain News

"There is a pleasantly nasty streak of mordant humor running just below the surface of this story . . . Billingham has such a command of his craft and his characters that he quickly lets us know Thorne will do his job—or die trying."
Chicago Tribune

Mark Billingham is the new-wave leader . . . Like the best of British and American crime writing rolled up together and delivered with the kind of punch you don't see coming."
Lee Child

Books by Mark Billingham

THE BURNING GIRL
LAZYBONES
SCAREDY CAT
SLEEPYHEAD

LAZY BONES

MARK BILLINGHAM

Avon Books
An Imprint of HarperCollins Publishers

This book was originally published in Great Britain in 2003 by Little, Brown and Company.

AVON BOOKS
An Imprint of HarperCollins*Publishers*
10 East 53rd Street
New York, New York 10022-5299

First Avon Books paperback printing: June 2005
First William Morrow hardcover printing: June 2004

For
Pat and Tony Thompson
and
Jeff and Pam Billingham

ACKNOWLEDGMENTS

Thanks are due to those people who helped this particular lazybones get this one done. . . .

DI Neil Hibberd of the Serious Crime Group (again) for his insight, for fighting off the desire to sleep, and for providing the usual invaluable advice.

Victoria Jones, for answering a thousand stupid questions, and, ironically, opening the right doors.

The governor, staff, and inmates of HMP Birmingham.

Sarah Kennedy, for kind words, very early, where the pictures are best.

Wendy Burns—supervising social worker (Fostering)—and Louise Spanner—family placement panel administrator—at Essex Social Services.

And of course . . . Hilary Hale, Sarah Lutyens, Susannah Godman, Mike and Alice Gunn, Paul Thorne, Wendy Lee, and Peter Cocks.

And my wife, Claire. I still demand a recount . . .

For one night or the other night,
will come the Gardener in white, and
gathered flowers are dead . . .

—James Elroy Flecker,
Golden Journey to Samarkand

Prologue

Prologue

13 March

Dearest Dougie,

I'm sorry about this being another typed letter, but as I explained before, it's difficult for me to write to you from home, so I do it at work when the boss isn't looking, or in my lunch hour (like today!) or whatever. So, sorry if it seems a bit formal. Trust me, when I'm writing to you, the <u>last</u> thing I'm feeling is formal!

I hope things with you are OK and even if they're not brilliant, I hope that my letters are making you feel a bit better. I like to dream that you look forward to them and that you think of me sitting here, thinking about you. At least you have the pictures now (did you like them?), so you don't have to use your imagination <u>too</u> much . . . (wicked grin!)

I know that it's really horrible in there but you must believe that things will get better. One day you will be out, with a bright future. Is it silly of me to hope that perhaps I can play a part in that future? I know that you are in there when you should not be. <u>I know that you being in that place is unjust!!</u>

I should sign off now, because I want to get this in the post before the lunch hour is over and I haven't had anything to eat yet. Writing to you, feeling near to you, is more important than a cheese sarnie anyway (she sighs!).

I will write again soon, Dougie, maybe with another picture. Do you put them on the wall? I don't even know if you have a cell all to yourself or not. If not, I hope whoever you are sharing with is nice. They are very lucky!!

It will all be over soon and when you are out of there, who knows, perhaps we can finally get together. I'm sure the wait will have been worth it.

Please look after yourself, Dougie. Hope you're thinking about me.

Yours, VERY frustrated . . .

Jane ☺
xxx
xx
x

Part One

Births, Marriages and Deaths

August 10, 1976

He inched himself toward the edge, each tightening of the sphincter muscle moving him a little farther across the narrow breadth of the banister's polished surface. He twisted his wrists, wrapping the towel once more tightly around them. Not giving himself the get-out, knowing his body would look for it. Knowing he would instinctively try to free himself.

His heels bounced rhythmically against the banister spindles below him. The blue tow rope that he'd found at the back of the garage was itchy against his neck. He smiled to himself. Scratching it, even if he could, would have been stupid. Like dabbing at the skin with disinfectant before slipping in the needle to administer a lethal injection.

He closed his eyes, bowed his head, and let his weight tip him forward and over and down.

It felt as if the jolt might take his head off, but it was not even enough to break a bone. There hadn't been time to do the math, to set weight against height. Even if there had been, he wasn't sure he'd have known what the relationship between them was. He remembered reading somewhere that the proper hangmen, the Pierrepoints or whoever, could do the calculation, could figure out the necessary drop, based on nothing more than shaking the condemned man's hand.

Pleased to meet you—about twelve feet, I reckon . . .

He clenched his teeth against the pain in his back. The skin had been taken off his spine by the edge of the stair rail as he'd dropped. He could feel warm blood trickling down his chin and he realized that he'd bitten through his tongue. He could smell the motor oil on the rope.

He thought about the woman, in bed, not ten feet away.

It would have been lovely to have seen her face when she found him. Her liar's mouth falling open as she reached up to stop his body swinging. That would have been perfect, but of course he would never see it. And she would never find him.

Somebody else would find both of them.

He couldn't help but wonder what the authorities would make of it all. What the newspapers would say. Their names would be spoken, would be whispered again in certain offices and living rooms. His *name*, the one he'd given her, would echo around a courtroom as it had done so often before, dragged through the mud and the filth that she'd spread before her like an oil slick. This time they themselves would be mercifully absent as others talked about them, about the tragedy, about the balance of their minds being disturbed. It was hard to argue with that now, this very moment. Him waiting to die, and her upstairs, thirty minutes ahead of him, the blood already soaking deep into their mushroom-colored bedroom carpet.

She had disturbed both their minds. She had asked for everything she'd got.

Half an hour before, her hands reaching to pro-
tect herself.

Eight months before that, her hands reaching,
her legs spread, on the floor of that stockroom.

She'd asked for everything . . .

He gagged, spluttering blood, sensing a shadow
preparing to descend, feeling his life beginning,
thankfully, to slip away. How long had it been
now? Two minutes? Five? He pushed his feet
down toward the floor, willing his weight to do its
work quickly.

He heard a noise like a creak and then a small
hum of amazement. He opened his eyes.

He was facing away from the front door, looking back at the staircase. He shifted his shoulders
violently, trying to create enough momentum to
make himself turn. As he spun slowly around, seconds from death, he found himself staring down,
through bloodied and bulging retinas, into the
flawless brown eyes of a child.

ONE

The look was slightly spoiled by the training shoes.

The man with the mullet haircut and the sweaty top lip was wearing a smart blue suit, doubtless acquired for the occasion, but he'd let himself down with the bright white Nike Airs. They squeaked on the gymnasium floor as his feet shifted nervously underneath the table.

"I'm sorry," he said. "I'm really, really, sorry."

An elderly couple sat at the table opposite him. The man's back was ramrod straight, his milky blue eyes never leaving those of the man in the suit. The old woman next to the old man clutched at his hand. Her eyes, unlike those of her husband, looked anywhere but at those of the young man who, the last time he'd been this close to them, had been tying them up in their own home.

The trembling was starting around the center of Darren Ellis's meticulously shaved chin. His voice wobbled a little. "If there was anything I could do to make it up to you, I would," he said.

"There isn't," the old man said.

"I can't take back what I did, but I do know how wrong it was. I know what I put you through."

The old woman began to cry.

"How can you?" her husband said.

Darren Ellis began to cry.

In the last row of seats, his back against the gym wall-bars, sat a solid-looking man in a black leather jacket, forty or so, with dark eyes and hair that was grayer on one side than the other. He looked uncomfortable and a little confused. He turned to the man sitting next to him.

"This. Is. Bullshit," Thorne said.

DCI Russell Brigstocke glared at him. There was a *shush* from a red-haired grunt type a couple of rows in front. One of Ellis's supporters, by the look of him.

"Bullshit," Thorne repeated.

The gymnasium at the Peel Centre would normally be full of eager recruits at this unearthly time on a Monday morning. It was, however, the largest space available for this "Restorative Justice Conference," so the raw young constables were doing their press-ups and star jumps elsewhere. The floor of the gym had been covered with a green tarpaulin and fifty or so seats had been laid out. They were filled with supporters of both offender and victims, together with invited officers who, it was thought, would appreciate the opportunity to be brought up to speed with this latest initiative.

Becke House, where Thorne and Brigstocke were based, was part of the same complex. Half an hour earlier, on the five-minute walk across to the gym, Thorne had moaned without drawing breath.

"If it's an invitation, how come I'm not allowed to turn it down?"

"Shut up," Brigstocke said. They were late and he was walking quickly, trying not to spill hot coffee from a polystyrene cup that was all but melting. Thorne lagged a step or two behind.

"Shit, I've forgotten the bit of paper, maybe they won't let me in."

Brigstocke scowled, unamused.

"What if I'm not smart enough? There might be a dress code . . ."

"I'm not listening, Tom . . ."

Thorne shook his head, flicked out his foot at a stone like a sulky schoolboy. "I'm just trying to get it straight. This piece of pond life ties an old couple up with electrical tape, gives the old man a kick or two for good measure, breaking . . . how many ribs?"

"Three . . ."

"Three. Thanks. He pisses on their carpet, fucks off with their life savings, and now we're rushing across to see how sorry he is?"

"It's just a trial. They've been using RJCs in Australia and the results have been pretty bloody good. Reoffending rates have gone right down . . ."

"So, basically, they sit everybody down presentence, and if they all agree that the guilty party is really *feeling* guilty, he gets to do a bit less time. That it?"

Brigstocke took a last, scalding slurp and dumped the half-full cup in a bin. "It's not quite that simple."

A week and a bit into a steaming June, but the day was still too new to have warmed up yet. Thorne shoved his hands deeper into the pockets of his leather jacket.

"No, but whoever thought it up is."

In the gym, the audience watched as Darren Ellis moved balled-up fists from in front of his face to reveal moist, red eyes. Thorne looked around at those watching. Some looked sad and shook their heads. One or two were taking notes. In the front row, members of Ellis's legal team passed pieces of paper between them.

"If I said that *I* felt like a victim, would you laugh?" Darren asked.

The old man looked calmly at him for fifteen seconds or more before answering flatly. "I'd want to knock your teeth out."

"Things aren't always that clear-cut," Darren said.

The old man leaned across the table. The skin was tight around his mouth. "I'll tell you what's clear-cut." His eyes flicked toward his wife as he spoke. "She hasn't slept since the night you came into our house. She wets the bed most of the time." His voice dropped to a whisper. "She's got so bloody thin . . ."

Something between a gulp and a gasp echoed around the gymnasium as Darren dropped his head into his hands and gave full vent to his emotions. A lawyer got to his feet. A senior detective stood up and started walking toward the table. It was time to take a break.

Thorne leaned across and whispered loudly to Brigstocke. "He's very good. What drama school did he go to?" This time, several of the faces that turned to look daggers at him belonged to senior officers . . .

Ten minutes later, and everybody was mingling in the foyer outside. There was a lot of nodding and hushed conversation. There was mineral water and biscuits.

"I'm supposed to write a report on this," Brigstocke mumbled.

Thorne waved across the foyer to a couple of lads he knew from Team 6. "Rather you than me."

"I'm trying to decide the right word to use, to describe the attitude of certain attending officers on my team. Obstructive? Insolent? You got any thoughts . . . ?"

"I *think* that was one of the stupidest things I've ever seen. I can't believe people sat there and took it seriously and I don't care *what* the results were in sodding Australia. Actually, no, *not* stupid. It was obscene. All those silly bastards studying every expression on that little prick's face. How many tears? How big were they? How much shame?" Thorne took a swig of water, held it in his mouth for a few seconds, swallowed. "Did you see *her* face? Did you look at the old woman's face?"

Brigstocke's mobile rang. He answered it quickly, but Thorne kept on talking anyway. "Restorative Justice? For who? For that old man and his skeletal wife?"

Brigstocke shook his head angrily, turned away.

Thorne put his glass down on a windowsill. He moved suddenly, pushing past several people as he walked quickly toward where he'd seen a group emerging from a door on the other side of the foyer.

Darren Ellis had taken his jacket and tie off. He was handcuffed, a detective on either side of him, their hands on his shoulders.

"Good show, Darren," Thorne said. He raised his hands and started to clap.

Ellis stared, his mouth opening and closing, an uneasy expression that had definitely *not* been rehearsed. He looked for help to the officers on either side of him.

Thorne smiled. "What do you do for an encore? Always best to finish on a song, I reckon . . ."

The officer to Ellis's left, a stick-thin article with dandruff on his brown polyester jacket, tried his best to look casually intimidating. "Piss off, Thorne."

Before Thorne had a chance to respond, his attention was caught by the figure of Russell Brigstocke marching purposefully across the room toward him. Thorne was hardly aware of the two detectives leading Ellis away in the other direction. The look on the DCI's face caused something to clench in his stomach.

"You want to restore some justice?" Brigstocke said. "Now's your chance." He pointed at Thorne with his mobile phone. "This sounds like a good one . . ."

It was called a hotel. They also called MPs "right," "honorable," and "gentlemen" . . .

The sign outside *said* HOTEL, but Thorne knew full well that certain signs, in less salubrious parts of London, were not to be taken too literally. If they all meant exactly what they said, there would be a lot of frustrated businessmen sitting in saunas, waiting for hand jobs they were never going to get.

The sign outside should have read SHITHOLE.

It was as basic as they came. The maroon carpet, once the finest offcut the warehouse had to offer, was now worn through in a number of places. The green of the rotting rubber underlay beneath matched the mold that snaked up the off-white wallpaper below the window. A long-dead spider plant stood on the window ledge, caked in dust. Thorne pushed aside the grubby orange curtains, leaned against the ledge, and took in the breathtaking view of the traffic inching slowly past Paddington Station toward the Marylebone Road. Nearly eleven o'clock and still solid.

Thorne turned around and sucked in a breath. Opposite him in the doorway, DC Dave Holland stood chatting to a uniform—waiting, like Thorne, for the signal to step in and start. To sink both feet deep into the mire.

In different parts of the room, three scene-of-crime officers crouched and crawled—bagging and tagging and searching for the fiber, the grain that might convict. The life sentence hidden in a dustball. The truth lurking in detritus.

The pathologist, Phil Hendricks, leaned against a wall, muttering into the new digital voice recorder he was so proud of. He glanced up at Thorne. A look that asked the usual questions. Are we up and running again? When is this going to get any easier? Why don't the two of us chuck in this shit and sit in a doorway for the rest of our lives drinking aftershave? Thorne, unable to provide any answers, looked away. In the corner nearest him, a fourth SOCO, whose bald head and bodysuit gave him the look of a giant baby, dusted the taps of the brown plastic sink with fingerprint powder.

It was, at least, a shithole with en suite facilities.

Altogether, seven of them in the room. Eight, if you counted the corpse.

Thorne's gaze was dragged reluctantly across to the

chalk-white figure of the man on the bed. The body was nude and lay on the bare mattress, the spots of blood joining stains of less obvious origin on the threadbare and faded ticking. The hands were tied with a brown leather belt and pushed out in front of him as he lay, prostrate, his knees pulled up beneath him, his backside in the air. His head, which was covered in a black hood, was pressed down into the sagging mattress.

Thorne watched as Phil Hendricks moved along the bed, lifted the head, and turned it. He slowly removed the hood. From behind, Thorne saw his friend's shoulders stiffen for an instant, heard the small, sharp intake of breath before he laid the head back down. As a SOCO moved across to take the hood and drop it into an exhibits bag, Thorne took a step forward so that he could see the face of the dead man clearly.

His eyes were closed, his nose small and slightly upturned. The side of the face was dotted with pinprick-size blood spots. The mouth was a mask of dried gore, the lips ragged, the whole hideous mess crisscrossed with spittle strings. The stained, uneven teeth were bared and had gnawed through the bottom lip as the ligature had tightened around the neck.

Thorne guessed that the man was in his late thirties. It was just a guess.

From somewhere above them, Thorne became aware of a rumble suddenly dying—a boiler switching itself off. Stifling a yawn, he looked up, watched cobwebs dancing gracefully around the plaster ceiling rose. He wondered if the other residents would care too much about their morning hot water when they found out what had happened in Room 6.

Thorne took a pace toward the bed. Hendricks spoke without looking around.

"Bar the fact that he's dead, I know nothing, so don't even ask. All right?"

"I'm fine. Thanks for asking, Phil, and how are you?"

"Right, I see. Like you only came over here for a fucking chinwag . . . ?"

"You are *such* a miserable sod. What's wrong with exchanging a few pleasantries? Trying to make all this a bit easier?"

Hendricks said nothing.

Thorne leaned over to scratch at his ankle through the bodysuit. "Phil . . ."

"I told you, I don't know. Look for yourself. It seems pretty obvious how he died, but it's not that simple. There's . . . other stuff gone on."

"Right. Thanks . . ."

Hendricks moved back a little and nodded toward one of the SOCOs, who moved quickly toward the bed, picking up a small toolbox as he went. The officer knelt down and opened the box, revealing a display of dainty, shining instruments. He took out a small scalpel and leaned across, reaching toward the victim's neck.

Thorne watched as the SOCO pushed a plastic-covered finger down between the ligature and the neck, struggling to get some purchase. From where Thorne was standing, it looked like washing line, the sort of stuff you can get in any hardware shop. Smooth blue plastic. He could see just how tightly it was biting into the dead man's neck. The officer took his scalpel and carefully cut away the line in such a way as to preserve the knot that was gathered at the back of the neck. This was, of course, basic procedure. Sensible and chilling.

They'd need it to compare with any others they might find.

Thorne glanced across at Dave Holland, who raised his eyebrows and turned up his palms. *What's happening? How long?* Thorne shrugged. He'd been there more than an hour already. He and Holland had been over the room, taking notes, bagging a few things up, getting a feel for the scene. Now it was the technicians' turn and Thorne hated the wait. It might have made him feel better, were he able to put his impatience down to a desire to get involved. He wished he could say honestly that he was itching to begin doing his job, to kick off the process that might one day bring this man's killer to justice. As it was, he just wanted to do what had to be done quickly, and get out of that room.

He wanted to strip off the plastic suit, get in his car, and drive away.

Actually, if he were being *really* honest with himself, he would have had to admit that only *part* of him wanted that. The other part was buzzing. The part that knew the difference between some murder scenes and others; that was able to *measure* these things. Thorne had seen the victims of enraged spouses and jealous lovers. He had stared at the bodies of business rivals and gangland snitches. He knew when he was looking at something out of the ordinary.

This was a significant murder scene. This was the work of a killer driven by something special, something spectacular.

The room stank of hatred and of rage. It also stank of pride.

Hendricks, as if reading Thorne's mind, turned to him, half smiling. "Just another five minutes, okay? I'm not going to get anything else here . . ."

Thorne nodded. He looked at the dead man on the bed—the position of him, as if he were praying. Had it not been for the belt, for the livid red furrow that circled his neck, for the thin lines of blood that ran down the backs of his pale thighs, he might have been praying.

Thorne guessed that at the end, he probably had been.

The room was hot. Thorne raised an arm to rub a sore eye and felt the tickle as a drop of sweat slid down his ribs then took a sudden, sharp turn across his belly.

Down below, a frustrated driver leaned on his horn . . .

Thorne was not even aware that he'd closed his eyes, and when he heard a phone ring, he snapped them open, convinced for a few wonderful moments that he'd woken suddenly from a bad dream.

He turned, a little disoriented, and saw Holland standing next to the bedside table. The phone was an off-white seventies model, the dial cracked, the grimy handset visibly jumping in its cradle. Thorne was now fully alert but he was still somewhat confused. Was this a call for them? Was it police business? Or was it possible that whoever was down at what passed for a reception desk had not been told what was happening and had put a caller through from the outside? Having met one or two of the staff, Thorne could well believe that even knowing exactly what had happened, they might still be dim enough to put a call through to the occupant of Room 6. If that was the case, it would certainly be a stroke of luck . . .

Thorne moved toward the ringing phone. The rest of the team stood frozen, watching him.

The victim's clothes—it had to be presumed they *were* the victim's—lay strewn about the floor nearby. Trousers—minus their belt—and underpants were next to the chair. Shirt, crumpled into a ball. One shoe under the bed, up near the headboard. The brown corduroy jacket, slung across the back of a chair next to the bed, had contained no personal items. No wallet, no bus tickets, no crinkled photographs. Nothing that might help identify the dead man . . .

Thorne did not know if the phone had already been dusted for fingerprints, and he had no time to check. He reached out to grab a plastic evidence bag from the fat, babyish SOCO and wrapped it around his hand. He held the hand up, wanting silence. He didn't need to ask.

He took a breath and picked up the receiver. "Hello . . . ?"

"Oh . . . hi." A woman's voice.

Thorne locked eyes with Holland. "Who did you want to speak to?" He was holding the phone an inch or so away from his ear and didn't hear the answer properly. "Sorry, it's not a very good line, could you speak up?"

"Is that any good?"

"That's great." Thorne tried to sound casual. "Who do you want to speak to?"

"Oh . . . I'm not really sure, actually . . ."

Thorne looked at Holland again and shook his head. *Fuck.* It wasn't going to be that easy. "Who am I talking to?"

"Sorry?"

"Who are you?"

There was a short pause before she spoke. The voice was suddenly a little tighter. Confident, though, and refined. "Listen, I don't want to sound rude, but it was somebody there who called *me.* I don't particularly want to give out—"

"This is Detective Inspector Thorne from the Serious Crime Group . . ."

A pause. Then: "I thought I was calling a hotel . . ."

"You *have* called a hotel. Could you please give me your name?" He looked across at Holland, puffed out his cheeks. Holland was poised, notebook in hand, looking utterly confused.

"You could be anybody," the woman said.

"Listen, if it makes you happier, I can call you back. Better still, let me give you a number to call so you can check. Ask for DCI Russell Brigstocke. And I'll give you my mobile number . . ."

"Why do I need your mobile number if you're calling me back?"

The conversation was starting to get faintly ridiculous.

Thorne thought he could detect a note of amusement, perhaps even flirtation, creeping into this woman's voice. Pleasing as this was on an otherwise grim morning, he wasn't really in the mood.

"Madam, the phone I'm speaking on, the phone you've called, is located at a crime scene and I need to know why you're calling."

He got the message across. The woman, though suddenly sounding a little panicky, did as she was asked.

"It was on my answering machine. I got here, I got into work this morning, and checked my messages. This one was the first. The man who called left the name of the hotel and the room number for delivery . . ."

The man who called. Was that the man on the bed or . . . ?

"What was the message?"

"He was placing an order. Bloody funny time to be doing it, though. That was why I was a bit . . . cautious about calling. I thought it might be a joke, you know, kids messing about, but kids wouldn't give you the right address, would they?"

"Did he leave a name?"

"No, which is one of the reasons I'm calling. And to get a credit card number. I don't do cash on delivery . . ."

"What do you mean, 'bloody funny time'?"

"The message was left at ten past three this morning. I bought one of those flashy machines that tells you the time, you know?"

Thorne pressed the mouthpiece to his chest, looked across at Hendricks. "I know the time of death. A tenner says you don't get within half an hour either side . . ."

"Hello?"

Thorne put the phone back to his ear. "Sorry, I was conferring with a colleague. Can I ask you to keep the tape from the machine, Miss . . . ?"

"Eve Bloom."

"You said something about placing an order?"

"Oh sorry, didn't I say? I'm a florist. He was ordering some flowers. That's why I was slightly freaked out, I suppose . . ."

"I don't understand. Freaked . . . ?"

"Well, to be ordering what he was ordering in the middle of the night . . ."

"What exactly did the message say?"

"Hang on a minute . . ."

"No, just . . ."

She'd already gone. After a few seconds, Thorne heard the click of the button being hit and the noise of the tape rewinding. There was a pause and then a bang as she put the receiver down next to the machine.

"It's coming up," she shouted.

Then a hiss as the tape began to play.

There was no discernible accent, no real emotion of any sort, in the voice. To Thorne, it sounded as if someone was trying hard to *sound* characterless, but there was a hint of something like amusement in the voice somewhere. In the voice of the man Thorne had to assume was responsible for the bound and bloodied corpse not three feet away from him.

The message began simply enough.

"I'd like to order a wreath . . ."

December 3, 1975

He inched the Maxi forward until the bumper was almost touching the garage door before yanking up the handbrake and turning off the ignition.

He reached across for his briefcase, climbed out of the car, and nudged the door shut with his backside.

Not six o'clock yet and already dark. Cold as well. He was going to have to start putting his vest on in the mornings.

As he walked toward the front door he began whistling it again, that bloody song he couldn't get out of his head. It was on the radio every minute of every day. What the hell was a "silhouetto" anyway? Do the bloody fandango? The thing went on for hours as well. Weren't pop songs supposed to be short?

He shut the front door behind him and stood on the mat for a second, waiting for the smell of his dinner to hit him. He liked this moment every day, the one where he could pretend he was a character in one of those programs on the TV. He stood and imagined that he was in the Midwest of America somewhere and not stuck in a shitty little suburb. He imagined that he was a rangy executive with a perfectly presented wife who would have a pot roast in the oven and a cocktail waiting for him.

Highballs or something they called them, didn't they?

It wasn't just his little joke, it was theirs. Their silly ritual. He would shout out and she would shout back, then they would sit down and eat the frozen crispy pancakes or maybe one of those packaged curries with too many raisins in.

"Honey, I'm home . . ."

There was no reply. He couldn't smell anything.

He dropped his briefcase by the hall table and walked toward the lounge. She probably hadn't had time today. Wouldn't have finished work until gone three and then she would have had shopping to do. There was only a fortnight until Christmas and there was loads of stuff still to get . . .

The look on her face stopped him dead.

She was sitting on the settee, wearing a powder-blue housecoat. Her legs were curled underneath her. Her hair was wet.

"You all right, love?"

She said nothing. As he took a step toward her, his shoe got tangled in something and he looked down and saw the dress.

"What's this doing . . . ?"

He flicked it up and caught it, laughing, looking for a reaction. Then, letting the length of it drop from his fingers he saw the rip, waggled his fingers through the rent in the rayon.

"Christ, what have you done to this? Bloody hell, this was fifteen quids' worth . . ."

She looked up suddenly and stared at him as if he was mad. Trying not to make it obvious, he began looking around for an empty bottle, making an effort to keep a smile on his face.

"Have you been to work today, love?"

She moaned softly.

"What about school? You did pick up . . . ?"

She nodded violently, her hair tumbling damp across her face. He heard the noise then from upstairs, the crash of a toy car or a pile of bricks coming from the loft they'd turned into a playroom.

He nodded, puffed out his cheeks, relieved.

"Listen, let's get you . . ."

He had to stop himself taking a step back as she stood up suddenly, her eyes wide and wet, folding herself over slowly, as if she were taking a bow.

He said her name then.

And his wife gathered up the hem of the powder-blue housecoat and raised it above her waist to show him the redness, the rawness, and the darker blue of the bruising at the top of her legs . . .

TWO

Thorne lost his bet with Phil Hendricks.

He answered the phone barely four hours after they'd found the body and within a few seconds he was lobbing his half-eaten sandwich across the office, missing the bin by several feet. He chewed what was left in his mouth quickly, knowing that his appetite was about to disappear.

Hendricks was calling from Westminster Mortuary. "Pretty quick," he said. He sounded extremely chipper. "You've got to bloody admit—"

"Why do you always manage to do this when I'm eating lunch? Couldn't you have left it another hour?"

"Sod that, mate, there's money at stake. Right, you ready? I'm going for time of death at somewhere around quarter to three in the morning."

"Shit." Thorne stared out of the window at a row of low gray buildings on the other side of the M1. He didn't know if the window was dirty or if that was just Hendon. "This had better be worth a tenner. Go on . . ."

"Right, how d'you want it? Medical jargon, layman's terms, or pathology-made-easy for thick-as-shit coppers?"

"That's cost you half the tenner. Get on with it . . ."

Hendricks spoke about death and its intimacies with considerably less passion than he demonstrated for Arsenal Football Club. Being from Manchester and not supporting the dreaded Manchester United was far from being the only finger he stuck up at convention. There were the clothes in varying shades of black, the shaved head, the ludicrous number of earrings. There were the mysterious piercings, one for each new boyfriend. . . .

He might have *spoken* dispassionately, almost matter-of-factly, but Thorne knew how much Phil Hendricks cared about the dead. How hard he listened to their bodies when they spoke to him. When they gave up their secrets.

"Asphyxia due to ligature strangulation," Hendricks said. "Plus, I think it happened on the floor. He had carpet burns on both knees. I think the killer put the body on the bed afterward. Posed it."

"Right . . ."

"Unfortunately, I still can't tell for sure whether or not he was strangled before, after, or during the sodomy."

"So, you're not perfect, then?"

"I know one thing. Whoever did it has a big future in gay porn. Our killer's hung like a donkey. He did quite a bit of damage up there. . . ."

Thorne knew he'd been right to get rid of the sandwich. He'd lost count of the conversations like this he'd had with Hendricks over the years. His head was used to them, but his stomach still found them tricky.

Thorne called it the H-plan diet . . .

"What about secretions?"

"Sorry, mate, bugger all. Only thing up there that shouldn't have been was a trace of spermicidal lubricant from the condom he was wearing. He was careful, in every sense . . ."

Thorne sighed. "Where's Holland? He still with you?"

"No chance, mate. He shot away first chance he had. Why did you send him down anyway? Actually, I'm hurt you didn't want to watch me work . . ."

These conversations, the ones that followed bodies, always ended on something lighthearted. Football, TV, anything . . .

"DC Holland hasn't seen you work nearly *enough,* though, Phil," Thorne said. "It still gives him the heebies. I'm doing him a favor, toughening him up . . ."

Hendricks laughed. "Right . . ."

Right, Thorne thought. He knew very well that when it came to slabs and scalpels you never toughened up. You just pretended you had . . .

Standing in the Incident Room, preparing to brief the team, Thorne felt, as he often did on these occasions, like a teacher who was feared but not particularly liked. The slightly psychotic PE teacher. These thirty or so people in front of him—detectives, uniformed officers, civilian and auxiliary staff—might just as well have been children. There were as many different types as could be found sitting in any drafty school hall in London, even as Thorne was speaking.

There were those who appeared to be listening intently but would have to check with colleagues later to find out exactly what they were supposed to be doing. Some, on the other hand, would be overkeen, asking questions and nodding eagerly, with every intention of doing as little as possible when the time came. There were the bullies and the picked upon. The geeks and the morons.

The Metropolitan Police Service. *Service,* note, with the emphasis on caring and efficiency. Thorne knew very well that most of the people in the room, himself on some occasions included, were happier back when they were a *force.*

One to be reckoned with.

It was four days since that first postmortem conversation with Hendricks, and if the pathologist had been quick, the team at Forensic Science Services had outdone him. Seventy-two hours for DNA results was really going some, especially when the crime scene was as much of a DNA nightmare as that hotel room had been. One notch up from a homeless shelter, it had yielded hair and skin samples from upward of a dozen individuals, male and female. Then there were the cats and dogs and at least two other animal species as yet unidentified.

And yet, incredibly, they'd found a match.

They were no nearer finding the killer, of course, but now they were at least certain who his victim had been. The dead man's DNA had been on file, for a very good reason.

Thorne cleared his throat, got a bit of hush. "Douglas Andrew Remfry, thirty-six years of age, was released from Derby Prison ten days ago, having served seven years of a twelve-year sentence for the rapes of three young women. We're putting together an accurate picture of his movements since then, but so far it looks like a pretty consistent shuttle between pub, betting shop, and the house in New Cross where he was living with his mother and her . . . ?" Thorne looked across at Russell Brigstocke, who held up three fingers. He turned back to the room. "Her *third* husband. We'll hopefully have a lot more in terms of Remfry's movements and so on later today. DCs Holland and Stone are there at the moment with a search warrant. Mrs. Remfry was somewhat less than cooperative. . . ."

An acnefied trainee detective near the front shook his head, his face screwed up in distaste for this woman he'd never met. Thorne gave him a good, hard stare. "She's just lost a son," he said. Thorne let his words hang there for a few seconds before continuing. "If the landlady is to be believed, Remfry, unless his killer happens also to be his double, booked the room himself. He didn't feel the need to give a name, but he was happy enough to hand over the cash. We need to find out why. Why was he so keen to go to that hotel? Who was he meeting . . . ?"

Thorne, in spite of himself, was smiling slightly as he recalled the interview with the hotel's formidable owner—a bottle blonde with a face like a bulldog chewing a wasp and a sixty-fags-a-day rasp.

"And who pays for the replacement of those sheets?" she'd asked. "All them pillows and blankets that this nutter nicked? They were one hundred percent cotton, none of 'em was cheap . . ." Thorne had nodded, pretended to write something down, wondering if her memory was as good as her capacity to talk utter shite with a straight face. "And the stains on the mattress. Where do I get the money to get that lot cleaned?"

"I'll see if I can find you a form to fill in," Thorne said, thinking, *Will I fuck, you hatchet-faced old mare . . .*

In the Incident Room, the trainee detective Thorne had stared at before poked a single finger up. Thorne nodded.

"Are we looking at the prison angle, sir? Someone Remfry was in Derby with, maybe. Someone he got on the wrong side of . . ."

"Someone he got up the *back*side of!" The comment came from a mustached DC sitting off to Thorne's left toward the back of the room. Thorne did not know the man. He'd been brought in, like many in the room, from different squads to make up the numbers. His "backside" comment got a big laugh. Thorne manufactured a chuckle.

"We're looking at that. Remfry's sexual preference was certainly for women before he got put away . . ."

"Some of them develop a taste for it inside, though, don't they?" This time the laugh from his mates felt forced. Thorne allowed it to die away, let his voice drop a little to regain attention and control.

"Most of you lot are going to be tracing the most likely group of suspects we've got at the moment . . ."

The trainee nodded knowingly. One of the clever ones.

He thought this was some kind of conversation. "The male relatives of Remfry's rape victims."

"Right," Thorne said. "Husbands, boyfriends, brothers. Sod it, fathers at a push. I want them all found, interviewed, and eliminated. With a bit of luck we might eliminate all of them except one. DI Kitson has drawn up a list and will be doing the allocations." Thorne dropped his notes onto a chair, pulled his jacket from the back of it, almost done. "Right, that's it. Remfry's were particularly nasty offenses. Maybe someone wasn't convinced he'd paid for them . . ."

The DC with the porno mustache smirked and muttered something to the uniform in front of him. Thorne pulled on his jacket and narrowed his eyes.

"What?"

Suddenly he might just as well have been that teacher, holding out a hand, demanding to see whatever was being chewed.

The DC spat it out. "Seems to me that whoever killed Remfry did everyone a favor. Fucker asked for everything he got."

It was far from being the first such comment Thorne had heard since the DNA match had come back. He looked across at the DC. He knew that he should slap the cocky sod down. He knew that he should make a speech about their jobs as police officers, their need to be dispassionate, whatever the case, whoever the victim. He should talk about debts having been paid and maybe even drag out stuff about one man's life being worth no more and no less than any other.

He couldn't be bothered.

Dave Holland was always happiest deferring to rank or, if he got the chance, pulling it. When it was just himself and another DC, things were never clear-cut and it made him uncomfortable.

It was simple. As a DC, he deferred to a DS and above, while *he* was able to play the big man with trainee detectives and uniformed officers. Out and about with a fellow DC, and things *should* just settle into a natural pattern. It was down to personality, to clout.

With Andy Stone, Holland felt outranked. He didn't know why and it peeved him.

They'd got on well enough so far, but Stone could be a bit "up himself." He had a coolness, a *flashiness,* Holland reckoned, that he turned on around women and superior officers. Stone was clearly fit and good-looking. He had very short dark hair and blue eyes, and though Holland wasn't certain, when Stone walked around, it looked as though he knew the effect he was having. What Holland *was* sure of was that Stone's suits were cut that bit better, and that around him he felt like a ruddy-cheeked boy scout. Holland would probably still get the vote as housewives' choice, but they all wanted to mother him. He doubted they wanted to mother Andy Stone.

Stone could also be overcocky when it came to badmouthing their superiors, and though Holland wasn't averse to the game himself, it got a bit tricky when it came to Tom Thorne. Holland knew the DI's faults well enough. He'd been on the receiving end of his temper, had been dragged down with him on more than one occasion . . .

Yet, for all that, having Thorne think well of him, consider that something *he'd* done was worthwhile, was, for Holland, pretty much as good as it could get.

He'd been on the team a lot longer than Andy Stone, and Holland thought that should have counted for something. It didn't appear to. It had been Stone who'd done most of the talking when they'd shown up bright and early on Mary Remfry's doorstep with a search warrant.

"Good morning, Mrs. Remfry." Stone's voice was

surprisingly light for such a tall man. "We have a warrant to enter and . . ."

She'd turned away then and, leaving the door open, had trudged away down the thickly carpeted hallway without a word. Somewhere inside a dog was barking.

Stone and Holland had entered and stood at the bottom of the stairs deciding who should start where. Stone made for the living room, where, through the partially opened door, they could see a silver-haired man slumped in an armchair, lost in morning TV trivia. As Stone leaned on the door he hissed to Holland, nodding toward the kitchen, where Mrs. Remfry had seemed to be heading.

"Cup of tea likely, you reckon?"

It wasn't.

It seemed odd to Holland, needing a warrant to search a victim's house. Still, like Stone had said, Remfry *was* a convicted rapist and the mother's attitude hadn't really given them a lot of choice. It wasn't just the grief at her son's death turning to anger. It was a genuine fury at what she saw as the implication in one particular line of questioning. Considering the manner and circumstances of her son's death, it was a necessary line to pursue, but she was having no truck with it at all.

"Dougie was a ladies' man, always. A proper ladies' man."

She was saying it again, now, having suddenly appeared in the doorway of her son's bedroom, where Holland was methodically going through drawers and cupboards. Mary Remfry, midfifties, tugging a cardigan tightly over her nightdress, watched, but did not really take in what Holland was doing. Her mind was concentrated on talking at him.

"Dougie loved women and women loved him right back. That's gospel, that is."

Holland was considerate going through the room. He

would have been whether Mrs. Remfry had been watching or not, but he made the extra effort to be respectful as he sorted through drawers full of vests and pants and thrust a gloved hand into pillowcases and duvet covers. In the short time since his release, Remfry had obviously not acquired much in the way of new clothing or possessions, but there seemed to be a good deal still here from the time before he went to prison. There was plenty from before he ever left school . . .

"He never missed out where birds was concerned," Remfry's mother said. "Even after he came out, they was still sniffing round. Calling him up. You listening to me?"

Holland half turned, half nodded, and, as if on cue, pulled out a decent-size stash of porn magazines from beneath the single bed.

"See?" Mary Remfry pointed at the magazines. "You won't find any men in *them*." She sounded as proud as if Holland were dusting off a degree certificate or a Nobel Prize nomination. As it was, he squatted by the bed, flicking through the pile of yellowing *Razzle*s, *Escort*s, and *Fiesta*s, feeling his face flush, turning away from the proud mother in the doorway. The magazines all dated from the mid to late eighties, well before Dougie began his days at Her Majesty's pleasure, banged up with six hundred and fifty other men.

Holland pushed the dirty mags to one side, reached back under the bed, and pulled out a brown plastic bag, folded over on itself several times. He let the bag drop open and a bundle of envelopes, bound with a thick elastic band, fell on to the carpet.

As soon as he saw the address, neatly typed on the topmost envelope, Holland felt a tingle of excitement. Just a small one. What he was looking at would probably mean nothing, but it was almost certainly more significant than fifteen-year-old socks and ancient stroke mags.

"Andy . . . !"

Mary Remfry wrapped her cardigan a little tighter around herself and took a step into the room. "What have you got there?"

Holland could hear Stone's feet on the stairs. He slipped off the elastic band, reached inside the first envelope, and pulled out the letter.

"So we can definitely rule out autoerotic asphyxiation, then?" DCI Russell Brigstocke, a little embarrassed, looked around the table at Thorne, at Phil Hendricks, at DI Yvonne Kitson.

"Well, I'm not sure we can rule *anything* out," Thorne said. "But I think the 'auto' bit implies that you do it yourself."

"You know what I mean, smart-arse . . ."

"Nothing erotic went on in that room," Hendricks said.

Brigstocke nodded. "No chance it was an extreme sex game that went wrong?" Thorne smirked. Brigstocke caught the look. "What?" Thorne said nothing. "Look, I'm just asking the questions . . ."

"Asking the questions that Jesmond told you to ask," Thorne said. He made no secret of his opinion that their detective chief superintendent had sprung fully formed from some course that turned out politically astute, organizationally capable drones. Acceptable faces with a neat line in facile questions, a good grasp of economic realities, and, as it happened, an aversion to anybody called Thorne.

"They're questions that need answering," Brigstocke said. "Could it have been some sort of sex game?"

Thorne found it hard to believe that the likes of Trevor Jesmond had ever done the things that he, Brigstocke, or any other copper did, day in and day out. It was unimaginable that he had ever broken up a fistfight at closing time, or fiddled his expenses, or stood between a knife and the body it was intended for.

Or told a mother that her only son had been sodomized and strangled to death in a grotty hotel room.

"It wasn't a game," Thorne said.

Brigstocke looked at Hendricks and Kitson. He sighed. "I'll take your expressions of thinly disguised scorn as agreement with DI Thorne, then, shall I?" He pushed his glasses up his nose with the crook of his first finger, then ran the hand through the thick black hair of which he was so proud. The quiff was less pronounced than usual, there was some gray creeping in. He could cut a vaguely absurd figure, but Thorne knew that when Brigstocke lost it, he was as hard a man as he had ever worked with.

Thorne, Brigstocke, Kitson, Hendricks the civilian. These four, together with Holland and Stone, were the core of Team 3 at the Serious Crime Group (West). This was the group that made the decisions, formulated policy, and guided the investigations with—and even on occasion *without*—the approval of those higher up.

Team 3 had been up and running a good while, handling the ordinary cases but specializing—though that was not a word Thorne would have used—in cases that were anything but ordinary . . .

"So," Brigstocke said, "we've got everybody out chasing down all the likely relatives of Remfry's victims. Still favorite with everybody?"

Nods around the table.

"A long way from odds-on, though," Thorne said. There were things that bothered him, that didn't quite mesh with the vengeful relative scenario. He couldn't picture an anger carried around for that many years fermenting into something lethal, corrosive, then manifesting itself in the way it had in that hotel room. There was something almost stage-managed about what he had seen on that filthy mattress. *Posed,* Hendricks had said.

And he was still troubled by the early morning call to the florist . . .

Thorne thought there was something odd about the message. He couldn't believe that it was simple carelessness, so the only conclusion was that the killer must have *wanted* the police to hear his voice on that answering machine. It was as if he were introducing himself.

"What came up at the briefing," Kitson said, "the stuff about Remfry turning queer inside? Worth looking into . . . ?"

Thorne glanced toward Hendricks. A gay man who was choosing to ignore the word Kitson had used, or else genuinely didn't give a fuck.

"Yeah," Thorne said. "Whatever he might or might not have got up to when he was inside, he was definitely straight before he went in. Don't forget that he raped three women . . ."

"Rape's not about sex, it's about power," Kitson said.

Yvonne Kitson, together with DC Andy Stone, had come into the team to replace an officer Thorne had lost, in circumstances he tried every day to forget. Of all the murderers he'd put away, Thorne was happy to remember that the man responsible was serving three life sentences in Belmarsh Prison.

Thorne looked at Phil Hendricks. "Never mind Remfry, can we be certain the *killer*'s gay?"

Hendricks didn't hesitate. "Absolutely not. Like Yvonne says, the rape's got nothing to do with sex, anyway. Maybe the killer wants us to *think* he's gay. He may well be, of course, but we have to consider other possibilities . . ."

"Whether it was a gay thing or not," Kitson said, "he could still have been set up by someone he did time with, someone with a major grudge . . ."

Brigstocke cleared his throat, at some level finding this all a bit embarrassing. "But the buggery . . . ?"

Hendricks snorted. "Buggery?" He dropped his Manchester accent and adopted the posh bluster of the gentleman's club. "Buggery!!"

Brigstocke reddened. "Sodomy, then. Anal intercourse, whatever. How could you do that if you weren't homosexual?"

Hendricks shrugged. "Close your eyes and think of Claudia Schiffer . . . ?"

"Kylie Minogue for me," Thorne said.

Kitson shook her head, smiling. "Dirty old man."

Brigstocke was unconvinced. He stared hard at Thorne. "Seriously, though, Tom. This might be important. Could *you?*"

"It would depend how much I wanted to kill somebody," Thorne said.

There was a silence around the table for a while. Thorne decided to break it before it became too serious. "Remfry went to that hotel willingly. He booked the room himself. He knew, or thought he knew, what he was getting into."

"And whatever it was," Hendricks added, "it looks as though he went along with it for a while."

"Right," Kitson said. She turned the photocopied pages of Hendricks's postmortem report. "No defense wounds, no tissue underneath the fingernails . . ."

The phone on the desk rang. Thorne was nearest.

"DI Thorne. Yes, Dave . . ."

The others watched for a few seconds as Thorne listened. Brigstocke hissed at Kitson. "Why the fuck did Remfry go to that hotel?"

Thorne nodded, grunted, took the top off a pen with his teeth. He took it out of his mouth, put it back on the pen. He smiled, told Holland to get his arse in gear, and ended the call.

Then he answered Brigstocke's question.

December 4, 1975

They sat in the Maxi, outside the house.

She'd held it together all morning, through all the really hard parts, the personal stuff, the intrusion. Then, when it seemed the worst was over, she'd begun to wail as she'd stepped through the doors he'd held open for her. Out of the police station and running down the steps toward the street, her heels noisy on the concrete, her sobbing uncontrollable.

In the car on the way back, the crying had gradually given way to a seething fury that exploded in fitful bursts of abuse. He kept his hands clenched tightly around the steering wheel as she rained blows down on his shoulder and arm. His eyes never left the road as she screamed words at him that he'd never heard her utter before. He drove carefully, with the same caution he always showed, and as he maneuvered the car through the lunchtime traffic on the icy streets, he absorbed as much of her pain and rage as he could take.

They sat in the car, both too shattered to open a door. Staring straight ahead, afraid to so much as look toward the house. The house, which was now simply the place where, the night before, she had told him what had happened. The collection of rooms through which they'd staggered and shouted and wept. The place where everything had changed.

The home they'd never feel comfortable in again.

Without turning her head, she spat words at him. "Why didn't you make me go to the police station last night? Why did you let me wait?"

The engine was turned off, the car was still, but his hands would not leave the steering wheel. His leather driving gloves creaked as he grasped it even tighter. "You wouldn't listen, you wouldn't listen to sense."

"What do you expect? Christ, I didn't even know my own name. I had no idea what I was fucking doing. I would never have had the shower . . ."

She'd been too upset to think clearly, of course. He'd tried to explain all this to the woman police constable that morning, but she'd just shrugged and looked at her colleague and carried on taking the clothes and putting them into a plastic bag as they were taken off and handed over.

"You shouldn't have had a shower, love," the WPC said. "That was a bit silly. You should have come straight in, last night, as soon as it had happened . . ."

The engine had been off for no more than a minute, but already it was freezing inside the car. The tears felt warm as they inched slowly down his face, running into his mustache. "You said you'd wanted to wash . . . to wash him off you. I said I understood but I told you you shouldn't have. That it wasn't a good idea. You weren't listening to me . . ."

Standing there in the lounge after she'd told him. The horrible minutes and hours after she'd *described what had been done to her. She wouldn't let him do a lot of things. She wouldn't let him hold her. She wouldn't let him ring anybody. She wouldn't let him go around to the bastard's house to kick what little he had between his legs into a bloody mush and punch him into the middle of next week.*

He looked at his watch. He wondered if the police would pick Franklin up at work or later on at his house . . .

He needed to call the office and tell them he wouldn't be in. He needed to call the school to check that everything was okay, that the previous night's explanations for why Mummy was so upset had been believed . . .

"What did that woman mean?" she said suddenly. "That WPC? When she asked if I always wore a dress that nice to go to work?" She slid her hands beneath her legs and began to rock gently in her seat.

Snow was starting to fall quite heavily, building up quickly on the hood and windshield. He didn't bother to turn on the wipers.

THREE

Later, when they talked about it, both Thorne and Holland admitted to fancying the deputy governor of Derby Prison. What neither of them *quite* got around to admitting was that, attractive as she undoubtedly was, they actually fancied her more *because* she was a prison governor.

They didn't really go into it all that much . . .

"He's certainly made a very good job of it." Tracy Lenahan put down the letter, actually a photocopy of one of twenty-odd letters written to Douglas Remfry during his last three months inside, plus a couple to his home address after he'd been released. The letters that Holland had found under Remfry's bed.

Letters written by a killer, pretending to be a twenty-eight-year-old woman named Jane Foley.

Thorne and Holland had already been taken through the procedure for the sorting of prisoners' mail. The letters—five sackfuls a day on average—would have been taken by two, perhaps three, operational-support-grade officers to the censor's room for sorting. The X-ray machine had been done away with by the present governor, but drug dogs might be used and each letter would be slit open and searched for illegal enclosures. The OSGs did not *read* the letters, and providing there was no good reason, they would not usually be seen by anyone else.

"A good job of sounding like a woman, you mean?"

Thorne asked. He thought the letters were pretty bloody convincing and so did Yvonne Kitson, but other opinions couldn't hurt.

"Oh yes, but I think he's been much cleverer than that. I've seen one or two letters like this before, genuine letters. You'd be amazed how much mail like this people like Remfry really get. This has that same odd tone to it. It's something slightly crazed . . ."

"Something a bit needy," Holland suggested.

Lenahan nodded. "Right, that's it. She's claiming to be a bit of a catch, a sexy bit of stuff looking for fun . . ."

"A sexy *married* bit of stuff," Thorne added. The fictitious Jane Foley was conveniently hitched to an equally fictitious and awfully jealous husband, so Remfry couldn't write back to her.

Lenahan read a few lines of the letter again, nodded. "All the suggestive stuff in the letter is bang on, but there's still a kind of hopelessness. Something sad underneath . . ."

"Like she's a bit desperate," Thorne said. "A woman who's desperate enough to write these sorts of letters to a convicted rapist."

Holland puffed out his cheeks. "This is doing my head in. A bloke, pretending to be a woman, pretending to be a different kind of woman . . ."

Lenahan pushed the letter back across her desk. "It's subtle, though. Like I said, he's bloody clever." She didn't need to tell Thorne that. He'd studied every one of "Jane Foley's" letters. He knew that the man who wrote them was very clever indeed. Clever, calculating, and extremely patient.

Lenahan picked up the photograph. "And this is the icing on the cake . . ."

Thorne was struck by her strange choice of phrase but said nothing. On the wall behind the desk was the regu-

lation portrait of the Queen, looking rather as if she
could smell something unpleasant wafting up from the
canteen. To Her Majesty's left were a series of framed
aerial views of the prison and, hung next to these very
modern images, a pair of large landscapes in oil. Thorne
knew next to bugger all about it but they looked pretty
old. Lenahan glanced up, followed Thorne's gaze.

"Those have been knocking around the place since it
opened in 1853," she said. "Used to be gathering dust
down in Visits. Then six months ago, we had an inmate
in for receiving stolen antiques. He took one look at
them and went pale. Worth about twelve thousand each,
so they reckon . . ."

She smiled and her eyes dropped to the black-and-
white photo in her hand. Thorne's went to the silver picture frame on her desk. From where he was sitting he
couldn't see the photo inside, but he imagined a fit-
looking husband—army perhaps, or maybe even a copper—and a smiling, olive-skinned child. He looked again
at the woman behind the desk, her dark eyes wide as she
stared at the picture. She was ridiculously young, probably not even thirty. Her black hair was shoulder length.
She was tall and large-breasted. It would have been clear
to a blind man that the deputy governor would figure
regularly in the fantasies of the men she locked up every
night.

Thorne glanced across at Holland and was amused to
see him struggling not to blush as he waited for Tracy
Lenahan to finish studying the photograph of "Jane Foley." The picture was of a woman kneeling, her head
bowed and hooded, the artful lighting concealing much,
but revealing tantalizing glimpses of the full breasts, the
neatly trimmed thatch of pubic hair. Of the leather belt
around the wrists.

Holland had earlier expressed surprise that the photos

had not been confiscated, especially as Remfry was a sex offender. Surely this kind of image was risky on "Fraggle Rock"—the term used by many police officers for the Vulnerable Prisoners wing. Lenahan, bridling slightly at the slang, had explained what she called the Page Three rule. Stuff like this was discretionary. Obviously images of kids were not allowed on the VP wing, but if it was harmless—the sort of thing you might see on Page Three of the *Sun*—then the OSGs would have a look, pass the odd comment, and put it back in the envelope.

"Jesus," Holland had said. "Page Three must be going seriously fucking arty . . ."

Lenahan put the picture down, scraped at the edge of it with a long red fingernail.

"This is clever, too. It's the ideal image to have chosen. Just what would be needed to hook an offender like Remfry, to tease him with the promise of something. This is a rapist's wet dream. Wherever your killer got it from, it's perfect." She swallowed, cleared her throat. "Remfry was a man who got off on submission . . ."

Thorne and Holland exchanged a glance. They hadn't told Tracy Lenahan, but they were pretty sure the picture wasn't one the killer had just gone out and bought. The naked woman was wearing a hood identical to the one that Phil Hendricks had taken off Douglas Remfry's body . . .

"There's half a dozen similar pictures," Thorne said. "They were sent with the most recent letters. They start to get more revealing the closer the letters get to his release date."

Lenahan nodded. "Increasing the excitement . . ."

"By the time he got out, he must have been gagging for it," Holland said.

She picked up the photograph again in her left hand and reached for the letter with her right. She brandished them both. "Your killer is sensitive to the way this kind of woman might think, *and* to what will best stimulate the man she's writing to."

Thorne said nothing. He was thinking that she sounded bizarrely impressed.

"Sensitive, like a gay man maybe," Holland said.

Thorne shrugged noncommittally. They were back to that. He had to agree it was possible, but he was growing irritated at the way the investigation was fixing on what they presumed the killer's sexuality to be. Yes, the violent sodomizing of the victim was clearly significant. The rapist had been raped and Thorne was sure that this would prove to be crucial in finding out why he'd been murdered. Thorne was *less* sure that who the killer chose to sleep with was as important.

Holland slid forward in his chair, looked at Tracy Lenahan. "This is an angle we obviously have to consider—that Remfry was killed by someone he'd known in prison. Someone with whom he'd possibly had a nonconsensual sexual relationship . . ."

Lenahan looked back at him, waiting for the question, not appearing terribly keen to do Holland any favors.

"Is that possible, do you think? Could Remfry have sexually assaulted another prisoner? Could he have been sexually assaulted himself?"

The deputy governor leaned back, something dark passing momentarily across her face. It vanished as she clasped her hands together and shook her head. Thorne thought that the laugh she produced sounded a little forced.

"I think you've been watching too many films set in American prisons, Detective Constable. There're some very nasty pieces of work in here, don't get me wrong, but very few of them are called Bubba, and if you're looking for bitches or puppies, you should look in a dogs' home. Prisoners form relationships, of course they do, but as far as I know, nobody's going to get gang-banged if they drop the soap in the shower."

Thorne couldn't help but smile. Holland smiled, too, but Thorne could see the skin tighten around his mouth and the reddening just above his collar. "As far as you know?" Holland said. "Meaning that it's possible."

"The week before last, in the kitchens, a prisoner had his ear cut off with the lid from a tin of peaches. That was an argument over a game of table tennis, I think." She smiled, sexy and very cold. "Anything's possible."

Thorne stood and walked away from Lenahan's desk toward the door. "Let's presume that the man we're looking for is *not* an ex-con. The obvious question is how he got the information. How did he find Remfry? How could he find out where a convicted rapist was serving his sentence and when he was going to get released, in enough time to set all this up?"

Lenahan swiveled in her chair to face the computer screen on the corner of her desk. She hit a button on the keyboard. "He would have had to have got it from a database somewhere." She continued typing, watching the screen. "This is a LIDS computer. Local Inmate Data System, which has everything on the prisoners in here. I can send stuff down the wire to other prisons if I need to, but I wouldn't have thought this would be enough . . ."

Thorne looked at the nearer of the two landscapes. The dark, thick swirls of the paint on the canvas. He thought it might be somewhere in the Lake District. "What about national records?"

"IIS. The Inmate Information System. That's got everything—locations, offense details, home address, release date." She looked up and across at Thorne. "But you'd still need to type a name in."

"Who has access to that?" Holland asked. "Do you?"

"No . . ."

"The governor? Police liaison officer?"

She smiled, shook her head firmly. "It's headquarters-based only. The system's pretty well restricted, for obvious reasons . . ."

Thanks and good-byes were brisk and Thorne would have had it no other way. Though he hadn't so much as glimpsed a blue prison sweatshirt the whole time they'd been there, he was aware of the prisoners all around him. Beyond the walls of the deputy governor's office. Above, below, and to all sides. A distant echo, a heaviness, the *heat* given off by over six hundred men, there thanks to the likes of him.

Whenever he entered a prison, moved around its green, or mustard or dirty cream corridors, Thorne mentally left a trail of bread crumbs behind him. He always needed to be sure of the quickest way out.

For most of the drive back down the M1, Holland had his nose buried in a pamphlet he'd picked up on his way out of the prison. Thorne preferred his own form of research.

He eased *Johnny Cash at San Quentin* into the cassette player.

Holland looked up as "Wanted Man" kicked in. He listened for a few seconds, shook his head, and went back to his facts and figures.

Thorne had tried, *once,* to tell him. To explain that *real* country music was fuck all to do with lost dogs and rhinestones. It had been a long night of pool and Guinness, and Phil Hendricks—with whichever boyfriend happened to be around at the time—heckling mercilessly. Thorne had tried to convey to Holland the beauty of George Jones's voice, the wickedness in Merle Haggard's, and the awesome rumble of Cash, the dark daddy of them all. A few pints in, he was telling anybody who would listen that Hank Williams was a tortured genius

who was undoubtedly the Kurt Cobain of his day and he
may even have begun to sing "Your Cheating Heart"
around closing time. He couldn't recall every detail, but
he *did* remember that Holland's eyes had begun to glaze
over long before then . . .

"Fuck," Holland said. "It costs twenty-five grand a
year to look after one prisoner. Does that sound like a lot
to you?"

Thorne didn't really know. It was twice what a lot of
people earned in a year, but once you took into account
the salaries of prison staff and the maintenance of the
buildings . . .

"I don't think they're spending that on carpets and
caviar, somehow," Thorne said.

"No, but still . . ."

It was roasting in the car. The Mondeo was far too old
to have air con, but Thorne was very pissed off at being
completely unable to coax anything but warm air from a
heating system he'd had fixed twice already. He opened
a window but shut it after half a minute, the breeze not
worth the noise.

Holland looked up from his pamphlet again. "Do you
think they should have luxuries in there? You know, TVs
in their cells and whatever? PlayStations, some of them
have got . . ."

Thorne turned the sound down a little and glanced up
at the sign as the Mondeo roared past it. They were ap-
proaching the Milton Keynes turnoff. Still fifty miles
from London.

Thorne realized, as he had many times before, that for
all the time he spent putting people behind bars, he gave
precious little thought to what happened when they got
there. When he *did* think about it, weigh all the argu-
ments up, he supposed that, all things considered, a loss
of freedom was as bad as it could get. Above and beyond
that, he wasn't sure exactly where he stood.

He feathered the brake, dropped down to just under seventy, and drifted across to the inside lane. They were in no great hurry . . .

Thorne knew, as much as he knew anything, that murderers, sex offenders, those who would harm children, had to be removed. He also knew that *putting these people away* was more than just a piece of argot. It was actually what they did. What *he* did. Once these offenders were . . . elsewhere, the debate as to where punishment ended and rehabilitation began was for others to have. He felt instinctively that prison should never become . . . the phrase *holiday camps* popped into his head. He chided himself for beginning to sound like a right-wing nutcase. Fuck it, a few TVs was neither here nor there. Let them watch the football or join in with game shows if that was what they wanted . . .

Sadly, by the time Thorne had formulated his answer to the question, Holland had moved on to something else.

"Bloody hell." Holland looked up from the pamphlet. "Sixty percent of goal nets in the English league are made by prisoners. I hope they've made the ones at White Hart Lane strong enough, the abuse Spurs get from other teams . . ."

"Right . . ."

"Here's another one. Prison farms produce twenty million pints of milk every year. That's fucking amazing . . ."

Thorne was no longer listening. He was hearing nothing but the rush of the road under the wheels and thinking about the photograph. He pictured the hooded woman, the make-believe Jane Foley, feeling a stirring in his groin at the image in his head of her shadowy nakedness.

Wherever he got it from . . .

Suddenly Thorne knew where he might go to find the answer, at least any answer there was to be found. The

woman in that photo might not be Jane Foley, but she
had to be somebody, and Thorne knew just the person to
come up with a name.

When he started to listen again, Holland was in the
middle of another question.

". . . as bad as this? Do you think prisons are any better than they were back in . . . ?" He pointed toward the
cassette player.

"Nineteen sixty-nine," Thorne said. Johnny Cash was
singing the song he'd written about San Quentin itself.
Singing about hating every inch of the place they were all
stood in. The prisoners whooping and cheering at every
complaint, at each pugnacious insult, at every plea to
raze the prison to the ground.

"So?" Holland waved his pamphlet. "Are prisons any
better now than they were then, do you think? Than
they were thirty-odd years ago?"

Thorne pictured the face of a man in Belmarsh Prison,
and something inside hardened very quickly.

"I fucking hope not."

At a little after six o'clock, Eve Bloom double-locked the
shop, walked half a dozen paces to a bright red front
door, and was home.

It was handy renting the flat above her shop. It wasn't
expensive, but she'd have paid a good deal more for the
pleasure of being able to tumble out of bed at the last
possible minute, the coffee steaming in her own mug
next to the till as she opened up. Every last second in bed
was precious when you had to spend as many mornings
as she did, up and dressed at half past stupid. Walking
around the flower market at New Covent Garden, ordering stock, chatting with wholesalers, while every other
person she could think of was still dead to the world.

She liked this time of year. The few precious weeks of
summer, when she wasn't forced to choose between

working in scarf and gloves or punishing her stock with central heating. She liked closing up when it was still light. It made the early starts less painful, gave that couple of hours between the end of the day and the start of the evening a scent of excitement, a tang of real possibility.

She closed the door behind her and climbed the stripped wooden stairs up to the flat. Denise had wielded the sander and done the whole place in a weekend, while Eve had taken responsibility for the decorating. Most domestic chores got split fairly equally between them, and though there were the sulks, the occasional frosty silences that followed a pilfered yogurt or a dress borrowed without asking, the two of them got on pretty well. Eve knew that Denise could be quite controlling, but then she also knew there were occasions when she herself needed to be controlled. She tended to be more than a little disorganized, and though Den could be Mother Hen–ish at times, it was nice to feel looked after. The endless list making could get wearing, but there *was* always food in the fridge and they never ran out of toilet roll!

She dropped her bag on the kitchen table and flicked on the kettle. "Oi, Hollins, you old slapper, you want tea?" Almost before she'd finished shouting she remembered that Denise was going straight out from work, meeting Ben in the pub next to her office. Denise had called the shop at lunchtime, told her she wouldn't be home for dinner, asked her if she fancied joining them.

Eve walked through to her bedroom to put on a fresh T-shirt while she was waiting for the kettle to boil. No, she'd stay in, veg out in front of the TV with a bottle of very cold white wine. She couldn't be bothered to change and go out. It was sticky outside and uncomfortable. She'd feel dirty by the time she got there. The pub would be loud and smoky and she'd only feel like a third wheel anyway. Denise and Ben were very touchy-feely . . .

She stared at herself in the mirror on the back of her bedroom door, striking a pose in bra and pants. She saw herself smiling as she thought again about the policeman who had answered the phone a week before. Impossible to picture from just the voice, of course, but she'd tried anyway and was pretty keen on what she'd come up with. She was fairly sure that, crime scene or no crime scene, he'd been flirting with her on the phone, and she knew full well that she'd been flirting right back. Or had she been the one to start it?

She pulled on a white, FCUK T-shirt and went back into the kitchen to make her tea.

They'd sent a car around the day after she'd called, to collect the cassette from her answering machine. She told the two officers that she'd have been more than happy to bring it into the station, but, understandably, they seemed eager to take it with them.

Walking around the flat opening windows, she debated whether a week was quite long enough. She couldn't decide whether she should just turn up, or if it might be better to call. The last thing she wanted was to look pushy. She had every right of course, being involved, to see what was going on. It was only natural that she should be a bit curious after the business with the phone call, wasn't it? Surely, going along to inquire if there had been any progress in the case was no more than any other concerned citizen would do.

She suddenly realized that, wandering around the flat, she'd put her tea down and couldn't remember where. Screw it, the kitchen was close and she knew *exactly* where the fridge was.

Opening the wine, she wondered if Detective Inspector Thorne was one of those funny blokes who got put off by women who appeared a bit keen.

Maybe she'd leave it another day or two . . .

* * *

The evening was ridiculously warm.

Elvis, Thorne's emotionally disturbed cat, looked un-comfortable, following him from room to room, yowl-ing like she was asking to be shaved. Thorne got sweaty, cooking and eating cheese on toast, wearing an open Hawaiian shirt and a pair of shorts he'd bought during a short-lived dalliance with a nearby gym.

Thorne lay on the sofa and watched a film. He turned the sound on the TV down and looked at the pictures with the radio on. He flicked through the music section in the previous week's edition of *Time Out*, trying to find the band with the most ridiculous name. Finally, just before midnight, his empties cleared away and noth-ing else to do that might put it off any longer, he reached for the phone.

It didn't matter that it was late. His father's body clock was only one of the systems that had broken down.

In some ways, the Alzheimer's diagnosis had come as something of a relief. The eccentricities were now called symptoms and, for Thorne, the vagaries of old age be-coming certainties, however unpleasant, had at least pro-vided a focus. Things had to be done, simple as that. Thorne still got irritated with the terrible jokes and the pointless trivia, but the guilt didn't last as long as it had before. Now he just got on with it, and the shape of the guilt had changed. Hammered into something he could recognize as anger, at an illness that took father and son and forced them to swap places.

There was a financial burden now that wasn't always easy to meet, but he was getting used to it. Jim Thorne was, at least physically, in pretty good shape for seventy-one, but still, a carer needed to visit daily and there was no way an old-age pension was going to cover it. His younger sister, Eileen, to whom he had never been close, traveled up from Brighton once a week, taking care to keep Thorne well informed of his dad's condition.

Thorne was grateful, though it seemed like a terribly British thing to him. Families eventually behaving well when it was practically too late.

"Dad . . ."

"Oh, thank Christ, this is driving me mad. Who was the first Doctor Who? Come on, this is doing my head in . . ."

"Was it Patrick somebody? Dark hair . . ."

"Troughton was the second one, the one before Pertwee. Oh shit and bloody confusion, I thought you might know."

"Look in the book. I bought you that TV encyclopedia . . ."

"Fucking Eileen's tidied it away somewhere. Who else might know . . . ?"

Thorne started to relax. His father was fine.

"Dad, we need to start thinking about this wedding."

"What wedding?"

"Trevor. Eileen's son. Your nephew . . ."

His dad took a deep breath. When he breathed out again, the rattle in his chest sounded like a low growl. "He's an arsehole. He was an arsehole when he got married the first time. Don't see why I should have to go and watch the arsehole get married again."

The language was unimaginative, but Thorne had to admit that his father had a point.

"You told Eileen you were going."

There was a heavy sigh, a phlegmy cough, and then silence. After a few seconds, Thorne began to think his father had put the phone down and wandered away.

"Dad . . ."

"It's ages. It's ages away, isn't it?"

"It's a week on Saturday. Come on, Eileen must have talked to you about it. She talks to *me* about nothing else."

"Do I have to wear a suit?"

"Wear your navy one. It's light and I think it's going to be warm."

"That's wool, the navy one. I'll bloody roast in the navy."

Thorne took a deep breath, thinking, *Please your bloody self.* "Listen, I'm going to come and pick you up on the day and we're stopping the night down there . . ."

"I'm not going down there in that bloody death trap you drive . . ."

"I'll hire a car, all right? It'll be a laugh, we'll have a good time. Okay?"

Thorne could hear a clinking, the sound of something metallic being fiddled with. His dad had taken to buying cheap secondhand radios, disassembling them, and throwing the pieces away.

"Dad? Is that okay? We can talk about the details closer to the day if you want."

"Tom?"

"Yeah?"

To Thorne, the silence that followed seemed like the sound of thoughts getting lost. Slipping down cracks, just beyond reach and then gone, flailing as they tumbled into darkness. Finally, there was an engagement, like a piece of film catching, regaining its proper speed. Holes locking onto ratchets.

"Sort that Doctor Who thing out for me, will you, son?"

Thorne swallowed hard. "I'll ask around and call you tomorrow. Okay?"

"Thanks . . ."

"And listen, Dad, dig out that navy suit. I'm sure it's not wool."

"Oh shit, you never said anything about a suit . . ."

December 22, 1975

They were both in the kitchen. A few feet apart, and nowhere near each other.

Just a couple of days till Christmas, and from the radio on the windowsill the traditional songs did a good job of filling the silences. Seasonal stuff from Sinatra or Elvis mixed in with the more recent Christmas hits from Slade and Wizzard. That awful Queen song looked like it was going to be the Christmas Number One. He didn't like it much anyway but he knew that he'd never be able to hear it again without thinking about her. About her body, before and after. Her face and how it must have looked, Franklin pushing her down among the cardboard boxes . . .

She stood with her back to him, washing up at the sink. He sat at the table and looked at the Daily Mirror. *The newsprint, the soapsuds, the absurdly cheery DJ—things to look at and listen to as, separately, they both went over and over it. Remembering what had happened at the station that morning.*

Thinking about the police officer, pacing around the Interview Room, winking at the WPC in the corner, leaning down on the desk and shouting.

He thought about the copper's face. The smile that felt like a slap.

She was thinking about the way he'd smelled.

"Right," the officer had said. "Let's go over it again." And then, afterward, he'd said it again. And again. Shaking his head indulgently when she'd finally broken down, beckoning the WPC, who strolled across, pulling a tissue from the sleeve of her uniform. A minute or two, a glass of water, and then they were back into it. The detective sergeant marching around the place, as if in all his years of training he'd never learned the difference between victim and criminal.

He'd done nothing, said nothing. Wanted to, but thought better of it. Instead, he'd sat and watched and listened to his wife crying and thought stupid thoughts, like why, when it was so cold, when he was buttoned up in his heaviest coat, was the bastard detective sergeant in shirt-sleeves? Rings of sweat beneath both beefy arms.

Now there was a choir singing on the radio . . .

He stood up and walked slowly toward the sink, stopping when he was within touching distance of her. He could see something stiffen around her shoulders as he drew close.

"You need to forget everything he said, okay? That sergeant. He was just going over it to get everything straight. Making sure. Doing his job. He knows it'll be worse than that on the day. He knows how hard the defense lawyer's going to be. I suppose he's just preparing us for it, you know? If we go through it now, maybe it won't be so hard in court." He took another step and he was standing right behind her. Her head was perfectly still. He couldn't tell what she was looking at, but all the while her hands remained busy in the white plastic washing-up bowl . . .

"Tell you what," he said. "Let's just get through

Christmas, shall we, love? It's not just for us after all, is it? New year soon, and then we can just keep our heads down, and get on with it, and wait for the trial. We could go away for a bit. Try and get back on an even keel maybe . . ."

Her voice was a whisper. He couldn't make it out.

"Say again, love."

"That policeman's aftershave," she said. "I thought at first it was the same as Franklin's. I thought I was going to be sick. It was so strong . . ."

She began to scream the second his hand touched the back of her neck and it grew louder as she spun around, the water flying everywhere, her arm moving hard and fast, striking out instinctively, the mug in her hand smashing across his nose.

Then she screamed at what she had done and she reached out for him and they sank down onto the linoleum, which quickly grew slippery with blood and suds.

While the voices of young boys filled the kitchen, singing about holly and ivy.

FOUR

Back when the Peel Centre had been the home of cadets in training, Becke House had been a dormitory building. To Thorne it still felt utilitarian, dead. He swore, on occasion, that rounding a corner, or pushing open an office door, he could catch a whiff of sweat and homesickness . . .

No surprise when, a month or so earlier, everyone on Team 3 had got very excited at news of improved facilities and extra working space. In reality, it amounted to little more than an increased stationery budget, a reconditioned coffee machine, and one more airless cubbyhole, which Brigstocke had immediately commandeered. There were now three offices in the narrow corridor that ran off the major incident room. Brigstocke had the new one, while Thorne shared his with Yvonne Kitson. Holland and Stone were left with the smallest of the lot, negotiating rights to the wastepaper basket and arguing about who got the chair with the cushion.

Thorne hated Becke House. Actually it *depressed* him, sapped his energy to the point where he hadn't enough left to hate it properly. He'd heard somebody once joking about Sick Building Syndrome, but to him the place wasn't so much sick as terminally ill.

He'd spent the morning catching up. Sitting at his gunmetal gray desk, sweating like a pig, and reading every scrap of paperwork there was on the case. He read the postmortem report, the forensic report, his own report on the visit to Derby Prison. He read Holland's notes on the search of Remfry's house, the interviews with relatives of the women Remfry had raped, and the statements from some of the men he'd shared cells with in three different prisons.

Inches thick already and only one promising lead. An ex-cellmate of Remfry's had mentioned a prisoner named Gribbin, whom Remfry had talked about falling out with, back when the pair of them were on remand in Brixton. Gribbin had been released from prison himself only four months before Remfry and had skipped parole. There was a warrant out . . .

When Thorne had finished reading, he spent some time fanning his face with an empty folder. He stared at the mysterious scorch marks on the polystyrene ceiling tiles. Then he read everything again.

When Yvonne Kitson came in, he looked up, dropped the notes down onto his desk, and gazed toward the open window.

"I've been thinking about jumping," he said. "Suicide seems like quite an attractive option, and at least I'd get a breeze on the way down. What d'you reckon?"

She laughed. "We're only on the third floor." Thorne shrugged. "Where's the fan?"

"Brigstocke's got it."

"Typical . . ." She sat down on a chair against the wall and reached into a large handbag. Thorne laughed when she pulled out the familiar Tupperware container.

"Wednesday, so it must be tuna," he said.

She peeled the lid off and took out a sandwich. "Tuna *salad,* actually, smart-arse. My old man went a bit mad this morning and stuck a slice of lettuce on . . ."

Thorne leaned back in his chair, tapped a plastic ruler along its arm. "How do you do it, Yvonne?"

She looked up, her mouth full. "What?"

Still holding the ruler, Thorne spread his arms wide, waved them around. "This. All of it. As well as three young kids . . ."

"The DCI's got kids . . ."

"Yeah, and he's a fucking mess like the rest of us. You seem to manage it all without breaking a sweat. Work, home, kids, dogs, *and* your sodding lunch in a box." He held out the ruler toward her, as if it were a microphone. "Tell us, DI Kitson, how do you manage it? What's your secret?"

She cleared her throat, playing along. Truth be known, they were both glad of a laugh. "Natural talent, an old man who's a pushover, and ruthless organizational skills. Plus, I never take the job home."

Thorne blinked.

"Right, any more questions?"

Thorne shook his head, put the ruler down on his desk.

"Good. I'm going to get a cup of tea. Want one . . . ?"

They walked along the corridor, past the other offices, toward the Major Incident Room.

"Seriously, though," Thorne said, "you do amaze me sometimes." He meant it. Nobody on the team had known Yvonne Kitson for very long, but bar the odd comment from older, less efficient male colleagues, nobody had a bad word to say about her. At thirty-three, she would almost certainly have been furious about the fact that many of them, Thorne included, found her comfortingly mumsy. This had more to do with her personality and style than with her face or figure, both of which were more than attractive. Her clothes were never flashy, her ash-blond hair was always sensible. She had no sharp edges, she did her job, and she never seemed to get rattled. Thorne found it easy to see why Kitson was already earmarked for bigger and better things.

At the coffee machine, Kitson leaned down to take

Thorne's cup from the dispenser. She handed the tea to him. "I meant it, about taking the job home." She began to feed more coins into the machine. "Couldn't if I wanted to, there's no bloody room . . ."

Every window in the Incident Room was open. Bits of paper were being blown from the tops of desks and filing cabinets. Thorne sipped his tea, listened to the flutter of paper, to the grunts of those bending to pick it up, and he thought how different he was from this woman. He took the job everywhere, home included, though there wasn't usually anybody there to bring it home *to*. He and his ex-wife, Jan, had divorced five years earlier, after she'd started getting distinctly extracurricular with a fine-arts lecturer. Thorne had had one or two "adventures" since then, but there hadn't been anyone significant.

Kitson dropped the red-hot plastic cup into another empty one and blew across the top of her drink. "By the way, the Remfry case?" she said. "Is it just me, or are we getting seriously fucking nowhere?"

Thorne saw Russell Brigstocke appear on the far side of the room. He beckoned, turned, and headed back in the direction of his office. Thorne took a step in the same direction, and, without looking, he answered Kitson's question.

"No, it isn't just you . . ."

When Russell Brigstocke was really pissed off, he had a face that could curdle milk. When he was *trying* to look serious, there was a hint of the melodramatic, a cocking of the head, and a pursing of the lips that always made Thorne smile, much as he tried not to.

"Right, where are we, Tom?"

Thorne tried and failed not to smile. He didn't bother to hide it, deciding that a more upbeat response than the one he'd just given Yvonne Kitson might not be a bad idea anyway. "Nothing earth-shattering, but it's ticking along, sir." It was always *sir* after one of Brigstocke's looks. "We've traced most of the male relatives now. Nothing that hopeful, but we might get lucky. Spoken to most of Remfry's former cellmates and the Gribbin thing looks the most likely . . ."

Brigstocke nodded. "I think it sounds promising. If someone bit half my nose off, I think *I'd* bear a fucking grudge."

"Remfry *said* it was him that did it. Probably just showing off. Anyway, we can't find Gribbin . . ."

"What else?"

Thorne held up his hands. "That's it. Apart from chasing up the computer side of it. We can start looking at the Inmate Information System as soon as Commander Jeffries reports back."

"He has," Brigstocke said. "Don't get too excited . . ."

Stephen Jeffries was a high-ranking police officer who actually worked for HM Prison Service. As the official police adviser, he was based at Prison Service Headquarters, in a grand-looking building off Millbank, from where he could stare directly into the offices of MI6 on the opposite side of the river.

Jeffries had been looking, *quietly,* into the feasibility of a leak from the Inmate Information System. If this was where the killer was getting his information, an awful lot of people would be wanting to know how.

"Commander Jeffries has delivered an interim judgment, suggesting that as an avenue of inquiry, this would be unlikely to prove fruitful."

"You'll have to help me," Thorne said. "I haven't got my 'bullshit to English' dictionary handy at the minute . . ."

"Don't be a smart-arse, Tom. All right? That would really help *me*."

Thorne shrugged. It sounded as if Jeffries came from

the same place that shat out Chief Superintendent Trevor Jesmond. "I'm listening."

Brigstocke glanced down at the piece of paper on his desk, speed-read a section out loud. "'Individuals with computer access to the system are based at the main HQ building as well as the twelve regional offices nation-wide—London, Yorkshire, the Midlands, et cetera . . .'"

Thorne groaned. "We're talking hundreds of people . . ."

"Thousands. Checking them all out would be a major drain on manpower, even if I had it."

Thorne nodded. "Right. So even if that *were* to prove fruitful, it wouldn't be proving very fruitful very bloody quickly." He picked up his empty teacup from Brigstocke's desk, spun around on his chair, and took aim at the wastepaper basket in the corner.

"No," Brigstocke said.

The paper cup missed by more than a foot. Thorne spun around again. "What about somebody hacking into the system?"

"Bloody hell, thousands of suspects is bad enough, now you want millions . . ."

"I don't *want* them, but if the system isn't secure . . ."

"If that system isn't secure, a lot of people are going to get their arses severely kicked. The IIS has information on the whereabouts of every prisoner in the country, terrorists included. There's all sorts of stuff on there. If it turns out that somebody's been able to break into it, for *whatever* reason . . . Jesus, they'll be talking about Douglas Remfry in Parliament."

"They're looking into it, though?" Thorne asked.

"As far as I know . . ."

"They've got things that tell them, haven't they? If they've been hacked. Like alarms. If somebody's been trying to break into the system?"

"Don't ask me," Brigstocke said. "I can barely send a fucking e-mail . . ."

Not long ago, even doing *that* would have been beyond Thorne, but he'd made an effort and was starting to get to grips with the technology. He'd even bought a computer to use at home. He hadn't used it very much yet.

"So, one thing's a drain on manpower, the other's politically sensitive. Has Commander Jeffries got any suggestions as to what we *can* do?"

Brigstocke took off his glasses, wiped the sweat from the frames with a handkerchief, and put them back. "No, but *I* have. I think there are other ways that the killer could have got the information he needed about Remfry."

"Go on . . ."

"What about if he got it from the victim's family? Gets his mum's name out of the phone book, rings up, and says he's an old friend who wants to visit . . ." Thorne nodded. It was possible. "Once he finds out where Remfry is and when he's coming out, he starts sending the letters . . ."

"He gets everything from Remfry's mother?"

"Remfry's mother . . . maybe one of the prison staff. I just think there are other things we could be looking at . . ."

"What's the motive, Russell?" Still the big question. "Why was Remfry killed?"

Brigstocke puffed out his cheeks, leaned back in his chair. "Fucked if I know. Got to be worth talking to Mrs. Remfry again, though . . ."

Thorne couldn't see it, and yet there was something in what Brigstocke had said. *Something* that had caused Thorne's heart to beat faster, just for a second; but, like the face of someone in a dream, like an object he ought to recognize, glimpsed from an unfamiliar angle, it had faded away before he could see it for what it was.

He was still trying to work it out when he spoke. "I'm chasing something else up. Something with the photos . . ."

Brigstocke leaned forward, raised an eyebrow.

"I'll tell you if it comes to anything," Thorne said. He looked at his watch. "Fuck, I'm going to be late . . ."

As he was standing up, the phone began to ring in his office next door . . .

Holland's mobile had rung just as he was heading across to the pub, for what was becoming something of a regular lunchtime pint. Andy Stone had given him that look. The one he'd been getting from a few of the lads, whenever the mobile rang, and they saw his face as HOME came up on caller ID.

"Shit," Holland said.

Stone took a few steps toward the pub doorway and stopped. "Shall I get you a beer, Dave?"

Holland pressed a button on the phone and brought it to his ear. After a few seconds he caught Stone's eye and shook his head.

Sophie was still crying when he walked through the door twenty minutes later.

"What's the matter?" He wrapped his arms around her, knowing what the answer would be.

"Nothing," she said. "I'm sorry . . . I know I shouldn't call." The words sputtered into his collar between sobs.

"It's okay. Look, I've only got about a quarter of an hour, but we can have a quick bit of lunch together. I'll go back when you're feeling calmer."

The baby was three months away. It was easy enough to put these weekly collapses down to hormones, but he knew that there was much more going on. He knew how frightened she was. Frightened that he would make a choice between her and the job. That he would think she was *forcing* him to make a choice. That the baby would not be enough to make him choose her. He understood because he was twice as scared.

They sat on the sofa and cuddled until she grew quiet. He whispered and squeezed, feeling the bump against his leg that was the child inside her, staring across the living room and watching the minutes go by on the video recorder display.

"Thorne."

"This is Eve Bloom . . ."

It took him a second to place the name, the voice. To put the two of them together. "Oh . . . hello. Sorry, I was miles away. Already thinking about lunch."

"Is this not a good time? Because . . ."

"It's fine. What can I do for you?"

"Just being nosy, if I'm honest. Wondered how it was all going. Stupid really, when I haven't the faintest idea what *it* actually is. Just, you know, curious as to whether that tape you took away has helped you . . . solve . . . *it!*"

He remembered hearing the amusement in her voice before. The phone in that hotel room, pressed tight to his ear. Happy to hear it this time.

"Fine, but I have to be somewhere about ten minutes ago, so . . ."

"That's okay, I didn't really mean now anyway . . ."

"Sorry?"

"What about lunch on Saturday? You can ask me a few pointless questions about answering machines, claim that I'm still helping you with your inquiries, and stick it all on expenses. Twelve-thirty any good . . . ?"

He hung up a few minutes later, just as Yvonne Kitson

strolled back into the office. "What on earth are you grinning about?" she said.

"Forget it, Mr. Thorne. No fucking way am I eating duck's feet."

The fact that Dennis Bethell was built like a brick shithouse and had a voice like a chorus girl on helium made most things he said sound vaguely ludicrous, but this was up there with the best of them . . .

It had been Thorne's idea. The last time they'd met had been in a pub and the voice, as it often did, had caused something of a scene. A sedate lunch sounded like a better idea and Thorne was fond of this place. The New Moon in the heart of Chinatown served the best dim sum in town. Thorne loved the ritual every bit as much as the food. He enjoyed watching the grumpy-looking old women as they wheeled their trolleys around the place. He liked stopping them, asking them to lift the lids, making his selections.

Thorne had had to explain the system to Bethell, who'd been sitting in a corner looking very confused when he got there. He was twenty minutes late, but Bethell hadn't been difficult to find. He was six feet three with the build of a WWE wrestler, spiky peroxide hair, and a great deal of gold jewelry. Spotting him in a restaurant where the clientele was almost entirely Chinese was not exactly taxing.

Today, Bethell was wearing camouflage combats and a bright blue T-shirt stretched across his enormous chest, bearing the slogan BITCH.

"Shark's fin soup and all that, fine. Duck's *feet*? That's horrible . . ."

"Relax, Kodak," Thorne had said. He smiled at the old woman as she lifted another bamboo lid. "I'll order for you . . ."

They'd chatted for a while, Thorne putting his man at

ease but also enjoying the to and fro of it. He was comfortable in these places, around the likes of Dennis Bethell.

Thorne popped a wafer-wrapped prawn into his mouth and slid the photograph of Jane Foley across the table. Bethell wiped soy sauce from his fingers with a napkin and picked it up.

"Nice," he said. "Very nice . . ."

Thorne knew that Bethell would be talking about the picture itself. The composition, the lighting. As a hardened pornographer, he was way past appreciation of the models themselves.

"I knew you'd like it," Thorne said.

"I do. It's very tasty. Who took it?"

"Well, do you know what, Kodak? I said to myself that if anybody could find out for me, it would be you . . ."

A bit more chat. Business, Bethell said, was booming. Though the dot-com filth merchants had once threatened the likes of him, Bethell was delighted to report that his work was more in demand than ever. Thumbnails from his legendary 1983 "Barnyard" series of pictures were being eagerly downloaded, having acquired almost legendary status among smut surfers . . .

Dennis Bethell's high-quality porno work had been getting men off for about as long as Thorne had been on the job. From slightly saucy to graphic glamour spreads, Bethell was a deft hand at anything that involved a lens and nipples. He was harmless enough and had been a reliable informant for a good many years. Thorne had come to regard him as one of the city's great eccentrics. A pumped-up East End vaudevillian with a hair-trigger temper, a talent for making girls take their clothes off, and his own catchphrase, "Nothing with children!"

"So, come on, then," Thorne said. "Is it professional or not?"

Bethell peered at the image, held it up to the light, sucked his teeth. "Yeah, maybe . . ."

"Not good enough, Kodak." Thorne raised a finger to attract the attention of the woman behind the small bar. He held up his empty bottle of Tsing Tao, ordering another.

"It's complicated," Bethell said. "These days there's a huge market for professionally taken stuff that's *made* to look like it was snapped by an amateur. Like it's a picture of someone's girlfriend. See what I mean? Especially with this sort of stuff."

"What sort of stuff?"

"This S-and-M stuff. Handcuffs and whips and chains. Fetishism." Bethell held up the picture that Thorne had looked at a hundred and more times. He looked at it again. This one had been taken from above, the woman flat on her face, hands bound behind her back. The hood tied at the bottom this time, like a noose.

"You ever do this sort of thing?" Thorne asked.

By now Bethell had a mouthful of minced crab dumpling. He answered cautiously, as if he thought the question was meant to catch him out somehow. "Yeah, I *have* done. Plenty of these pervy mags around. My stuff's better than this, though . . ."

"Naturally. Listen, if this *is* a professional job, can you find out who took it?"

"I could ask around, I suppose, but—"

"What about where the film was developed?"

"Waste of time. Unless the bloke's a moron, he'd have done it himself. Digital camera, straight to his PC. Piece of cake . . ."

"Find out what you can, then. I want to know who the model is and who paid for the shoot."

Bethell looked pained. "Oh, be fair, Mr. Thorne. A bit of info is all well and good, but that's like doing your job for you. Like being a bloody detective."

The waitress delivering Thorne's beer giggled at Bethell's despairing squeak and hurried away. Thankfully Bethell didn't catch it.

"Think of it as another string to your bow, Kodak. You might fancy a change of career. The force is always on the lookout for eager young lads like yourself . . ."

"You can be a right bastard sometimes, Mr. Thorne . . ."

Thorne leaned across the table and held a chopstick inches away from Bethell's face. "Yes I can, and just to prove it, if you don't do a decent job on this for me, I will come round to your dwelling slash business premises, take your zoomiest zoom lens, and stick it so far up your arse, you'll be taking pictures of your large intestine with it. Pass the prawn crackers, will you . . . ?"

Bethell sulked for a few minutes. Then he picked up the photograph and slid it into the pocket of his combat trousers.

"You really should try one of these duck's feet, Kodak," Thorne said. "Did you know, they can actually make you swim faster?"

Bethell's eyes widened. "Are you winding me up, Mr. Thorne . . . ?"

Welch was standing, waiting in the doorway, when Caldicott appeared at the other end of the landing with the mail trolley. As it got closer, agonizingly slowly, stopping at almost every door, it became clear that Caldicott's face still hadn't healed properly.

One side, from mouth to forehead, was shiny, like it was slick with sweat, and the color of something that might have been skinned. Against the raw, weeping red, the lines of tiny white rings stood out clearly, the ones on what was left of his lips looking like a row of cold sores . . .

The mail trolley squeaked that little bit nearer. Caldicott grinning as best he could, the mail round a nice cushy number. A sweetener from the caring sharing screws on the VP wing, after the weeks spent in hospital.

A couple of morons from B-wing had caught him in the laundry room. They shouldn't have been anywhere near the place by rights, should have been locked up, but someone somewhere had turned a blind eye. Left a door open.

One of Caldicott's women had *actually* been a girl. A fourteen-year-old. Caldicott had told Welch, sworn to him that he thought she was older, that he wasn't into meat that tender. Surely, Caldicott pleaded, surely *he* must be able to understand. He must have been in a similar position. I mean, come on, some of the girls around these days! Welch had admitted that, yes, he knew what Caldicott meant and he *had* been there himself, several times, and he mentally thanked his lucky stars that the girl he'd been caught for had been over sixteen, if not by a great deal. Caldicott had probably told *them* as well, the animals down in the laundry room. He'd have pleaded, told them that he thought the girl was older, but they wouldn't have been interested in that kind of bullshit from a pervert. These were men who dealt in facts.

While one held Caldicott calmly by the cock and balls, the other had emptied the dryer, dropping the laundry neatly into the red plastic bucket. Then, his screams unheard or ignored, they had bent Caldicott over and forced his head and shoulders into the massive steel drum, pressing his face down onto the red-hot metal . . .

Caldicott holding out a letter, a smile pulling the seared skin up and back across his yellowing incisors. Welch, thinking he looks like the phantom of the fucking opera, snatching the envelope and stepping quickly back behind the door . . .

The envelope has been opened, of course, but he's long past caring about privacy or any of that. He has a few precious minutes alone and the chance to read her letter, the last one he will be forced to read in a tiny room that stinks of his cellmate's shit.

There's another photo. It's the first thing he looks for and he almost shouts out loud when he feels it tucked down between the pages of the letter itself. He pulls it out and slaps it down flat on his chest without looking. Then slowly he lifts it up, little by little, moaning out loud as he catches his first glimpse of her. The hood has gone, but this time her back is to the camera, her head lowered. Just a glimpse of shortish hair, the face hidden. She is sitting on her heels, her wrists fastened securely behind her, the shadows falling across her shoulder blades and beautiful round arse . . .

The door opens and he is not alone anymore. He quickly draws his knees up to hide the erection and presses the picture flat against his chest again. As his cellmate drops with a grunt onto the bed opposite, Welch is already closing his eyes, every last detail of Jane's nakedness clearly recalled and perfectly visible on the back of his eyelids.

May 7, 1976

"Ladies and gentlemen, you may find this surprising, but I wish, for the next few minutes, to concentrate on the evidence of a witness called by the defense . . . I invite you to consider the evidence given here by Detective Sergeant Derek Turnbull. Sergeant Turnbull's record as a police officer is exemplary and I believe we should set great store by his testimony. We should take seriously the words we have heard him speak during this very disturbing case.

"I want you to remember these words . . .

"We should remember Sergeant Turnbull's words about the interviews he carried out with the woman who accuses my client of this serious offense. He spoke about the 'confusion,' about the 'lack of focus,' he conceded under cross-examination that this woman's thinking 'seemed to be all over the place.' I ask you, should an incident that was allegedly so distressing not be easy to recall accurately? Should it not be seared into the memory? Yes, of course. And yet this woman cannot be sure about exact times. There is no consistent description of what my client was wearing at the time of the supposed attack. Just a good deal of hot air and a lot of irrelevant nonsense about aftershave . . .

"We should remember Sergeant Turnbull's words when he described the results of the physical examination. Nothing was found beneath this woman's fingernails. Nothing was found to suggest any resistance whatsoever. Sergeant Turnbull repeated to the court what she said when questioned about this fact. 'I couldn't fight back,' she said.

"Could not? Or did not want to?

"We should remember, too, the sergeant's words when describing the circumstances of the first interview, the first physical examination. This examination was, in his words, 'worse than useless,' taking place as it did the morning after the alleged attack and after the so-called victim had showered. Remember his colleague's words when describing the dress which you have been shown as Exhibit A? 'Too nice to wear to work.' I put these things together, ladies and gentlemen, and I come up with an altogether different version of what happened in that stockroom in December of last year . . .

"Could not that dress have been torn during the frenzied, and consensual, bout of lovemaking to which my client freely admits? Could not the bruising be no more than the marks of excessive passion? Could not that shower have been taken, yes, to wash away the smell of my client, but only so as to hide the truth of her ongoing sexual relationship with him from her husband?

"I have asked you to remember the words of a police officer whose evidence was intended to damn the man I represent here today. Instead, unwittingly, I'm sure, he has done quite the opposite. I have asked you to consider these words and I can see that you are doing just that. I can see from *your faces, ladies and gentlemen of the jury, that these words have caused you, quite rightly, to doubt. If you doubt, as you surely must, the truth of what this woman claims to have happened, then I know that your deliberations in the jury room will be very short.*

"The law, of course, is quite clear about reasonable doubt. I feel sure that this being the case, doubting as you must, you will do the right thing. You will do the just thing. You will do as His Honor must instruct you so to do, and acquit my client . . ."

FIVE

Another hot, humid evening. The air outside heavy with the taste of a storm on the way. Tantalizing snippets of conversation from people walking past drifted into the living room through the open windows.

Thorne had sat eating in T-shirt and shorts, listening to the noise from a party on the other side of the road. He didn't know what annoyed him more—the raised voices and the cranked-up sound system, or the good time that some people he didn't know were clearly having.

His plate licked clean by Elvis, Thorne had opened a can of cheap lager, tuned out the sounds of music and laughter, and spent a couple of hours reading. A summer's evening absorbed in violent death.

These were the reports based on searches of CRIM-INT—the Criminal Intelligence database—looking for any cases whose parameters might overlap with the Remfry killing . . .

Holland and Stone had been thorough. It was largely about trial and error, about narrowing the search down and coming up with hits that might be significant. Key words were entered. Matches were sifted and examined in relation to those from other searches. *Rape/murder* produced few cases where the victim was male, but the results were still cross-referenced with those that came up when other, more specific key words were punched into the system.

Sodomy. Strangulation. Ligature. Washing line.

And up they'd come . . .

A series of unsolved murders going back five years. Eight young boys brutally abused and strangled, their bodies dumped in woods, gravel pits, and recreation grounds. A pedophile ring that was too well organized or too well connected. Uncatchable.

A man attacked in his own home. Tied up with washing line while his home was ransacked, then kicked to death for no good reason. Thorne thought about Darren Ellis, the old couple he'd tied up and robbed . . .

A catalog of vicious sexual assaults and murders, many still unsolved. The grim details now little more than entries in a uniquely disturbing reference library. A resource to be accessed, in the hope that a past horror might shed light on a present one.

Not this time.

Holland *had* actually pulled the files on two cold murder cases: a young man, thirty or so, found in the boot of a car in 2002. Raped and choked to death with an unidentified ligature. A man in his sixties, attacked in a multistory car park and strangled with washing line in 1996.

Thorne had agreed both with Holland's initial assessment and his final conclusion. Both files had been worth a closer look. Both had been put back.

Once he'd stuffed the report away in his briefcase, Thorne went over and stood by the open window. For ten minutes or so he'd stared across at the house where the party was, trying and failing to identify a song from its annoyingly familiar bass line. Trying and failing to stop thinking about bodies years dead and a body as yet unburied and the photograph he'd given Dennis Bethell . . .

Then he'd called his father.

After he'd hung up, twenty frustrating minutes later, Thorne stood, holding the phone, and tried to imagine the synapses in his father's brain misfiring, the thoughts exploding in a shower of tangential sparks . . .

The cascade of color blackened. It became the dark hood that covered the head of a naked woman and masked the terror on the face of a pale, stiffening corpse. Life choked off and arse exposed and a thin line of brown blood on rusty bedsprings.

Thorne took off what few clothes he still had on, walked through to the bedroom, and dropped down onto the mattress. He lay there in the semidarkness, staring up at the outline of the lampshade that had cost a pound from IKEA, realizing that it was cheap because it was also nasty.

The bed felt as if it were full of grit.

He could feel the dreadful, delicate weight of the case upon him. Like the dark tickle of something unwanted crawling across his body. The sharp, spindly legs of it picking their way across the sheen of sweat on his chest.

Thorne closed his eyes, remembering a moment of calm and contentment on a bracken-covered hillside.

Except that he was unsure it *was* a memory. If it had ever happened, the details had slipped away over time. Perhaps it was the memory of a dream he'd once had, or a fantasy of some sort. Maybe it was a scene from a long-forgotten film or TV show he'd once watched and into which he'd projected himself . . .

Wherever it came from, two others were always there with him, lying on the hillside among the bracken. A man and a woman, or perhaps a girl and a boy. Their ages were as unclear as their relationship to him or each other, but all three of them were happy. Where they actually were never seemed to matter. The geography of the place was changeable. Sometimes he was sure there was a river down below them. At other times it was a road, the hum of insects becoming the distant drone of traffic.

The only constants were the bracken and the presence of the pair lying just a few feet away, the ground beneath and the sky above the three of them . . .

It seemed as if they'd eaten something, a picnic maybe. Thorne felt full, lying there, his arms spread out wide, six inches off the ground, moving lazily back and forth through the bracken. He had a smile on his face and his stomach still jumped and fluttered with the final bursts of laughter. He could never be sure who or what had caused them all to laugh such a lot. He could never be sure of much beyond the fine, unfamiliar feeling that surged through him as he remembered. As he imagined. As he *lay* on that hillside.

Blurred as the edges of Thorne's reality on that hillside were—the whys and whens and whos so indistinct as to be virtually nonexistent—it still seemed, at moments such as these, ankle-deep in madness and butchery, a pretty good place to be.

With the first fat raindrops beginning to fall outside, he pressed his head back into the pillow and imagined the fronds of bracken, feathery against his neck.

As the headlights from passing cars played across the bedroom window, Thorne felt only the sunlight on his face.

June 12, 1976

They moved through the shopping center, almost touching, their faces blank, each carrying a bag. A couple walking around the shops together. Seeing them, no one could ever have known.

The enormity of the space between them.

The pain that grew to fill it.

How little time they had left . . .

They touched things in shops, picked up items to get a closer look, occasionally made the same banal comments they might have made six months before. "We could put that in the kitchen." "Do you think one of those would look nice in the bedroom?" "That color really suits you."

They walked into a shop that sold ugly ornaments, useless knickknacks, like two people in a dream . . .

Since the day the trial had ended, they had been going through the motions. Shopping, eating, tidying toys away. Sitting on the settee together and watching It's a Knockout *and* George and Mildred. *Getting through the days. The only obvious change being that she hadn't gone back to work. Unlike Franklin. He'd been welcomed back with apologies and open arms.*

Out of one shop and into another. They strolled through a department store, taking care, of course, to avoid the cosmetics department. The perfumes, and especially the aftershave. These days, the great smell of Brut was liable to make her throw up all over the place.

They were almost perfect, like the victims of bodysnatchers. They were a "Spot the Difference" competition that was unwinnable. The "before" and "after" were, to all intents and purposes, identical, but what was in their heads and their hearts would never be seen, could never be imagined. Least of all by them.

She had retreated into herself and he had become unbearably buoyant. Around the house their bodies did the normal things, while her silence and his false cheer chased each other from room to room. While the mania and the suspicion festered and matured.

It was my fault . . .

Why didn't she struggle . . . ?

He was looking at picture frames, remembering the face of the jury foreman. A few feet away, she stood, spinning a display of postcards, seeing only stubby fingers reaching into trousers, scrabbling at her crotch. He caught her eye but she looked away before he could smile.

The next second, Franklin's wife had stepped from behind a glass display case and was standing in front of her.

He took a step toward them, then stopped as his wife raised a hand, reached toward this woman who had looked down on her, at her, every day from the public gallery. He watched as Franklin's wife ignored the hand that reached out to her, pulled back her head, and snapped it forward, releasing a thick gobbet of spittle into his wife's face.

There was a gasp from a woman nearby. An-

other stepped back, openmouthed, and knocked a glass decanter crashing to the floor.

He stepped in front of his wife then, and guided her gently but firmly toward the exit. As they left she never took her eyes from the woman who had spat at her. She never made a move to wipe the spit away.

She didn't speak a word as she was taken back to a house she would never leave again.

SIX

From Kentish Town, Thorne took every shortcut he knew, cutting through side streets until he reached Highbury Corner and then heading east along the Balls Pond Road toward Hackney.

Thorne took a quick glance at his *A–Z*. The florist's was tucked away somewhere behind Mare Street, a stone's throw from London Fields. This area of parkland stood alone in the midst of one of the most depressed areas in the city. It was once grazed by sheep and prowled by highwaymen. Now up-and-comers who directed videos or worked in advertising sat on benches sipping their skinny lattes or walked their pit bulls across the green, doing their best to look like hard men.

Thorne drove along streets bustling with Saturday morning shoppers. Noisy with the cries of greeting, the shouts of traders in the markets. And every few hundred yards, a look on a face or a hand thrust into a pocket that Thorne recognized as the signs of an altogether different kind of business.

Here, as in a dozen other boroughs, street crime was out of control. Phone jacking was virtually a form of social interaction, and if you walked around with a Walkman, you were a tourist who couldn't read a street map.

These days, the highwaymen prowled in gangs.

So the powers that be, in their infinite wisdom and desire for good press, were targeting areas like Hackney, piloting schemes that would involve the youth of an area. Thorne had read a report of one such scheme involving a couple of earnest young officers trading in the blue serge for hooded tops, and getting down with the kids in a local community center. One had asked a thirteen-year-old gang member if he could think of ways he might avoid getting into trouble with the police.

The kid had answered without a trace of irony. "Wear a ski mask."

It was a small place, sitting between a minicab firm and a locksmith's. The shopfront was pleasingly old fashioned; the window display minimalist, the name painted in a green, creeping-ivy design on a plain cream background.

BLOOMS.

Inside, the shop was lit by candles. There was classical music playing quietly in the background. There wasn't a single flower Thorne recognized . . .

"Are you looking for something in particular?" A man, thirty or so, with a paperback in his hand, stood behind a small wooden counter.

Thorne moved toward him, smiling. "Do people not buy daffodils anymore? Roses, chrysanthemums . . . ?"

A woman carrying an enormous assortment of flowers stepped through a door at the back of the shop. She looked to be in her midthirties. As soon as she spoke, Thorne recognized the voice—gabbling, confident, *amused*. It was clear that Eve Bloom had recognized him as well.

"Well, we can get that sort of specialized stuff in if you want, Mr. Thorne, but it *will* be very expensive . . ."

He laughed, sizing her up in a few seconds. Though her hands stayed busy among the stems she was carrying, he could tell that she was doing the same.

She was short, maybe five feet two, with blond hair

held up by a large wooden clip. She wore a brown apron over jeans and a sweatshirt. Her face was dotted with freckles, and the smile revealed a gap between her two front teeth.

Thorne fancied the pants off her on sight.

The man behind the counter had picked up a notepad. "Shall I put in an order, Eve? For the roses and those other things . . . ?"

She put down the arrangement, lifted the apron over her head, smiled gently at him. "No, I don't think so, Keith." She turned to Thorne. "I thought we could go to this great little tearoom just around the corner. Cream teas to die for. What do you think? We've got the weather for it after all. We can pretend we're in Devon or somewhere . . ."

As they strolled, she talked virtually constantly. "Keith helps me out on a Saturday morning. He's fantastic with flowers, and the customers are very fond of him. Rest of the week I can manage the place on my own, but Saturday, early, that's when I have to make up most of the wedding arrangements, get ahead on the paperwork, accounts, and what have you. Anyway, screw it! Today, Keith can keep an eye on things for an hour or so while we pig out. He's not a genius, bless him, but he works his socks off for . . . well, for almost nothing, if I'm honest."

"What does Keith do the rest of the time?" Thorne said. "When you're not exploiting him."

Eve smiled and shrugged. "Don't really know, to be honest. I think he has to look after his mother a lot. Maybe she's well-off, because he never seems to be short. He's certainly not working in *my* shop for the money, not on what I can afford to pay him. God, I am *so* gasping for a cup of tea . . ."

The tearoom was kitsch beyond belief, with check

tablecloths, art deco tea sets, and Bakelite radios dotted around on shelves and window ledges. The cream tea for two arrived almost instantly. Eve poured Earl Grey for herself, ordinary tea for Thorne. She lathered jam and clotted cream onto her scone, grinned across the table.

"Listen, when I'm eating is probably the best chance you'll have to get a word in, so I should take your chance if I were you. I know I talk *way* too much . . ."

"The man who left the message on your answering machine, has he been in touch with you again?" She looked at him, confused. "Follow-up question," Thorne explained. "Justify the expenses claim, like you suggested. Bit of a long shot, but it seemed as good a question as any . . ."

She cleared her throat. "No, Detective Inspector, I'm afraid that I never heard from the man again."

"Thank you. If you think of anything else you will get in touch, won't you? And I needn't tell you that we'd prefer it if you didn't leave the country . . ."

She laughed and pushed the last piece of a scone into her mouth. When she'd finished it she looked straight at him, raising a hand to shield her eyes against the sunlight that streamed in through the picture window. "I take it you haven't caught him yet?" Thorne looked back at her, still eating. "Did he kill somebody?"

Thorne swallowed. "I'm sorry, I shouldn't . . ."

"I'm just putting two and two together, really." She leaned back in her chair. "I know it's a man, because I've heard his voice, and you told me you were with the Serious Crime Group, so I'm guessing that you're not after this bloke because he hasn't taken his library books back."

Thorne poured himself another cup of tea. "Yes, he did kill somebody. No, we haven't caught him yet."

"Are you going to?"

Thorne poured *her* a cup . . .

"Why me?" she said. "Why did he pick me to order the wreath from?"

"I think he picked a name at random," Thorne said. They'd found a tattered Yellow Pages in the cupboard beneath the bedside table. It had been covered in fingerprints. Thorne doubted any belonged to the killer. "He just let his fingers do the walking."

She pulled a face. "I knew I shouldn't have shelled out for that bloody box ad . . ."

Though she talked twice as much and ten times as quickly as he did, Thorne still talked more, and more easily, in the hour or so that followed than he could remember doing to almost anybody for a long time. To any woman, certainly . . .

"When's the wedding?" Eve asked as their plates were cleared away.

Thorne was struck then by how much ground they'd covered and how quickly. "A week today. God, I'd rather stick needles in my eyes . . ."

"Do you not get on with your cousin?"

Thorne smiled at the waitress as she popped the bill down on the table. "I barely know him. Probably wouldn't recognize him if he walked in here. Just family functions, you know . . ."

"Right. You choose your friends, but you can't choose your relatives."

"Yours as bad as mine, then?"

She brushed a few stray crumbs from the tabletop into her hand, emptied it onto the floor. "Is he the same sort of age as you? Your cousin?"

"No, Eileen's a lot younger than my dad, and she had Trevor pretty late. He's still only early thirties, I think . . ."

"What are you?"

"How *old*, you mean?" She nodded. Thorne opened his wallet, dropped fifteen pounds on top of the bill. "Forty-two. Forty-three in . . . fuck, in ten days."

She clipped up a few stray hairs that had tumbled loose. "I won't say that you don't look it, because that always sounds so false, but looking at you, I'd say that they were forty-three pretty interesting years."

Thorne nodded. "I'm not going to argue, but just so you know . . . I don't mind about the sounding-false thing."

She smiled, put on a pair of small almond-shaped sunglasses. "Forty, then. Late thirties at a push."

Thorne stood up, pulling his leather jacket from the chair behind him. "I'll settle for that . . ."

Back at the shop they swapped business cards, shook hands, and stood together, a little awkwardly, in the doorway. Thorne looked around. "Maybe I should get a plant or something . . ."

Eve bent down and picked up what looked like a miniature metal bucket. A cactuslike plant sprouted from a layer of smooth white pebbles. She handed it to him. "Do you like this?"

Thorne was far from sure. "What do I owe you?"

"Nothing. It's an early birthday present."

He studied it from every angle. "Right. Thanks . . ."

"It's an aloe vera plant."

Thorne nodded. Over her shoulder, he could see Keith watching them closely from behind the counter. "So I should be all right for shampoo . . ."

"There's a gel in the leaves, very good for cuts and scrapes."

Thorne looked at the fierce-looking spikes growing along the edges of the plant's sword-shaped leaves. "That'll come in handy."

They stepped out onto the pavement, the slight awkwardness returning. Thorne noticed a silver scooter parked by the side of the shop—one of the latest Vespas, based on the classic design. He nodded toward it. "Yours?"

She shook her head. "God, no. That's Keith's." She pointed to the other side of the road. "That's me over there . . ."

Thorne looked across the road at the grubby white van behind which he'd parked the Mondeo. The name of the shop was painted on its side, in the same creeping-ivy design as was on the shopfront.

"The name certainly fits," he said.

She laughed. "Right. Like being an undertaker called De'Ath. What else could I do? Flowers are the only thing I can think of that bloom . . ."

Thorne could think of several other things, but he shook his head, not wanting to say anything that might spoil a nice afternoon. "No, you're right," he said.

Thinking . . .

Bruises. Tumors. Bloodstains . . .

For the fourth time in the last hour, Welch was answering the same stupid set of questions.

"Date of birth?"

Maybe the officers just passed the list among themselves. You'd have thought that at least one of them could have come up with something more interesting . . .

"Mother's maiden name?"

But no. Same tired old teasers designed to catch out the impostor. The process had gone unchanged for many years, but these days they really weren't taking any chances. Not since the incident a couple of months earlier. A couple of Pakistanis in a prison up north had swapped places on release day and the silly bastards had let the wrong one out. Several guards had blown their pensions that day and, once the jungle drums had finished beating, given every con in the country a fucking good laugh . . .

"Do you have any tattoos?"

"Can I ask the audience?"

"You want to be a smart-arse, Welch, we can start the whole thing over again . . ."

Welch smiled and answered the questions. He wasn't going to do anything silly at this stage of the game. Each door he walked through, each successfully completed series of questions, each tick on a chart took him one step farther away from the center of the place. One step closer to the final door.

Answering pointless questions and signing his name over and over. Taking receipt of his travel warrant and discharge grant. Taking back his property. The battered wallet, the wristwatch, the ring of yellow metal. Always "yellow metal." Never "gold" in case the bastards lose it . . .

Then through another door and on to another guard, and all this one gets to say to him is "good-bye."

Welch walked away toward the gate. He moved slowly, savoring every step, seconds away from the moment when he would hear the clang of the heavy door behind him and feel the heat of the day on his face.

And look up at a sun the color of yellow metal.

For Thorne and Hendricks, a Saturday night in front of the television with beer and a takeaway curry was a regular pleasure. For nine months of the year there was football to watch, to argue about. Tonight, the start of the new season still seven weeks away, they would probably watch a film. Or just sit through whatever was on until, a couple of cans in, they stopped really caring. Maybe they would just put some music on and talk.

It was nearly nine o'clock and the light was only just starting to fade. They walked down Kentish Town

Road, away from the restaurant and back toward
Thorne's place. Both wore jeans and a T-shirt, though
Thorne's were far and away the baggier and less eye-
catching. Hendricks carried a plastic bag, heavy with
cans of lager, while Thorne took responsibility for the
curry. The Bengal Lancer delivered, but it was a nice evening for a walk and there was the added attraction of a
cold pint of Kingfisher while they'd waited, the smell
coming from the kitchens sharpening the edges of their
appetites.

"Why the rape?" Thorne asked suddenly.

Hendricks nodded. "Right. Good move. Let's get the
shoptalk out of the way—you know, the rape and murder stuff—then we can relax and enjoy *Casualty* . . ."

Thorne ignored the sarcasm. "Everything else so well
planned, so meticulously done. He takes no chances. He
strips the bed even after he's killed Remfry on the floor.
Takes everything away to make sure he leaves nothing of
himself behind . . ."

"Nothing strange about not wanting to get caught."

"No, but it was all so careful. Ritualized almost.
Whether it happened before or after the murder, I don't
see the rape as part of that. Maybe he just snapped at
some point, lost it . . ."

"I can't see it myself. The killer didn't just go mental
and do it without thinking. He knew what he was doing.
He wore a condom, so he was still wary, still in
control . . ."

There were dozens of people gathered outside the
Grapevine pub. They spilled across the pavement, laughing and drinking, enjoying the weather. Hendricks was
forced to drop behind Thorne as they stepped into the
road to skirt around the crowd.

"You think the rape wasn't part of the plan?" Hendricks was abreast of Thorne again. "You think he just
decided to do it once he'd got there?"

"No, I think he planned the whole thing. The rape just seems—"

"It was more violent than most, I agree, but rape's hardly delicate, is it?"

An old man waiting at a zebra crossing to cross the road caught just enough of the conversation. He jerked his head around and, ignoring the signal to cross, watched them walk away. A frustrated driver waiting at the crossing glared at the old man and leaned on his horn . . .

"I'm not sure why it bothers me," Thorne said. "It's a murder investigation but it's the rape part that feels significant . . ."

"You think the killer was making a point?"

"Don't you?" Hendricks shrugged and nodded, heaved the bag up, and slid a protective arm underneath. "Right," Thorne said. "So why is the simple grudge scenario not playing out . . . ?"

They walked on past the sandwich bar and the bank. Music was coming from behind open windows, drifting out of bars and down from roof terraces. Rap and blues and heavy metal. To Thorne, the atmosphere on the street seemed as relaxed as he could remember. Warm weather did strange things to Londoners. On sweaty rush-hour tube trains, tempers shortened as temperatures rose. Later, when it got a few degrees cooler and people had a drink in their hands, it was a different story . . .

Thorne smiled grimly. He knew it was only a small window of opportunity. Later still, when darkness fell and the booze began to kick in, the Saturday-night soundtrack would become a little more familiar.

Sirens and screaming and breaking glass . . .

As if on cue, as Hendricks and Thorne walked past the late-night grocers, two teenagers, standing outside, began to push each other. It might have been harmless, it might have been the start of something.

Thorne stopped, took a step back.

"Oi . . ."

The taller of the two turned and looked Thorne up and down, still clutching a fistful of the other's blue Hilfiger shirt. He was no more than fifteen. "What's your fucking problem?"

"I don't have a problem," Thorne said.

The shorter one shook himself free and turned square on to Thorne. "You will have in a minute if you don't piss off . . ."

"Go home," Thorne said. "Your mum's probably worried."

The taller one sniggered, but his mate was less amused. He looked quickly up and down the street. "You want me to smack a couple of your teeth out?"

"Only if you want me to arrest you," Thorne said.

Now they both laughed. "You a fucking copper, man? No way . . ."

"Okay," Thorne said. "I'm not a copper. And you're just a couple of innocent young scallywags minding your own business, right? Nothing I should have to worry about, you know, if I *were* a police officer, in any of your pockets." He saw the eyes of the taller boy flick toward those of his friend. "Maybe I should check, though, just to be on the safe side . . ."

Thorne leaned, smiling, toward them. Hendricks stepped forward and hissed in his ear. "Come on, Tom, for fuck's sake . . ."

A girl, two or three years older, walked out of the shop. She handed each of the boys a can of strong lager, opened one herself. "What's going on?"

The boy in the blue shirt pointed at Thorne. "Reckons he's a copper, says he's going to arrest us."

The girl took a noisy slug of beer. "Nah . . . he's not going to arrest anybody." She pointed with the can toward the bag Thorne was holding. "Doesn't want to let his fucking dinner go cold . . ."

More laughter. Hendricks put a hand on Thorne's shoulder.

Thorne carefully put the bag on the ground. "I'm not hungry anymore. Now turn out your pockets . . ."

"You love this, don't you?" the girl said. "Have you got a hard-on?"

"Turn out your pockets."

The boys stared at him, cold. The girl had another swig of beer. Thorne took a step toward them and *then* they moved. The shorter boy stepped around his friends and away, running a step or two before slowing, regaining his composure. The girl moved away more slowly, dragging the taller of the boys by the sleeve. They stared at Thorne as they went, walking away backward up the street.

The girl lobbed her empty can into the road and shouted back at Thorne.

"Poofs! Fucking queers . . ."

Thorne lurched forward to chase after them but Hendricks's hand, which had never left his shoulder, squeezed and held on. "Just leave it."

"No."

"Forget it, calm down . . ."

He yanked his shoulder free. "Little fuckers . . ."

Hendricks stepped in front of Thorne, picked up the bag, and held it out to him.

"What are you more pissed off about, Tom? The fact that I was called a queer? Or that *you* were?"

Unable to answer the question, Thorne took the bag and they carried on walking. They veered almost immediately right onto Angler's Lane, a one-way street that would bring them out close to Thorne's flat. This narrow cut-through to Prince of Wales Road had once been a small tributary off the River Fleet, now one of London's "lost" underground rivers. Here, when Victoria took the throne, local boys would fish for carp and trout, before the water became so stinking and polluted that no fish could survive, and it had to be diverted beneath the earth, confined and hidden away in a thick iron pipe.

Now, as Thorne walked home along the course of the lost river, it seemed to him that nearly two centuries later the stench was just as bad.

By a little after ten, Hendricks was fast asleep on the sofa, and likely to remain so well into Sunday morning. Thorne tidied up around him, switched off the TV, and went into the bedroom.

He got no reply from the flat. She answered her mobile almost immediately.

"It's Thorne. I hope it's not too late. I remembered from the sign on the door of the shop that you weren't open on Sundays, so I thought you might—"

"It's fine. No problem . . ."

Thorne lay back on the bed. He thought that she sounded pretty pleased to hear from him.

"I wanted to say thanks," he said. "I enjoyed today."

"Good. Me, too. Want to do it again?"

During the short pause that followed, Thorne looked up at the cheap, crappy lampshade, listened to her laughing quietly. There was a noise he couldn't place in the background. "Bloody hell," he said. "You don't waste a lot of time . . ."

"What's the point? We only saw each other a few hours ago and you're ringing up, so *you're* obviously pretty keen."

"Obviously . . ."

"Right, well, tomorrow's for sleeping and I'm busy in

the evening. So, how keen would you say you are, *really*? On a scale of one to ten . . ."

"Er . . . how does *seven* sound?"

"Seven's good. Any less and I'd've been insulted and more would have been borderline stalker. Right then, what about breakfast on Monday? I know a great caff . . ."

"Breakfast?"

"Why not? I'll meet you before work."

"Okay, I'll probably have to be at work about nine-ish, so . . ."

Eve laughed. "I thought you were keen, Thorne! We're talking about when *I* start work. Half-past five, New Covent Garden flower market . . ."

July 17, 1976

It was more than half an hour since he'd heard the noises. The grunting and the shouting and the sounds of glass shattering. He heard her footsteps as she moved around, from her bedroom across that creaky floorboard that he'd never got around to fixing, into the bathroom, and back again.

He spent that half hour willing himself to get up off the settee and see what had happened. Not moving. Needing to build up some strength, some control before he could venture upstairs . . .

Sitting in front of the television, wondering how much longer this was going to go on. The doctor had said that if she kept taking the tranquilizers, then things would settle down, but there was no sign of that happening. In the meantime, he was having to do all the stuff that needed doing. Everything. She was in no state to go to the shops or to the school. Christ, it had been over a week since she'd last come downstairs.

Walking across to the foot of the stairs, stiff and slow as a zombie . . .

Listening to it, watching it, feeling it all come apart. They'd given him the time off work, but the sick pay wasn't going to last forever and she was contributing nothing and now the debts were growing as thick and fast as the suspicion. Mush-

rooming, like the doubts that sprouted in every damp, dark corner of their lives; had been, ever since that moment when the foreman of the jury had stood and cleared his throat.

He walked into the bedroom, feeling the carpet crunch beneath his feet. He glanced down at a dozen distorted reflections of himself in the shards of broken mirror, then across to where she lay, no more than a lump beneath the blankets. He turned and walked back the way he'd come. Back across the creaky floorboard.

In the bathroom, he skidded in the puddles of ivory face cream. He stepped across the piss-colored slicks of perfume. He kicked away the broken bottles into every corner.

So much that was designed to smell alluring, desirable, mingled unnaturally on floor and walls, making him heave . . .

He moved across to the sink, afraid he would retch. He found it filled with the contents of the cabinet that stood empty above it.

Blusher and lipstick and eye shadow ground into the porcelain.

Moisturizer clogging the plug hole like poisonous waste.

Powder and shampoo and bath oil, thrown and poured and sprinkled.

The edges of her fancy soaps blunted against the walls. Dents in the plasterboard, pink as babies, blue as bruises. The mirror cracked, and spattered with nail polish, red as arterial spray . . .

He ran a tap into the perfumed swamp, splashed water onto his face. He looked around at her handprints in talcum, the fingertrails dragged through brightly colored body lotion. Hints of *herself left behind in everything she was trying to discard.*

She'd been fine until they'd found her out, hadn't she? Fine with the knowledge of what she'd done as long as it stayed just between her and Franklin. Now the guilt was eating at her, wasn't it? Sending her fucking mental or making her pretend that she was, it didn't really matter which.

Half a minute later he was walking back down the stairs, thinking, *She lied, she lied, she lied, she lied . . .*

She. Lied.

SEVEN

Thorne might well have gone right off Eve Bloom had she been a morning person—one of those deeply annoying types who is always bright-eyed and bushy-tailed whatever the ungodly hour. As it was, he was relieved to find her wedged into a quiet corner, clutching a polystyrene cup filled with seriously strong tea and grimacing at nothing in particular. She clearly felt as much like a warmed-up bag of shit as he did . . .

Thorne cranked his face into action and forced a smile. "And there I was, thinking that you'd be full of the joys of it." She stared at him, said nothing. "Fired up by the noise and the color, intoxicated by the sweet smell of a million flowers . . ."

She scowled. "No chance."

Thorne shivered slightly and rubbed his arms through the sleeves of his leather jacket. It might have been the hottest summer for a good few years, but at this time in the morning it was still distinctly bloody nippy.

"Like that, then?" he said. "Floristry losing its appeal, is it?"

She took a noisy slurp of tea. "Some aspects get ever so slightly on my tits, yes . . ."

They stepped back as a trolley piled high with long, multicolored boxes came past. The porter behind it winked at Eve, laughed when she gave him the finger.

"You know you want me, Evie," he shouted, wheeling the trolley away.

She turned back to Thorne. "So, you love *everything* about your job, do you?"

"No, not everything. I'm not big on postmortems or armed sieges. Or team-building seminars . . ."

"There you go, then . . ."

"Most of the time, though, I *think* I love it . . ."

There was the first hint of a smile. She was starting to enjoy their double act. "Sounds to me like maybe you love it, but you're not *in* love with it . . ."

"Right." Thorne nodded. "Problems with commitment."

She blew on the tea, her pale face deadpan. "Typical bloke," she said. Then she laughed and Thorne got his first glimpse that day of the gap in her teeth that he liked so much . . .

They moved methodically through the vast indoor market. Up and down the wide concrete aisles. He followed a few steps behind her, cradling his own cup of rust-colored tea and feeling himself coming slowly to life, the creases cracking open. Taking it all in . . .

The shouts and whistles of traders and customers alike echoing through the gigantic warehouse. Twenty- and fifty-pound notes counted out and slapped into palms. Porters humping boxes or steering noisy forklifts in their fluorescent green jackets. *All* the colors—the stock, the signs, the customers' fleecy tops and puffa jackets—all standing out against the dazzling white buzz of a thousand strip lights, dangling from the girders forty feet above.

Eve Bloom clearly knew every inch of this space the size of two football fields; where to find every wholesaler and specialist; where to get the pots, the bulbs, the sundries; the location of any plant, flower, or tree among tens of thousands of others. Thorne watched as she ordered, as she haggled, and as she connected with stall holders and market staff.

"All right, Evie darlin' . . ."

"How are you, sweetheart . . . ?"

"Here she is! Where you been hiding yourself, love . . . ?"

Despite her earlier stab at grumpiness, Thorne could see that she really enjoyed *this* part of the job. The smile was instant, the banter good-natured and flirtatious. If her customers liked her half as much as those she was buying from, her shop was probably doing pretty well. For all this, it was clear that she drove a hard bargain and would take nothing unless the price was right. The wholesalers shook their heads as they tapped at their computer keyboards or scribbled in their pink order books. "I'm cutting my throat selling at this price . . ." Within half an hour she was done and there was no shortage of porters volunteering to load up her boxes and take them out to where her small white van was parked.

Once business was out of the way, she took Thorne on one last circuit of the market. She showed him a bewildering selection of different flowers—the ones she liked or hated, the sweetest smelling and the oddest looking. She pointed out the red-and-yellow gerberas, lined up neatly in rows and stacked in small square boxes like fruit. The pink peonies, the orange protea like pincushions, and the phallic anthuriums, their heads like something Dennis Bethell might photograph. Thorne saw enough Jersey carnations to fill every buttonhole at a century's worth of society weddings and enough lilies for a thousand good funerals. He looked at daisies and delphiniums, the stuff of cheap and cheerful bouquets for desperate men to buy from gas station minimarts in the early hours. Then there were gangling blue-and-orange birds of paradise at five pounds a stem and fruiting lemon trees in vast pots, both surely destined for the dining tables and bespoke conservatories of Hampstead and Highgate.

Thorne nodded, asked the occasional question, looked keen. When she asked, he told her he was enjoying himself. In truth, though he was impressed by her knowledge and touched to a degree by her enthusiasm, he was dreaming of bacon sandwiches . . .

Half an hour later, and Thorne's fantasy had become greasy reality. Eve had kept him company, working her way through sausage, egg, and chips like a long-distance truck driver. It might or might not have been her breakfast of choice, but the café was not the sort of place that offered much in the way of a healthy alternative.

"How often do you do this?" Thorne asked.

"Harden my arteries or get up horribly early?"

"The market . . ."

"Just one day a week, thank God. Some people do it two or three times a week, but I'm much too fond of my bed."

Thorne swallowed another mouthful of tea. In the two and something hours he'd been up, he'd already drunk more tea than he'd normally consume in a week. He could feel it, sloshing about in his belly like dirty water at the bottom of a tank.

"So what you bought this morning's going to last you the week, then?"

"Well, if it does, the business is in big trouble. The rest of the stock I need comes over from Holland. This mad Dutchman drives a big van over on a Friday, goes round every small florist in East London. It's more expensive than coming down here, but I get to stay in bed . . ."

She reached into a small leather backpack, pulled out a packet of Silk Cut. She offered it to Thorne. "Want one?"

"No, I don't, thanks." This wasn't strictly true. Fifteen and more years he'd been off the fags, and he *still* wanted one . . .

She lit up, took a long drag. Drew the smoke down deep and let it out slowly with a low hum of contentment. "It's your birthday a week today, isn't it?"

"You've got a good memory," he said. He puffed out his cheeks. "Mine's getting worse the older I get." He pulled a mock-sulky face. "Thanks for reminding me about *that*, by the way . . ."

A spark flared briefly inside his head, then fizzled and died. There was something he was trying to remember, something he knew was important to the case. It was something he'd read. Or maybe something he hadn't read . . .

He brought his eyes back to Eve and saw that she was speaking. Saying something he couldn't hear. "Sorry, what . . . ?"

She leaned across the table. "Be a nice birthday present to yourself if you solved your case, wouldn't it?"

Thorne nodded slowly, smiled. "Well, I *had* promised myself some CDs . . ."

She flicked ash from her cigarette, rubbed the tip around the edge of the ashtray. "You don't like talking about your job, do you?"

He looked at her for a few seconds before answering. "There's things I *can't* talk about, especially with you being involved. The stuff I *can* talk about just isn't very exciting . . ."

"And you think I'd be as bored as *you* were when I showed you round the market . . . ?"

"I wasn't bored."

"Do the criminals you interview lie as badly as you do?"

Thorne laughed. "I wish."

She stubbed out her cigarette, leaned back in her chair, and looked at him. "I'm interested. In what you do."

He remembered the way he'd felt talking to her in the tearoom. How it had seemed like a long time since he'd spoken to a woman like that. It was a hell of a lot longer since he'd talked about the job. "Murder cases go cold very quickly . . ."

"So you need to catch the killer straightaway?"

Thorne nodded. "If you're going to get a result it tends to happen in the first few days. It's been two weeks already . . ."

"You never know . . ."

"I do, unfortunately."

She pushed her chair away from the table and stood up. "I need to go and get rid of some of that tea . . ."

While she was in the toilet, Thorne stared out of the steamy window. The café was in a side street between Wandsworth Road and Nine Elms Lane. From where he was sitting, Thorne could see the rush-hour traffic moving slowly across Vauxhall Bridge. Cars carrying their occupants north toward Victoria and Piccadilly, or south to Camberwell and Clapham. Toward shops and offices and warehouses where they would moan and joke about another bloody Monday and then not spend it failing to catch a killer.

It was a close call, but Thorne would not have swapped places with them.

Eve rejoined him. Above them, a train rumbled by on its way into Waterloo. She had to raise her voice. "I forgot to ask," she said, "how's the plant?"

"Sorry?"

"The aloe vera plant . . ."

Thorne blinked, remembering the vision that had greeted him on stumbling bleary-eyed into the living room at five o'clock that morning. Elvis, squatting awkwardly atop the small metal bucket. Keeping his belly low to avoid the spikes. Looking Thorne straight in the eye as he pissed happily into the white pebbles . . .

"It's doing fine," Thorne said.

Thorne's phone rang.

"Where are you?" Brigstocke said. "We've got Gribbin—"

"I'm on my way in . . ."

"When I say 'got him' I just mean we know where he is, all right? We've got to go and *get* him. Holland's waiting on your doorstep."

"Tell him I'll be back home in half an hour."

"Where the hell are you?"

Thorne looked across at Eve, who smiled and shrugged. "I've been jogging . . ."

What does a child-sex offender look like?

Thorne knew this to be a pointless question. Pointless because, truthfully, it was unanswerable. It was also extremely dangerous.

And yet people had been taught to believe that they knew the answer. That they should stick their hands up and shout it out. It was always an answer that came too late, though, wasn't it? After the damage had been done and the children had been hurt. After the man had been caught and that first fuzzy photo had appeared on the front of the newspapers. Then it was as though everything that people already knew had been confirmed. Of course! It was so bloody obvious, wasn't it? *That* was what one of those men looked like. Knew it all along . . .

If it was so obvious, if the evil that these men did was written clearly across their faces for all to see, then why did they live next door and go undetected? If you could see it in the bastards' eyes, then why did they pass by un-noticed on the streets? Why did they teach your kids? Why were you married to one?

Because, as Thorne knew all too well, you couldn't see it, no matter how much you wished that you could or how hard you looked. Nobody looked like a child-sex offender. *Everybody* did.

Thorne looked like one. And Russell Brigstocke. And Yvonne Kitson . . .

What Ray Gribbin did *not* look like was the *popular perception* of a child-sex offender. He was not your typical tabloid kiddie-fiddler. He did not have bad skin or lank, greasy hair. He did not wear thick glasses, carry a bag of boiled sweets, or wear a dirty raincoat. As well as the misshapen nose that Douglas Remfry had claimed responsibility for, Gribbin had a shaved head, cold eyes, and a smile that said "fuck right off." He was a child-sex offender who looked like an armed robber.

Whatever the hell an armed robber looked like . . .

Thorne put the photo together with the other paperwork he had been studying, and handed the lot across to where Stone and Holland were sitting in the backseat. Stone looked at the photo. "Christ, he's not what I expected," he said.

Thorne said nothing, stared out of the passenger window.

Brigstocke flashed the lights and put his foot down. The car in front of them pulled across to let the unmarked Volvo pass. "I know what you mean," he said. "Looks like the sort who might bear a grudge, though, doesn't he?"

Thorne couldn't argue with that. He watched, slightly dizzy, as the wheat fields that bordered the M4 flew past at ninety miles an hour. He made himself belch; reading had made him feel a little sick . . .

Brigstocke spoke up to get everybody's attention.

"Right, you should all have had a chance to look at the notes by the time we get there . . ." Thorne wound down his window an inch. Brigstocke glanced across at him, carried on. "This is a bit last minute, but we didn't have a lot of choice. We're doing this in a hurry, but let's all make sure we do it right, shall we?" There were grunts from the two in the back. Thorne turned to look at him. "Gribbin's got a history of violence, and if Remfry's story is to be believed, that's the *only* time Gribbin's come off worse. He's been picked up with knives on him before, so we're taking no chances . . ."

Stone leaned forward, an arm on each headrest and his face pushed between the seats. "How many going in?"

"Probably be the four of us, plus a couple of the local boys . . ."

Stone nodded, carried on speed-reading the notes.

"Watch out for the woman as well," Brigstocke said. "Sandra Cook's got a decent-size criminal record. Drug abuse, theft, prostitution. She did three months in Holloway for taking half a DC's face off with her nails . . ."

Holland shuffled forward. If Brigstocke had so much as touched the brakes, Holland would have smashed into the back of his head. "*Patricia* Cook's the woman who called up about Gribbin, right?"

Stone glanced at him. "Sandra's sister . . ."

Thorne took a gulp of cold air and shut his window.

"So why does she rat on her sister's boyfriend?" Holland asked.

Brigstocke tried to catch Holland's eye in the mirror. "That's the other reason we're not fucking around this morning," he said. "Nonattendance is not Gribbin's only violation of his parole conditions."

"Shit . . ." Stone had seen it. He held the notes out for Holland to take.

Thorne turned his head, looked at Holland. "There's

three people in the house, Dave. Gribbin, Cook, and Cook's eleven-year-old daughter . . ."

Thorne swiveled around again, pulled his seat belt taut. Beneath it, he could feel his heart start to thump that little bit faster and louder. Around the nape of his neck he could sense the smallest tingle beginning to build. He caught his breath as an insect hit the windshield in a mess of blood and wings.

It was a horseshoe-shaped cul-de-sac in a modern housing development and the property they were interested in was at the far end . . .

Thorne looked at the houses as the van slowly made its way past them up the drive. Taking in the detail, the attempts to personalize and gentrify. The bright, differently colored front doors; the hanging baskets overflowing with geraniums; the wooden signs for The Elms and The Thistles. Most of the houses and garages were empty, the occupants having left for work hours earlier, but still the occasional curtain twitched. This was probably as exciting as it would ever get.

It was one of those funny towns on the outskirts of the city that couldn't quite make its mind up if it was urban or rural. Twenty-odd miles to the west of central London, it lay uncomfortably between the M25 and the Chilterns. For its population of commuters, the proximity to rolling hills and quaintly named villages probably made the daily slog up the motorway worthwhile, but it was a different story for their teenage children. No amount of fresh air could make the place any less boring. Antique shops would not prevent them pissing it up the wall on a Friday night and cutting up rough in the center of town . . .

Thorne saw a woman staring down at him from an upstairs window. He read the alarm on her face and watched her back away quickly, almost certainly heading for the phone. It was understandable. Those who peeped from behind curtains on one side of the drive saw a blue Transit van. Those like her, in houses on the *other* side, could see the four men in jackets, jeans, and trainers, who crept slowly alongside it, moving at the same speed, the van's progress masking theirs.

When the van began a long, slow sweep around the curve of the horseshoe, the police officers behind it moved in a similar arc. As it slowed right down, they did the same, and when it stopped and the engine was switched off, the four men gathered into a tight huddle and waited.

Five hundred yards away, at the other end of the drive, two police vans had sealed off the entrance. Traffic police kept the vehicles moving as drivers slowed down to gawk. Half a dozen uniformed officers in shirtsleeves moved curious pedestrians along.

Behind the Transit, Thorne listened. He could hear the distant squawk of a two-way. The drone of traffic from the other side of the field behind the houses. Somewhere nearby there was a radio playing. He tuned the sounds out and tried to concentrate on what Brigstocke was saying . . .

"Are we clear?" Brigstocke asked. He looked hard at Thorne, Holland, and Stone. Thorne knew he was looking for focus. Nods all around. This was probably going to be straightforward enough, but it only took a second for something run-of-the-mill to go very wrong.

"Right . . ."

A beat, then Brigstocke hammered with his fist on the side of the van and two more officers jumped immediately from the front. The van doors still swinging, they began sprinting toward the house, the biggest one lugging a heavy, metal door ram.

Thorne and the others came around from the far side

of the van, running. Brigstocke and Stone went immediately left toward the gate at the side, making for the back of the house. Thorne and Holland veered away from them, following in the wake of the two from the front of the van . . .

Grunts, and short breaths, and the pounding of rubber soles across tarmac and pavement and grass, and still the sound of the radio coming from somewhere . . .

Thorne came up next to the officers at the front door. He crouched down, ready to spring forward, and nodded. A couple of deep breaths. The big officer gritted his teeth and swung the battering ram.

"Police . . . !"

Thorne could hear shouting from inside the house and from around the back. The door hadn't given. He began kicking at the lock, then moved quickly as the ram was swung into the door again. This time it crashed open and, leading with his forearm, Thorne rushed in.

"Police! Everybody in the property show themselves now . . ."

From behind him, Thorne heard the clang of the battering ram as it was dropped on to the doorstep. From somewhere up ahead he could hear a thump and, upstairs, a woman screaming . . .

A woman, Thorne thought. *Not a child* . . .

"Anybody here, show yourself!"

He saw a long hallway ahead of him. Two, three doors off to his right . . .

"In there!"

He glanced left at the big officer coming past him, at the bulk of his wide back moving beneath his car coat as he charged up the stairs two at a time.

At the other end of the hall was a kitchen, and through it he could see Brigstocke and Stone outside the back door. Holland pushed past him, ran to open it.

The doors clattered open, smashed in ahead of him.

In the first room, nothing . . . He stepped back out into the hall, turned to see Brigstocke and Stone running toward him.

From the second room, a shout . . .

"Here . . ."

Thorne shoved his way past the officer in the doorway and burst into the room. It was small—a sofa, an armchair, a wide-screen TV still on. At the other end was an archway leading off right to another room, a dining room, Thorne guessed.

Gribbin stood next to the armchair, his hands above his head. His face showed nothing. His eyes moved from Thorne's to the doorway through which Sandra Cook was being propelled by one of the local CID boys. She pushed her way past Brigstocke and Stone, all but dragged Holland out of the way.

"What the fuck do you want?" she shouted.

Thorne ignored her, turned to look at Gribbin. "Raymond Gribbin, I'm arresting you in connection with breach of parole conditions, which—"

He stopped and looked toward the archway in the right-hand corner as a figure stepped cautiously through it. One by one the heads of the other seven people crowded into the small room turned, until everyone was looking at the girl.

"Is everything going to be okay, Ray? I'm scared . . ."

Gribbin took his hands from above his head, opening his arms as he stepped toward her. "It's all right, sweetheart . . ."

It all happened in a few seconds. It was a testament to Andy Stone's speed and strength that he was able to do so much before being dragged away by Thorne, Holland, and a screaming Sandra Cook.

"Don't fucking touch her . . ."

As Gribbin's hands slid across the girl's shoulders, Stone was halfway across the room. He was on him by the time Gribbin was reaching to pull the small blond head to his barrel chest, the girl squealing as he pushed her away and turned to defend himself . . .

Gribbin reached up and grabbed Stone around the collar, staggering back into the television, which tipped against the wall. Stone brought both fists up fast into the thick, tattooed forearms and pulled them back down hard as he dropped his head into Gribbin's face. It was then that three pairs of hands grabbed Stone, around collar, belt, and sleeve, yanking him backward across the armchair as Gribbin dropped to his knees and the girl ran sobbing to her mother.

Stone tried to stand up, to tell those around him that he was calm, that they could get their bloody hands off him . . .

Thorne stepped across and knelt down next to Gribbin.

His head had fallen back against the television, one hand scrabbling at the carpet, balling itself into a fist. Blood dripped through the fingers of the other hand. On the screen behind Gribbin's head, there was applause as a woman welcomed viewers to her show and invited the studio audience to share their holiday nightmares.

Twenty minutes later, with the inhabitants of the quiet cul-de-sac pressed against their windows, Gribbin was led out, a bloody handkerchief pressed to what was left of his nose.

By teatime, the initial interviews had been completed. Heads were starting to hang. Though there were still a few things to check out, it was pretty clear, to Thorne at least, that Gribbin had nothing whatsoever to do with the murder of Douglas Remfry.

The phone rang just before eleven. The voice could have belonged to only one person.

"I think you might have had a bit of luck, Mr. Thorne."

"I'm listening, Kodak."

"Well, don't get too excited, because whatever happens we've got to wait a few days, but it looks good. Remember me joking about doing your job for you . . ."

Thorne listened. It did sound very promising, but after the fiasco with Gribbin he found it difficult to get excited. It was hard to see anything as more than just another straw to be clutched at.

He went into the bedroom and lay down.

It was starting to get cooler.

Beneath him, the bracken felt sodden, and above, the sky was darkening.

August 3, 1976

"*You smell. You smell like death. You fucking stink . . .*"

Her eyes showed nothing. Not hurt at the accusation, not denial, not pain at the weight of him pressed down onto her arms, his face inches from her own.

He pushed himself off her, moved down to the end of the bed to where the tray had been left untouched.

"*I'm fucking sick of this,*" *he said.* "*You want to starve yourself, that's up to you, but don't make me cook the shit for you, all right?*"

She raised herself up on the pillow, stared past him.

"*What?*" *he said, shouted.* "*What?*"

He looked at her for a minute or more. Her face was, as always, blank enough for him to imagine it changing, to create the expression that he knew should be there as large as life. To picture the eyes dropping, the tightness around the lips, and the clenching of the jaw. To see shame.

He grabbed the plate and hurled it against the wall above her head. She didn't flinch. She didn't blink.

He stopped in the doorway, turned, and stared

at her. Her eyes flat as glass. Beans running down
the wall behind her.

"In court they tried to make out that if you had
been raped it was like you were asking for it anyway. The dress, other things. They just meant the
way you behaved, like you were flirting, coming
on to him. They didn't know the half of it, did
they? You did ask for it. I know what you did. You
literally asked him for it. Took him, dragged him
into that fucking stockroom, and asked him. Told
him what you wanted . . ."

As he closed the bedroom door behind him, he
could hear her saying the word over and over
again.

"If . . . if . . . if . . ."

She could not hear herself saying it. The sound
of the screaming inside her head was all she'd been
able to hear for a while.

EIGHT

Thorne turned right off the Charing Cross Road. Eleven o'clock in the morning or thereabouts and baking hot. He took off his jacket, threw it across his arm as he began walking up Old Compton Street.

Soho was a difficult area to categorize at the best of times, which had probably been its trouble down the years. Was it bohemian or squalid? Characterful or seedy? Thorne knew that today it was all these things and probably the better for it, but it had been a struggle. Four decades on and the villains that had run Soho in the fifties and sixties had become trendy. Thanks to the new wave of British gangster films, Billy Hill, Jack Spot, and their boys, with their sharp suits and slicked-back hair, were now officially iconic. For all their newfound sexiness, it was these men and those who followed in the seventies who had driven the resident population of the area away, who had silenced the noisy heart of it.

It was thanks mainly to the gay population that Soho's heart had begun to beat again. Now it was one of the few areas in the center of the city with a real sense of community; a sense that the horrific bombing of the Admiral Duncan pub a few years earlier had only strengthened. Though Thorne had not felt *totally* comfortable on the few occasions Phil Hendricks had brought him down here drinking, he couldn't deny that there was a good atmosphere to the place.

Thorne walked past Greek Street, Frith Street. The Prince Edward Theatre and the awning of Ronnie Scott's off to his right. Young men sat outside cafés, enjoying the hot weather, the chance to show off well-developed bodies. Soho was still a great place to eat and drink, but for every Bar Italia there was a Starbucks or a Costa Coffee; for every family-run deli, two branches of Pret A Manger . . .

Thorne suddenly felt hungry and realized that he had a problem. He knew that he didn't have time to grab an early lunch, but he also knew that if he ate any later he would run the risk of spoiling dinner, and he was really looking forward to that . . .

"Well, we might as well," Eve had said when he'd called. "We've already had breakfast and lunch . . ."

On the corner of Dean Street was a shop selling fetish wear. Thorne stopped and looked at the garish window display. A dummy was clad in rubber. A spiked dog collar around the neck and a gas mask obscuring the face. He thought about the photographs of Jane Foley; the reason he was here.

He looked at his watch. He was going to be late . . .

"Did you really look at this photo?" Bethell had asked on the phone.

"What?"

Bethell sounded cocky, pleased with himself. "Study it, you know . . ."

Thorne was not in the best of humors. "I'm tired and I've had a shit day, so get on with it, will you . . . ?"

"I mean *really* look at it, Mr. Thorne. In one of your labs or whatever. Get it onto some state-of-the-art magnifying equipment, break it down into pixels . . ."

"This is the Met, Kodak. I haven't even got a fan in my fucking office . . ."

"I've got some good gear indoors. I use it for airbrushing, you know? Stuck it on there and bingo!"

"What . . . ?"

"The picture's shot against a plain white backdrop, all right? Sheet on a roller, usual kind of thing. Now, there's a small mark bottom right-hand corner, looks like a smudge, remember?"

"No, I don't . . ."

Thorne turned right, then immediately left into Brewer Street. This, more than anywhere in Soho, was where you could see the sleazy and the sophisticated cheek by jowl. The peep show next door to the sushi bar. A place that offered shiatsu massage opposite premises delivering an altogether more intimate type of service.

A bored blonde in a cubicle beckoned him, inviting him into a show that promised a "live double act." Thorne wondered if there were any shows that offered dead ones.

"Come on in, love," the woman said. Thorne smiled and shook his head. She looked like she didn't give a damn. Of course, the sex industry had always been just that, had always been about the money, but Thorne had known hookers who did a better job of disguising it. He'd only ever *read* about his favorite hooker of all time, but he would have liked to have met her. A legendary whore called Miss Corbett who'd worked these streets in the eighteenth century, and had taxed her gentlemen an extra guinea for every inch that their "maypole" fell below the nine inches she deemed satisfactory.

Two hundred and fifty years on and now it was the drugs squad, not vice, who worked these streets every night. The sniffer dogs did what they'd been trained to do but Thorne thought it was pretty much a waste of time and effort. A lot of hard work and resources to nail the odd casual user, the occasional two-bit dealer if they had a bit of luck . . .

"You know you're always saying how you need a bit of luck sometimes?"

Thorne had stretched out on the sofa by now, the phone pressed to his ear, the other hand reaching down to rub Elvis's belly. "Are you ever going to get to the point, Kodak?"

"Well, this is it. Your bit of good luck. I scanned the photo into my computer, blew it up big-time, okay? You can do all sorts of stuff if the quality of the original's decent enough, yeah?" Thorne would have said it was impossible, but Bethell's voice was actually getting that little bit higher as he got more excited. "So, I pixel-ated the bastard, zoomed in, and then I could suddenly see what that brown smudge was. I recognized it, see."

"Recognized it?"

"It's a burn mark, like a scorch on the white back-cloth. I recognized it 'cause I was there when it happened. I was shooting a threesome nine months back and some silly tart, done a couple of pills too many, knocks over a big lamp. Fucking whole lot could have gone up, but all it did was leave this big burn mark up the roller. I remembered the shape of it. Tight fucker that runs the place never bothered to replace it . . ."

By now Thorne was sitting up. "Tight fucker's name and address would be good."

"Charles Dodd. Charlie, really, but he insists on Charles. Likes to pretend he's posh, even though the cunt comes from Canvey Island . . ."

"Kodak . . ."

"The place is above a fishmonger's on Brewer Street."

Thorne knew the shop. "Right, listen . . ."

"You'll have to wait a few days, I'm afraid, Mr. Thorne. He's in Europe. I checked."

Thorne was thinking it through. Should he wait? Could he get a warrant and turn the place over while Dodd was away . . . ?

"I think I did a pretty good job, Mr. Thorne," Bethell said. "What d'you reckon?"

"I want to know the second he's back . . ."

Now, three days since that conversation, Thorne watched Dennis Bethell in the bookshop on the other side of the street. He was browsing through the remaindered art books, though some of his own, slightly racier stuff was almost certainly on sale downstairs.

Thorne moved to cross the road and was bumped roughly by a man coming fast, from his left. Thorne's response was typically British. "Sorry," he said. The other man grunted, raised a hand, and carried on walking.

Bethell was waving at him now from inside the bookshop. Thorne nodded toward the other end of the street and began walking. Bethell put down a coffee-table book of nude freak-show photographs, squeezed out of the shop doorway, and followed.

Welch laughed as he strolled away up Wardour Street. He'd learned a few things during the years he'd spent in various institutions. Never say sorry was one. How to recognize a copper was another . . .

Since his release he'd spent a lot of time just walking around. The hostel was depressing, and he'd really enjoyed being out and about. The weather was amazing; a couple of days out in the open and he'd already got a bit of color back. If *he* looked better, less prison-pale, he thought that the women who were walking about, wearing next to nothing, looked *gorgeous*. Seriously horny. Fuck it, if this was global warming, then who gave a toss about the ozone layer?

There were windows all along the street with adverts in each for a new film. Welch stopped and looked at a couple that he liked the sound of. Maybe when his welfare money came through he might spend a couple of afternoons catching up. He'd enjoyed the cinema before he'd gone inside, tried to see most of the stuff that came out, providing it wasn't too arty.

He'd been to the pictures the night before he was arrested, of course. *The Blair Witch Project.* She'd been all over him then, snuggling up in the scary bits, hand on his knee all the way through. Well up for it, she was. He could read the signals. It was only later that the bitch decided to change her mind. To fuck him around.

To this day, it amazed him that they could do that. Take a bloke all the way there, get him worked up, get him so as his balls felt like they'd explode, and then just turn around and casually announce that they didn't feel like it. That it was too much too soon, or some such crap. He'd decided that it *was* crap, that she just didn't want him to think she was a whore. That all she needed was a little persuasion . . .

He'd been astonished when the police had come knocking the next afternoon. Couldn't fucking believe it. He was still shaking his head while they were taking the swabs.

He could see that the male copper, the detective sergeant, thought it was rubbish, that they were all wasting their time. When he'd told them how randy the silly bitch had been in the cinema, he was *nodding,* for fuck's sake. He could see exactly what had been going on. The woman officer was different, though; she'd had it in for him straightaway.

"Good at reading signals, are you?" she'd said. Her expression blank, the spools on the tape squeaking as they turned in the recorder. "Tell me what I'm thinking right now . . ."

"That you'd fancy me if you weren't a dyke?"

Looking into the window, he saw himself smile, remembering her face when he'd said it. The smile faded a little when he recalled the look on the same face eight months later; the grin from the other side of the court-room as he was taken down.

He moved on to the next window. There was a poster advertising the new Bruce Willis blockbuster. Some new missile and Bruce's cheeky smile and a tasty blonde with fake tits. Maybe next week, the week after, whenever he started getting the welfare checks, he might go and see it. He couldn't afford it just yet. The discharge grant wasn't going to stretch much further, and besides, he'd need a fair bit tomorrow night, to pay for the hotel.

"You sure he's in there?"

"He's in there, Mr. Thorne. Got back from Holland yesterday. Went over to pick up a few bits and pieces."

Thorne nodded. Flowers weren't the only thing that came across from Holland in vans . . .

They were standing across the road from the fishmon-ger's, the flashing neon sign above Raymond's Revue Bar reflected in the shop window. The reds and blues danc-ing across the shiny heads of salmon, herring, and tur-bot. Next to it, a narrow brown door.

Bethell forced his hands into the pockets of tight leather trousers. Shifted his weight from one expensive training shoe to the other. "Right, I'll get out of your way, then, shall I?"

Thorne reached for his wallet, wondering if the tight-ness of Bethell's trousers might have something to do with the height of his voice. He counted out fifty in ten-ners. Bethell took it and handed over an envelope in re-turn.

"There's your photo back . . ."

Thorne took a step into the road, turned, and held up the envelope. "I'd better not see this popping up on the Internet, all right?"

Bethell laughed. A series of shrill peeps. "I didn't know you visited those sorts of sites . . ." Thorne was already starting to cross. "Listen, you won't mention my name, will you . . . ?"

Thorne stopped to let a car pass, spoke without turning. "Oh, so I can't say, 'Dennis sent me,' then?"

"Seriously . . ."

"Relax, Kodak. Your reputation will remain squeaky-clean. No pun intended . . ."

Thorne pressed the button on the grimy white intercom and stepped back. He glanced up at an unmoving gray curtain, and right, into the black eye of a large, ugly-looking fish he couldn't put a name to. The shopfront was original, the tiling that edged the window ornate, but the prices and stock were firmly in line with the twenty-first-century trendiness of the location. Swordfish steaks at a fiver a pop, and not a clam to be seen . . .

"Yes . . . ?"

"Mr. Dodd? I was wondering if I could talk to you about renting some studio time . . . ?"

Thorne could hear suspicion in every crackle of the speaker. He looked back at the ugly fish, found himself raising his eyebrows. *What d'you reckon?*

He was buzzed up.

Charlie Dodd stood at the top of a narrow, carpetless stairway. He was in his fifties with thin lips and a comb-over. He smiled, barring the way and trying to make it look like a welcome.

By the time Thorne had reached the top of the stairs, warrant card in hand, the smile had become a grimace.

"Have you got a warrant?"

"I don't need one, you invited me up."

"Listen, you obviously aren't one of DCI Davey's boys. Everything's been sorted . . ."

Plenty of things in Soho were still the same forty years on. Thorne made a mental note of the name as he stepped past Dodd and pushed open an unpainted plywood door.

Dodd scuttled after him. "What the fuck's your game . . . ?"

The studio was no bigger than an average double bedroom and the main feature was indeed a double bed. *Unlike* the average bedroom, the walls were painted black, there were lights hung from a ceiling bar, and Thorne guessed that the array of sex toys and costumes on display was only likely to be replicated in the bedrooms of a few high-ranking members of Parliament . . .

A man turned from the foot of the bed, lifted a large video camera down from his shoulder. Behind him, a foot or so away from the bedstead, Thorne could see the white backdrop with the burn mark in the bottom right-hand corner.

Two thin, pale girls lay on the bed. One pulled her arm from beneath the other and reached down to pick up a pack of cigarettes from the floor. The other stared at him, her face blank and white as new paper.

"What's this?" the man with the camera said.

Thorne smiled. "Don't mind me . . ."

Dodd raised a placatory hand to the cameraman and turned to Thorne. "Now listen, there's nothing illegal going on here, so why don't you fuck off?"

"What about the stuff you've just brought back from Holland, Charlie?" Thorne stepped forward and steered Dodd into the corner of the room. "Sorry, I know you prefer Charles . . ."

The watery green eyes narrowed as Dodd's mind raced, trying to work out who had the big mouth. "What do you want?"

Thorne took the picture from the envelope. "This

photo was taken here." He handed it to Dodd. "I just
want to know who took it. Nothing too difficult . . ."

Dodd shook his head. "Not here, mate."

Thorne squeezed behind Dodd, stood close enough to
smell the sweat and hair oil. He jabbed a finger over his
shoulder at the smudge on the photo and then lifted up
Dodd's head and pointed it at the scorch mark on the
backcloth.

"Have another look, Charlie . . ."

Dodd turned back to the photo. The man with the
camera had put it back onto his shoulder. He was mum-
bling something to the girls, who were lazily shifting
their position on the bed.

"If it was taken here, I wasn't around at the time,"
Dodd said, handing the photo back to Thorne. He in-
clined his head toward the bed. "Stuff like this today,
run-of-the-mill, I usually stick around, get on with other
things . . ."

One of the girls began to moan theatrically. Thorne
glanced across. The camera was trained on one girl's
head as it busied itself in her friend's crotch. At the other
end of the bed, the girl who was moaning stared at the
ceiling, still smoking her cigarette.

"You saying you don't remember this picture being
taken?"

"There's times, customers would rather I wasn't here.
You understand what I'm saying? Maybe there's things
being shot I'd prefer I didn't witness anyway and they're
paying good money for the place, so—"

"Bullshit." Thorne pushed the photo into Dodd's face.
"Do you see any animals? Underage boys?"

Dodd swatted Thorne's arm away, shook his head.

"This is top-shelf stuff, no stronger than that. There's
a whole series of these and they're much the same, so
start remembering, Charlie . . ."

Dodd was starting to get upset. He ran his hands back and forth through the oily strands of hair. As he spoke, Thorne watched a white fleck of dried spittle move from bottom lip to top and back again. "I wasn't here. All right? I'd remember if I was, I can remember every fucking shot taken up here, ask anybody. Like you say, the picture's harmless enough, so what reason have I got to fuck you about . . . ?"

On the bed, the girl who was being worked on leaned across to stub out her cigarette on a saucer. The cameraman moved in closer. "Go on," he said to the other girl. "Get your tongue right up her arse . . ."

"All right," Thorne said. "Think about anybody who might have asked you to make yourself scarce while they were shooting. Last six months or so . . ."

"Jesus, d'you know how many people use this place?"

"Not a regular. Probably a one-off."

"Yeah, but still . . ."

"Just one man and a girl. Think . . ."

The cameraman kicked the end of the bed in annoyance and spun around. "For Christ's sake, can you two shut up? I'm recording sound here . . ."

The girl who had been going down on her friend raised her head and turned to look at Thorne. The lights washed out her face, exaggerating the job that the heroin had already done. Dodd opened his mouth to speak and Thorne was grateful for the chance to look away.

"There was one, four or five months ago. It was like you said, a one-off. He just wanted the place for a couple of hours. Normally, even if they want rid of me for the shoot I stick around to set the lights up, but this bloke said he was going to do all that himself. Said he knew what he was doing."

"What about the girl?"

"I never saw a girl. It was just him . . ."

"Give me a name."

Dodd snorted, looked at Thorne in disbelief. "Right. I'll check the files, shall I? Maybe ask my secretary to look it up. For fuck's sake . . ."

Thorne took a step toward the doorway. "Get your coat on, Charlie. I need a picture of this fucker, and for your sake your memory for faces had better be as good as it is for tits and arse . . ."

"Sorry, mate, it's not going to happen. That's why I remembered him, as it goes. First I thought he was a messenger, you know, dropping off some negs or something. Head to foot in leather, with a dark visor on his helmet . . ."

Thorne knew straightaway that Dodd was telling the truth. It felt like something starting to press heavily against the back of his head. His piece of good luck turning to shit.

"You must have seen him more than once. He didn't just turn up on the off chance . . ."

"Once to make the booking, once on the day." Dodd was starting to sound slightly smug. "Never got a look at him, though. Both times he had the motorbike outfit on. I remember him standing out there on the stairs, in all the leather gear like a fucking hit man, waiting for me to leave . . ."

On the other side of the room, a vibrator began to buzz. The camera was rolling again.

Thorne turned and yanked open the door. The statement could be taken later, for what it was worth. He'd run headlong into another wall, and right now it felt as real, as black, as the one that ran around the tatty fuck parlor behind him.

He took the stairs down two at a time. The jolt that ran through his body at every step failed to dislodge the image that had fixed itself in his head. The face of the girl on the bed when she'd raised up her head and turned to look at him . . .

Her mouth and chin glistening, but the eyes as black and dead as those of the fish that lay on slabs in the window of the shop next door.

August 10, 1976

It was the first time in a long while that he'd seen anything at all register on her face. He wasn't expecting a reaction, but it tickled him nevertheless. To see her jaw drop a little, watch her eyes widen when she saw his hand tighten around the base of the lamp . . .

"Please," she said. Please . . .

In the few seconds that he held the lamp high above his head, he thought about the different uses of that word. The meanings that it could take on. Its many subtle varieties, conjured by the tiniest changes in emphasis.

He thought about the number of ways it could mislead.

Please don't.

Please do.

Please don't stop doing . . .

Please me. Pleasure me. Please . . .

Pleading for it.

As he brought the lamp down with every ounce of strength he had, he thought that, all in all, it was a pretty appropriate word. For her very last.

At least, the way she meant it now, it was honest. With each successive blow he became more fo-

cused, his thinking becoming less cluttered, until finally, when she was unrecognizable, he could re-member where in the garage he'd last seen the tow rope.

NINE

That dreadful hiatus between arriving and anything actually happening . . .

The plastic wrap, they were assured, would be coming off the buffet platters *very* shortly, and the DJ wouldn't be too long setting his gear up. Until then, there was a hundred and fifty quid behind the bar, so everybody could get a couple down them and toast the bride and groom one more time while they were waiting for the fun to start. Everyone could mingle . . .

Tragically, there weren't quite enough people in the rugby club bar for a significant hubbub to develop; there was no comforting blanket of noise for Thorne to hide under. He got a pint of bitter for his dad, half a Guinness for himself, and looked for the nearest corner. He sat sipping his beer and tried to summon up the necessary enthusiasm for Scotch eggs and pork pie and cold pasta salad. Raised his glass to anyone whose eye he caught and tried not to look too bored or miserable or, God forbid, in need of cheering up.

His father was *certainly* in no need of it. Jim Thorne sat on a chair at the bar holding court. Telling jokes to a couple of teenage boys who laughed and sipped their weak lagers. Informing any woman who would listen that he had a memory like a goldfish, because he had that disease with the funny name. He'd forgotten, *what* was it called again? Asking with a twinkle to be forgiven if he'd slept with any of them and couldn't remember.

Thorne was delighted to see his dad in such good form. To see him enjoying himself. It was a huge relief after the phone call twenty-four hours earlier that had ruined his evening with Eve Bloom . . .

The large, stripped-pine table in the kitchen had been set for four. Thorne had yet to encounter anybody else. Eve turned from the cooker.

"In case you're wondering, they're in her room." She spoke at the level of a stage whisper. "Denise and Ben. I think they've had a row . . ."

Thorne was pouring wine into two of the glasses. He whispered back. "Right. Was it a big one? Should I start clearing away a couple of these place settings . . . ?"

Eve moved over to the table and picked up her wine. "No chance. Ben won't let an argument get in the way of his dinner. Cheers." She took a sip and carried the glass back across to where several large copper pans sat on the halogen burner. She nodded toward the door at the sound of footsteps and raised voices coming from else-where in the flat. "Those two enjoy a good row anyway. They're pretty violent, but usually short-lived . . ."

Thorne tried to sound casual. "Violent?"

"I don't mean like that. Just a lot of shouting. Bit of throwing stuff, but never anything breakable . . ."

Thorne glanced across at her. She was busy at the cooker again, her back to him. He stared at the nape of her neck. At her shoulder blades, brown against the cream linen of her top.

"I'm more of a seether myself," she said.

"I'll watch out for that."

"Don't worry, you'll know it when it happens . . ."

Thorne looked around the kitchen. A couple of

framed black-and-white film posters. Chrome kettle, toaster, and blender. A big, expensive-looking fridge. It looked like the shop was doing pretty good business, though he couldn't be sure which things were Eve's and which belonged to her flatmate. He guessed that the vast array of herbs in terra-cotta pots were probably down to Eve, as were the scribbled Latin names of what Thorne presumed to be flowers on the enormous blackboard that dominated one wall. He was pleased to see his own name and mobile-phone number scrawled in the bottom left-hand corner.

"So, what are they arguing about? Your friends. Nothing serious . . . ?"

She turned, licking her fingers. "Keith. Remember? The guy that helps me out on a Saturday. He was here when Ben arrived. Ben reckons he's got a bit of a thing for Denise, and Denise told him not to be such an idiot . . ."

Thorne remembered the way Keith had looked at him when he was talking to Eve in the shop. Maybe Denise wasn't the only one he had a bit of a thing for . . .

"What do you think?" he asked. "About Keith and Denise . . ."

A door squeaked and slammed and a moment later the door to the kitchen was pushed open by a slim, fair-haired woman. She was barefoot, wearing baggy, combat-style shorts and a man's black vest. She marched up behind Eve and gave her backside a healthy tweak.

"That smells fucking gorgeous!"

She turned and beamed at Thorne. Her hair was a little shorter and a shade lighter than Eve's. Though she seemed slight, the vest she was wearing showed off well-defined arms and shoulders. Her delicate features sharpened as an enormous smile pushed up cheekbones you could slice bacon on.

"Hello, you're Tom, aren't you? I'm Denise." She all but ran across the kitchen, grabbed his outstretched hand,

and flopped down in a chair on the other side of the table. "So, Tom? Thomas? Which?" She reached for the wine bottle and began pouring herself a very large glass.

"Tom's fine . . ."

She leaned across the table and spoke as though they were old friends. "Eve's been going on at *nauseating* length about you, do you know that?" Her voice was surprisingly deep and a little theatrical. Thorne couldn't think of anything to say. Took a sip of wine instead. "Bloody *full of it*, she is. I'm guessing that the only reason she is resolutely refusing to turn around from the oven, *at this very moment*, is that she's gone bright red . . ."

"Shut your face," Eve said, laughing and without turning around.

Denise swallowed a mouthful of wine, gave Thorne another massive smile. "So, in the flesh," she said. "A man who catches murderers."

Thorne needed to relax after the morning he'd spent in Soho. Now he was starting to enjoy himself. This woman was clearly as mad as a hatter but likable enough.

"Right at this very minute, I'm a man who *isn't* catching them . . ."

"We all have off days, Tom. Tomorrow you'll probably catch a bagful."

"I'll settle for just the one . . ."

"Right." She raised her glass as if in a toast. "A really *good* one."

Thorne leaned back on his chair and glanced across at Eve. As if she sensed him looking, she turned, caught his eye, and smiled.

Thorne turned back to Denise. "What about you? What do you do?" He stared at the tiny, glittering stud in her nose, thinking, *Actress, poet, performance artist* . . .

She rolled her eyes. "God, Information Technology. Sorry. Dull as fuck, I'm afraid."

"Well . . ."

"Don't bother, I can see your eyes glazing over already. Bloody hell, how d'you think *I* feel? All day surrounded by *Lord of the Rings* readers, making jokes about floppy *this* and hard *that*. PCs going down on them . . ."

At the cooker, Eve laughed. Thorne knew straightaway that she was thinking the same thing that he was. "I know," he said. "Where *I* work, having a PC go down on you means a *very* different thing . . ."

When the man whom Thorne presumed to be Ben strolled into the kitchen, it was Denise who stopped laughing first. He walked over, leaned against the worktop next to where Eve was cooking, and began chewing a fingernail. He tilted his chin toward Thorne. "Hiya . . ."

Thorne nodded back. "Hi. Are you Ben?"

Denise spoke pointedly over the noise of the wine glugging into her glass. "Oh yes, he's Ben." Ben looked none too pleased at the horribly fake smile she gave him as she spat out his name.

Eve lobbed a tea towel at her. "All right you two, stop it." She leaned across and kissed Ben on the cheek. "This'll be ready in about five minutes . . ."

Ben moved across to the fridge, opened it, and took out a can of lager. He turned to Thorne, held it up. "Want one?"

Thorne lifted his glass of wine. "No, thanks . . ."

Ben moved around behind his girlfriend and sat next to Thorne. He was tall and well built, with fair, wavy hair, a gingerish goatee beard, and neatly trimmed, pointed sideburns. Although in his thirties, and clearly fifteen years too old for it, he was wearing what Thorne guessed was skateboarding gear. He stuck out a hand, introduced himself. "Ben Jameson . . ."

Thorne did the same, suddenly feeling a little awk-

ward, and somewhat overdressed in his chinos and black
Marks & Spencer polo shirt . . .

"I'm starving," Ben said.

Eve carried four plates across to the table. "Good.
There's loads . . ."

For half a minute there was only the sound of china
and glassware clinking. Of cutlery scraping against
dishes, and chairs against the quarry-tiled floor as the
meal was dished up.

"This looks amazing," Thorne said.

Nods and grunting from Denise and Ben, a smile from
Eve, and then silence. Thorne turned to his right. "You in
IT as well, Ben?"

"Sorry?"

"I wondered if the two of you had met up at
work . . . ?"

"God, no. I'm a filmmaker."

"Right. Anything I might have seen?"

"Only if you watch a lot of corporate training
videos," Denise said.

Thorne could feel his foot pressing against something
underneath the table. He pushed, hoping it was Eve's
foot. She looked up at him . . .

"Yeah, that's what I'm doing at the moment," Ben
said. He drummed his fork against the edge of his plate.
"But I've got some stuff of my own I'm trying to get off
the ground as well."

Denise reached across and laid a hand across Ben's,
stilling the movement of the fork. Her tone was blatantly
patronizing. "That's right, darling. 'Course you
have . . ."

Ben pushed his pasta around a little, spoke without
looking up from the plate. "So, what's new at your
place, then, Den? Any riveting system crashes? Any interesting computer viruses to tell us about . . . ?"

Thorne took his first mouthful, caught Eve's eye. She smiled and gave a small shrug. He glanced across at Denise and Ben, who were looking anywhere but at each other. The row might be officially over, but they were clearly intent on scoring a few points off each other.

"Right." Eve folded her arms. "If you two don't kiss and make up, you can fuck off next door and ring out for pizza. Fair enough?"

First Denise and then Ben raised their eyes to Eve, who was doing her best to look serious. The antipathy between the couple seemed to melt away in the face of her mock annoyance, the two quickly shaking heads and nuzzling necks and saying sorry for being stupid. Thorne watched all three clutching hands—apologizing without embarrassment to him and to each other—and he was struck by the dynamic between these people who were clearly great friends, by the warmth and strength of it.

He smiled, waving away their apologies. Impressed by them, and envious . . .

When his phone rang, Denise leaned forward, seeming genuinely excited. "This could be the first of those murderers, Tom . . ."

Something tightened inside Thorne when he saw the name come up on the phone's display. For a second he thought about leaving the room to take the call, maybe even pretending it *was* work. He decided he was being overdramatic, mouthed "sorry," and answered the phone.

"This is bad, Tom. Very bad. I've been getting my things ready for tomorrow. Ready for the trip. Laying it all out on the bed, trying to choose, and there's a problem with this blue suit . . ."

Thorne listened, watching Eve and her friends pretending *not* to, as his father moved from panic to complete hysteria at frightening speed. When all he could hear down the phone was sobbing, Thorne pushed back his chair, dropped his eyes to the floor, and stepped away from the table.

"Dad, listen, I'll be there first thing in the morning, like I said I would." He moved across to the kitchen window, stared out across London Fields. The light at the top of Canary Wharf winked back at him as he stood, wondering if Eve and the others could hear the crying, and trying to decide what to do.

Eve stood and moved across to him. She put a hand on his arm.

"It's all right, Dad," Thorne said. "Look, I'll have to go home first, all right? To get my stuff and pick up the hire car. Calm down, okay? I'll be there as soon as I can . . ."

The snotty cow behind the reception desk looked at Welch like she thought he was going to steal something. Like he was a piece of shit that one of those businessmen laughing loudly in the bar had brought in on their shoes. It wasn't like it was the fucking Ritz either . . .

"I rang a couple of days ago to book," Welch said.

The receptionist stared at her computer screen, plastered on a smile that was fake and frosty at the same time. "So you did," she said. "Just the one night, is it?"

Welch felt like reaching across the desk and slapping her. He had half a mind to ask for the manager, to demand the level of service and fucking courtesy to which he was entitled. "Yeah, one night. I get breakfast, don't I?"

The girl didn't look up. "Yes, sir, breakfast is included in your room rate."

Welch suddenly wondered what would happen if there were two of them coming down in the morning. He didn't know if she would want to stay for breakfast. He thought about asking, decided to leave it.

"I won't keep you a second, sir . . ."

While the receptionist punched her keypad, Welch stared around the lobby. The plants were plastic. The gray carpet looked like it would take your skin off if you fell on it. There was a sign next to the desk which said THE GREENWOOD HOTEL, SLOUGH, WELCOMES THOMPSON MOULDINGS LTD.

"There we go, sir. If you could just fill that in." She slid the booking form across to him. He had to think for a few seconds before he could remember the address of the hostel. "I'll need an imprint of a credit card. Nothing will be charged to it, but—"

"No need. I'm paying cash." He signed the form and reached into the pocket of his jacket for the roll of tenners.

"That's fine, sir . . ."

Welch took out the money. He had a card he could have used if he'd felt like it, but he wanted her to see the cash. He slipped off the elastic band, started counting it out. The hostel was fucking horrendous, but being released NFA—having No Fixed Abode—did have its advantages. The discharge grant was more than double what you'd get normally.

"No payment in advance, sir. You settle the bill when you check out." She placed a key card on top of the pile of cash and pushed the lot back toward him. "Room 313. Third floor."

He grabbed his money, tried not to shout. "I do bloody well know. I know what you're supposed to do, all right?"

The receptionist reddened and turned away from him.

Welch picked up the plastic bag that contained a toothbrush, condoms, clean pants and socks for the morning. He thought about joining the gang from Thompson Mouldings in the bar, having a quick one. On second thought, he'd go straight to the room, maybe have a shower, try to enjoy every single minute of it . . .

Grinning at nobody in particular, he walked toward the lift.

This was stuff that only went on at family weddings. That Thorne knew could never happen anywhere else: an old woman, seventy if she was a day, dancing awkwardly in the corner with a small boy; two women in their forties shouting at each other across the table, raising their voices so that their comments about the food/dress/service could be heard above the Madonna/Oasis/George Michael; small children sliding on their knees across the polished dance floor, while smaller ones screamed or struggled to stay awake in spite of the loud music.

Some related by blood, forever, and some for only an hour or two. Eyeing one another up and staring one another down. A fuck or a fight not much more than a look or a lager away . . .

Twenty minutes since the happy couple had taken to the floor to dance the first dance to "Lady in Red," and Thorne hadn't moved from his seat in the corner. From there he could watch what was happening in the main hall and keep an eye on his old man.

He looked across. His father was no longer sitting at the bar. Thorne got up, ordered himself another Guinness, and while he was waiting for it to settle, wandered through into the main hall.

He passed people he knew not well or not at all, their faces colored by the DJ's piss-poor lighting rig—red, then green, then blue. At the far end of the hall, Thorne looked to his right, and through the archway that led to another, smaller room, he could see his father shuffling along the buffet table, muttering to himself, piling food he would never eat onto a paper plate . . .

"Go easy, Dad. How many chicken legs can one man eat?"

"Mind your own fucking business . . ."

"It's too much . . . look, get your hand underneath it . . ."

"Shit . . ."

The flimsy cardboard unable to sustain so much food. The plate collapsing in on itself. *The mattress sagging beneath the weight of the dead man . . .*

Thorne was suddenly angry with his father, at having to play nursemaid. Then angrier still at knowing that if he *were* at home there would be fuck all happening, the leads dried up, the new angles nonexistent. There was no reason for him to be missed.

He bent to pick up the food that had spilled onto the floor, thought better of it, and kicked it under the table.

The room was absolutely fucking huge. Or perhaps it just *seemed* huge. He knew that his sense of perspective was still a little skewed. Christ, having a crap without company felt like luxury . . .

It was all Welch could do to stop himself running into the bathroom to rub one off. That had been exactly what he'd done when Jane had got in touch with him at the hostel. Grabbed one of her photographs and thrown one off the wrist, hardly able to believe what she was suggesting.

He'd been amazed, how had she known where he was? He didn't bloody care, mind you, he'd been fucking delighted. He hadn't thought he'd hear from her again. He'd presumed she was one of those silly tarts who got off on writing to cons while they were inside, but would run a mile once they got out. He'd been so sure that he'd actually chucked away the letters she'd sent him in prison when he got out. He kept the photos, obviously. No way was he getting rid of *them* . . .

He pulled out the one photo of Jane that he'd brought with him. God, she looked gorgeous. He dreamed that perhaps she would bring the hood with her, maybe even the handcuffs. He'd secretly brought the picture along in the hope that they could try to re-create it.

He'd spent such a long time imagining what she looked like underneath the hood, or with her face lifted up out of the shadow, and now, when he was about to see her, the truth was that he didn't care. He knew what her body was like, that she would surrender it to him, allow him to take it. Besides, when it came to it, he'd always been a firm believer in not looking at the mantelpiece when you were poking the fire.

Welch let out a long, slow breath. Looked at his watch. He stroked himself through his trousers, unsure that he'd be able to contain himself if she didn't get a bloody move on . . .

Somebody knocked at the door. Three times. Softly.

On the way back to the bar, his father out of harm's way, Thorne had been collared by his auntie Eileen, who asked if he was having a good time and would he mind having a quick word with one of her nephews who was thinking of joining the police force? Thorne thought that he'd rather wash a corpse and said that yes, of course he would, and pushed his way back toward where he hoped his drink would still be waiting . . .

He downed a third of the pint in one, and as it went down, he watched as hard glances were exchanged on the other side of the bar. Some cousin or other and the bride's mate, looking like they wanted trouble. Thorne decided that even if they started punching seven shades of shit out of each other right there and then, he wasn't going to raise a finger.

He realized that he was wrong about this stuff only happening at family weddings. With the possible exception of the disco, you could get it all at family funerals as well. The key word was *family,* that first syllable stretched out and said with a metaphorical jab of the finger, if you were a character on *EastEnders,* or a fake Cockney TV celebrity, or from a particular part of Southeast London.

Thorne looked across. He guessed that the trouble would kick off a little later. In the car park, maybe.

It was events like these, he thought, *births, marriages, and deaths,* that saw the undercurrents rise to the surface and become unstable. Bubbling up and swirling in eddies of beer and Bacardi. Sentimentality, aggression, envy, suspicion, avarice.

History. The ties that bind, twisted . . .

This was the stuff that was reserved for those closest to us, that was hidden away from strangers, even when that was *exactly* what most of your family were.

Thorne saw a lad, sixteen or seventeen, walking across the bar toward him. This was probably the nephew in search of career advice. On second thought, Thorne was in just the mood to give him some . . .

He might start with a few statistics. Such as the number of murders committed by persons unknown to the victim, and how tiny they were compared to those committed by persons to whom the victim was actually *related.* He would tell the boy that when it came to families, to the tensions within them and the acts carried out in their name, he should never, *ever* be surprised. He would tell the stupid, eager young idiot that families were dangerous.

That they were capable of anything.

When the man had come through the door, Welch could see straightaway that he was in trouble.

There was a look on the man's face that Welch recognized, that he'd spent years in prison trying to avoid. It was the look he'd seen often on the faces of ordinary honest-to-goodness murderers and armed robbers. The same look of contempt, of threat, that Caldicott must have seen down in that laundry room before they flash-fried his face . . .

Welch thought that perhaps he should have struggled more, but there was little he could do. The man was far stronger than he was. The years inside had toughened him up mentally, but his body had gone soft and flabby. Too much time reading and not nearly enough in the gym . . .

Welch spent his last moments thinking that pain was so much worse when you were unable to fight it, when you could not protest its presence . . .

The scream in his throat was stopped by whatever had been thrown around his neck and pressed back into a strangled, bubbling hiss. His body, too, could do nothing. It drew itself instinctively from the agony, but each jerk away from the tearing, from the stabbing, just tightened the grip of the line that was crushing the breath out of him.

Welch pushed his head down toward the carpet, feeling the line bite farther into his neck, his teeth deeper into his tongue. He strained against the hands that dragged his neck back, contorting himself, his body fetal in the seconds before death.

I'm dying like a baby, Welch thought, his eyes wide but seeing nothing inside the hood, a softer, blacker darkness beginning finally to come over him . . .

Thorne had just put his father to bed. He was walking across the corridor to his own room when the phone rang. He let it ring until he was inside the room.

"You're up late . . ."

"Great, isn't it?" Eve said. "Lie-in tomorrow. So, how was the wedding?"

"Perfect. Dull speeches, shit food, and a fight."

"What about the actual *wedding* . . . ?"

"Oh, *that*? Yeah, that was okay . . ."

She laughed. Thorne sat on the bed, wedged the phone between shoulder and chin, and started to take his shoes off. "Listen, I'm really sorry about last night . . ."

"Don't be silly. How's your dad?"

"You know, annoying. Mind you, he was annoying before . . ." Thorne thought he could hear the sound of traffic at the other end of the line. He guessed Eve was out somewhere, but thought better of asking where. "Seriously, though, sorry about rushing off. Did the food get eaten?"

"Don't worry, it will . . ."

"Sorry . . ."

"It's fine, there would have been tons left anyway. I'd made loads and Denise eats nothing, so I wouldn't worry about it."

Thorne began to unbutton his shirt. "Say thanks to her and Ben for the entertainment, by the way . . ."

"Good, wasn't it? I think I broke it up too early, though. Another minute, and I'm sure we'd have seen a glass of wine thrown in someone's face . . ."

"Next time."

She yawned loudly. "God, sorry . . ."

"I'll let you get to bed," he said. He was imagining her in the back of a cab, pulling up outside her flat.

"Sleep well, Tom."

Thorne lay back down on his bed. "Listen, you know that scale of one to ten? Can I move up to an eight . . . ?"

Thorne's phone rang again eight hours later. Its insistent chirrup pulled him up from the depths of a deep sleep. Dragged him from a dream where he was trying to stop a man bleeding to death. Each time he put his finger over a hole, another would appear, as if he were Chaplin trying to plug a leak. Just when it seemed he had all the wounds covered, the blood began to spurt from a number of holes in *him* . . .

"You'd better get back, sir," Holland said.

"Tell me . . ."

"The killer's ordered another wreath . . ."

Part Two

Like Light

November 27, 1996

Stooping to pick up the car keys he'd dropped, Alan Franklin winced in pain. A fortnight shy of retirement, and his body, like a precision alarm clock, was telling him that it was just the right time. The back pain and the talk of retirement cottages abroad had begun on almost exactly the same day . . .

He straightened up, his noisy exhalation echoing around the almost deserted car park. They'd probably talk about it again tonight, the two of them, over a bottle of wine. Sheila was leaning toward France, while he fancied Spain. Either way, they would be off. There was nothing to keep them, after all. The children he'd had with Celia were grown up with kids of their own. Not that he had any contact with his boys anymore, and he'd never seen the grandchildren they'd produced. There were friends, of course, and they'd be missed, but it wasn't like he and Sheila were going to be far away. They had no real ties . . .

He fumbled for the key to the Rover, pushed it toward the lock.

Sheila would probably get her way in the end, of course, she usually did. It had to be said that more often than not she was right. She'd been right this morning, telling him that it was going to freeze, that he needed to wrap up warm.

He turned the key, popped up the central locking.

As he reached for the door handle, something passed in front of his eyes with a swish and bit back, hard into his neck, pulling him off his feet . . .

He hit the floor before his briefcase did, before he had a chance to cry out, one leg broken and bent behind, the other straight out in front of him, hands flying to his throat, fingers wedging themselves between line and neck.

Hands scrabbled at his own, tearing at his fingers, pulling them away. A fist crashed into the side of his head, and as he rocked with the impact, he felt his fingers, numb and running with blood, slipping from beneath the line. And hot breath on the back of his neck . . .

He watched his leg shooting out, the foot kicking desperately against the Rover's dirty gray hubcap.

He remembered suddenly the face of the woman underneath him. Smelled himself, the aftershave he used to love. Felt again that strength in his arms.

He saw her legs kicking out against the boxes piled high on either side of the stockroom. Heard the dull thud of her stockinged feet on the cardboard. He felt the movement beneath him die down and then stop, saw her eyes close tight.

It seemed to be getting dark very quickly. Perhaps the lights in the car park were on some sort of timer. Fading to save electricity. He could just make out his foot, the heel of his brogue still crashing into the hubcap, again and again. Cracking the cheap plastic.

Then, just black and the rushing of his blood, and the sound of his heartbeat, which thumped inside his eyeballs as the line tightened.

He saw his wife, smiling at him from the garden, and the woman beneath him trying to turn her head away, and his wife, and then the woman, and finally the woman where his wife should have been, telling him how cold it was going to get.

Laughing, and reminding him not to forget his scarf . . .

TEN

Carol Chamberlain had always been an early riser, but by the time her husband shuffled, bleary-eyed, into the kitchen at a little after seven o'clock, she'd already been up a couple of hours. He flicked on the kettle, nodded to himself. He'd known very well she would have trouble sleeping after the phone call.

It had come the evening before, in the ad break between *Stars in Their Eyes* and *Blind Date*. As soon as the caller had identified himself, begun to tell her what he wanted, Carol had understood the quizzical look on Jack's face when he'd handed her the receiver.

She'd listened to everything that the commander had to say. From the audible exasperation in his voice it was clear that she'd asked a lot more questions than he'd been expecting. After fifteen minutes she had agreed to think about what she'd been asked.

The new team had been set up, she was told, to utilize some of the resources that had been—how had he put it?—*wasted* in previous years. The basic idea was that highly capable ex-officers could bring years of valuable experience to bear on reexamining old, dead cases. Would be able to cast a fresh eye across them . . .

For most of the time since she'd hung up, since they'd gone back to watching Saturday-night TV, Carol had been in two minds. She was certainly a "wasted resource," but much as she was happy, no, *desperate*, to do something, she had also heard something dubious in the voice of the unspeakably young commander. She knew immediately that he and many others would be picturing hordes of aged ex-coppers shuffling in from Eastbourne, on sticks and Zimmer frames, waving dog-eared warrant cards and shouting: "I can still cut it. I'm eighty-two, you know . . ."

Jack put a mug of tea down in front of her. He spoke softly. "You're going to do it, aren't you, love?"

She looked up at him. Her smile was nervous, but still wider than it had been in a while.

"I can still cut it," she said.

While Thorne had been racing back from Hove, shagging the hired Corsa up three different motorways, Brigstocke had made the scene at the Greenwood Hotel secure. By the time Thorne arrived, it was nearly three hours since the body they would later identify as Ian Welch had been discovered, and more than twelve since he'd been killed. There was little else for Thorne to do but stare at him for a while.

"Well, it's a slightly nicer hotel anyway," Hendricks said.

Holland nodded. "They even sent us up some coffee . . ."

"There's a CCTV set-up in the lobby as well," Brigstocke said. "It's pretty basic, I think, but you never know."

It was a classic businessman's hotel. Trouser presses, Teasmades, and bog-standard soap in the bathroom. The simple, clean room couldn't have been more different from the pit they'd stood in three weeks earlier. Save, of course, for the one gruesome feature they had in common.

As with the murder scene in Paddington, the bed had been stripped and the bedding taken away. The clothes

lay scattered, but the body itself had been precisely posi-
tioned. Dead center with head toward the wall, belt
around the wrists, white hands bloodless. The hood, the
line around the neck, the dried red-brown trails snaking
down the thighs like gravy stains . . .

This one looked a little older than Remfry. Late forties
maybe.

Brigstocke gave Thorne what little they had. Thorne
took the information in, standing by the window, one
eye on the fields beyond the main road. They were two
minutes from the motorway, fifty yards from a major
roundabout, but on this Sunday morning, Thorne could
hear nothing but birdsong and the rustle of a body bag.

This time the killer had ordered his floral tribute personally. The order had been placed with a twenty-four-
hour florist at just after eight-thirty the evening before
and paid for with the victim's debit card. Thanks to that,
they already had a name for the dead man . . .

"He didn't fancy leaving a message this time," Brigstocke said.

Thorne shrugged. Either the killer had learned from
his mistake or had done what he needed to do in leaving
his voice on Eve Bloom's machine.

"Twenty-four-hour florists?" Thorne shook his head.
"Who the hell needs flowers in the middle of the night?"

"They're not *actually* twenty-four hours," Brigstocke
said. "But there's always somebody there until at least
ten o'clock. They don't guarantee to get your flowers delivered by the next morning, but apparently they made a
special effort in this case, due to the nature of the
order . . ."

At 9 A.M., a deliveryman had waltzed into hotel reception carrying the wreath. The receptionist, somewhat
taken aback, had rung room 313 and, on getting no reply, had asked the deliveryman to wait, and had gone up

to the room. Five minutes later, her screams had woken most of the hotel.

"Sir . . . ?"

Thorne turned from the window to see Andy Stone coming through the bedroom door. He was clutching a piece of paper, grinning, and moving quickly across to where Thorne and Brigstocke were standing.

"The victim checked in under his own name . . ." Stone said.

Brigstocke shrugged. "No real reason for him not to, was there? He thought he was coming here to get fucked."

"Looks well and truly fucked to me," Holland said.

When Stone had finished laughing, Thorne caught his eye. "Go on . . ."

Stone glanced down at the piece of paper. "Ian Anthony Welch." He half turned toward the body. "Released eight days ago from Wandsworth. Three years of a five-stretch for rape."

Thorne spoke to nobody in particular. "I don't know why we never considered it. Remfry wasn't killed because of who he was. He and Welch were killed because of *what* they were. Christ, this is the sort of case we normally get brought *in* for . . ."

Brigstocke stretched, his plastic bodysuit rustling. "Well, this time, we've got our very own."

Now things were going to change: in the previous week and a half, priorities had shifted. Older cases that had been downgraded in the immediate wake of the Remfry murder had, suddenly, three unsuccessful weeks on, been shunted forward again. Members of the team found themselves knee-deep in court preparations for a domestic, processing the arrest of a teenager who'd stabbed his friend for a computer game or gathering the papers on a drug-related shooting. This reallocation of resources was normal and now it would need to be done all over again. Now that the Remfry murder was the Remfry and Welch murd*ers,* the more straightforward cases would slide back onto the back burner.

Now Team 3 would be handling no other cases at all . . .

"One, two, three . . ."

Thorne watched as four officers heaved the body off the mattress and onto the black body bag that had been stretched out on the floor next to the bed. The belt had been removed but the hands were still clenched tightly together behind the back, fingers entwined. Rigor mortis had set in hours ago and the body rolled awkwardly onto its side, knees drawn up to the chest. The officers looked at one another and, after a few moments, a DS stepped forward. He placed a hand on the chest, and as he rolled the body onto its back, he pushed the legs downward as far as they would go. Flattening the body just enough to zip the bag up.

"I forgot to ask," Brigstocke said. "How was the wedding?"

Thorne was still watching the sergeant, whose eyes were closed the whole time his hands were on the naked body.

"Not a lot more fun than this," Thorne said.

Fifteen minutes later, just after midday, the core of the team gathered in the lobby. They were about to go their separate ways. The postmortem was being rushed through at two o'clock, and while Thorne would be following Hendricks to Wexham Hospital, Brigstocke and the others would be heading back to the office.

While the DCI spoke on the phone to Jesmond and then to Yvonne Kitson back in the Incident Room, the others sat on mock-leather armchairs and shared a pot of coffee. Less animated than the small gaggle of hotel staff and guests, they stared out through the plate-glass windows in reception at the body being loaded into the mortuary van.

Brigstocke joined them, sliding his mobile back into the inside pocket of his jacket. "Well, that's everybody up to speed, me included . . ."

"What words of wisdom from the all-knowing detective chief superintendent?" Thorne asked. Outside, the mortuary van was moving away. Hendricks waved as he climbed into his car to follow it. Thorne raised a hand in return.

"Nothing I can argue with," Brigstocke said. "We'll have reporters here before they've put new sheets on the bed. So here it is. Officially, we can't confirm *or* deny a link with the Remfry murder." He paused, making sure the message was sinking in. "It makes sense. The tabloids would have a fucking field day with this one. Screaming about vigilantes, running polls. *Is the killer doing a good job? Yes or no?*"

"Is that a possibility, you think?" Stone asked. "Could this be some sort of vigilante thing?"

Thorne reached for the coffeepot, poured himself another cup. "This is something very personal. The man who's doing this isn't doing it for you or me . . ."

"Maybe," Brigstocke said. "But all the same, there *will* be people asking whether or not we should be grateful . . ."

The hotel manager walked through reception, talking quietly to a small group of guests in golfing gear. They stopped at the main doors and chatted some more. The manager shook their hands before watching the bemused golfers duck underneath the police tape and walk away, shaking their heads. It was a game Thorne had little time for, but he guessed they'd have something other than new cars and holidays to talk about on the first tee.

Brigstocke cleared his throat. "Right. Forensics will be moving as quickly as they can, but while we're waiting, there's plenty we need to do . . ."

"We'll get nothing," Thorne said. "It's cleaner than the last place, but it's still a hotel room. They'll be gathering samples into next week."

"We might get lucky," Holland said.

"More chance of six numbers coming up Saturday night . . ."

Brigstocke tapped a spoon against his coffee cup. "Let's cut the morale building short for a minute, shall we? Talk about what we *can* do . . ."

Holland raised a hand. "Sir. If I *do* get six numbers up on Saturday night, I'm officially requesting permission to resign from the case and fuck off to Rio de Janeiro with twin supermodels." The few seconds of laughter did everybody good.

"I want to know exactly what Ian Welch has been doing since he came out," Brigstocke said. "Where he's been staying, who he's been seeing—"

Stone cut in. "He came out NFA. The prison gave me the address of a hostel . . ."

Brigstocke nodded. "Good, and you're going to be calling a *lot* more governors before we're finished. We'll need to contact every prison in the country housing sex offenders, talk to anyone with an imminent release date. That's the easy bit. We're also going to trace every rapist, groper, and flasher who's been released in the last six months. Check that none of them have received letters. Warn them in case they get any."

"How many are we looking at?" Holland asked.

Brigstocke picked up a small pack of biscuits, sealed in plastic. He dangled it between two fingers. "Based on the last set of Home Office stats, probably one serious sex offender is released somewhere in the country every day." He tore open the packet with his teeth, spat out the plastic, looked at the faces of the other men around the table. "I know. Frightening, isn't it? Just going back to the start of this year, we're going to be looking for something like a hundred and fifty offenders . . ."

Stone raised his eyebrows. "Well, we should know where most of them are, in theory at least. Still might be a shitload of work, though."

"Yes, it might be," Brigstocke said.

"Are we going to be able to justify that? I mean, like you said, these aren't exactly innocent victims, are they?"

Brigstocke blinked, opened his mouth to shout. Thorne got in first. "Not your worry, Andy."

"I know. I was just saying . . ."

Thorne raised a hand. "What we *can't* justify are bodies . . ."

They walked out to their cars. Brigstocke drifted away from the others toward his Volvo, took Thorne with him. He glanced toward Andy Stone.

"Have a word . . ."

Thorne nodded. "Well, he *was* making the same sort of point you made yourself earlier. Remfry, Welch, doing what they did, being what they are. Some people might well think that . . ."

Brigstocke pressed the remote, deactivating the car alarm with a squawk. "I'm not talking about what he said back there. I'm talking about the Gribbin business."

Thorne had been waiting for this. He had known that Stone's behavior during the raid was not just going to be forgotten. "Right . . ."

"Don't worry, it's not going as far as the Funny Firm. All been put down to protecting the girl. Still, I want you to let him know he overstepped the mark."

"Fair enough . . ."

Brigstocke got into the car, started the engine. He began to pull slowly away. "Call me from the Wexham as soon as Phil's finished . . ."

Holland loped across the gravel as Thorne walked to the Corsa. "You up for a drink later?"

"I'm likely to be up for several," Thorne said.

Holland ran a hand along the front wing of the hire car. "This is the sort of thing *you* ought to get."

"Sort of thing I ought to get *when*?"

"Come on, your car is fucked. This is nice, though . . ."

"It's *white* . . . and my car is not fucked . . ."

"Name one thing that's good about it."

Thorne opened the Corsa's door, hesitated before getting in. "What? Straight off the top of my head?"

Holland laughed, leaned down as Thorne climbed in. "If this was a woman we were talking about, you'd dump her."

The electric window slid down. "You've got a very strange mind, Holland."

"How's it going with the florist, anyway?"

"Mind your own business."

There was a rumble as an engine started up. Thorne looked across to see Stone watching them from behind the wheel of his own car, a silver Ford Cougar. He nodded toward it. "What d'you think of Stone's motor?"

"It's a bit flash," Holland said.

Thorne could see Stone slapping his palm off the steering wheel. "Better get a move on. He looks keen to get back."

Holland took a step away from the car, stopped. "Did your dad have a good time at the wedding?"

"A good time? Yes. I think so . . ."

"I meant to tell you . . ." Stone sounded the horn. "William Hartnell was the first Doctor Who. I looked it up on the Internet."

"I'll tell him . . ."

Thorne turned the key in the ignition, watched as Holland ran across and climbed into Stone's car. He could hear the music being cranked up as the sports car roared past him and out onto the main road with hardly a look from Andy Stone toward anything that might have been coming.

Thorne looked at his watch and turned the engine off again. Not quite one o'clock yet. The postmortem wasn't until two and it was no more than a ten-minute drive to the hospital. He sat for a few minutes trying to decide between sleep and a Sunday paper and then he started to hear distant shouting, a cheer, a solitary handclap. The noise recognizable, tantalizing. Carrying easily on the warm, afternoon air.

It took him twenty minutes to find the game, a quarter of a mile away up the main road in a small park. The season was still a month and a half away, but Sunday footballers cared as little for the calendar as they did for other trivialities like fitness and skill. A team in red and a team in yellow and a dozen or so lunatics watching, living every less than beautiful second of it.

Thorne could not have been more content. He stood on the touchline and lost himself in the game. In a little over an hour he would be watching organs meticulously excised, the flesh expertly sliced and laid aside . . .

For a while, he was happy to watch a team in red and a team in yellow, running and shouting and kicking lumps out of each other.

Thorne picked up his pint and turned from the bar. Except for Russell Brigstocke, one of whose kids was unwell, and Yvonne Kitson, most of the senior members of the team had come out. There was an unspoken need to loosen up, to enjoy a night out that they might not have the chance to repeat for a while, now that the case had moved up a gear. Now that there was a second body.

Thorne wasn't planning on staying long. He was wiped out. One drink, maybe two, and then home . . .

They were gathered around a couple of smallish tables. Holland and Hendricks were sitting at one end with Andy Stone and Sam Karim, a DS who worked as office manager. They were playing Shag or Die, a game that involved choosing between a pair of equally undesirable sexual partners, which had swept through the entire Serious Crime Group in the last few weeks. The choice between Princess Anne and Camilla Parker-Bowles was prompting heated debate. Phil Hendricks was trying to make himself heard, claiming that as a gay man, he should not have to sleep with either of them. His point was eventually accepted as valid and he was given a choice between Saddam Hussein and Detective Chief Superintendent Trevor Jesmond to mull over . . .

If the Royal Oak had a theme other than drinking heavily, nobody had ever worked out what it was. Apart from being the *nearest* pub to Becke House, it had nothing whatsoever to recommend it. The fairly constant presence of police officers may have had something to do with it, but there was rarely anybody drinking in the pub who didn't have a badge.

Thorne looked around. Sunday night and the place was all but deserted: a couple at a table near the toilets, staring into their drinks like they'd had a row; the room quiet, save for his team's graphic deliberations and the tinny, musical stings from the unused arcade game in the corner.

Hardly any more there than had gathered earlier in the Dissecting Room: Phil Hendricks; a trio of mortuary attendants; the exhibits officer; a stills photographer; a video cameraman; the PC who had been first to arrive at the Greenwood Hotel, there to confirm that the body was indeed the same one he had seen on the bed in room 313. And Thorne . . .

Nine of them, gathered in a cold room with easy-to-clean surfaces and drains in the floor. The smallest murmur or the crunching of peppermints magnified, bouncing off the cracked, cream tiles. A small crowd, waiting for the body of Ian Welch to be uncovered and taken apart.

Thorne had attended hundreds of postmortems, and though it was a process he had become resigned to, he had found that lately it was a difficult one to leave behind, to shed easily. The visceral onslaught disturbed him now far less than the tiny details, the sensory minutiae that might stay with him for days after each session . . .

Blinking awake in the early hours, as a brain plops gently into a glass jar.

Dabbing at his freshly shaved face, the water spiraling away, its momentary slurp like the sucking of the flesh at the finger that presses into it.

A smell at work, the odor of something very raw, lurking somewhere deep within the medley of sweat and institutional food . . .

Nine of them gathered. Waiting like embarrassed guests at a bizarre party, strangers to one another. *That dreadful hiatus between arriving and anything actually happening . . .*

Finally, Hendricks drew back the white sheet and asked the equally white PC to confirm it was the same body he'd seen earlier. The constable looked as though the only thing he could confirm was rising rapidly up from his stomach. He swallowed hard.

"Yes," he said, "it is."

And they were away . . .

Holland had moved across to the bar to get a round in and Thorne took his place next to Andy Stone. Karim leaned across, eager to involve Thorne in the game. Before he had a chance to speak, Thorne angled his body away, turned into the corner, toward Stone.

"Idiotic, bloody game," Stone said. Thorne had only

just got there, but Stone sounded like he was three or four drinks ahead of him. "If it's shag or *die,* you'd shag anybody, wouldn't you? So what's the point?"

Thorne swallowed a mouthful of lager and leaned a little closer to Stone. "I need to have a quick word about what happened when we picked Gribbin up."

If Stone had been on the way to being drunk, he sobered up very quickly. "I was protecting the kid. I didn't know what he was going to do . . ."

"Which is exactly what the DCI is going to say. Still, I'm here to tell you, off the record, that you overstepped the mark. That nobody wants to see it happen again, okay?" Stone stared forward, said nothing. "Andy . . . ?" Thorne took another drink. Half the pint had gone already. "Nobody's very fond of guys like Gribbin, but you were over the top."

"There's just so bloody many of them. I don't understand how there can be so *many* of them walking about."

"Listen . . ."

Stone turned. He spoke low and fast as if imparting dangerous information. "I've got a mate on the Child Protection Team over at Barnes. He told me about this time they were after a child killer up in Scotland. This bloke had already killed three kids, they had a description, and some woman claimed she'd spotted him on a beach one bank holiday, right? So they appealed for people to come forward with their holiday snaps, see if anybody might have got a picture of this fucker accidentally . . ."

Thorne nodded. He remembered the case. He had no idea what Stone wanted to tell him.

"So, they get hundreds of films handed in. They develop them all and go through the pictures. Thousands of them." Stone picked up his glass, stared into it for a moment. "The woman couldn't pick out the man she'd seen, but the police identified thirty known child-sex offenders. In *one* fucking weekend, on *one* beach. Thirty . . ."

Stone drained his glass. "Right. Toilet, I think . . ."

Thorne watched Stone go, and drained his. He decided to leave the Corsa in the car park at Becke House. It was easy enough to get the tube home . . .

The rest of the evening passed quickly and easily. Thorne had some success with a couple of his dad's jokes; Holland argued with Sophie on the phone, pulling faces for the lads, doing his best to laugh it off; nobody could choose between Margaret Thatcher and the Queen; Holland spoke to Sophie again, then turned his phone off; Thorne bet Hendricks ten pounds that Spurs were going to finish above Arsenal the following season; Hendricks had one Guinness too many and told Holland that several of his gay friends fancied him . . .

Stone grabbed Thorne's arm as they were all stepping out into the clear, warm night. Saying their good-byes.

"Something else my mate told me. They arrested this one bloke who had all these pictures of kids off the Internet, you know? Downloaded them onto his computer, hundreds of them. He said that he was searching through all these pictures, looking at them all, at their faces, hoping that one day he might find the pictures of himself . . ."

Thorne tried gently to pull away. Stone was squeezing his arm tightly.

"That's rubbish, isn't it?" Stone said. "That's crap. That's an excuse, don't you think? That's not really true, is it, sir . . . ?"

Thorne stepped through the front door into the communal hall he shared with the couple in the flat upstairs.

The breath he let out was long and noisy. He picked up the mail, sorted the bills from the pizza delivery menus, fumbled for his flat key.

As soon as the door was open he knew. He could feel the breeze where there should be none. The scent of something carried on it . . .

He moved quickly into his own small hallway. The cat was rubbing itself against his shin. He put down his bag, dropped the letters onto the table next to the phone, and stepped around the corner into the living room.

He stared at the space where the video had been. Looked up at the dusty shelf he'd never bothered to paint, on which his sound system had sat. The leads were gone, which meant they'd obviously been in the place for a while. The ones who were in a hurry just ripped the spaghetti out of the back, left it still plugged in.

He reached to pick up the few scattered paperbacks that had previously been held upright by his Bose speakers. Clearly, whoever now had his speakers wasn't a great reader. They *had* taken every single CD . . .

Fuckers would hand over his entire collection for a day's worth of smack.

Thorne walked through to the kitchen, stared at the small window they'd climbed through. The window he'd left open. In a hurry two nights earlier, throwing his stuff for the wedding together and not locking up properly because he was rushing across to calm his fucking stupid father down . . .

Aside from the obvious gaps, the place seemed pretty much as he'd left it. He guessed that there would be a suitcase or two missing from the wardrobe in the bedroom. Away out of the front door, casual as you like, as if they were taking something very heavy on their holidays.

The smell hit him the second he opened the bedroom door, and Thorne had a pretty good idea where it was coming from. He moved his hand to cover his mouth, needing to unclench the fist as he did so. His first thought when he threw back the duvet was that it must have taken a good deal of skill to have done the job so accurately, smack in the center of the bed.

Thorne backed quickly out of the room, his guts bubbling. Elvis yowled at his feet; hungry, or keen to deny responsibility for the turd on the bed, one or the other. Thorne wondered if it was too late to ring his father and shout at him for a while.

He looked at his watch. It was ten past twelve . . .

He'd just turned forty-three.

*All through Sunday, every time he was beginning
to enjoy himself, he'd remembered the bloody message and become prickly, irritated. It had been
there on his answering machine, waiting for him
when he'd got back from Slough on Saturday
night. He'd ignored it, collapsed exhausted into
bed, and played it back first thing the next morning. It was exactly what he did not need. It was
spoiling things.*

He needed to deal with it.

*As he moved around his flat, dressing himself, he
remembered the look on Welch's face when he'd
walked into the hotel room. The face was the very
best thing. Remfry's had been the same. It was the
look that passes across the face of someone who
thinks that they are about to get one thing, and
then realizes that they are in for an altogether different sort of experience.*

*He wondered if they saw that expression on the
faces of the women they raped.*

*He didn't know the details of their particular of-
fenses, he didn't care. Rape was rape was rape. He
did know that most attacks did not involve dark
alleys and deserted bus stops. He knew that most
rapists were known to their victims. Were trusted
by them. Friends, colleagues, husbands . . .*

They would have seen that terrible realization on the faces of the women they attacked. The horror and surprise. The very last thing they were expecting.

The very last person they were expecting it from.

He'd enjoyed watching that same expression distort the smug, expectant features on the faces of these men. He'd savored it for a few seconds before taking out the knife and the washing line . . .

Creating an entirely new expression.

He pulled on his jacket and picked up his keys. Checked himself in the mirror by the front door. He glanced down at the answering machine.

He would definitely sort the message business out later.

ELEVEN

It was no more than a ten-minute walk from the tube station, but Thorne had a healthy sweat on by the time he reached Becke House. A figure loitered by the main doors, wreathed in cigarette smoke. Thorne was amazed when it turned around and revealed itself to be Yvonne Kitson.

"Morning, Yvonne."

She nodded, avoiding his eye and blushing like a fourth-former caught smoking behind the bike sheds. "Morning . . ."

Thorne pointed at the cigarette, almost burned down to the butt. "I didn't know you . . ."

"Well, you do now." She tried her best to smile and took another drag. "Not quite so perfect, I'm afraid . . ."

"Thank Christ for that," Thorne said.

Kitson's smile got a little warmer. "Oh, sorry. Was I starting to intimidate you?"

"Well, not *me*, obviously. But I think one or two of the younger ones were a bit scared." Kitson laughed, and Thorne saw that she was still carrying her bag across one shoulder. "Have you not even been *in* yet?" he asked. She shook her head, blowing smoke out the side of her mouth. "Bloody hell, how stressed out can you possibly be, then?" Kitson raised her eyebrows, looked at him like he didn't know the half of it.

They stood for a few seconds, looking in different directions, saying nothing. Thorne decided to make a move before they were forced to start discussing the hot weather. He put one hand on the glass doors . . .

"I'll see you upstairs . . ." he said.

"Oh shit." Like she'd just remembered. "Sorry to hear about the burglary . . ."

Thorne nodded, shrugged, and pushed through the doors. He trudged up the stairs, marveling at the incredible speed and efficiency of the Met's jungle-drum system.

A desk sergeant in Kentish Town, who knows a DC in Islington, who calls somebody at Colindale . . .

Throw a few Chinese whispers into the mix and you had a culturally diverse ensemble of rumor, gossip, and bullshit that outperformed any of the systems they actually used to fight crime . . .

It took Thorne almost five minutes to get from one side of the Incident Room to the other. Running the gauntlet of digs and wisecracks. A cup of coffee from the reconditioned machine in the corner the prize that awaited him.

"Sorry, mate . . ."

"You look a bit rough, sir. Sleep on the sofa?"

"Never done a crime prevention seminar, then, Tom?"

"Many happy returns . . ." This was Holland.

Thorne had wanted to keep it quiet. He'd deliberately said nothing in the pub the night before. He must have mentioned the date to Holland sometime. "Thanks."

"Not a very nice present to come home to. I mean the burglary, not—"

"No. It wasn't."

"Somebody said they took your car . . ."

"Is that a smirk, Holland?"

"No, sir . . ."

The night before. Thorne, hauling the mattress out through the front door when he remembered that he hadn't seen the Mondeo outside when he'd arrived home. He didn't recall seeing his car keys on the table as he'd come in either. He *had* been worrying about other things at the time . . .

He dropped the mattress and stepped out into the street. Maybe he'd parked the car somewhere else.

He hadn't. Fuckers . . .

"Birthday drink in the Oak later, then?" Holland said.

Thorne stepped past him, almost within reach of the coffee machine now. He turned and spoke quietly, reaching into his pocket for change. "Just a quiet one, all right?"

"Whatever . . ."

"Not like last night. Just you and Phil, maybe."

"Fine . . ."

"I might ask Russell if he fancies it . . ."

"We can do it another day if you're not up for it."

Thorne slammed his coins into the coffee machine. "Listen, after dealing with the fallout from our second body, and spending fuck knows how long I'm going to have to spend on the phone to house insurance companies and car insurance companies and whichever council department is responsible for taking shitty mattresses away, I think I might need a drink . . ."

After Holland had gone, Thorne stood, sipping his coffee and staring at the large white write-on/wipe-off board that dominated one wall of the room. Crooked lines scrawled in black felt-tip, marking out the columns and rows. Arrows leading away to addresses and phone numbers. The ACTIONS for the day, each team member's duties allocated by the office manager. The names of those peripheral to the investigation. The names of those central to it: REMFRY, GRIBBIN, DODD . . .

In a column of all its own: JANE FOLEY??

And now a second name added beneath Dougie Remfry's, with plenty of empty space for more names below that one. The heading at the top of the column hadn't been altered yet. Nobody had thought to add an s to VICTIM, but they would.

Thorne heard a sniff and turned to find Sam Karim at his shoulder.

"How's the head?"

Thorne glanced at him. "What?"

"After last night. I feel like shit warmed up . . ."

"I'm fine," Thorne said.

Samir Karim was a large, gregarious Indian with a shock of thick silver hair and a broad London accent that was delivered at a hundred miles per hour. He planted half of his sizable backside onto the edge of a desk. "Fuck all off those tapes, by the way . . ."

"Which tapes?"

"CCTV tapes from the Greenwood."

Thorne shrugged, unsurprised.

"Couple of possibles," Karim said. "But only from the back. The cameras only really cover the bar and the area around the desk and the lifts. You can walk in and go straight up the stairs without being seen at all, if you know where the cameras are . . ."

"He knew where they were," Thorne said.

They stared at the board together for a moment or two. "That's the difference between our team and all the others, isn't it?" Karim said.

"What?"

"They have a victim. We have a list . . ."

There's a moment in film and TV shows, a particular shot, a cliché to signify that moment when the penny drops. For real people this means remembering where they've left their car keys, or the title of a song that's been annoying them. For the screen copper, it's usually a darker revelation. The instant that provides the break in the case. Then, when that pure and brilliant comprehension dawns, the camera zooms toward the face of the hero, crashing in quickly or sometimes creeping slowly up on them. Either way, it goes in close and it stays there, showing the light of realization growing in the eyes . . .

Thorne was not an actor. There was no nod of steely determination, no enigmatic stare. He stood holding his coffee cup, his mouth gaping, like a half-wit.

A *list* . . .

The certainty hit him like a cricket ball. He felt a bead of sweat surface momentarily from every pore in his body before retreating again. Tingling; hot, then cold.

"Feeling okay, Tom?" Karim asked.

Zoom in close and hold . . .

Thorne didn't feel the hot coffee splashing across his wrist as he marched across the room, up the corridor, and into Brigstocke's office.

Brigstocke looked up, saw the expression on Thorne's face, put down his pen.

"What . . . ?"

"I know how he finds them," Thorne said. "How he finds out where the rapists are . . ."

"How?"

"This *could* all be very simple. Our man might work for the prison service, or hang about in pubs around Pentonville and the Scrubs, hoping to get matey with prison officers, but I doubt it. At the end of the day, finding out where rapists are banged up isn't that hard. Families, court records . . . he could just go to newspaper archives and sift through the local rags if he felt like it . . ."

"Tom . . ."

Thorne stepped quickly forward, put his coffee cup down on Brigstocke's desk, and began to pace around the small office. "It's about what happens *afterward*. It's about release dates and addresses. I *had* thought that maybe there was some connection with the families, but

Welch was NFA. His family disowned him and moved away years ago." He glanced across at Brigstocke as if he were making everything very obvious. Brigstocke nodded, still waiting. "Release details are fluid, right? Prisoners move around, parole dates change, extra days get tagged onto sentences. The killer has to have access to up-to-date, accurate information . . ."

"Do I have to phone a friend?" Brigstocke said. "Or are you going to tell me? How does he find them?"

Thorne allowed himself the tiniest flicker of a smile. "The same way we do."

Behind his glasses Brigstocke blinked twice, slowly. The confusion on his face became something that might have been regret. Or the anticipation of it. "The Sex Offenders Register."

Thorne nodded, picked up his coffee. "Jesus, we need shooting 'cause it took us *this* long . . ."

Brigstocke took a deep breath. He began stepping slowly backward and forward in the space between the wall and the edge of the desk. Trying to take this vital but daunting piece of new information on board. Trying to shape it into something he could handle. "I don't need to say it, do I?" he said finally.

"What?"

"About this not getting out . . ."

Thorne looked up, past Brigstocke. The sun was moving behind a cloud but it was still baking in the tiny office. He could feel the sweat gathering in the small of his back. "You don't need to say it."

"Not just because it's . . . sensitive. Although it *is*."

Thorne knew that Brigstocke was right. The whole issue of the Register had been what the tabloids were fond of calling a "political hot potato" for years. This was just the sort of thing to blow the whole "naming and shaming" debate wide open again. When he looked back to Brigstocke, the DCI was smiling.

"This might be the way we get him, though, Tom."

Thorne was counting on it . . .

Brigstocke came around his desk. "Right, let's start with the bodies that are informed about an offender's registration requirements. The ones that get fed the notification details as a matter of course." He started to count them off on his fingers. "Social services, probation . . ."

"And us, of course," Thorne said. "We'd better not forget the most interesting one, had we, Russell?"

Macpherson House was located in a side street off Camden Parkway. In the course of a century, the building had been a theater, cinema, and bingo hall. Now it was little more than a shell, within which was situated temporary hostel accommodation.

"Fuck me gently," Stone said. He was craning back his head, staring at the grimy, crumbling ceiling high above him.

Holland looked up. There were still traces of gilt on the moldings. Decorative swirls of plaster leaves trailed across the ceiling and then down toward four ornate columns in each corner of the vast room. "Must have been amazing . . ."

There was a week-old copy of the *Daily Star* on the floor. Stone pushed it aside with his foot. He sniffed at the stale air and pulled a face. "It's a bloody shame . . ."

As they walked, Holland took Stone through the simple, ironic history of the place. The theater that had become a cinema. The cinema done for in the seventies by the more popular entertainment of the bingo hall. The bingo hall itself made redundant thirty years later by the easy availability of scratch 'n' win cards and the National Lottery.

"From music hall to the Stupid Tax," Holland said.

Stone snorted. "I take it those six numbers never came up, then?"

"I'm still here, aren't I?"

Their footsteps echoed off the scuffed stone floors, else were muffled as they walked across the occasional threadbare rug or curling square of carpet. "Can't see what's going to replace the Lottery, can you?"

Holland shook his head. "Not as long as there's a call for it."

They were walking ten yards or so behind Brian, the hostel supervisor, a big man in his fifties with long gray hair, a large hoop earring, and a multicolored waistcoat. Without turning around, he held out both arms. Taking in the place.

"Always be a call for *this*, though . . ."

Now, forty feet below the faded rococo grandeur, the space was taken up with cracked sinks and metal beds. A kitchen and a serving hatch. A pair of small televisions, each attached with a padlock and chain to nearby radiators. Behind the beds, along the walls, stood row upon row of scratched and dented lockers—some without locks, many without doors. All rusting and covered in graffiti.

"Council got them for a song," Brian said. "When the swimming pool down the road was knocked down. Same week they got this place off Mecca . . ."

Holland looked down at the floor as he walked. Shoes under many of the beds, trainers, mostly. The occasional tatty suitcase. Dozens of plastic bags.

Stone took off his jacket. "Tramps by and large, is it?"

Brian looked back over his shoulder. Holland thought he looked powerful, like he could handle himself. He probably needed to on occasion. "All sorts. Long-term homeless, runaways, addicts. The odd ex-con like Welch . . ."

"Where do they go during the day?" Holland asked.

The big man slowed, let Holland and Stone draw level

with him. "Wandering about. Begging. Trying to find somewhere to sleep." He smiled when Holland looked confused. "This place is warm and they can get something to eat, but there's not a lot of sleeping goes on. Most of them are scared of getting stuff stolen. Even if they do want to sleep, a hundred blokes coughing and shifting around on creaky bedsprings is worse than a neighbor with a drum kit . . ."

"My ex-girlfriend kept me awake half the night," Stone said. "Talking in her sleep, grinding her teeth . . ."

Brian smiled thinly. "It's quiet enough in here now, but you won't be able to hear yourself think by dinnertime. They'll start drifting back as soon as it starts to get dark. Be rammed in here by nine o'clock."

Holland looked at the lines of beds, three and four deep. Imagined it.

Eyes down for a full house.

The supervisor stopped. He tapped on the open door of a locker and immediately began moving away again. "This was Mr. Welch's. I'll be in the front office if you need anything . . ."

They both pulled on gloves. While Stone went through the locker, Holland got down on his hands and knees and, for the second time in a little over a fortnight, went rummaging under the bed of a recently murdered rapist.

It took less than two minutes to gather together Welch's worldly goods: a battered green holdall full of clothes that smelled of charity shops; a plastic bag of dirty pants and socks; a radio spattered with white paint; an electric razor; a couple of tatty paperbacks . . .

At the back of the locker, between the pages of one of the books, the photographs of Jane Foley.

"Here she is," Stone said, holding one of the pictures up between his fingertips. "Lovelier than ever."

Holland got to his feet, moved across to take a look. "How many?"

"Half a dozen. Can't see any letters. Must have chucked them . . ."

Stone slid the photos into an evidence bag, popped it into an inside pocket. Holland shoved everything else into a black bin-liner. When he'd finished he picked the bag up. It wasn't heavy.

"Not a lot, is it?" he said.

Stone pushed the locker door closed and shrugged. "That's what you get."

It was nearly midday and starting to get really warm. Holland rubbed the sweat off the back of his neck. He thought about what he guessed was going through Stone's mind. "Do you not give a shit because Welch was an ex-con?" he said. "Or because he was an ex-con who was also a rapist? Honestly, I'm interested . . ."

Stone thought about it. Holland bounced the bin bag against his knees.

"I suppose I'd give a bit *more* of a shit if he'd been a forger," Stone said. "Less if he'd murdered half a dozen schoolgirls . . ."

Holland looked at the expression on Stone's face. He couldn't help but laugh as they began to move away, back toward the entrance. "I don't believe it. You've actually got a fucking sliding scale . . ."

They walked up Parkway, where Stone had parked the Cougar. At regular intervals, rubbish bags like the one Holland was carrying were piled high on the pavement. After Madame Tussaud's, Camden's Sunday market was now the second most popular tourist attraction in the city, and cleaning up after it was becoming a little like painting the Forth Bridge.

"So, what is it now? Couple of months till the baby?" Stone asked.

Holland swung the bin bag from one hand to the other. "Ten weeks."

"Sophie must be the size of a house . . ."

Holland smiled, turned to look into the window of a Japanese restaurant. The plates of plastic sushi, red and yellow and pink. He promised himself that one of these days he'd try some.

They turned left and Stone unlocked the car with a remote. "So? Excited, then?"

"Yeah, she's very excited."

Stone opened the car door. Looked at Holland across the roof. "I meant *you* . . ."

"Get your arse up. Right up in the air, that's it. Now let your fingers do the walking . . ."

Charlie Dodd was making himself useful. The place had been hired out for a webcam session and he'd thrown in his services, gratis. He was cheerfully relaying on-screen instructions to the bored-looking girl on the bed when the phone rang.

"Just do some moaning for a minute, sweetheart . . ."

His hand was slippery against the receiver as he mumbled a greeting and waited.

"I got your message . . ."

Dodd recognized the voice straightaway. Without looking around, he used his hand to indicate to the girl on the bed that she should carry on, then brought it to his mouth and took out the cigarette.

"I was wondering when I was going to hear back from you."

"I've had a busy weekend."

Dodd reached for a plastic cup, flicked fag ash into the inch of cold tea at the bottom. "Anything interesting?"

For a few seconds there was nothing but the crackle of static. "You said something about doing me a favor."

"*Done* you a favor, mate," Dodd said. "Already did it. A big favor."

"Go on . . ."

Dodd thought that the man on the other end of the phone sounded relaxed. He was probably putting it on, of course, trying to sound cool because he could guess what was coming. Because he knew he might have to part with some money and wanted to be in control in case there was haggling to do. It was a pretty convincing act, though. Sounded like he knew what Dodd was going to say . . .

"The police were here with one of the photos you did. A photo of the girl with the hood on." Dodd waited for a reaction. Didn't get it. "I got asked a lot of questions . . ."

"And did you tell any lies, Mr. Dodd?"

Dodd pinched the cigarette between thumb and fore-finger, took a final drag. "A couple of little white ones, yeah. And one dirty big fucker." He dropped the nub end into the plastic cup, turned, and watched the girl on the bed. "I told them I never saw your face. Said you never took the crash helmet off . . ."

The girl's rear end bobbed and swayed. Dodd thought the moaning was a bit over-the-top—silly cow sounded like she had food poisoning. There were red blotches at the top of her legs. Finally, the man on the other end of the phone spoke . . .

"Come on, Mr. Dodd, spit it out. Don't be shy."

Dodd reached into the top pocket of his shirt for an-other cigarette. "I'm not fucking shy, mate . . ."

"Good, because there's really no need to be . . ."

"Not about money, anyway."

The man laughed. "There we are. No point in going around the houses. Now, if I remember rightly, there's a cash-point machine just around the corner from your studio, isn't there . . . ?"

Thorne was somewhere between Brent Cross and Gold-ers Green when he began finding it hard to stay awake . . .

He had been as good as the promise he'd made to himself and Holland that morning, having left the Royal Oak in time to make the last tube going south. He was tired and there was still plenty to sort out back at the flat, so it was no great wrench to walk out of the pub before closing time.

He'd left just as Phil Hendricks was starting to let rip. He'd made his feelings about the Sexual Offences Act clear plenty of times before. In the pub, once the subject of the Register had come up, there was no stopping him . . .

"Don't forget the gay men," Hendricks had said. "Those evil bastards who are twisted enough to enjoy loving, consensual sex with their seventeen-year-old boyfriends." The words were spat out, the flat Manchester vowels lending an edge of real anger to the irony.

Thorne knew that Hendricks had every right to be pissed off. It was ridiculous that men convicted of what was still termed "gross indecency" should be lumped together with child abusers and rapists. Even when the age of consent for gay men was lowered to sixteen, as one day it would be, Thorne knew that those convicted prior to its equalization would remain on the Register.

Thorne could only agree with his friend's pithy assessment, the last words he'd caught as he walked out of the pub.

"It's a queer basher's charter," Hendricks had said.

Eve had called to wish him a happy birthday as he was heading for the tube station at Colindale. As they talked, Thorne walked past the KFC, the chippy, more than one kebab shop. His stomach urged him to go in, then changed its mind as he told Eve about the burglary and the little gift that had been left for him.

"Well, it's certainly original," Eve had said.

Thorne laughed. "Right, and a homemade present's *so* much more thoughtful, isn't it?"

Thorne was walking slowly, absorbed in the conversation but keenly aware, as always, of exactly where he was and what he was doing. Keeping track of any movement on the other side of the street, at the corners up ahead, behind parked cars. This wasn't Tottenham or Hackney, but still, there was no point in being stupid when people were getting shot for £9.99 handsets . . .

"So . . . when are you going to replace that bed?" Eve had asked.

"Oh, I suppose I'll get around to it eventually . . ."

"I sincerely hope so."

They were joking, but suddenly Thorne sensed a real shift. A hint of impatience. Like she was making the running and wanted him to do some catching up.

"Well, we can always go to your place, can't we?" Thorne said.

There was a pause. Then: "It's a bit tricky. Denise can be funny about that sort of thing . . ."

"About you having men over?"

"About men *staying* over . . ."

Thorne heard Eve sigh, as if this was a conversation she'd had before. With Denise herself, most probably. "Hang on, she has Ben around, doesn't she?"

"I know, it's mad. But trust me, it isn't worth going into . . ."

Then Thorne had arrived at the station and they'd wound it up. While he fed coins into the ticket machine they'd made a hasty arrangement to meet the following week. She'd said good-bye as he went down on the escalator and he lost the signal before he could say it back.

The train was all but deserted. A teenage couple sat at the far end of the carriage, the girl's head on her boyfriend's shoulder. He was stroking her hair and muttering things that made her smile.

Thorne took a deep breath. His brain felt fuzzed up. He'd only had a couple of pints but his head was thickening, getting heavier with every lurch and sway of the train. He needed to stay awake. Tempting as it was to close his eyes, to let his head drop back, the last thing he wanted to do was to nod off and wake up in Morden.

He thought about the conversation with Eve. When they'd arranged to meet, why hadn't he pushed to make it sooner? Was that panic he'd felt when she'd been talking about the bed? Maybe with the case and his old man and the burglary there was too much other stuff going on. Maybe he was just subconsciously prioritizing. He was *definitely* feeling far too fucked to think straight about anything . . .

At Hampstead, a man got on through the doors to Thorne's right, and despite the availability of seats chose to stand at the end of the carriage, clutching onto the rail above his head. Thorne looked at the man. He was very tall and thin with chiseled features and a frenzy of graying hair and a battery of bizarre visual tics from which Thorne found it impossible to avert his gaze . . .

It quickly became clear that the tic, which Thorne guessed to be Tourette's syndrome, was in three parts. First the man would raise his eyebrows theatrically and his chin would jerk up. A second later the entire head would be wrenched round to the side, and finally, the jaws would snap noisily together, the teeth clacking like castanets. Thorne watched guilty and mesmerized as this three-part pattern repeated itself over and over, and he found himself assigning a word, a sound effect, to each distinct spasm. The eyebrows, the wrench of the neck, the snap of the jaws. Three movements that in rapid succession seemed to display surprise, interest, and then ultimately a bitter disappointment. Movements that sounded to Thorne like "Ooh! Whay-hay! Clack!"

Oh really? Sounds interesting! Ah, fuck it . . .

After a minute or two the man seemed to be bringing the seizure under control and Thorne finally dragged his own head around and his eyes away. The young couple in the left-hand carriage had got off and had been replaced by a pair who were a good deal older and less tactile. The woman caught Thorne's eye and dropped her gaze to the carriage floor like a piece of litter.

When Thorne turned back and looked to his right, the man who was holding on to the rail was now still, and staring straight at him.

Thorne leaned back until he felt his head, big and wobbly as a baby's, hit the window. The glass was cool against his scalp.

He closed his eyes.

He was only a couple of stations away from where he'd need to change at Camden. He could afford to spend just a minute or two drifting, wide-awake and counting the stops, and floating toward his hillside . . .

Almost as soon as Thorne had completed the thought, he was asleep.

He had plenty of stuff to do, a few more images to download from the camera and print, but he thought he deserved a quick break. Ten or fifteen minutes messing about on the Net wouldn't hurt and then he'd get back to business. Put all the pictures together and stick them in the post . . .

He enjoyed working at the computer, now that he felt like he'd mastered it. He'd needed to learn, so he'd learned. In just a couple of years he'd gone from being a novice to being more than comfortable with pretty much any machine.

He opened the bookmark, drummed his finger against the mouse as he waited for the page to appear . . .

Once you became skilled at something, it was easy to enjoy it. Like the work he did on those fuckers with the knife and the washing line. He was certainly enjoying that. It was funny, he thought, that the word skilled *had* kill *sitting right there in the middle of it.*

He'd first found the site when he was looking for inspiration, for help with the photos of Jane. Now he just popped back every now and then to keep abreast of it all. Just to see . . .

It had been a strange week, all in all. By rights he should have been doing other stuff, but he'd been forced to tweak the schedule, to rearrange things a bit in view of the hiccup with Dodd. That's all it had been. It was easily fixed.

There were several new links from the site since the last time he'd been here. One or two were begging to be checked out. He pointed and clicked, held his breath . . .

He was itching to get back to the serious work. Apart from anything else there was the challenge of a change in routine. Now that the prisons had been warned, there couldn't be any more letters.

"Jesus . . ."

The woman's head was shaved and she had been hog-tied. A chain ran from a ring in her collar down to the leather strap between her ankles. The buckled harness snaked across her face like a spider's web, her mouth at its center filled by a large red ball gag . . .

It was a shame. If he was going to use more pictures, this was just the sort of thing he might have gone for, but now it was academic. With Remfry and Welch it had been a lovely, long, slow tease. With the next one things would have to be simple and direct. A bit more "in your face."

He hoped it would be as much fun as wooing.

TWELVE

Carol Chamberlain felt twenty years younger. Every thought and sensation was coming that bit quicker, feeling that bit stronger. She felt hungrier, more awake. The night before in bed, she'd leaned across and "helped herself," for heaven's sake, which had certainly surprised and delighted her old man. Maybe the battered green folder on her lap would prove to be the saving of both of them . . .

Jack was still smiling twelve hours later as he brought a plate of toast through to her. She blew him a kiss. He took his overcoat from the stand in the corner, off to pick up a paper.

Carol had been fifty-two, a DCI for a decade, when the Met's ludicrous policy of compulsory retirement after thirty years had pushed her out of the force. That had been three years ago. It had rankled, for each day of those three years, right up to the moment when that phone call had come out of the blue.

Carol had been amazed, and not a little relieved . . .

She knew how much she had to offer, *still* had to offer, but she also knew that this chance had come along at the very last moment. If she was being honest, she would have to admit that recently she'd felt herself slowly giving in, throwing in the towel in much the same way that her husband had.

She heard the gate creak shut. Turned to watch Jack

walking away up the road. An old man at fifty-seven . . .

Carol picked up the folder from her knees. Her first cold case. A sticker on the top right-hand corner read AMRU.

The Area Major Review Unit was what it said at the top of the notepaper. The Cold Case Team was how they thought of themselves. In the canteen they were just called the Crinkly Squad.

They could call her whatever they liked, but she'd do the same bloody good job she'd always done . . .

The day before at Victoria, when she'd collected the file from the General Registry, she'd noticed straight-away that it had been pulled only three weeks earlier by a DC from the Serious Crime Group. That was interest-ing. She'd scribbled down the officer's name, made a mental note to give him a call and find out what he'd been looking for . . .

Three years away from it. Three years of reading all those books she'd never got around to, and cooking, and gardening, and catching up with friends she'd lost touch with for perfectly good reasons, and feeling slightly sick when *Crimewatch* came on. Three years out of it, but the flutter in her stomach was still there. The butterflies that shook the dust from their wings and began to flap around as she opened the folder and started to read.

A man throttled to death in an empty car park, seven years earlier . . .

A week into his forty-fourth year. The discovery of his burned-out car being far from the low point, Tom Thorne was already pretty sure that the year was not go-ing to be a vintage one. Seven days since he'd rushed back from a wedding to attend a postmortem. Seven days during which the only developments on the case had been about as welcome as the turd he'd found wait-ing for him in his bed.

Welch's movements between his release from prison and the discovery of his body, painstakingly reconstructed, had yielded nothing.

Forensically, the photos recovered from the locker in Macpherson House had been a black hole.

A hundred and more interviews with *anybody* who could feasibly have seen *anything,* and not a word said that might raise the blood pressure.

The ACTIONS outlined and ticked off on the white board. Allocated and diligently carried out. Contacting the sex offenders who had themselves been diligent about signing the Register at the right time. Tracking down those who were not *quite* so assiduous, who had perhaps forgotten, or mixed up the days in their diaries, or buggered off to another part of the country and gone underground. Checking and double-checking the statements of everyone from the traumatized receptionist at the Greenwood Hotel to the semipickled tramp who had been occupying the bed next to Ian Welch for the few days before he was killed . . .

This was what 99 percent of police work really consisted of. It was procedure like this, together with a little bit of luck, that would provide pretty much the best chance, the *only* chance, of getting a result. And Thorne, of course, hated every tedious minute of it.

While he was waiting for that elusive bit of luck to arrive, even his one moment of genuine inspiration was proving to have been useless . . .

Sitting in Russell Brigstocke's office—Monday morning and feeling like it—Thorne listened as he was told *just* how useless it was. He had thought that the killer's access to the Sex Offenders Register might hold the key to catching him. Detective Chief Superintendent Trevor Jesmond was more than happy to disillusion him . . .

"Fact is," Jesmond said, "tabloids or no tabloids, the

information's already public property. Every force has a community notification policy. Supposed to be on a case-by-case, need-to-know basis. Information gets released to schools, youth clubs, and so on, but, as with anything else, we can't know for certain where that information goes later on."

Brigstocke glanced at Thorne, raised his eyebrows. Jesmond was just getting warmed up . . .

"Yes, we *might* be looking for a prison officer. But we might also be looking for someone who's a friend of a friend of a teacher with a big mouth. Or someone who lives next door to an indiscreet social worker, who likes to natter while they're washing their cars on a Sunday morning . . ."

"Are you saying that we've been wasting our time for a week?" Thorne said.

The detective chief superintendent shrugged, like he'd been asked if he'd lost weight. "Ask me that again when we've caught him . . ."

Jesmond seemed to relish moments like this. Thorne looked across at him and thought, *You really enjoy raining on my fucking parade, don't you?*

"I see what you're getting at, sir," Thorne said. "But it can't hurt, I mean, at least in the short term, to carry on assuming that the killer has a direct contact with one of the bodies we're talking about. Social services, the probation service . . ."

Jesmond cocked his head to one side, waiting to be unconvinced. Brigstocke tried to help out. "It's a decent avenue of inquiry, sir," he said.

Thorne sniffed. "Our *only* decent avenue of inquiry . . ."

"Well, I think you'd better go out and find us another one," Jesmond said. "Don't you?"

Thorne said nothing. He watched the hand pushing

back the wisps of sandy hair. The strange area on either side of the nose where webs of veins met spatters of freckles. He looked at the dry lips cracking themselves into a smile and it struck him, as it always did, that Jesmond smiled with his eyes closed.

Thorne smiled himself, remembering how he'd once described Jesmond's face to Dave Holland. "You know the sort of face," he'd said. "If you hit it once, you couldn't stop."

Jesmond leaned forward across the desk. "Seriously, though, let's think about what you're saying. As an example, why don't we look at the possibility that the killer has a direct connection with the police service . . ."

"A police officer," Thorne said.

Jesmond simply repeated himself and pressed on. "A direct connection with the police service. Now, apart from the sheer numbers involved, the methods employed to access and utilize the Sex Offenders Register vary wildly from force to force. Some access it via the Police National Computer. Some graft Register information onto existing systems, or create dedicated databases . . ."

Brigstocke puffed out his cheeks. Thorne could already sense things going away from him, could feel himself starting to drift.

"Some are still using manual, paper-based systems, for heaven's sake," Jesmond said. "And we all know just how secure *they* are."

Brigstocke nodded. "How secure *anything* is!"

Thorne was tuning it out. Thinking about those jungle drums . . .

"The fact is, the whole system's a mess," Jesmond said. "There is no single strategy for managing and sharing sex offender information, either with other agencies or with one another. Some believe that general access to local officers is vital to obtain the full intelli-

gence benefit. Other areas, other stations, simply have a
nominated officer who gets informed whenever the Register is updated . . ."

Thorne could smell another turd in his bed . . .

The way it was being laid out, the killer could have
found his rapists almost anywhere. On the Internet or in
a wastepaper basket. It was clear that if they had ten or a
hundred times as many officers working on this, tracking down the man they were after the way he'd been
hoping to was a nonstarter.

"It isn't just us, either," Brigstocke said. "The courts
are supposed to notify us when there's a need for an individual to register, and for how long, and it should be
confirmed by the prison or the hospital or wherever
when he gets released. Well, that's the bloody theory,
anyway. Sometimes the first you hear about a sex offender on your block is when they tell you *themselves*,
for fuck's sake . . ."

Jesmond leaned back in his chair and smiled. Eyes
closed. "So, when I say you'd better find us another decent avenue of investigation, I'm simply being practical.
I'm thinking of the best way, the fastest way, to catch
this man . . ."

Thorne nodded. Said it under his breath . . .

"Ooh! Whay-hay! Clack!"

In the Major Incident Room, business carried on as
usual, but each officer was keenly aware that things
might be about to change. Each man or woman on the
end of a phone or hunched over their paperwork glanced
across occasionally in the direction of Brigstocke's office, knowing that behind its closed door, decisions were
being made that would affect them all.

Each casual conversation full of unspoken concerns.
Some less to do with overtime than others. Some, at bottom, fuck all to do with work at all . . .

"Jesmond had a face like fourpence when he marched through here," Kitson said.

Holland glanced up from his computer screen. "Looked much the same as he always does, if you ask me . . ."

"I know what you mean," Kitson said. "He's a miserable sod. Still, I think we must be doing *something* wrong. They've been in there awhile." She looked across to where the Incident Room led out onto the corridor that housed the small suite of offices—Brigstocke's, the one she shared with Tom Thorne, Holland and Stone's . . .

Kitson sat down on the edge of the desk. She placed a hand on top of the computer Holland was working at. "Can't you do this in your office?"

Holland peered at his screen. "Andy's working in there . . ."

There was grime on the top of the computer. Kitson took out a tissue, spat on a corner, and began rubbing at the heel of her hand. "Not a problem, is there?"

Now Holland looked up at her. "No, it's fine. Just easier to concentrate in here sometimes . . ."

Kitson nodded, carried on rubbing, though her hand was clean. "Sam Karim tells me you've been putting yourself up for quite a bit of overtime lately. Working all sorts of hours . . ."

Holland clicked furiously at his mouse. "Shit!" He looked up, blinked. "Sorry . . . ?"

"It's a good idea. Trying to stash a bit of money away before the baby arrives."

Holland's face darkened for a second. The smile he conjured didn't altogether chase the shadows from around his eyes.

"Right," he said. "I mean, they're expensive, aren't they?"

"You think nappies are a price, mate, wait until he

wants CDs and the latest trainers. Is it a he or a she? Do you know . . . ?"

Holland shook his head, his eyes meeting Kitson's for half a second and then sliding away to her chin. "Sophie doesn't want to know."

"*I* did." Kitson's voice dropped down a tone. She opened up the tissue and began to tear it into small pieces. "My other half wanted to wait and see, but I've never really liked surprises. I sent him out of the room after we'd had the scan so they could tell me. Did it with all the kids. Managed to keep it secret right up until the births . . ."

Holland smiled. Kitson crushed the pieces of tissue into her fist and stood up. "Are you going to take any time off afterward?"

"Afterward?"

"All this overtime you're piling up now, you can probably afford a break, spend a bit of time at home with Sophie and the baby. Mind you, the Federation's still fighting to get paternity leave up from two days. Two days! It's a bloody disgrace . . ."

"We haven't really talked about it . . ."

"I bet she'd like you to, though." Kitson saw something in Holland's eyes, nodded sympathetically. "She must hate all this extra work you're having to do . . ."

Holland shrugged. Let his head drop back to his computer screen. "Oh, you know . . ."

Kitson took a step away from the desk. She opened her hand above a wastepaper bin and sprinkled the pieces of dirty tissue into it.

Holland watched her go, thinking, *Actually, you probably don't.*

Thorne stuck his head around the door of the Incident Room, tried not to gag on a breath of late afternoon hot air and fermenting aftershave. He waved to Yvonne Kitson. She clocked him and walked quickly across.

"Get everyone together at the far end," Thorne said. "Briefing in fifteen minutes."

Without waiting for a response, Thorne turned and moved away, back up the corridor toward his office . . .

Sensing that Jesmond was probably right. Knowing that *he* was right about the Register, but that even if the killer was a social worker or a probation officer or a copper, they were going to have to get him some other way.

He threw his jacket across the desk, dropped down into the chair. There was a small pile of mail he hadn't dealt with. He began to sort through it . . .

If he was a copper?

Thorne would not have bet on it. In all his years he'd known plenty of bad apples, worked with his fair share of shitbags, but never a killer. It was an interesting idea, a seductive one even, but beyond being convenient in TV shows, it was not much use to him.

He dropped a bunch of envelopes into the bin, those that obviously contained circulars or dreary internal memos going in unopened. He always saved the interesting-looking ones until last . . .

There were still aspects of the case that bothered him, that he'd flag up at the briefing. The bedding that had been removed for starters. And the other thing. The thought he couldn't articulate, couldn't shape and snap up.

Something he'd read and something he hadn't . . .

It pretty much amounted to less than fuck all. Not a decent lead, not a bit of luck. He could only hope that some bright spark came up with something useful at the briefing.

When the photographs tumbled out of the white envelope, it took Thorne a few seconds to understand what he was looking at. Then he saw it. Then his heart lurched inside him and began to gallop.

As an athlete's heart rate recovers more and more quickly as his fitness increases, so Thorne reacted less and less, physically at least, to images like those that would soon be scattered across his desk. The thumping in his chest was already slowing when he reached into a drawer, took out a pair of scissors, and snipped away the elastic band that held the bundle of pictures together. The breaths were coming more easily as he used the tip of a pencil to separate them. By the time he'd decided that he wanted a closer look, remembered where he could find the gloves he needed, his heartbeat was slow and steady again.

There was no longer any visible movement, no judder of the flesh where his shirt stuck damp against his chest . . .

Thorne stood, moved out into the corridor, and turned toward the Incident Room. As he walked, he felt amazingly calm and clearheaded. Coming to shocking conclusions and making trivial decisions.

The killer was even more cold-blooded than he had imagined . . .

He was supposed to be seeing Eve later on. Obviously, he would have to call and cancel. Perhaps she would be free tomorrow . . .

Into the Incident Room, and Kitson was moving across from the right of him, eager to talk about something. He held up a hand, waved her away. The box stood, a little incongruously, on a filing cabinet in the far corner of the room, exactly where he'd remembered seeing it. He pulled out the plastic gloves, like snatching tissues from a cardboard dispenser, revealing the transparent fingers of the next pair.

Holland was behind him, saying something he didn't catch as he turned to walk back . . .

The briefing, whenever they had it, would certainly be a bit more lively. Whatever Jesmond thought about the route the investigation was taking, it had definitely become heavy going. Those photos, what was in them, would get it started again.

Jump leads.

Not a bit of luck, exactly, but fuck it, close enough . . .

Thorne walked into his office and straight across to his desk. He knew even as he was doing it, even as he pulled on the gloves and delicately picked up a photo by its edge, that he was probably wasting his time. He had to go through the motions, of course, but the gloves were almost certainly unnecessary. Though he knew the surface of a photograph was as good as any at holding a fingerprint, he also knew that the man who had taken it was extremely cautious. Aside from the prints of postal workers and prison officers, or the hair and dead skin of the victims themselves, they'd got nothing from any of the photos or letters thus far. This was, after all, a killer who removed the bedding from his murder scenes.

Still, everybody made mistakes now and again . . .

Thorne flicked quickly through the photos. The close-ups of the battered and bloodied face, those thin lips thickened, then burst. The movement in the full-length pictures captured in a sickening blur. Pictures taken, unbelievably, while the victim was still alive. Thrashing . . .

He pushed aside the interior shots and lowered his head, checking to see if the killer had made one mistake in particular. He stared closely at the photo that had been very deliberately placed on the top of the pile. The first picture he had been intended to see. The window of the shop next door . . .

A killer's little joke.

Thorne was dimly aware of the figures of Holland and Kitson, watching him from the doorway as he squinted at the picture. Hoping to see a distorted image that would probably be worse than useless, but would show him that he was dealing with fallible flesh and blood. Searching in vain for a reflection of the cameraman in a tiny black mirror.

Looking for the killer's face in the eye of a dead fish.

He was pretty sure he'd picked a good one.

The list had to be looked at carefully. He couldn't just print off a copy and stick a pin in. Not that there was that much time to look at it when he had the chance, but he was getting better at selecting the likely candidates quickly. With the previous two he'd chosen a couple of decent-looking ones and gone through the details more carefully later, when he could take his time. He'd done the same thing with this one, rejecting a couple of names for various practical reasons—location, domestic setup, and so on—and coming up with a winner.

Christ, though, there were plenty to choose from. The serious cases, the ones he was interested in, would be on the Register indefinitely, and those that did eventually come off the list, after five, or seven or ten years, had been replaced a hundred-fold by the time their names were removed.

It was a growth industry . . .

This one would shape up very nicely, by the look of it. He lived alone in a nice, quiet street. Friends were an unknown quantity as yet, but it didn't look like there was any family around. It might even be possible to avoid using a hotel alto-gether . . .

He was ambivalent about that. Doing it in a

house or flat would be simpler, but there was an unpredictability that made him uncomfortable. It would be tricky to get inside in advance and look at the layout of the place. He couldn't count on the place being as forensically friendly as the average hotel room. An unexpected visit from a neighbor couldn't be prevented with a Do Not Disturb sign on the door.

He hadn't had the choice with Remfry or Welch, but using hotels had worked out well so far and he was somewhat reluctant to change a winning formula. Hotels did mean a lot more possible witnesses and a security system to get around but that wasn't too much of a problem. He'd learned that people saw fuck all when they weren't really looking, and cameras saw even less if you knew how to avoid them.

He'd avoided being seen, being really seen, for a very long time.

THIRTEEN

"I was wondering how much it would cost to send a bouquet of flowers . . ."

"Well, we charge five pounds fifty for delivery, and the bouquets start at thirty pounds."

"Christ, I don't want to spend *that* much. I haven't even kissed her yet . . ."

Eve laughed. "Are you sure kissing is likely?"

"Definitely," Thorne said. "She's *well* up for it . . ."

"Shit, I've got a customer. Better go . . ."

"Listen, I'm sorry about canceling last night. I couldn't—"

"It's fine. Hold that thought, all right? The kissing, I mean. I'll see you later."

"Yeah . . . I can't say what time, though."

"Call me when you're about to leave. We can just grab a quick drink or something . . ."

"Right . . ."

"Seriously, if you *are* ever tempted, flowers wouldn't guarantee kissing. *Chocolates*, on the other hand, will get you just about anything . . ."

She hung up.

Smiling, Thorne reached inside the bodysuit, dropped the phone into his jacket pocket. He took a long swig from a bottle of mineral water and turned, to find himself confronted by a family of backpackers. Mum, Dad, and two blond children were all sporting backpacks of decreasing size, and staring at him expectantly from the other side of the cordon. Thorne stared back at them until eventually, having decided that nothing much was going to happen, they wandered away.

Six hours earlier, when there *had* been something they might have been able to tell their friends back home about, the onlookers had been a little harder to dissuade. With the nightclubs emptying and the streets buzzing, a sizable crowd had quickly gathered and gawked from behind the lines of police tape. A hundred yards back toward Wardour Street one way and Regent Street the other, they had stood and watched excitedly. The drunks heckled and the tourists took pictures as the body of Charles Dodd was carried out.

Once the body had been loaded up and taken away, the cordon had been relaxed a little. Now there was just a square of blue tape running from the narrow doorway leading up to Dodd's studio, around to the farthest side of the fishmonger's shop next door. Fluttering ever so gently . . .

"What's going on in there, mate?"

Thorne looked up at a small, skinny individual with birdshit highlights and an improbable amount of jewelry, nodding at him from behind the tape. The man, who was wearing satin tracksuit bottoms and a sleeveless camouflage vest, took three drags of a cigarette in quick succession, then flicked it into the gutter.

"It's a raid," Thorne said. "Fashion Police. I'd be on my way, if I were you . . ."

The man bounced twice on the balls of his feet, grimaced, and jogged away. On the other side of the narrow street, a girl in a tiny leather skirt and crop top was leaning against the kiosk of a peep show, eating a bacon sandwich. She grinned over at Thorne, having clearly heard the exchange. Thorne smiled back at her. It was a little after nine in the morning but evidently not too early to try to get something going inside the shorts of the passing male trade. Already warm enough for the tables of a pavement café to be filled with customers downing cappuccino and munching on pastries. Pretending they were somewhere more exotic.

Thorne watched them. Wishing *he* was somewhere else. Thinking of things that would put anybody off their breakfast . . .

When they'd battered down the door early the previous evening, Thorne had known exactly what they would find. The smell, thick against his face mask, would have told him anyway, but as he'd climbed the narrow staircase, Thorne had been very well aware of what was waiting for him at the top. He'd already seen the pictures.

The real thing, several long, hot days after the event, was a whole lot worse.

The body had been strung up. The washing line had been tied in a makeshift noose around Dodd's neck and thrown over one of the lighting bars above the studio floor. It was tied off around the foot of the bed, the weight of the body lifting one end of the bed twelve inches off the ground. The pictures, taken while Dodd was still alive, had shown the spasms, the desperate clawing at the neck and kicking of the legs. Several days dead, the corpse hung, stiff and still. It was only the rumble of the tube trains passing beneath them on the Bakerloo Line that caused the slightest tremor, that made the body start to swing just a little . . .

Each time, Thorne had fought a bizarre urge to stop the movement. To step across and grasp the legs that protruded from dirty shorts like bloated blood sausages. To clutch the feet, purple with lividity, straining against the straps of the plastic sandals.

Thorne had stood by the bed in the middle of the studio, remembering a pair of pale girls, writhing on nylon sheets.

He had watched a scene-of-crime officer leaning across the mattress, scraping at whatever had dripped down from the body that dangled above it.

He had looked up at the tongue that stuck out from Dodd's mouth. Blue, and big as a man's hand. Telling him to fuck off.

Once it had been cut down and loaded up, Thorne had been only too grateful to do precisely as Dodd's corpse had seemed to be requesting. Home for a change of clothes, and food he couldn't finish. Four hours not sleeping, and then back to the murder scene.

Opposite him, the girl finished the last mouthful of her sandwich. She wiped the back of a hand across her mouth, reached down behind the kiosk for her handbag. She shrugged at Thorne and began to apply lipstick.

Thorne turned at the sound of the door opening. Holland stepped out. He moved across to join Thorne, unzipping his bodysuit and gulping down the fresh air as he walked.

"Fuck, it's hot in there."

Thorne handed Holland the bottle of water. "How much longer?"

"Almost done, I think."

Holland stood next to Thorne, leaning back against the window of the fishmonger's shop. They stared across at the peep show and the pavement café. A waiter smiled across at them. They might just have been friends enjoying the good weather, their plastic outfits far from being the most outlandish on display.

"So he's probably just cleaning up after himself," Holland said. "He kills Dodd to make sure he can't say anything."

"Maybe . . ."

Holland turned, pressed his hands against the window, already dusted for fingerprints. The fishmonger had been given very little time to get his stock into the freezer room and no time at all to clean up afterward. Holland looked at the pink swirl of blood and fish guts floating on top of the water in a metal tray. "He knew you'd get it." He nodded toward the window. Flies bumped against the glass, buzzing around the scattered flaps of puckered skin. "He knew you'd understand what that photo meant."

Thorne nodded. "Oh, he knew I'd been here all right." Holland looked sideways at him, raised an eyebrow. "Don't get excited. Yeah, he might have followed me, or he *might* be Trevor Jesmond hearing voices from the devil, but I think there's probably a simpler explanation." Holland turned, listening. "I think you were right. I think Dodd was killed because of what he could tell us. And because he was threatening to."

"Dodd tried to blackmail the killer?"

Thorne folded his arms. "Only the idiot didn't *know* he was a killer, did he? I can't prove any of it, obviously . . ."

"It sounds feasible," Holland said.

"Dodd was lying, of course he was. That crap about the killer keeping his crash helmet on, about not having any records. I should have fucking pulled him on it . . ."

"You weren't to know."

"Yes, I was. If people like Dodd are breathing, they're lying. He didn't know who we were after, or why, but that didn't matter. If he thought I was chasing someone who hadn't paid their parking ticket, he'd have lied through his back teeth, as long as he could see a way to make money out of it."

They watched as a middle-aged man handed over his

money at the peep-show kiosk and hurried inside. The girl caught Thorne's eye, put her thumb to the tips of her fingers, and made a masturbatory gesture. Thorne didn't know whether she was indicating what the man would be doing or what she thought of him. Or what she thought of *them* . . .

Holland cleared his throat and took a drink. "So, after you come round and show him the photo of Jane Foley, he contacts the killer . . ."

Thorne stepped away from the window, turned, and looked up toward the second floor, where the studio was. "I've been through the place and there's no sign of an address book or anything like that anywhere . . ."

"Maybe the killer took it," Holland said.

"He might have done." Thorne put his hand up to shield his eyes from the sun. "Let's go over every inch again, anyway. If there's a scrap of paper with an address or phone number on it, I want it found."

"What about phone records?"

Thorne nodded, pleased that Holland was thinking so fast, was so close behind him. "I've got Andy Stone onto it. I want everything, landline and mobile, if Dodd had one. Every call he made since the day I was here . . ."

"He might have just gone round, if he had an address . . ."

"In which case we're stuffed." Thorne reached across for the water bottle. He took a swig, held the now tepid water in his mouth for a while before swallowing. "We're still none the wiser as to how the killer hooked up with Dodd in the first place. People like Dodd don't advertise. It's word of mouth, it's *contacts* . . ."

"We've already spoken to everybody we could find," Holland said. "Anybody who's ever taken so much as a snap of their wife's tits in that studio has made a statement."

"So talk to them again. And find me some you haven't

spoken to at all." Holland groaned, let his head drop back against the glass. "Just get on it, Dave," Thorne said. "Yvonne can work up a new list. I'll catch up with you later."

While Holland climbed out of his bodysuit, Thorne watched as two young media types stood up from their table at the café opposite and shook hands. They were dressed casually in shorts and trainers, but their top-of-the-line mobiles and designer sunglasses gave them away. An advertising campaign agreed maybe, or a TV project given the green light.

He wondered if they knew that only a few hundred yards away, in an attic room over a coffee shop on Frith Street, John Logie-Baird had given the first-ever public demonstration of television nearly eighty years before.

Thorne opened the door, took a second or two before heading back inside . . .

Christ, a commercial break *would* be nice. A catchable made-for-TV killer would be even nicer. He might just as well have *been* a TV cop. For the umpteenth time that morning, Thorne watched a passerby notice him, the bodysuit, the police tape . . . and look around eagerly for the camera.

After the postmortem at Westminster Mortuary, they walked over to a small Italian place near the Abbey. Talked about murder over pizzas and Peroni beer.

"I think Dodd was beaten until he was more or less unconscious," Hendricks said. "Then the killer tied the line around his neck, tossed it over the lighting bar, and hauled him up." Thorne nodded, took a swig of beer. "Would have taken a fair bit of strength . . ."

"So we know he's not a nine-stone weakling. What else?"

"He's a nasty fucker . . ."

"We knew that already."

Hendricks poured more chili oil over what he had left of a large pepperoni and cheese. "Dodd wakes up pretty bloody quickly when he works out what's going on, but it's far too late by then. The killer ties the line off, picks up his camera, and starts taking pictures."

"How long?" Thorne asked.

"He'd have blacked out in a couple of minutes." Hendricks speared a slice of pepperoni, popped it into his mouth. "Death through cerebral hypoxia pretty quickly afterward . . ."

Thorne thought about it. Dodd had been a sleazy piece of shit, but he hadn't deserved that. Dancing at the end of a line, like something in the shop next door. Tearing at the flesh of his own neck. Staring through half-closed eyes at the maniac responsible, calmly snapping away, trying to capture his best side . . .

"When they talk about killers like this, they use words like *organized* and *disorganized*," Thorne said. "Two basic categories. The ones who plan carefully, who follow an almost ritualized pattern of killing, of cleaning up after themselves. And those who just act on instinct, who don't have as much control over what they're doing . . ."

"So where does this nutter fit in?"

Thorne put down his knife and fork. There was half a pizza left but he'd had enough. "That's what I was thinking. Part of him is organized. The letters to the men in prison. Dodd needs to be got rid of, so he gets rid of him. The washing line, the lack of forensics, the photos he sent to me . . ."

"He's getting off on *that*, definitely . . ."

"Why beat the bloke half to death, though? Dodd's face looked like cheap mince. Why not just smash him across the back of the head, then string him up?" A waitress was hovering, trying not to eavesdrop. Thorne held up his plate. She took it gingerly and moved quickly away. "At some level, they're always angry, you know? I haven't met a killer yet who wasn't pissed off somewhere about *something*." Thorne downed the last of his beer. He swallowed, seeing the bodies of Welch and Remfry, the mess that had been made of their necks. Of their insides. "This bloke, though? He's off the fucking scale . . ."

"You doing anything tonight?" Hendricks wiped his mouth. "I could come over."

"What?"

Hendricks glanced across to where the waitresses were gathered near the till. "I'm changing the subject. Before they call the police."

"They're staring because of what you look like, mate, not because of our interesting table conversation. And no, you can't come over. I'm meeting someone a lot better looking than you."

"Surely not."

"With no embarrassing piercings . . ."

Hendricks grinned. "You never know. She might have them in special, secret places."

The waitress was there again. She took the plate from in front of Hendricks. He'd left a perfect ring of pizza crust.

"If you don't eat your crusts, you won't get curly hair," Thorne said.

Hendricks ran a hand across his shaved head. "With the look I'm cultivating, that's not really a problem . . ."

The afternoon had bled into the evening, and by the time Thorne pushed through to where Eve was sitting, at a small table next to the cigarette machine, it was almost last orders. Plenty of time to get through a bottle of wine between them. For Thorne to apologize for messing her about, and for Eve to tell him he was being stupid. More than enough time for Thorne to tell her almost nothing about the sort of day he'd had.

It was a small, friendly pub near the Hackney Empire. They stepped out onto Mare Street and looked up and down the road. They fastened unnecessary buttons on jackets, studied parked cars, filling up a suddenly awkward moment.

Eve stepped over to him, put her hands on his shoulders. "Now, about that kiss . . ."

Thorne didn't need asking twice.

They kissed, his hands moving around her waist and hers to the back of his head and neck. She bit softly on his lower lip. He pushed the tip of his tongue into the gap between her teeth. Then his mouth widened into a grin and they leaned away from each other.

"I *knew* you were well up for it," Thorne said.

She dropped her hand down, gave his backside a good hard squeeze. "I'm well up for anything."

They were a few minutes' walk from Eve's flat. A short bus or cab journey from Thorne's. This wasn't the reason for the uncertainty that Eve saw in Thorne's expression.

"You still haven't bought a new bed, have you?" she said.

Thorne tried his best to look like a guilty schoolboy. He imagined that it made him look endearing. "I haven't had time . . ."

She grabbed his hand and they began to walk.

"I've only really had last Sunday and there was all manner of shit that needed doing." Thorne decided not to elaborate. He didn't explain that the shit in question had involved replacing his stereo system and those twenty-five or so CDs that he *really* couldn't do without. Spending his nights curled up on the sofa as he was, some people might have questioned his priorities. With the prospect of a night curled up with Eve Bloom looking distinctly achievable, even *he* had to agree that they seemed completely bonkers.

They walked a little way up Mare Street and then

turned left, crossing the railway line and cutting across London Fields. The night wasn't as muggy as some had been recently, but it was still warm. There were plenty of people around.

"You're not waiting for the insurance, are you?" Eve asked suddenly.

"What?"

"To pay for a new bed."

Thorne laughed. "I think I can afford a new bed. It's actually only a new mattress, so it won't break the bank. I'll need the insurance to sort out a new car, though. I'm getting pissed off with buses and junk heaps from the car pool . . ."

"What are you going to get?"

Thorne wasn't sure whether he'd spent more time the previous week on the phone chasing the insurance company or sitting at his kitchen table poring over car magazines. "It doesn't really matter," he said.

Eve leaned in close to Thorne to let a jogger go past. "Do coppers cheat on their insurance like everybody else?"

"Well, cheat is putting it a bit strong. I may have got the make and model of the stereo ever so slightly wrong. All right, *and* the price. I might have thrown the odd boxed set in when I was doing my CD inventory, but fuck 'em, I probably forgot stuff as well."

They walked on in silence for a minute or so and then stopped at the edge of the park. They watched a group of lads kicking a ball around, floodlighting courtesy of a couple of lampposts and a full moon.

Thorne remembered the game he'd watched just over a week earlier. The park near the hotel in Slough. That one had been just *before* a postmortem . . .

"There was another body today," Thorne said. "Well, last night and today. That's why I had to cancel."

Eve squeezed his hand. "Is it the same man? The one who left the message on my machine?"

They moved away from the game and out onto the road that ran parallel to the one where Eve lived and worked.

"He kills men who have assaulted women," Thorne said. "Who've raped them and been to prison for it. The one we found yesterday was slightly different, but that's basically what he does. Fucked if I know why he does it, or when he's going to do it again, and fucked if I know how I'm going to stop him."

"So don't."

Thorne laughed. Stared at the pavement. Stepped around the dogshit. "I'm not the one who decides . . ."

"It's not like he's chopping up old ladies, is it?"

They turned onto a small side street and walked slowly up the middle of the road.

Hand in hand, at arm's length.

"I'm always reading about how stretched police resources are," Eve said. "So why not use them on something a bit more worthwhile?"

"More worthwhile than a murderer?"

"Yeah, but look at who he's murdering . . ."

Thorne took a deep breath. He shouldn't have said anything. He did *not* want to get into this. "Look, whatever you think about what those men had done, whatever any of us thinks, they'd been to prison for it. I haven't got a *lot* of respect for the legal system, but surely—"

"All right. Just think of this bloke as cutting reoffending rates, then."

Thorne looked at her. She was smiling, but there was something set around her eyes. She clearly felt strongly about what she was saying, and Thorne knew that it was tough to argue with. "I can't think like that, Eve. I can't go down that road . . ."

"As a police officer, you mean? Or just . . . personally?"

They emerged from the side street. Eve's shop stood in darkness on the corner opposite.

"Listen, just how much of a problem would it really be with Denise? If I was to stay?"

Eve sighed heavily. "I told you. She gets a bit weird . . ."

"Aren't there nights when she's not there? Doesn't she ever stay at Ben's?" Eve shook her head. "Why not?"

"I don't know. He's just as batty as she is. Come on, you've seen them together . . ."

They walked past the shop, stopped at Eve's doorstep. Eve reached into her bag for the door keys.

"She's got no right to tell you who you can have staying," Thorne said.

Eve pressed her palms against his chest. "She doesn't exactly tell me. Listen, it's just not worth the hassle." She grabbed the lapels of Thorne's leather jacket, pulled him toward her. "Especially when you can just buy a mattress. I could do it for you, if you like . . ."

They stopped kissing when the front door of Eve's flat suddenly swung open from the inside. Denise stood in the doorway, looking surprised. A figure loomed behind her, and Thorne recognized the man he'd seen working in the florist's that first day he'd been in there.

"Hello, Eve," he said.

Denise stepped out into the street. The man followed her. "Keith just dropped round to say he won't be able to make it again on Saturday," Denise said.

Eve moved forward, put a hand on Keith's shoulder. "Everything okay, Keith?"

He shook his head, reddening. "It's difficult . . ."

Eve turned to Thorne. "Keith's mum hasn't been well . . ."

The four of them stood there a little awkwardly. Denise's arms were bare and she rubbed at them, shivering slightly as a breeze began to pick up.

Keith pulled on the denim jacket he'd been carrying. "I'm going home." He nodded to himself a couple of times, then turned and marched quickly away. The others watched him go.

"I'm going to bed, hon," Denise said. "I'm utterly fucked." She bounded across and threw her arms around Eve's neck. "See you in the morning . . ."

Thorne watched as she kissed Eve on both cheeks. He was slightly taken aback when she leaned over and kissed him, too. Half on the cheek and half on the mouth.

" 'Night, Tom . . ." She turned and stepped smartly back inside the flat, pushing the door behind her until it was almost, but not quite, closed.

Thorne checked his watch. There was probably still time to make a late bus to Kentish Town or Camden.

"I'd better be getting off as well," he said.

Eve gave him a theatrical leer. "You won't be getting off with anyone if you don't buy yourself a bed. I'll take you to IKEA at the weekend . . ."

"Oh, please God, no," Thorne said.

Thorne could see Keith striding along the street a hundred yards or so ahead of him. He hung back, trying not to catch up. Feeling awkward, the good nights having been said, and not wanting to go through it again. Thorne was relieved when he saw Keith turn off onto a side street. Keith looked back and stared at him for a few seconds before he moved out of sight.

When Thorne reached the corner and looked, there was no sign of him.

As he hurried toward the bus stop on Dalston Lane, Thorne admitted something rather puzzling to himself. He'd asked Eve about staying the night at her place only because of what she'd already told him about Denise. Because he'd known very well that it wasn't going to happen. He actually felt comfortable that it hadn't . . .

There was a seedy-looking burger van opposite the

bus stop and Thorne was suddenly starving. The late-night bagel bakery was five minutes' walk away. It was a toss-up between food poisoning and the risk of missing the last bus.

Ten minutes later the bus rumbled into view and he was already wishing he hadn't had the burger. As he rummaged in his jacket for the exact change, Thorne wondered why on earth he should be feeling something like relief that he was on his way home alone.

The man on the machine next to him stopped pedaling and sat for a few moments, eyes closed, getting his breath back. The man climbed off and
walked across to the water fountain. Still pedaling
fast, he watched as the man gulped down water,
flung his sweat towel around his neck, and walked
through into the weight room.

When the song he was listening to had finished,
he unplugged his headphones, got off the bike, and
followed him.

Howard Anthony Southern was a creature of
habit and was serious about looking after himself.
These two things meant that keeping an eye on
him, getting to know him, was not only easy but
fairly enjoyable. He worked out anyway, but a
few extra hours a week couldn't hurt. It was easy
enough to join the same gym and make sure he
was here at the same time that Southern was as often as he could. That wasn't always straightforward, of course. Sometimes he couldn't get away,
but he'd seen enough to know what he was dealing
with.

He knew enough already. That Southern had
done what he'd done, that his name was on the
list, was more than enough. Still, it was good to

find out a bit more. To know for certain how much stronger than Southern he was, how easy it would be to take him when the time came. To see his face contorted and running with sweat. To glimpse in advance what it would be like as he strained against the ligature . . .

He walked through into the weight room. Southern was on the pec-fly. He took a seat next to him on the mid-row, began to work.

He could see instantly that Southern was eyeing up a woman on the other side of the room. She was bending and stretching, her flesh taut against the black Lycra. Southern pressed his forearms toward each other, grunting with the effort, all the time watching the woman in the mirror that ran along one wall.

He knew this was why Howard Southern came here.

He wondered if Southern had offended again since his release. Was he more careful having been caught once? He might have been getting away with it for years. Was he watching the woman in the mirror and thinking about forcing himself on her? Working himself into a lather, his eyes like sweaty hands on her, convincing himself just how much she wanted it . . .

The weights dropped back with a clang as Southern released the handles. He turned and puffed out his cheeks.

"Why do we do it?"

This was a bonus. He'd been planning to talk to Southern today anyway. To strike up a casual conversation at the juice bar maybe, or in the locker room . . .

"It's bloody madness, isn't it?" Southern nodded toward the woman in the black leotard. "Here I am killing myself for the likes of her."

He smiled back at Southern, thinking that the idea was right, but that he had an altogether different reason.

FOURTEEN

Carol Chamberlain was three quarters of a team of two.

She had been assigned a research officer, but ex–Detective Sergeant Graham McKee was, to use a favorite phrase of her husband's, about as useful as a chocolate teapot. When he wasn't in the pub, he made it perfectly clear that he thought Carol should have been the one making coffee and phone calls, while he was out doing the interviews.

A few years ago, she'd have had his undersized balls on a platter. Now she just got on with doing the job, his as well as her own. It might take a bit longer, but at least it would get done properly. She believed in that. She couldn't be sure yet, but if the case she was on now had been handled properly first time around, there might well have been no need for her to be doing anything at all.

The drive to Hastings hadn't taken her as long as she'd thought, but she'd left early to be on the safe side. Jack had got up with her, made her some breakfast while she got ready. She could see that he was unhappy that she was going out on a Sunday, but he'd tried to make a joke of it.

"Bloody unsociable hours. Sunday down the drain. Now I *know* you're working for the police force again . . ."

She checked her makeup in the mirror before she got out of the car. Maybe she'd overdone the foundation a little, but it was too late now. She was pleased with her hair, though; she'd run a rinse through it the night before to get rid of most of the gray.

Jack had told her she looked great.

She walked up to the front door and knocked, telling herself to calm down, that she'd done this a thousand times, that there was no need to grip the handle of her briefcase as though it were stopping her from falling . . .

"Sheila? I'm Carol Chamberlain from AMRU. We spoke on the phone . . ."

Carol could see that the woman who answered the door was clearly not expecting someone who looked like her, rinse or no rinse. She had gained a stone in weight for each year that she'd been out of the force, and at a little over five feet tall she knew very well how it looked. Her hair could be as fashionable and artificially auburn as she wanted, but—whatever lies Jack might tell her— she could do little about the rest of it. However sharp she *felt,* she knew that those thirty years on the job showed in her face. Some mornings she stared at herself in the bathroom mirror. Her eyes were like currants sinking into cake mix . . .

The woman opened the front door a little wider. However disappointed or confused she might be, Carol hoped that good old British reserve would prevent Sheila Franklin saying anything about it.

"I'll put the kettle on," she said eventually.

In the kitchen, while tea was being made, they spoke about weather and traffic. Sheila Franklin wiped down surfaces and washed up teaspoons as she went. Settled a few minutes later in the small, simply furnished living room, her face crinkled into a frown of confusion.

"I'm sorry, but I thought you said that the case was being reopened . . ."

Carol had said no such thing. "I'm sorry if you were

misled. I'm re*examining* the case, and if it's considered worthwhile, it might be reopened."

"I see . . ."

"How long were you and Alan married?"

Alan Franklin's widow was a tall, very thin woman whom Carol would have put in her mid to late fifties. Not a great deal older than she was herself. Her hair was pulled back from a face dominated by green eyes that did not stay fixed on any one spot for more than a few seconds. From behind the rim of her teacup, her gaze darted around like a ferret's as she answered Carol's questions.

She'd met Franklin in 1983. He would have been in his late forties by then, ten years older than she was. He'd left his first wife and a job in Colchester a few years before that and moved to Hastings to start again. They'd met at work and married only a few months later.

"Alan was a fast worker," she said, laughing. "Very smooth, he was. Mind you, I didn't put up much of a struggle."

As always, Carol had done her homework. She was up to speed with what very few background details there were. "How did Alan's kids react? What would they have been then? Sixteen? Seventeen . . . ?"

Sheila smiled, but there was something forced about it. "Something like that. I'm not even sure how old they are now. In all the time we were married, I think I saw the boys once. Only one of them bothered to show his face at Alan's funeral . . ."

Carol nodded, like this was perfectly normal. "What about the first wife?"

"I never met Celia. Never spoke to her on the phone. I'm not even sure that *Alan* ever did, to be honest, after they split up."

"Right . . ."

Sheila leaned forward and put her cup and saucer down. "I know it probably sounds odd, but that's just the way it was. It was Alan's *past* . . ."

Carol tried not to let any reaction, any *judgment* of these people's lives, show on her face, but it was hard. She and Jack had married relatively late, and there were times when relations with his ex-wife were a little strained, but they were civil. They acknowledged each other. And Jack's daughter had *always* been a part of their lives.

"I did make an effort with the children," Sheila said. "For a while I tried to persuade Alan that he should see them, that he should try and build bridges. He was always a bit funny about it."

"Perhaps he thought his ex-wife had turned them against him."

"He never said so. The kids were more or less grown up anyway, and we did try briefly to have our own." She began piling the tea things back onto the tray she had brought them through on. She took hold of the tray and stood up. "I was nearly forty by then, and it never happened . . ."

Carol followed Sheila as she walked back toward the kitchen. "Did Alan never talk about why he and Celia had divorced?"

"Not really. I think it was unpleasant."

From what Carol was hearing, that was probably an understatement. "Presumably there was alimony, though? They must have communicated through solicitors . . . ?"

"For the last few years we didn't even know where they were living. The son who turned up at the funeral only knew Alan was dead because he saw it on the news."

"I see . . ."

The cups and saucers were already being washed up. When Sheila turned from the sink, Carol saw her read something in her face. Maybe that judgment she'd been trying to hide . . .

"Look, it was always just Alan and me," Sheila said. "We were self-sufficient. Anything that happened before didn't seem to matter. And I was the same, honestly. I never bothered with old boyfriends or what have you, and we never saw much of my family. Alan had no contact with the family he had before, because he had me." She took a step toward Carol, who was standing in the doorway, water dripping from a teacup onto the linoleum. Her face seemed to soften as she spoke. "That's what he always used to say. That I was his life now. What he had before hadn't worked out and so he didn't want to think about it. Alan was trying to get away from his old life . . ."

Carol nodded. "Could I use your loo . . . ?"

She leaned against the sink, letting the water run awhile.

She had never worked much on instinct, but in thirty years Carol Chamberlain had learned to give it breathing space. Back in 1996, Alan Franklin's murder had gone unsolved. Unsolved, largely because it had been seemingly motiveless.

She smelled the soap, began to wash her hands . . .

It was at least possible that whatever Alan Franklin had been trying to escape from, here in this house with his new job and nice new wife, had finally caught up with him in that car park.

Sheila Franklin was waiting for her at the foot of the stairs.

"Do you have any of Alan's old things?" Carol asked. "I don't mean clothes or—"

"There's a couple of boxes in the loft. Papers and what have you, I think. Alan put them up there when we moved in."

"Would you mind if I had a look?"

"God, no, not at all. Actually, you could do me a favor and take them with you." Sheila looked past Carol, back up the stairs. She blinked slowly and a film appeared over her eyes. "I could do with getting things tidy . . ."

It wasn't exactly a photo fit, but then there wouldn't have been a lot of point . . .

Thorne had taken the picture out of his bag while the train was pulling out of King's Cross, laid it out on the table in front of him, stared at it for ten minutes.

The waiter from the café opposite Dodd's studio had made his statement the day after the body had been found. He'd described a motorcycle courier who'd been hanging around a few days before. He hadn't actually seen the man in the dark crash helmet and leathers go in through the door, or even go up to it. It was a hot afternoon. He'd had a lot of tables to look after . . .

A Wednesday, nearly a fortnight ago. Five days before they'd broken down the narrow brown door and smelled a murder scene.

So, Charlie Dodd had not been *completely* full of shit. The man to whom he had rented out his studio *had* worn a crash helmet. The lie, Thorne guessed, had been about not seeing the face underneath it. It was a lie that Charlie Dodd thought might make him some money and had ended up costing him a lot more.

At the noise of the buffet trolley squeaking down the carriage Thorne glanced up. Thameslink food would not be his Sunday morning breakfast of choice, but he was hungry. He felt in his pocket for change.

Dodd had probably felt totally safe as the man in the motorbike gear had strolled up the stairs in the middle of the afternoon. As likely as not, he'd felt in control, ready to squeeze the mug for whatever he could get. He'd had no idea of the kind of man he was dealing with.

No witness from the Remfry or Welch killing had mentioned seeing anybody in a crash helmet, but all the same, it needed to be checked out. On any given afternoon, Soho was thick with bikes, scooters, and mopeds, delivering scripts and videos, sandwiches and sushi. It had taken the best part of two days to trace every courier who had been in the area on legitimate business and eliminate them. Two days dicking about to confirm what Thorne had known to be true from the moment the waiter had described what he'd seen.

The face behind that visor had belonged to the killer, and the black rucksack slung across his shoulder had contained a length of blue washing line.

"What can I get you, love?"

The trolley was at Thorne's table. He asked for tea and a Kit Kat. He took the top off the cardboard cup, mopped up the inevitable spillage with his napkin, and began to dunk the tea bag.

He stared again at the picture he had begun to draw a few days earlier. A man in a crash helmet was too generic to have justified any kind of official image, but Thorne had begun scribbling at his kitchen table and added to it on subsequent days at his desk, or on the tube to and from Hendon. Thorne was about as competent an artist as he was a medieval dancer, but he could see *something* in his thick and clumsy shading. Something about the heavy, crosshatched pencil lines suggested a darkness behind the visor. Blacker and harder than tinted plastic . . .

He looked up, and out at the scenery moving past. He watched it get greener, saw the houses get bigger, as the train moved into Hertfordshire.

Thorne drank his tea and ate his chocolate. Reflected in the window, he watched as the old boy sitting across from him dithered over what to order. One of the women working the trolley rolled her eyes at the other, and a teenager in a tracksuit sighed loudly, impatient to get past.

Eileen had rung him from Brighton a couple of nights before. His father's home help had come down with shingles and there was a bit of a flap on. Eileen had called a neighbor who was coming over with a casserole on Friday, and arranged for a temporary home help to come in, but *she* wouldn't be able to start until Monday, and with nobody there to make sure . . . the old man wouldn't eat a thing . . .

Thorne had felt guilty that she'd asked him like it was a favor. A few miles away from St. Albans, a packet of his dad's favorite mints in his pocket, he felt guiltier still that he was wishing he was somewhere else. Thinking about a Sunday in a pub by the river with Eve.

The automatic door at the end of the carriage slid open. The two women maneuvered the trolley past the teenager in the tracksuit, now enjoying a crafty fag by the toilets. He shrugged at them, turned, and blew his smoke out of the window.

Thorne remembered Yvonne Kitson with her cigarette outside Becke House. He didn't really think of her as a friend, they had never socialized outside work, but something about that encounter pricked at him. Without thinking too much about it, Thorne reached into his bag for the contact sheet, looked up Kitson's home number, and dialed. She was probably up to her elbows in getting Sunday lunch ready . . .

A man, presumably Kitson's husband, answered.

"Hi, could I speak to Yvonne, please?" Thorne said.

"She's not here."

Thorne waited for a bit more information, but none was forthcoming. "It's not important. Could you just tell her that Tom Thorne rang? I'll maybe try later . . ."

"You can try, but I don't know when she'll be back. She said she'd only be a couple of hours . . ."

Thorne was still thinking about the conversation five minutes later as he walked out of St. Albans Station looking for a taxi. Maybe Yvonne Kitson's husband was a naturally surly bastard. Maybe he was in a foul mood because he'd got the kids to look after when he wanted to be out playing golf or reading the Sunday papers. Maybe it was something else altogether. Whatever the reason he was pissed off, he didn't seem bothered about letting a total stranger know about it.

She said *she'd only be a couple of hours . . .*

Ahead of him, Thorne watched a young couple climb into the only available cab. He thought about Eve again, the things they could be doing. What the hell, he'd managed to avoid a Sunday being dragged around IKEA . . .

In the living room, when Thorne had suggested cooking something, his father had reddened and called him a "silly little bastard." Half an hour later in the pub, his dad seemed an awful lot happier. A pint of bitter and a plate of sausage and chips could cause mood swings in the old man every bit as radical as those brought on by the changing chemistry of his brain.

"This is number three on my list of rules, you know?" his dad said.

They were sitting at a table in the corner: Thorne, his father, and his father's friend Victor. There used to be quite a gang of them, regulars in this pub two or three nights a week. Since the Alzheimer's had been diagnosed, his dad's other old friends tended not to be around quite as much. Victor was the only one who didn't seem to think he could catch it . . .

"What is?" Thorne said.

His father held up his pint, pleased as punch. "This. '*No beer.*' Number three, coming after 'no going in the kitchen' and 'no going out alone.' My list of stupid rules, you know?"

Thorne nodded. He knew . . .

"No booze." Jim Thorne cleared his throat, lowered his voice, tried to sound like a DJ. "Straight in at number three in the Alzheimer's Hit Parade . . ." Thorne and Victor laughed. Thorne's father began to hum the theme to *Top of the Pops,* then stopped suddenly and looked across at Victor, his face creasing with panic. "Who are the top three chart acts of all time? In terms of weeks on the chart, I mean . . ."

Victor leaned forward, the mood suddenly urgent. "Elvis . . . Cliff Richard . . ."

"Obviously, yeah," Jim said, agitated. "It's the third one I can't bloody think of. Christ, I know this . . ."

Thorne tried to help. "The Beatles . . . ?"

With the perfect timing of a music-hall double act, his dad and Victor looked at each other, then at Thorne, before answering simultaneously, "No . . ."

Thorne could see his father beginning to sweat, to breathe heavily. The fact that he was wearing two sweaters was not helping. "I can see his bloody face. You know, bloke who fancies other blokes." He began to raise his voice. "Christ, he plays the . . . the thing with keys on, black and white keys . . ."

"Piano," Thorne said. His father often spoke like this, when the right word wouldn't come. *The thing you put in your mouth to clean your teeth with. Bacon and . . . those things that come out of a chicken.*

Victor thumped his fist on the table triumphantly. "Elton John," he said.

"I know," Jim said. "I fucking know . . ." He began stabbing at the chips on his plate, one after the other, looking as if he might weep at any moment.

"I'll get some more drinks in," Thorne said quickly. "If you're going to break one of your rules, you might as well really break the fucker . . ."

Victor drained his pint, handed Thorne the empty glass. " 'Course, your dad might not have Alzheimer's at all . . ."

Thorne shot him a look. This kind of discussion was pointless, though Victor was, strictly speaking, correct. Alzheimer's could not be, could *never* be, confirmed. They were 90 percent sure, though, which was about as good . . . or bad, as it got.

"Same again, Victor . . . ?"

"Are you listening, Jim?" Victor said. "You can't be *certain* it's Alzheimer's . . ."

Thorne put a hand on Victor's arm. "Victor . . ."

Then Victor shot *him* a look, and Thorne suddenly saw what was happening. He saw that he was trampling all over one of his dad's favorite lines. He felt sick with shame . . .

His father put down his knife and fork, picked up his cue. "That's right, Vic. The consultant told me that the only way they can be sure is to perform a postmortem. I said, 'No, thank you very much. I don't think I'm too keen on one of those just yet!' "

Victor and his father were still laughing loudly as Thorne stood at the bar waiting to get served . . .

The "middle stage" of the dementia was how it had been described to him. It all sounded a bit vague, but Thorne figured that as long as there was another stage to go, things would be all right for a while longer. As long as the bad jokes outnumbered the moments of terror and despair, he would try not to be too worried.

* * *

Just briefly, for a minute or two, Carol had wondered
about what she was doing, had thought about swapping
places with her husband. She was a middle-aged woman,
for heaven's sake! She ought to be inside like Jack, curled
up on the sofa in front of the TV instead of wrapped up
in an overcoat, rummaging through filthy cardboard
boxes in their freezing garage.

That had been before she got into it. As soon as she
began to delve into all that was left of Alan Franklin's
past—his *first* past—she'd stopped feeling the cold.
She'd rediscovered that bizarre and exciting feeling of
looking for something, *getting after it,* without having
the foggiest bloody idea of exactly what "it" was.

All around her, in front rooms and kitchens on her
quiet little road in Worthing, women her age were doing
crosswords, or losing themselves in crappy romances or
pouring breakfast cereal into bowls ready for the morning . . .

Carol pulled a pile of dusty blank paper out of one of
the boxes, swept away the grime with the side of her
hand. She wouldn't have swapped places with any one of
those women . . .

There was lots of paper in both boxes; reams of the
stuff in a variety of sizes, once presumably white, but
now yellowed and slightly damp. There were envelopes,
too, and smaller packages of file cards, sticky labels, and
rusted staples. Franklin had met Sheila while working
for an insurance firm in Hastings, but had clearly
wanted to hold on to a few odd souvenirs of the working
life he'd had before.

None of the other stuff would have caused pulses to
quicken at the *Antiques Roadshow:* a couple of unused
diaries from 1975 and 1976; a bunch of keys on a Ford
Escort key ring; plates and teacups wrapped up in old
newspaper; a couple of Polaroids inside a manila envelope—two boys; one a baby, the other a toddler, and

later the same two as a pair of gawky, unsmiling teenagers.

Carol unwrapped the dry newspaper from around what turned out to be a large silver tankard. She laid it to one side and smoothed out the crumpled page on the garage floor. It was from a local paper. She looked at the date—presumably the day Franklin had walked out on, or been thrown out by, his wife. Not a great deal seemed to have happened in Colchester that day: a small protest about a proposed ring road; a leisure center reopening after a refit; a smash-and-grab at the jeweler's on the High Street . . .

Carol smiled at a phrase she hadn't heard for many years. *Smash-and-grab*. Not much more than twenty years ago and even the crimes seemed more innocent somehow . . .

She picked up the tankard, which, after a closer look, she could see was silver-plated. In spite of the newspaper, it had blackened slightly on one side, but she could make out an engraving. She held it up to the light from the bare bulb, and read:

From the boys at Baxters, May 1976.
Welcome back.
Have one to celebrate or <u>more</u> than one to forget the whole thing!

Carol thought about ringing Sheila Franklin, but knew instinctively that she wouldn't be a great deal of help. Her husband had not shared his past with her. Maybe he went up into the loft once in a while and peered at it, or perhaps he was trying to forget it himself. Either way, Carol was pretty sure that she would have to work it out on her own. She'd start tomorrow. It couldn't be that hard. She'd get that lazy bastard McKee to make a few calls.

Wincing, Carol hauled herself up from where she'd been kneeling on the floor. She'd put a cushion down on the concrete, but her knees still felt very sore. She switched off the garage light and stood for a few seconds in the darkness before going inside.

Wondering what Alan Franklin had cause to celebrate back in 1976. And what he might have wanted to forget . . .

On the twenty-five-minute train journey back from St. Albans, Thorne had the entire carriage to himself.

He reached into his bag for his CD Walkman and a couple of discs. He opened up an album by a band called Lambchop—a birthday present from Phil Hendricks that, until he'd shelled out three hundred pounds in Tower Records, had been the *only* CD he'd owned for a day or two after the burglary. It was "alt. country," Hendricks had told him. Apparently, Thorne needed to move with the times a little . . .

Thorne pressed PLAY, let it come, and thought about the curious good-bye he and the old man had shared.

Half an hour after Victor had left and whatever tea was still in the pot had gone stone-cold, Thorne and his father had stood together on the doorstep. Both, for very different reasons, trying to find the right thing to say.

Jim Thorne had never been one for tactile displays of affection. Occasionally a handshake, but not today. Instead, with a twinkle in his eye, he had leaned in close and, as if imparting a great pearl of wisdom, told Thorne that "Three Steps to Heaven" by Eddy Cochrane had been number one in the hit parade on the day he'd been born.

Thorne kicked off his shoes, put his feet up on the seat opposite. What his father had said, what he'd *remembered*, was, he supposed, touching in its own way . . .

The music in his headphones was slow, and lush and

strange. Thorne couldn't make head or tail of the lyrics and there were horns, for crying out loud. Not *Ring of Fire*–style Tijuana trumpets, or mariachi, but proper *horns*, like you'd hear on a soul record . . .

Thorne ejected the Lambchop CD, put it back into its jewel case. Another time, perhaps. He put on Steve Earle's "Train a Comin' " and closed his eyes.

Soul was all well and good, but there were times when guts sounded a whole lot better.

It was stupidly easy.

He never ceased to be amazed at how pathetic these animals were. How simple it was to lead them by the nose. By the nose between their legs . . .

It was less than a week since the first casual remarks had been exchanged and already he could start thinking specifically about when and where Southern was going to be killed. It had been such a piece of cake that he half regretted all that effort with the others. The months of planning, the buildup, the letters. It might have been just as easy to wait until after they'd been released and collar them in a bar somewhere. Just smile and say hello.

People like that, like Southern, didn't need subtlety. Fuckers didn't understand it, wouldn't recognize it. Using their cocks like blunt instruments . . .

He'd won Southern's trust quickly, and now that he had it, the rest was fairly straightforward. Times and places. Arrangements.

It was all about trust, about getting it and keeping it. The gaining of trust was something he was good at. People gave it to him all the time, like a gift, without his needing to ask for it.

By contrast, he never, ever gave it. Not anymore. He knew very well what could happen if you did.

FIFTEEN

Carol lifted the handset and dialed, checking the number on her pad twice as she pressed each button carefully. She reached over to straighten a picture on the wall as the phone at the other end began to ring.

She had only been able to stand watching McKee mess around for so long before she'd taken over herself. Two and a half days spent on the phone, digging through records at Companies House, getting wound up. Reminding herself of how shit the job was most of the time.

"Nobody made you do it," Jack had said. "Nobody would think any the worse of you if you chucked it in."

Nobody except her . . .

Tracking down Baxters, the company Alan Franklin had worked for in Colchester nearly thirty years before, had proved enormously frustrating. She'd discovered quickly that the company, a stationery wholesaler, had not only left the area in the early eighties, but had changed its name. She was pretty much starting from scratch. She had spoken to every company in the south of England able to provide so much as a plain brown envelope, and got precisely nowhere. Then, just at the point when Jack was starting to talk about divorce, she got lucky. The personnel manager of a firm in Northampton knew *everybody* in the stationery supply business, played golf with most of them, God help him! He was only too delighted to tell her *exactly* where to

find the person she needed to talk to, and gave her the
name of a company in King's Lynn . . .

"Hello, Bowyer-Shotton, may I help you?"

"Yes, please," Carol said. "I'd like to speak to Paul
Baxter."

"I'll put you through . . ."

Andy Stone sat, sweating through his white linen shirt,
some small fraction of his mind on the report he was
writing up . . .

He thought about the woman he'd woken up next to.
He remembered the look on her face the night before,
and the look she'd given him as she'd slipped out of his
bed that morning without a word . . .

She'd been attending a tedious conference at the
Greenwood Hotel a couple of weeks earlier, when Ian
Welch had been killed. Stone had interviewed her, given
her his number in case there was anything else she remembered. She'd remembered that she fancied him,
rung, and asked if he wanted to go for a drink.

He guessed that she was turned on by the fact that he
was a copper. A lot of women seemed to find it exciting.
The power, the handcuffs, the war stories. Whatever the
reason, once the novelty wore off, most of them seemed
to lose interest in him very quickly.

Meantime, the sex was usually pretty good . . .

He wanted to control things in bed. He liked to be on
top, the woman's arms flung above her head, his hands
around her skinny wrists, pushing himself up and away
from her while he was doing it. He'd done weights, built
up his chest and arms so that he could hold the position
for as long as he needed to.

Last night had started really well. She'd looked up at
him, her eyes wide, and said all the right things, *just* the
sort of words he imagined hearing whenever he thought

about it. She told him he was too big, that he might hurt her. He threw back his head, gritted his teeth, pushed harder . . .

Then she'd spoiled things. She'd begun to moan, to grab at his shoulders, to say that she liked it rough. Then, between ragged breaths, she'd told him that she *wanted* him to hurt her.

In seconds he had shrunk and slipped out of her. He dropped down and rolled onto his side, listening to her sigh, aware of her inching across to her own side of the bed so that no part of their bodies were touching . . .

Stone looked up at the greeting of a colleague passing his desk. He smiled and continued to type. He remembered the warm feeling of his hand, cupped between his legs, and the sound of the woman's body sliding across the sheet as it edged away from him.

Carol had been put on hold . . .

She had probably been listening to Celine Dion for no more than a couple of minutes, but she could feel herself growing a hell of a lot older.

Moments like this, the empty minutes that made up so much of any case, made her glad she'd agreed to take the job on the clear understanding that she could work from home. She'd guessed that AMRU would not be given the swankiest office facilities, and working as they did (or were supposed to do) in teams of just two, she'd have been lucky to get a cupboard.

Jack had cleared a space for her in the spare room. They set up the old computer that his daughter had used, and shelled out twenty pounds on an extra handset for the cordless phone. Her filing system consisted of yellow Post-it notes stuck around a picture frame, her husband doubled as a coffee machine, and when Carol glanced at the mirror above her desk, she saw dusty hatboxes, old lamps without plugs, and a collection of china dogs that had seemed like a good idea a couple of years before.

It was cramped, but she liked her things around her.

The day she'd taken up residence in her new office, Jack had stood behind her and they'd both stared into the mirror. Carol sat at her desk and smiled at the rubbish they'd amassed together down the years, piled up on the single bed behind her. The reflection of her retired self.

"That'll stop you getting too carried away," Jack said.

The Muzak came to an abrupt and merciful halt. "Can I help you?" a man asked.

"Yes. Paul Baxter, please . . ."

"Wrong department, love. You've come through to accounts. Let me try and transfer you . . ."

Ten seconds of clicking and then a familiar voice. Carol's heart was already sinking as she spoke.

"Paul Baxter, please . . ."

"Is that you again? Sorry, dear, you've come back to the switchboard. I'll put you through . . ."

The sun, blazing through even the grimiest of the big windows, had turned the Major Incident Room into a sauna by midday. Yvonne Kitson didn't really need to reapply her lipstick, but did it all the same. Any excuse to spend a few minutes in the cool of the toilets was welcome.

She didn't usually wear a great deal of makeup. Just enough to feel good, but that was all. In this job more than most, people were quick to judge, to form instant opinions that would be passed around and set in stone before you'd so much as got your workstation organized.

She knew very well what people thought about her. She knew what the likes of Tom Thorne thought she *was*, thought she *did*. She knew just how wide of the mark they were.

Makeup—the colors, how much, when you wore it—
gave off a signal. It said you were this or that. Concealing, lying, *making it up* . . .

She stood for a few moments, looking at herself in the
cracked mirror. She moved her head a few inches, until
the crack ran right down the middle of her face. Until it
looked about right.

She would give it one more minute . . .

She began to count down the time in her head. Fifty-
five seconds more, then she would slam the phone down,
make some tea, and go and shout at her old man for a
while. No, she would snatch the phone back up, call
McKee and shout at *him* . . .

Carol began to swear repeatedly under her breath.
Fuck, fuck, fuck. She'd turned her back on gardening,
and old films in the afternoon, and the *Reader's Digest*,
for *this* . . .

"Paul Baxter's phone . . . ."

She almost cheered. "Thank God. Is Mr. Baxter
there?"

The woman sounded unsure. "Well, he was here a
minute ago. He might have grabbed an early lunch. Let
me see if I can find him for you . . ."

There was a clatter as the receiver was dropped, then
silence. Thirty seconds later Carol heard voices, then
muffled laughter, which grew suddenly louder before the
receiver was picked up and abruptly replaced. Then she
just heard a dial tone.

Carol took a deep breath and dialed again, jabbing at
the buttons as if each were the eyeball of a Bowyer-
Shotton employee.

"Hello, Bowyer-Shotton, can you hold for a moment . . . ?"

Carol shouted. "No!"

It was too late . . .

* * *

Dave Holland was in a reasonable mood until the little fucker started to get cocky.

"Listen, I don't think I have to go into the details . . ."

"Well, that depends, doesn't it?" Holland said. "On just how much of a pain in the arse you want me to be."

"I did some modeling up there. Fair enough?"

"Right. Catalog stuff, was it? The Marks & Spencer autumn collection . . . ?"

"You want to know my connection with Charlie Dodd, so I'm telling you. I was booked to do some filming, all right?"

"Did you ever mention it to anybody else?" Holland asked. "Pass Dodd's name on? Maybe you told somebody about the studio?"

There was a hollow-sounding bark of laughter down the line. "Yeah. I was so proud of the work, wasn't I? I mean, *London Cock Boys* and *Borstal Meat* are fucking classics. Maybe you've seen them . . ."

Holland hung up, put a line through another name on the list.

Charlie Dodd had known a lot of people. They'd worked their way through every number on his phone records and everyone appeared to have a valid, if occasionally sordid, reason for being a friend, or "business associate." Photographers, film developers and suppliers, video production companies, prostitutes. Each person was asked to give the name of anybody else they thought might have known Dodd, and this, together with a few more contacts provided by Thorne's squeaky-voiced informant, had generated another, much bigger list to be worked through.

Holland stifled a yawn. At the end of the day, it would probably result in nothing more than a handy contact list to pass on to Vice. It was certainly unlikely to provide any link to the killer as, contrary to what Thorne had said, Dodd had discovered that it *did* pay to advertise. One of the first numbers on the list had turned out to be a specialist S&M magazine. They were suitably saddened at the news that a much-valued client would not be placing any further small ads to advertise his facilities . . .

Holland leaned back in his chair, thrust up his arms, and stretched. Wasting his time, as he'd wasted it the night before at home. Making calls that could have waited, crossing names off the list. An excuse, an escape . . .

Sophie had come through in her dressing gown. One hand cradling her stomach and the other holding a mug of tea. She'd put it down in front of Holland and stood looking over his shoulder at the paperwork on the tabletop, her hand resting on the top of his head.

She'd laughed softly. "Little bastard's been kicking the shit out of me all day . . ."

When Holland had looked up half a minute later, she'd been standing in the doorway. He'd picked up his tea, smiled a thank-you at her.

"I know you think I want you to choose," she'd said. "And I really don't. Yes, I sometimes hate what you do, and I get pissed off at your pigheaded boss and the fact that you worship the ground he walks on, but you know all that. Yes, I would be happy if you took some time off and, no, I don't want you doing anything stupid. Not now. I wouldn't ask you to make a choice, though, Dave." Then she'd turned to stare out of the window for a moment. "I'd be too scared . . ."

For a few seconds there had been only the sound of the traffic rumbling up the Old Kent Road and a radio from the flat downstairs. Holland had picked up the phone from its cradle, reached for his pen. "Can we talk about it later?" He'd looked down at the papers on the desk, at the pointless list of names. "This is really important . . ."

Thorne watched his team going through the motions. Holland, Stone, Kitson . . .

He saw dozens of other officers and civilian staff talking and writing and thinking—the impetus running out. As if the heat had thickened the air, made it a little harder to move through.

Thorne stood watching from the doorway of the Incident Room, thinking about the thrashing limbs of a body near to death . . .

It was always the same pattern. In the days that followed the discovery of a murder victim, the activity was frantic. An urgency seized the team, the knowledge that the hours, the days immediately following, would be when they had their best chance. After Dodd, they'd run around like blue-arsed flies, checking records and tracing contacts and taking statements and chasing couriers. Waiting for *anything*.

And, gradually, as always, the flurry of activity on the case had slowed, like the movements of the victim himself as death had approached. The frenzy became drudgery. The phone was picked up and the statement taken reflexively, the small spark of hope fizzling to nothing, until the body of the investigation itself began to stiffen and cool, to swing aimlessly . . .

Something would be needed. The case, and those working it, needed a jolt to kick some life back into them. An external force, like the passing train that had given movement to Charlie Dodd's corpse.

Thorne had no idea what it was or where it might come from.

"Paul Baxter . . ."

"Am I *speaking* to Paul Baxter?"

"Yes, who's this?"

Carol felt a little of the tension in her back and neck begin to ease. "My name's Carol Chamberlain, from the Metropolitan Police Area Major Review Unit. You would not believe the trouble I've had trying to get hold of you . . ."

"Get hold of *me* . . . ?"

"You, your company . . ."

"We're in the phone book . . ."

"Right, but I was looking for *Baxters*."

There was a pause. Carol could hear Baxter taking a drink of something, swallowing. "That was a long time ago. My dad got bought out in . . . '82. I think. I stayed on as head of sales when we moved up here, that was part of the deal . . ."

"Anyway . . ."

"So how can I help you?" Paul Baxter laughed. He had a low, sexy voice. Smooth, like a DJ. "Does the Met need some new headed notepaper?"

"Do you remember an employee called Alan Franklin? He would have left in—"

Baxter cut her off. "God, yes, of course I do. I was helping out in the warehouse when all that happened, working for my old man. Just before Christmas, I think . . ."

"When all *what* happened?"

She could hear confusion, suspicion even, in Baxter's voice as he answered. "Well, I don't suppose we'll ever know for sure, but I remember the court case obviously. God, and all that dreadful stuff afterward . . ."

Carol realized suddenly that she was on her feet, leaning on her desk. In the mirror she saw the face of a woman who, for the first time in three long years, was feeling the buzz. Feeling it across her chest like a heart attack. In her head like a hole that sucked away the breath in a second. Rushing through her blood and bone like light.

Like a lease of life.

"Hello . . . ?"

She became dimly aware of Baxter's voice on the other end of the phone. She lowered herself into the chair, took just another second before moving on.

"Okay, Mr. Baxter, when can I come and see you?"

Done and dusted . . .

The suggestion had come from Southern himself. How brilliant was that?! An invitation back to Southern's small flat in Leytonstone had been politely declined. He'd already decided that he would be sticking with the hotel. Southern had gone for that idea straightaway—same as the others had. There was something about a hotel that gave the rendezvous an excitement for them. It was the same for him as well, of course, but then he knew just how exciting it was really going to be . . .

The hotels he'd chosen, on each occasion so far, had suited the mood of the event and the character of the individual concerned perfectly. He always gave some thought to that, as well as to the necessary issues of security. Remfry, if he'd had the chance, would have done it up a back alley, across a rusty oil drum. The place in Paddington had the seediness that got him off, the squalor that turned him on. Welch, on the other hand, had wanted somewhere a bit nicer. He was clearly a man with aspirations, ideas above his station. The Greenwood had fitted the bill nicely.

The place that he'd found for Howard Southern would be ideal. It was a small, country-house-type *hotel in leafy Roehampton, on the outskirts of Richmond Park. There was a romantic, woodland view from some of the bedrooms.*

He was sure that it would go down well. Howard Southern loved the countryside. Hadn't he brutally beaten and raped his first victim on a disused bridle path in Epping Forest?

Done and dusted.

SIXTEEN

Two B's and a C. Two B's and a C . . .

The results she needed to see when she opened that envelope at the end of August. The offer from the university she wanted. The grades that she had to get if she was going to take up her place in the drama course in Manchester. Two B's and a C. It had become Fiona Meek's mantra in the weeks since her final paper.

Most of her friends were still celebrating the end of the exams. One or two of those with parents richer than her own were away traveling, and the rest were just pissing the time away. There were only a couple, like her, who had decided to put a bit of money away and take summer jobs. She knew she could be a bit too sensible sometimes, but she didn't mind missing out. She didn't care if her friends made fun of her. They wouldn't be laughing when their student loans ran out halfway through the first term.

It was the perfect job, and plenty of people wanted it. A friend of her dad's was the corporate hospitality manager and had put in a good word. Working the two shifts suited her. It was an early start, but she was finished midmorning and not on again until teatime, so she had her days to herself.

Fiona waved as, farther up the corridor, she saw one of the other girls coming out of a room, dumping dirty towels into the laundry hamper. She parked her own trolley, began loading soap and shampoo into a small basket. The smell was familiar from the mountain of stuff she now had in her own bathroom at home.

The seven-to-ten bedroom shift was the hardest. She'd been amazed these last couple of weeks to see just what pigs some people lived like when they weren't at home. She hadn't had any *really* bad ones yet—no used condoms, or what have you—but still, some people behaved like animals. Equally weird were the rooms that barely looked lived in at all. Towels neatly folded and beds made. These were the sort of people, Fiona supposed, who tidied their houses before their cleaning ladies came around.

Either way, as she moved around the bedrooms, replenishing toiletries and coffee sachets, smoothing sheets and checking minibars, she tried to get inside the heads of these people whom she rarely ever met. She tried to flesh out lives she could only guess at by the labels on strangers' shoes, the smells in their bathrooms, and the paperbacks by the sides of their beds.

It was all good practice, she reckoned, for being an actress. If she ever got the chance. Two B's and a C. Two B's and a C . . .

She slid the plastic passkey into the lock and shoved open a bedroom door.

A lot of murders went unsolved, but compared to the cleanup rates for burglary, Thorne reckoned that he, and others like him, were doing pretty bloody well.

"For fuck's sake, Chris, it's been nearly three weeks. You must know *most* of the likely lads in the area . . ."

On the other end of the phone, Chris Barratt enjoyed a good laugh. It sounded to Thorne as if this conversation was making the Kentish Town crime-desk sergeant's day.

"You know what it's like, Tom," Barratt said. "This

early on a Saturday morning, you want to count yourself lucky there was anybody here to answer the bleeding phone . . ."

Thorne knew how stretched things were in many areas. Violent street crime was, quite rightly, being targeted, and uniformed manpower was being taken away from such everyday London trivialities as common housebreaking. He was aware that because he was on the job, they were probably making twice the effort they would normally be making to lay hands on whoever had turned his flat over. He also knew that twice nothing was pretty much fuck all.

"Three weeks, though, Chris . . ."

"We found your car."

"Yeah, and got nothing off it . . ."

"It was burned out . . ."

"Only on the inside."

The Mondeo had been found on an estate behind Euston Station. The inside had been torched, the wheels nicked, and the words POLICE ARSEHOLES spray-painted on the roof. Yet more cause for amusement around the Incident Room at Becke House . . .

"What about fences?" Thorne asked. "The bastard should have got something for my CD system . . ."

"Duh! We never thought about that . . ."

Thorne sighed. He took the gum he'd been chewing out of his mouth and lobbed it out of the open window. "Sorry, Chris. Any kind of fucking result would be good at the minute, you know?"

"You're sorted with the insurance, aren't you?" Barratt said.

"Yeah, fine." Thorne was still waiting for the money to come through, car and contents, but there was no reason why it shouldn't . . .

"So are you really that bothered?"

A clammy Saturday morning. Working up a sweat in slow motion. The arse end of a week that felt like a tight space he was too big to squeeze through.

"Yes, I'm bothered," Thorne said. "So should you be. And when you eventually catch the little bastard who used my bedroom as a toilet, he's going to be *very* fucking bothered . . ."

A guest in a smart suit hurried past her toward the lift. Fiona said good morning and put the back of a rubber-gloved hand across her mouth to stifle a yawn. She moved up the corridor toward the next bedroom, thinking about what she might do later on.

The early evening shift was usually a cinch. A chance to flirt with her favorite waiter as she cleaned the tables in the bar, or to gossip with the girls in reception while she vacuumed. A couple of times she'd managed to finish all her jobs double-quick and find a quiet corner, somewhere out of sight, where she could sit and open a book.

If she wasn't too tired, she might go out for a couple of drinks, catch up with some of her mates. Maybe she could slip away from work a few minutes early . . .

No such luck the evening before. There was a dose of summer flu going around and the place was short-staffed. She'd had to do the whole of main reception herself and was just thinking she might finally be able to get away when she'd been roped into lending a hand up in the Conference Room, laying the table for a Saturday-morning business breakfast the following day.

She'd wheeled the trolley laden with cutlery and table linen into the lift and pressed the button for the top floor. Just as the doors were closing, a couple had stepped in. She was attractive, wearing a smart skirt and silk blouse. He was *very* attractive, and dressed a little more casually.

On the first floor, the woman got out. They hadn't

been a couple after all. As the doors closed, the man turned to her and smiled. Feeling herself redden, Fiona looked down and began to count the knives and forks.

The bell rang as the lift reached the top floor and she straightened her wheels, nudged them toward the door. The man took a step forward to hold the door for her. He gave her another smile as she pushed the trolley out, the cutlery clattering noisily as she moved past him.

A few feet up the corridor, she'd turned and looked at him, a little confused that he hadn't stepped out of the lift himself. Just as the doors began to shut, the man in the leather biker's jacket had caught her looking at him. He turned his palms upward and shook his head at his own stupidity.

"Miles away. Missed my floor . . ."

There were times when investigations seemed shrouded in darkness. When the light, no matter the season or time of day, seemed to have faded away in those rooms where a case was worked, where progress in catching a killer was discussed and evaluated. For those groping around in the dark, there was always the frustrating feeling that if someone could just shine a light in the right direction, something important would be revealed. Then the shadows would shorten and slip away.

The day was getting off to a slow start, but Brigstocke seemed in no mood to crack the whip. It was fine with Thorne. He sensed that an extra ten minutes or so spent sitting around together, talking about nothing much for a while before they got down to it, might do everybody some good.

Might shorten a few shadows . . .

They sat on and around three different desks in the Incident Room. The coffees and teas were being eked out. Magazines and papers were being flicked through, space stared into, clocks glanced at.

"Anybody have a decent Friday night?" Thorne said. Nobody seemed awfully keen on answering one way or the other. Thorne laughed. "Fuck me, what a bunch of party animals!" He turned to look at Stone. "Come on, Andy, you're young and single . . ."

Stone looked up, but only for a second. "Too worn out . . ."

Holland laughed. "You big girl . . ."

"You won't be laughing once your missus has a kid," Brigstocke said.

"Right." Kitson walked across to the recently installed watercooler. "You should be making the most of your Friday nights, Dave. Soon be a thing of the past . . ."

Holland grunted, turned his attention back to the sports page of the *Daily Mirror.* Thorne craned his head to look at the headline. The latest on a story that Spurs were about to sign some temperamental Italian midfielder.

"What about the rest of the weekend, then?" Thorne threw the question open to any of them. "Any plans?"

The reaction—a lot of noncommittal shrugging—was much the same as before. Thorne began to think that his own social life, such as it was, looked pretty bloody exciting by comparison. Mind you, it had picked up a lot lately . . .

"Sundays in the Brigstocke household are sacred and unchanging." The DCI picked up his briefcase, moved away in the direction of his office. "Dog walking, laundry, the bloodbath of Sunday lunch with one set of parents or another. Oh, and a trip to the garden center, or maybe the supermarket if I'm *really* lucky . . ."

Thorne laughed, looking around, sharing it. He thought about the last Sunday *he'd* spent. Something Brigstocke had said sparked another memory and Thorne turned to watch Yvonne Kitson heading back across the room, drinking from a paper cone filled with cold water.

"Did you get my message last Sunday?" She swallowed, looked at him blankly. "I called. Late morning, I think . . ."

Kitson dropped the empty cone into a wastepaper basket. "Any particular reason?"

"Well, if there was, I'll be damned if I can remember it," Thorne said.

Kitson looked at him for a second or two, her face showing nothing. "I didn't get the message."

Thorne shrugged. "Doesn't matter." He nodded toward where Brigstocke had been just a minute before. "I'd thought it would be a good time to catch you, you know? Reckoned you'd be another one with a family routine on a Sunday."

Kitson moved past him, picked up the magazine she'd been reading, and dropped it into her bag. She took a step toward the toilets, then turned to Thorne, nodding as though she'd just remembered something. "I was at the gym . . ."

The Incident Room was coming to life, starting to fill with noise and movement. Holland walked across it, evidently catching the tail end of Thorne and Kitson's conversation.

"You should get together with Stoney," he said. "He's well into weights and all that." Holland looked over to where Andy Stone was sitting on the edge of a desk, chatting to a trainee detective. "He might be a lanky so-and-so, but he looks like a light heavyweight with his shirt off . . ."

Kitson looked at Thorne and raised her eyebrows. Her face was open and relaxed again. Her tone, when she spoke to Holland, was matey and suggestive. "Easy, tiger," she said.

Holland started to say something else, but Thorne was

already moving away from them. He knew that by the end of the day the heat and the frustrations of the case would combine to leave him as tightly wound as the E-string on a pedal-steel guitar. He wanted to get into his office, call Eve, and organize something that would help lessen that tension just a little.

"Christ, you sound even more harassed than *I* am . . ."

"I told you, Saturdays are the busiest day."

"Keith's mum still no better, then?"

"Sorry?"

"Keith not around to help out?"

"Oh. No . . ."

Thorne looked up as Kitson walked in and moved across to her desk. Her look told him that she knew exactly whom he was talking to. Thorne lowered his voice . . .

"Fancy going to see a film tonight?"

"Yeah, why not. There's a copy of *Time Out* in the flat, I'll see what's on . . . "

From nowhere, and for no immediately obvious reason, the case burst its way into their conversation. Into Thorne's head. The image that would not focus. The thought that would not reveal itself.

Something he'd read and something he hadn't . . .

At the sound of Eve's voice, the phantom thought vanished as suddenly as it had arrived. "Tom?"

"Yeah . . . that's fine. Maybe we could do a bit of shopping tomorrow."

There was a pause. "Anywhere in particular?"

Thorne dropped the volume even further, cupped his hand around the mouthpiece.

"The bed shop . . ."

Eve laughed, and when she spoke again, *her* voice was lowered. Thorne guessed from the noise that she had a shop full of customers. "Thank fuck for that," she said.

"I'm pleased you're pleased," Thorne said.

"Yes, well, it's about bloody time. I'd decided I wasn't going to mention it again. I didn't want to sound desperate."

Thorne glanced up. Kitson was hunched over some paperwork. "Listen, I had a long look at myself in the mirror this morning. I'd say 'desperate' is a pretty good word for it . . ."

Fiona only had a couple of rooms left.

The girls usually worked to a set pattern in terms of floors, corridors, and so on, but the order in which individual rooms were cleaned varied from day to day. Rooms with a Do Not Disturb sign hung on the door would obviously get done later than those with used breakfast trays left outside, while some rooms would get knocked onto a later shift.

There were two rooms at the end of her corridor on the first floor that still needed doing. She looked at her watch. It was twenty to ten . . .

Fiona grabbed a bucket crammed with sponges, sprays, and bottles, nudging the vacuum cleaner toward the bedroom door with her foot. She knocked on the door and counted to five, thinking about eggs and bacon and bed. It was the same most mornings. By this time, by the end of this corridor, she would be thinking about home, a late breakfast, and a few more gorgeous hours wrapped up in her duvet.

Twenty minutes. She might get both rooms done before the end of her shift if she was lucky, though it would obviously depend on what sort of state they were in.

She reached down for the passkey card hanging from a curly plastic chain around her waist . . .

There was a tune going through her head. The song that had woken her on the clock radio, a present from her grandma when the exams had finished. The song was very old-fashioned, just a singer and a guitar, but the tune had stayed with her all morning.

She eased the card into the lock and slid it out again. The light below the handle turned green. She pushed down and leaned against the door . . .

From the corner of her eye, she saw someone coming toward her along the corridor. It looked like one of the snotty old cows that ran housekeeping. She couldn't be sure because the woman's face was all but hidden behind an enormous arrangement of lilies.

Turning sideways, she eased open the door with her hip. The vacuum was kicked across the threshold, left to hold the door ajar while she turned back to the trolley to grab her other bits and pieces . . .

Two months later, Fiona would be offered her chance, her place in the drama course in Manchester, but she would not take it up. Not *that* September, at any rate. She would get her two B's and a C but it would not mean a great deal to her. Two months later, her mother would remove the slip of paper from the envelope and read out the results and try to sound excited, but her daughter would still not be hearing very much. The scream that had torn through her body eight weeks earlier would still be echoing in her head and drowning out pretty much everything.

The sound of a scream and a picture of herself, of a young girl stepping through a doorway and turning. Faced with a peculiar kind of filth. Stains that she could never hope to remove with the bleaches and the waxes and the cloths that spill from a bucket, tumbling noisily to the bedroom floor.

*   *   *

It wasn't much past ten yet, but Thorne was already starting to wonder what the lunchtime special at the Royal Oak might be when the middle-aged woman walked into his office.

"I'm looking for DC Holland," she said.

She'd marched in without knocking, so Thorne wasn't keen from the start, but he tried to be as nice as he could. The woman was short and dumpy, probably pushing sixty. She reminded him a bit of his auntie Eileen, and he suddenly had a good idea who she was.

"Oh, right, are you Dave's . . . ?"

The woman cut him off and, as she spoke, she dragged a chair from behind Kitson's desk, plonked it in front of Thorne's, and sat herself down.

"No, I'm not. I'm Carol Chamberlain. Ex-DCI Chamberlain from AMRU . . ."

Thorne reached for a pen and paper to take notes, thinking, *Fucking Crinkly Squad, all I need*. He leaned across the desk and proffered a hand. "DI Thorne . . ."

Ignoring the hand, Carol Chamberlain opened her briefcase and began to rummage inside. "Right. *You'll* do even better. I only asked for Holland"—she pulled out a battered green folder covered in yellow Post-it notes, held it up—"because his was the name . . . attached to *this*." Emphasizing the last word, she dropped the folder down onto Thorne's desk.

Thorne glanced at the file and held up his hands. He tried his best to sound pleasant as he spoke. "Listen, is there any chance we can do this another time? We're up to our elbows in a very big case and—"

"I know *exactly* what case you're up to your elbows in," she said. "Which is why we should really do it now."

Thorne stared at her. There was a steel in this woman's voice that suggested it would not be worth his while to argue. With a sigh, he pulled the folder across the desk, began to leaf through it.

"Five weeks ago, DC Holland pulled the file on an unsolved murder from 1996." Aside from the steel, her voice had the acquired refinement that often came with rank, however distant, but Thorne thought he detected the remnants of a Yorkshire accent beneath. "The victim's name was Alan Franklin. He was killed in a car park. Strangled with washing line."

"I remember," Thorne said. He flicked a couple of pages over. It was one of the cases Holland had pulled off CRIMINT. "There were a couple of these that we looked at and then dismissed. Nothing suggested that . . ."

Chamberlain nodded, dropped her eyes to the folder. "This was handed to me as a cold case. My *first* cold case, as it happens . . ."

"I read about the initiative. It's a good idea."

"I've been looking at the Franklin murder again . . ."

"Right . . ." Thorne stopped, noticing the faintest trace of enjoyment then, another tiny line around her mouth that cracked open for just half a second and was gone. It was enough to prompt a reaction in *him*, a flutter of something that began, as always, at the nape of his neck . . .

"Alan Franklin should have been known to us, to those who were investigating his murder back in '96. His name should have come up on a routine check . . ."

Thorne knew there was no need to ask why. He knew she was about to tell him. He watched, and listened, and felt the tingle grow and spread around his body.

"In May 1976, Franklin stood trial at Colchester Crown Court. He was accused of rape. Accused and acquitted."

Thorne caught a breath, let it out again slowly. "Jesus . . ."

Like a beam of light in the right direction . . .

Later, when Thorne and the woman he'd thought was Dave Holland's mother knew and liked each other better, Carol Chamberlain would confess to him that *this* was one of those rare moments she'd missed more than anything. The seconds looking at Thorne, just before she revealed the most significant fact of all. When she'd had to fight very hard to stop herself grinning.

"Alan Franklin was accused of raping a woman named Jane Foley . . ."

Part Three

Harm's Way

The grunting seemed to be coming from somewhere very deep down. A noise of effort and of immense satisfaction. Rising up from his guts and exploding, carried on hot breath from between dirty, misshapen teeth. Beneath these animal sounds—dog noise, monkey noise, pig noise—the counterpoint provided by the dull slapping of hot flesh against cold as he pushes himself harder, again and again.

Refusing to speed up. Giving no sign that it might soon be over.

Taking his pleasure.

Inflicting his pain.

How was this allowed to happen? Naïveté and trust had proved to be the perfect complements to frustration and hatred. It had happened in a moment. How long ago was that? Fifteen minutes? Thirty?

There seems little point in struggling. It will be over eventually, it must be. No point in thinking about what happens afterward. Probably a shy smile, maybe an apology and a cigarette and a speech about signals and crossed wires.

Fucker. Fucker. Fucker.

Until then . . .

Eyes that cannot bear to stay open, shut tight

and a new picture presents itself. Small at first, and far away. Posed, waiting in a distant circle of light at the end of a tunnel.

Now it is the grunting and the slapping that begin to recede into the distance as the picture gets closer, rushing up the tunnel, sucking up the darkness until it is fully formed and clearer than it has ever been.

Clearer even than it ever really was. The colors more vivid: the red wetness against the white shirt; the cobalt blue of the rope's coils around the neck like an exotic snake at his throat. The sounds and smells of the body and the rope, deafening and pungent. Creaking and fecal.

The feeling: the unique horror of seeing it. Seeing the indescribable pain in those eyes at being seen.

Then, at the end, watching it. Sensing something struggle to escape, and finally float free, up and away from the body that twirls slowly at the end of a frayed and oily rope.

SEVENTEEN

It was as grim a story of broken bodies and bruised lives as Tom Thorne had ever heard . . .

A week since Carol Chamberlain had sat in Thorne's office and blown everything wide open. Holland was at the wheel of a car-pool Laguna as they drove into Essex, heading toward Braintree. The two men were comfortable enough with each other to let silences fall between them, but today's was particularly heavy. Thorne could only hope that what was in Holland's head was a sight less dark than what was in his own.

As grim a story . . .

Jane Foley was raped by Alan Franklin. Thorne was convinced of it, though if it had not been proved *then*, there was very little chance that the truth would emerge over twenty-five years later. What nobody doubted, then or now, were the bizarre and brutal actions taken by her husband, Dennis. What he had done to Jane, and then to himself, on the afternoon of August 10, 1976.

Thorne would probably never know for certain *exactly* what had gone on in that house, what had passed between those two people and led to those last, intimate moments of horror. Thorne *did* know that he would spend a good deal of time imagining those moments: the terror of Jane Foley as her husband draws near to her; the guilt and the anguish and the fear of a man who has just committed murder; the blood not yet dry on his hands, the towrope slippy with it as he fashions a makeshift noose.

Worst of all, the incomprehension of the two children, finding the bodies of their parents . . .

Thorne started slightly as Holland smacked his palms against the wheel. He opened his eyes to see that they'd run into a line of slow-moving traffic. Ever since they'd come off the M11 it had been snarled up. Midmorning on a Saturday and no good reason for the jam, but it was there all the same.

"Shit," Holland said. It was the first word either of them had spoken in nearly an hour.

If Thorne was going to spend time thinking about what had happened between Jane and Dennis Foley, he was also going to be dwelling on something equally painful. Something that, God help him, might have been responsible for horrors all of its own.

Thorne had fucked up. He had fucked up as badly as he could remember and, for him, that was saying something . . .

Carol Chamberlain had presumed that the officers working on the Franklin murder in 1996 had also fucked up. It looked as if they'd failed to check Franklin's name against the General Registry at Victoria, which would have revealed his part in the Jane Foley rape case twenty years before that.

In fact, it was a matter of record that those officers *had* phoned the General Registry. What was *not* a matter of record, what would have to remain conjecture, was that the brain-dead pen pusher on the other end of the phone—a man long since retired and, Thorne hoped, long since dead—had missed Franklin's name. One eye on his crossword as the other had simply skipped past it. It had been a costly mistake.

But Thorne's had been costlier.

Unlike the officers in 1996, Thorne had *not* checked. Jane Foley's name had never been run past the General Registry, had never been put through the system. Strictly speaking, it had not been Thorne's job to do it, but that didn't matter. As far as Thorne was concerned, he carried the can. He never made sure, and even if he *had* thought of it, it would not have struck him as important.

Why would they need to check out the name of a woman who didn't really exist? Jane Foley was the made-up name of a made-up person, wasn't it? Jane Foley was a fantasy . . .

Thorne knew very well that if they . . . he . . . *anyone* had checked, made one simple phone call after they'd found Remfry's letters, that Ian Welch might still be alive. As might Howard Anthony Southern . . .

The traffic had begun to move again. Holland yanked the gear stick down, took the car up into second. "I wouldn't mind, but there's never a decent bloody pileup at the end of it . . ."

The body of the third victim had been discovered, in a hotel in Roehampton, at around the same time as the woman from the Crinkly Squad had walked into Thorne's office and dropped her very welcome bombshell. She had still been there when the call came through and Thorne had invited her along to the murder scene. It had seemed the very least he could do.

In that hotel room, with SOCOs and pathologists and an honest-to-goodness body, Thorne had thought that, even standing in the background as she was, Carol Chamberlain had looked as happy as a kid in a sweets factory . . .

In the days that followed, the investigation had begun to move forward in two distinct directions. While the latest victim was being processed, and the change in the pattern of the killings was being looked at, Thorne and those closest to him had begun to work on a new front. They would be chasing the major new lead that Carol Chamberlain had given them.

Holland steered the car into an ordinary-looking road lined with drab sixties houses, and spindly trees that didn't help a great deal. They'd managed to nab one of the few team vehicles with air-conditioning and the street felt like a sauna as they stepped out of the car. They pulled on their jackets, grimacing.

As they walked toward Peter Foley's house, Thorne thought about leads. Why on earth did they talk about "chasing" them? He wondered if it was because, no matter how inanimate they were, or how quick you thought *you* might be, some had a nasty habit of getting away from you.

Dennis Foley's younger brother, the only surviving relative of either Dennis *or* Jane they had yet been able to trace, was not the most gracious of hosts.

Thorne and Holland sat perched on the edge of stained velour armchairs, sweating inside jackets they had not been encouraged to take off. Opposite them on a matching sofa, Peter Foley sprawled in baggy shorts and a loud Hawaiian shirt, open to the waist. He clutched a can of cold lager, which, when he wasn't drinking from it, he rolled back and forth across his skinny chest.

"You were, what, eleven years younger than Dennis?" Holland said.

Foley swallowed a mouthful of beer. "Right, I was the mistake."

"So when it happened you'd have still been a student?"

He shook his head. "Nope. Least you could do is get your facts right. I was twenty-two in '76. I'd left college the year before . . ." His accent was pure Essex, the voice high and a little wheezy.

"And you were doing what?" Thorne asked.

"I was doing fuck all. Bumming around, being a punk. I was a roadie for The Clash at one point . . ."

Thorne had been a punk as well, though he was six years younger than Foley, who was pushing fifty. The man sitting opposite him certainly didn't look like he listened to "White Riot" much anymore. He was skinny, though his arms were well muscled; worked on, Thorne guessed, to better display the Gothic tattoos. His graying hair was tied back in a ponytail and the wispy beard teased into a point. From the look of him, and the copies of *Kerrang!* tossed under the coffee table, Thorne figured that Peter Foley was something of an aging heavy-metal fan.

"What do you think happened to Jane?" Thorne said.

Foley lifted himself up, pulled a pack of Marlboros from his shorts pocket, and sank back down again. "What? You mean when Den . . . ?"

"Before that. With Franklin."

"Fucker raped her, didn't he." It wasn't a question. He lit his cigarette. "He'd have gone down for it as well if it wasn't for you fucking lot . . ."

Holland bridled a little, opened his mouth, but Thorne cut across him. "What do you mean, Mr. Foley?" Thorne knew *exactly* what Foley meant and he knew that he was right. The force, back then, was not exactly famed for the sensitivity with which it treated rape victims.

"You get the transcripts of that trial, mate. Have a look at some of the things they said about Jane in court. Made her sound like a total slut. Especially that copper, talking about what she was wearing . . ."

"It was handled badly," Thorne said. "Back then a lot

of rapists got off, simple as that. I'm sure you're right about what happened to Jane, about Franklin."

Foley took a drag, then a drink, and leaned back, nodding. He looked across at Thorne, like he was reevaluating him.

Thorne glanced at Holland. Time to move on. As far as the interview went, they hadn't worked out a system—who would ask what, who was going to take the lead—they never did. Holland did the writing. That was about as far as it went.

"Did you know that Alan Franklin was dead?" Holland said. "He died in 1996."

Now it was Thorne's turn to do the evaluating. He studied Foley's face, trying to read the reaction. All he saw, or thought he saw, was momentary shock, and then delight.

"Fucking good," Foley said. "I hope it was painful."

"It was. He was murdered."

"Even better. Who do I send a thank-you letter to?"

Thorne stood up and began to wander about. Foley was getting altogether too comfortable. Thorne was not considering the man to be a suspect, not at the moment anyway, but he always preferred his interviewees a little off balance . . .

"Why do you think he did it, Peter?" Thorne said. "Why did Dennis kill her?" Foley stared back at him, sucked his teeth. He emptied the last of the lager into his mouth and crushed the can in his hand.

Thorne repeated the question. "Why did your brother kill his wife?"

"How should I know?"

"Did he believe what they said about Jane in court?"

"I don't—"

"He must have thought about it at least . . ."

"Den thought about a lot of things."

"Did he think his wife was a slut?"

"'Course he fucking didn't . . ."

"Maybe they had problems in bed afterward . . ."

Foley leaned forward suddenly, dropped the empty can at his feet. "Listen, Jane went weird afterward, all right? She had a breakdown. She stopped going out, stopped talking to anyone, stopped doing anything at all. She was mates with this girl I was seeing at the time, you know, we all used to go out together, but after the trial, no . . . after the *rape*, she just wasn't there anymore. Den pretended like everything was fine, but he was bottling it all up. He always did. So, when Franklin walked out of that court like Nelson fucking Mandela, like *he'd* been the victim . . ."

Thorne watched as Foley leaned back, *fell* back on the sofa, and began to spin one of the half-dozen silver rings on the fingers of his left hand.

"Look, I don't know what Den thought, all right? He said some mad stuff at the time, but he was all over the place. They make you doubt things, don't they? That was their job in that court, to make the jury doubt, and they did a bloody good job. I mean, you're *supposed* to trust the police, aren't you, to believe them . . . ?"

Foley looked up and across at Holland, then turned to look at Thorne. For the first time he looked his age. Thorne looked at the cracks across Peter Foley's face, saw hard drugs in his past and perhaps even in his present.

"Something snapped," Foley said quietly.

For no good reason that he could think of, Thorne took a step across the room and bent to pick up the beer can from the floor. He put it down on a dusty chrome-and-glass shelving unit next to the TV, then turned back to Foley.

"What happened to the children?"

"Sorry . . . ?"

"Mark and Sarah. Your nephew and niece. What happened to them afterward?"

"Straight afterward, you mean? After they found . . . ?"

"Later on. Where did they go?"

"Into care. The police took them away and then the social services got involved. There was some counseling went on, I think. More so for the boy, as I remember, he'd have been eight or nine . . ."

"He was seven. His sister was five."

"Yeah, that sounds right."

"So . . . ?"

"So, eventually, they were fostered."

"I see."

"Look, there was only Jane's mum and she was already getting on in years. No other way, really. I said I'd have the kids, me and my girlfriend, but nobody was very keen. I was only twenty-two . . ."

"And of course, your brother *had* just bashed their mother's brains out with a table lamp . . ."

"I said I'd have them. I *wanted* to have them . . ."

"So you stayed in touch with the kids?"

" 'Course . . ."

"Did you see much of them?"

"For a while, but they moved around. It wasn't always easy."

"You've got the names and addresses?"

"Which . . . ?"

"The foster parents'. You said the kids moved around. Were there many?"

"A few."

"You've got all the details?"

"Not anymore. I mean, I did then, yeah. There were Christmas cards, birthdays . . ."

"And then you just lost touch?"

"Well, you do, don't you?"

"So you'd have no idea at all where Sarah and Mark are living now?"

Foley blinked, laughed humorlessly. "What, you mean you lot *haven't*?"

"We've traced every Mark Foley in the country. Every Sarah Foley or Sarah Whatever *née* Foley, and none of them remembers wandering into the hall and seeing their father dangling from a towrope. Nobody recalls popping upstairs to find Mum lying in a pool of blood with her skull caved in. Call me old-fashioned, but I don't think that sort of thing would slip your mind."

Foley shook his head. "I can't help you, mate. Even if I could, it would go against the bloody grain . . ."

Thorne looked at Holland. Time to go. As they stood up, Foley swung his legs up onto the sofa, reached down beside it for another can of lager.

"Before everything happened, before it all went belly-up, Jane and Den were normal, you know? Just a normal couple with two kids and an okay house and all the rest of it. They were a good team, they were doing all right, and I reckon they'd have got over what that arsehole did to Jane. I mean, couples do, don't they, eventually, and Den would have helped her, because he loved her. But what came after, what happened to them in that trial, and the stuff later on . . . you don't get over that, ever. And that's thanks to *you*."

Foley was talking about something that had happened a long time ago. He was talking about mistakes that it was too late to put right, and about a police officer long since retired.

But he was pointing at Thorne.

EIGHTEEN

Thorne enjoyed expensive wine, but rather more often, cheap lager. This particular brand, which had caught his eye in the supermarket, was the same one Peter Foley had been drinking . . .

Another Saturday when he hadn't got home until gone ten o'clock. Eve would probably still have been up, he could have called, but he hadn't bothered. He had only managed to see her once in the last fortnight, and though they'd talked often on the phone, he'd sensed a tension starting to creep in. He was starting to use his workload as an excuse.

Thorne knew very well that when it came to relationships, he was basically bone idle. He'd been that way with the girls he'd got together with in the fifth form, he'd been that way with his first serious girlfriends, and he'd been that way with Jan. Happy to sink into a rut, wary of changing direction. Eventually, of course, Jan had changed direction herself. Got creative with her creative-writing lecturer . . .

All because he was comfortable being stuck in the mud, and now he could feel it going the same way with Eve.

There was the bed thing, for starters. As he lay with his feet up on the sofa that would soon become his bed for another night, he thought about the whole stupid business of his failure to buy a new mattress. The trip they'd arranged the week before had been canceled for obvious reasons. He'd joked with Eve about burglars and murderers conspiring to keep them from shagging, but in reality, the delays had been . . . convenient. There *was* a part of him, a nasty part he was reluctant to acknowledge, that worried about how interested in Eve he would really be once he'd got her into bed, but that wasn't really the problem. At the end of the day, he was just plain, bloody lazy . . .

From his brand-new speakers came the mournful tones of Johnny Cash, singing his sublime version of Springsteen's "Highway Patrolman." As Cash sang about nothing feeling better than blood on blood, Thorne thought that if any voice could capture the love and agony, the hatred and the joy, of family ties, it was his. It helped if you'd lived it, of course.

On the floor, the cat was yowling, begging to be picked up. Thorne leaned down, put his can on the carpet, and pulled her up on to his lap.

So often it came down to families . . .

He thought about Mark and Sarah Foley, whose family was torn apart in front of them, leaving each with no one save the other. A generation down the line and they were nowhere to be found. It could only be because they wanted it that way.

Mark Foley, now a man in his midthirties, once a terrified little boy in need of professional counseling. Had he grown up, the horror turning to hatred and festering inside him? Had he waited twenty years and then killed the man who'd raped his mother, the man he held responsible for her death and the suicide of his father? Right now, Mark Foley was as good a suspect as they had, but what had happened since 1996, between Alan Franklin's death and this new spate of killings? What had sparked off the cultivating and murdering of these completely unconnected rapists . . . ?

Thorne had always known, somehow, that rape was

key to the case. Hadn't he tried to explain it to Hendricks? The rape element in the killings of Remfry and Welch, and now of Howard Southern, had always felt significant. *More* significant than the killings themselves. Now Thorne knew why. If he didn't fully understand it, he at least understood that it had a history . . .

And still that ambivalence on the part of so many involved in the investigation. A third victim and another convicted rapist. Older, yes, and a lot longer out of prison, but still a sex offender. Still a perv. One for whom very few people, least of all those trying to catch his killer, seemed to be mourning.

And still that ambivalence, if Thorne was honest, on *his* part as well . . .

Seems to me that whoever killed Remfry did everyone a favor . . .

There will be people asking whether or not we should be grateful . . .

It's not like he's chopping up old ladies, is it?

Thorne found it hard to argue with the sentiments, but as someone who'd spent his entire adult life if not always catching killers, then at least believing that what they did was wrong, he had to try to stay out of it.

With some cases it was easy. Hate the killer, love the victim. Thorne would never forget the months he'd spent hunting a man who killed women while *trying* to put them into comas, into a state of living death. Or his last big one: tracking down a pair of killers, one a manipulative psychopath, the other who killed because he was told to . . .

Then there were the cases where it wasn't quite so clear-cut, where sympathies were not so easily divvied up: the wife, driven to murder an abusive husband; the armed robber, knocked off for squealing on his workmates; the drug dealer, carved up by a rival . . .

Then there was this case.

When Thorne swung his legs onto the floor and stood up, Elvis jumped off and skulked away, grumbling, toward the kitchen. Thorne followed her. He dropped his empties into the bin, and for half a minute he stared into the fridge for no particular reason.

He walked into the bedroom, gathered up his duvet and pillow from the bottom of the wardrobe.

Thorne despised rapists. He also despised murderers. To go into which he despised more or less was not going to help anybody.

Eve and Denise had finished the best part of a bottle of red wine each.

The laughter had been getting louder, and the language a good deal more earthy ever since the pizzas had been finished and the second bottle of red opened . . .

"Fuck him if he's not interested," Denise said.

Eve swirled the wine around in her glass, stared through it. "That's the thing, though. He *is* interested, definitely."

"Oh, you can tell, can you?"

"It wasn't hard . . ."

Denise gave a lascivious grin. "Well, *that* usually means they aren't interested at all."

Eve almost spat her wine across the table. When she'd finished laughing, she stood and began gathering up the pizza boxes. "I don't know what he's up to. I'm not sure *he* knows what he's up to . . ."

Denise reached over, grabbed a last piece of cold pizza crust before the box got taken away. "Maybe he's a schizo, like some of these nutters he tries to catch."

"Maybe . . ."

"Does he talk about his work much? About the cases he's working on?"

Eve was folding the pizza boxes in half, crushing them down into the bin. She shrugged. "Not really."

"Oh, come on, he must say something, surely?"

"We got into it a couple of weeks ago, this weird murder case." Eve stepped across to the sink and began washing her hands. "We ended up sort of arguing about it and he hasn't really mentioned it since."

"Right. Except when he's using it as an excuse?"

"Maybe I'm being paranoid about that . . ."

Denise poured what was left in the bottle into her glass. She held the empty bottle aloft triumphantly. The bell rang.

"That'll be Ben," Denise said. "He had to stay late, get an edit finished." She took a hearty mouthful of wine and all but skipped from the room.

Eve listened to her flatmate's feet as they hammered down the stairs. She heard the squeal when the door was opened, the low moans as Ben stepped in and they embraced on the doorstep . . .

She made a quick decision to get off to bed before Ben came up. She would read for a while and try not to think too much about Tom Thorne, about whether he might ring the next day. She moved out into the hall, shouting down the stairs to Denise and Ben as she opened her bedroom door.

"I'm going to turn in, I think. See you in the morning . . ."

The last thing she wanted to watch was those two all over each other.

The sun was streaming in through two vast windows at the far end of the narrow room, and yet the light was somehow cold, as if it were bouncing off the refrigerated doors and steel instruments of an autopsy suite.

Blinding white light, but Thorne knew very well that it was the middle of the night.

He wore pajamas, with his brown leather jacket over

the top. He moved quickly around the room, his steps
jaunty, bouncing in time to a tune he could hear but not
quite place.

The three beds were equidistant from one another,
lined up precisely. The metal bedsteads made them look
a little like hospital cots, but they were bigger, more
comfortable. They were identical, each with thick pillows, a clean white cotton sheet, and a body.

Thorne moved to the end of the first bed, wrapped his
hands around the metal rail, and peered down at Douglas Remfry. The arse poking into the air, the face buried
in the sheet. He began to shake the bed, rattling the
frame, shouting over the noise of it. He shook and shook
and shouted, filled with contempt for who this man had
once been, for what he had done.

"Come on, then, up you get, you idle bastard. There's
women out there begging for it. Up and at 'em . . ."

And as the body shook on the bed, the skin began to
slip off until it lay on the sheet, gathered about the bare
bones like dirty tights, rolled down around a pair of ankles.

Thorne laughed and pointed at what remained, at the
rapist's skin and skeleton, sloughed away and contorted.
"For heaven's sake, Lazybones, are you ever going to get
up out of that bed?"

He trotted across to the second bed, shook the flesh
from Ian Welch's bones. All the time taking the piss.
Feeling nothing for these dead men. For these lumps . . .

At Howard Southern's bed, Thorne paused and
watched as the bed began to vibrate, something passing
noisily beneath the floor. A shadow arced across the vast
windows and Thorne looked up. He watched the movement, back and forth, until the smell hit him.

He laughed when he looked back at the beds, and saw
what the bodies had become. What they had actually

been all the time. Thorne could only presume that each had been expertly expelled onto the center of his bed, from the body dangling at the end of a rope, high above them.

As soon as Thorne awoke, the dream began to slide away from him, the images sucked back into the darkness until only the feelings remained. Scorn and anger and shame.

It was a little after two-thirty in the morning.

When even the feelings had faded, there were only thoughts of the woman whose defilement and death long before had, it seemed, caused everything. Now she moved through his case as surely as if she were still corporeal and Thorne was ready to embrace her.

She was nearly thirty years dead, and so was her killer, but that didn't matter.

In Jane Foley, Thorne had finally got a victim he could care about.

NINETEEN

It was Monday morning. Seven weeks to the day since the body of Douglas Remfry had been found. More than twenty-five years since Jane Foley had been raped and subsequently battered to death. Thorne was still trying to work out the connection between the two murders. He hoped that the woman sitting opposite him might be able to help . . .

Despite its somewhat shady reputation, and the tired old jokes about the IQs and sexual habits of its women-folk, Essex was full of surprises. As the oldest recorded town in the country and the capital of Roman Britain, Colchester had more history than most places. Still, the last thing Thorne expected from a municipal building in the middle of town was what looked like a small stately home on its own grounds.

The area office for the Adoption and Fostering Service was somewhat run-down, admittedly, but amazing nonetheless. Thorne had thought that all the period or faux-period properties in the area had been snapped up by footballers and armed robbers a long time ago. The surprise was evidently clear in his face as he and Holland were greeted by the service manager and shown into a large office with dark oak paneling all around and heavy wooden beams crisscrossing an ornate ceiling above.

"This was originally the coach house. I know it looks nice, but trust me, it's a bastard to work in . . ." Joanne

Lesser was a light-skinned black woman in her midthirties, tall and—so Thorne thought—a little on the thin side. Her hair was straight and lacquered, the brows heavy, framing a face that was severe until it broke into a smile. Then it was all too easy to picture her laughing at a dirty joke in spite of herself, or tipsy at the Christmas party.

"The place is falling to pieces, basically," she said. "We can only put so much weight on the floors, the filing cabinets have to go against certain walls, and nothing's level. You can find your chair rolling from one side of the office to the other, if you're not careful . . ."

Thorne and Holland smiled politely, unsure about whether or not she'd finished. After a few seconds, she shrugged and raised an eyebrow to indicate that *she* was waiting for *them*.

The only sound in the room came from a noisy metal fan that looked like it might have been an antique itself. At the other end of the desk, an entire army of trolls, action figures, and plush toys was lined up across the top edge of a grimy, beige computer.

"You spoke to DCI Brigstocke on the phone," Thorne said. He raised his voice a little to make himself clearly heard above the fan. "Mark and Sarah Foley?"

Lesser reached for a piece of paper on her desk and studied it.

"Nineteen seventy-six," Holland added, trying to move things along.

"Right, well, I'm sure you weren't expecting it to be straightforward . . ." She looked up and across at them, smiling. Thorne couldn't quite manage one in return. "All I can really tell you with any certainty is that they were never fostered by anybody who is still registered with us as an active carer."

Holland shrugged. "I suppose it *would* have been too much to hope for . . ."

"Right," Thorne said. He had been hoping nevertheless.

"We're talking over twenty-five years ago," Lesser said. "It's possible that the people who fostered them *are* still active, but have moved to another area."

"How do we check that?" Thorne said.

She shook her head. "Not a clue. It's pretty unlikely anyway, I'm just thinking aloud, really . . ."

Thorne could feel a headache starting to build. He shuffled his chair a little closer to the desk, pointed to the fan. "I'm sorry, could we . . . ?"

She leaned across and switched the fan off.

"Thanks," Thorne said. "We'll try to get through this as fast as we can. Why was what you told us the only thing you could tell us 'with any certainty'?"

"Because the only files I have access to here are current. Those are the ones concerned with active carers."

"That's the stuff on computer?"

She snorted. "It wasn't until ten years ago that things even started being *typed,* and even now there's still a load of stuff that's handwritten. It's not just the building that's past it . . ."

Thorne blinked slowly. It was just his luck to need help from an organization whose systems were even more fucked up than the ones he worked with every day.

"But there *are* records, in one form or another, that go back further . . ."

"In one form or another, I suppose so. God knows what state they'll be in if you manage to lay your hands on them, a few scribbled pages nearly thirty years old. Hang on, some are on microfiche, I think . . ."

Thorne tried not to sound too impatient. "There are records, though?"

"Dead files . . ."

"Right, and the dead files, the files that would have the records from the midseventies, will be stored somewhere?"

"Yeah, they should be in Chelmsford, at County Hall. The law says we have to keep them."

Holland muttered. "Data Protection Act . . ."

"That's it. Everybody who's received a service from us has a right to see their records, to have access. Some people wait years. They come back in their forties or fifties, looking for details on people who fostered them when they were kids."

"How come it takes them so long?" Holland said.

"Maybe it's the distance that makes them appreciate it. At the time, when they're kids, it can be a bit traumatic . . ."

Thorne thought about Mark and Sarah Foley. Anything they went through as foster children could not possibly have been more traumatic than what had happened before. "What do you tell them?" he asked. "These people that come looking."

"Good luck." She leaned back on her chair, took the material of her blouse between thumb and forefinger, and pulled it from her skin. She flapped it back and forth, blew down onto her chest. "We've got the records, but I couldn't really tell you where. Like I said, they *should* be over at County Hall, but laying your hands on them is another matter."

Joanne Lesser smiled a "nothing I can do" smile and Thorne remembered a similar moment: he and Holland sitting in almost identical positions in Tracy Lenahan's office at Derby Prison. It seemed like a long time back. A few deaths ago . . .

Thorne rolled his head around on his neck. "I know that we're talking about stuff that dates back a long way and you've made it clear that the system's not all it should be, but surely there's some sort of central storage place . . . ?"

"Sorry, I thought I'd explained. We only have the active files because each time you move, each time the office relocates, you leave the dead files behind. Now, in theory, they should get taken back to County Hall and, like you say, stored somewhere. In reality, stuff just gets chucked in boxes. It goes missing . . ."

"Why would you move?"

"Council buildings are interchangeable. Somebody could decide tomorrow that this should be the new headquarters for the DSS or Refuse Collection. Unless the council renews the lease, this place might be a hotel in a couple of years."

"Right. So, have you moved often?"

"I've only been doing this ten years and we've moved three—no, four—times since I started." Thorne had to fight quite hard to stop himself from swearing or kicking a hole in the front of the desk. "It gets worse. I know that some stuff got destroyed a couple of years ago when part of the archive was flooded . . ."

Thorne and Holland exchanged a glance. They were catching every red light . . .

"What about school records?" Lesser said. "You might have more luck . . ."

Holland glanced down at his notebook. "They attended local primary and secondary schools until 1984, after which there's no record of them."

She considered this. "Are you sure they're still alive?"

"We're not really sure about anything," Thorne said. In truth, the idea that Mark and Sarah Foley might be dead was something that had been only briefly considered. It had even been suggested that the suicide of Dennis Foley might have been a second murder made to *look* like a suicide. That whoever had been responsible might have wanted the children dead, too. Half an hour spent looking at the files on the original case, at the postmortem report on Dennis Foley, had soon put an end to that clever theory.

"This is probably clutching at straws," Holland said,

"but I don't suppose there's anybody still working here, in your department, who was around back in 1976?"

"Sorry. Staff tend to move around as often as the offices do."

"A bit like footballers," Holland said.

"I wish we got paid as much." Thorne thought the smile she gave Holland was of an altogether different sort from the one she'd given him.

Thorne shifted on his chair. It was enough to drag Holland's eye from Joanne Lesser back to him. Time to go.

"Right, well, thanks . . ."

"It's a long way back," she said.

Holland reached for his jacket. "There shouldn't be too much traffic at this time of the day . . ."

"No, I meant you're going back a long way. To look for these people, for Mark and Sarah Foley. I mean, what about National Insurance? Vehicle Licensing? Sorry, I don't want to teach my grandmother to suck eggs, but—"

"It's okay," Thorne said.

She leaned forward in her chair. "Why do you want to find them?"

Holland stuffed his notebook away. "I'm sorry, but we can't really—"

Thorne cut him off. What did it matter? "They were fostered after their parents died. Their father killed their mother and then himself. The children discovered the bodies." Lesser's lower jaw sagged a little. "We think that what happened back then is connected with a series of murders that we're investigating now."

"A *series*?" She spoke it like it was a magic word.

"Yes."

"They're connected to it, you mean? Mark and Sarah Foley?"

Thorne could see a flush developing at the top of her

chest. Her voice was suddenly a little higher. She was excited.

Thorne stood up and began pulling on his leather jacket. "Listen, Joanne, we'll be sending someone down to County Hall to start looking for these records. I'm sure you're busy, but we'd be very grateful if you could give him as much help as you can . . ."

She rolled her chair back and stood, too. "You don't need to send anyone. I'd be happy to do it for you. I mean, yes, I *am* pretty busy, but I can find the time." The flush had moved up to the base of her throat. "I'll probably be quicker on my own, to be honest. You know, without somebody else getting in the way . . ."

Thorne thought about her offer. It sounded like such a wild-goose chase that he'd probably only be wasting an officer anyway. He nodded. "Thanks."

At the door, while Holland took down Lesser's phone number and handed her a card, Thorne stared at the posters on the wall next to the door. One image in particular caught his eye: a girl and a boy, hand in hand, staring straight at the camera, their moist round eyes begging. They were much younger than Mark and Sarah Foley would have been, no bigger than toddlers, and they were almost certainly actors. Still, their faces held Thorne's attention . . .

He tensed a little when he felt Lesser's hand on his arm.

"It's funny," she said, "to think that people can just slip through the net like that, isn't it?"

Thorne nodded, thinking that some people were a lot more slippery than others.

Driving back through the town center, Holland talked about Joanne Lesser. He joked about the sort of woman who looked like she was afraid of her own shadow and then went home and lay in the bath, one hand holding some gruesome true-crime book while the other . . .

Thorne wasn't paying too much attention. He felt as though someone had poured concrete in through his ears. The thoughts floundered in his head, sticky and dismal, while his face, as always, was easy to read.

"Like she said, we *were* going a long way back," Holland said. "Probably wasting our time. We'll find them somewhere else . . ."

Thorne grunted. Holland was right, but all the same, he had been counting on something a bit more positive.

Holland made for the motorway, heading out of town along the line of the Roman wall. From here at St. Mary's of the Wall, during the English Civil War, a vast Royalist cannon named Humpty Dumpty was said to have fallen, later to be immortalized in the children's nursery rhyme. They passed the ancient entrance to the town, through which Claudius, the invading emperor, had once ridden into Colchester on the back of an elephant. Thorne found it strange that two thousand years later, whether by accident or design, the far more recent history of ordinary people could be so impenetrable.

"I'm betting Miss Marple back there's already scrounging through her dead files," Holland said. He laughed, and Thorne dredged up something that might have been a smile, if one half of his face had been paralyzed. "What d'you reckon?"

Thorne reckoned that he'd been right about chasing leads. This one had sounded solid, like it wasn't going away. Now it had put on a burst of speed and Thorne felt as if he could do nothing but watch it disappear into the distance.

The slice of white bread in Peter Foley's hand was blackened with dabs of newsprint from his fingers. He looked at his hands. There were still scabs on a couple of the knuckles, and oil beneath his fingernails from where he'd spent the morning tinkering with his motorbike. He used the bread to mop up the last of his gravy, then picked up his mug of tea and leaned back against the red plastic banquette.

He stared out of the café window and watched the cars drift by. He thought about his family. The dead and the disappeared.

Bumming around . . .

That's what he'd told those fuckers when they'd asked what he was doing back when it had happened, and it was pretty much all he'd done since as well. Holding down a job, once he'd got back into the swing of things, had become difficult. He'd developed a tendency to take things the wrong way, to react badly to a tasteless comment or a funny look. He couldn't say for sure that what had happened was responsible. He might always have been destined to be a shiftless loser with a tendency toward casual violence, but what the fuck, it was comforting to have something to blame.

To have some*body* to blame.

He should have moved away from the area. There was always some old dear with an opinion, or a pair of young mums whispering and shielding their children. Always some interfering fucker, willing to tell any woman he got close to all about his happy family. People had good memories. Not as good as his, though . . .

He remembered the argument he'd had with Den a couple of days before it had happened. He'd wanted to come over, had asked Den why nobody had seen Jane for a while, if everything was all right. Den had lost it and told him to mind his own business, said that he knew very well what was going on. He remembered his brother's face, the trembling around the mouth as he'd accused him of fancying Jane, all but suggesting they'd been screwing behind his back. He remembered the guilt he'd felt, then and afterward, because he *did* fancy Jane and always had.

And he remembered the faces of the children, the last time he'd seen them, before that cow from the social services had driven them away. Sarah had been quiet, she'd probably not really understood what was going on, but the boy's face, *Mark's* face, pressed against the back window of that car, had been streaked with snot and tears.

He slid out of the booth, grabbed his paper, and strolled across to the counter to pay for his lunch.

He thought about his nephew and his niece and hoped that they were together somewhere a long way away. A place where nobody could ever find them and fuck their new lives up.

The afternoon stretched ahead. He would go back and lie down and wait for it to get dark. Then he would put some metal on and drink. He would empty can after can, until the noise inside his head was quieter than the screech and the smash of the music that would be filling his bedroom.

When they got back to Becke House, Thorne filled Kitson and Brigstocke in on how things had gone in Colchester. They conferred about progress on the other flank of the operation. The Southern killing had plenty in common with those that had gone before: the cause of death; the layout of the murder scene; the wreath ordered in person from an out-of-hours floristry service—this time delivered as far as the hotel-room doorway, then hurriedly dropped after one look at the state of its recipient.

But there were plenty of differences, too. There were new avenues that had to be explored . . .

Southern had been released from prison more than ten years previously. He hadn't been selected in the same way as the previous victims, and he was certainly approached differently. Unlike Remfry or Welch, he had a whole life that had to be sifted through if they were going to find out just how the killer had made himself part of it. Interviews, running into many hundreds, were still being conducted with anyone who had contact with Southern: the people he worked with; the friends he drank with; the members of the gym he worked out at; the girlfriend he'd recently broken up with . . .

These people who had been part of his new life would, for the most part, have had no idea that Howard Southern had once served time in prison. Even if he'd told any of them—and with some people it *might* have gained him kudos or a round of drinks—chances are he wouldn't have told them what for.

Unfortunately for him, someone had found out *exactly* what Howard Southern had once done, and had killed him for it.

In his office, Thorne went through his mail. As always, it was mostly junk. Pointless memos, press releases, crime statistics, new initiative outlines. He glanced through the monthly Police Federation newsletter, at a story about a local force recording themselves whistling the theme tunes to a host of well-known police TV shows. These recordings were being broadcast in some of the rougher housing developments and shopping centers in an effort to deter street criminals.

When Thorne had finished laughing, he checked his messages. There'd already been a call from Joanne Lesser to say that she'd start checking the records the following morning, and that some files had apparently been moved from County Hall to a new storage facility on an industrial estate just outside Chelmsford. The next one was from Chris Barratt at Kentish Town. There was nothing from Eve . . .

Thorne picked up the phone, wondering at the sharp

twinge of disappointment he felt. He marveled, as he dialed, at his seemingly endless capacity for indecision, for fucking off . . .

"About bloody time, too," he said.

"Calm down," Barratt said. "We haven't got him yet. But we know exactly who he is. We'll pull him first thing tomorrow morning."

"How did you find him?"

"Are you listening? This is funny as fuck . . ."

"Go on . . ."

"He'd got rid of the stereo, right? Probably sold it the same day, got himself blitzed on the proceeds. Then he has a problem . . ."

"Which is?"

"Your taste in music."

"Eh?"

"The idiot's had to make himself a bit conspicuous in the end. We got the nod eventually because by all accounts he's spent the last four weeks trying to get rid of your bloody CD collection."

"What?" Thorne's relief was all but canceled out by his outrage . . .

By now, Barratt was making no attempt to hide his enjoyment. "Couldn't *pay* anybody to take 'em off his hands, by all accounts. Been dragging them round every market and secondhand place in London . . ."

"Enjoy yourself, Chris. As long as I get them all back."

"Listen, if I was you, when you *do* get them back, why don't you stick a few by the window, where people can see them. You know, as a deterrent . . ."

"I'm not listening. Just call me when you've arrested him, all right?"

"Fine . . ."

"And I'll want five minutes."

"No problem. I'm here all day . . ."

"Not with you, smart-arse. With *him* . . ."

TWENTY

He'd seen comedians on TV talking about how women could hold a hundred thoughts in their heads at one time and juggle an assortment of tasks, while men were incapable of doing even two things at once. Masturbating and maneuvering a mouse was about as much as a man could manage.

Even though he knew it was nonsense, he still found the joke funny. Even as he sat working *and* planning the next killing . . .

Multitasking was something of a specialty, had to be, and even though the slightly more socially unacceptable stuff he did was the more exciting, he actually enjoyed the day job, too. He took pride in what he did. Of course he couldn't have done the other things without it.

The next killing . . .

He didn't know for certain yet if the next would also be the last, but in a lot of ways it made sense. It would round things off very nicely. This one would be different in many ways, of course, more symbolic than the others, but certainly no less enjoyable for it.

A date had yet to be set, but that was the final detail. The victim had been selected weeks ago. In fact, he'd pretty much selected himself.

Talk about being in the wrong place at the wrong time . . .

* * *

Thorne thought about the Restorative Justice Conference he'd sat through weeks earlier. He remembered Darren Ellis and the squeak of his shiny white training shoes. He pictured the face of the old man who'd been sitting more or less where he was now . . .

Opposite him, in the Interview Room at Kentish Town station, sat a boy who Thorne knew to be seventeen, but apart from the unexcited eyes, the rest of him might have belonged to any skinny fourteen-year-old. Noel Mullen had been stealing cars to order while others his age had been pinching chocolate bars from the nearest sweets shop. By the time his contemporaries were sneaking into pubs and feeling up girls, Noel had already acquired a decent-size drug habit and a growing reputation with the police in Northwest London. There was a room that should have had his name on the door, in the young offenders' institute that at one time had welcomed both his elder brothers.

He still looked as if his mum should be washing his underpants and pouring the milk on his Rice Krispies . . .

"Why did you shit in my bed?" Thorne said.

The boy did a pretty good job of looking unutterably bored, but there was a jerkiness to the seemingly casual roll of the head, a tremor at the ends of the fingers. Thorne wondered how long it had been since he'd had a fix. Maybe not since he'd failed to sell Thorne's CDs, to turn Cash into cash and score with it . . .

"Come on, Noel . . ."

"What's the fucking point? You going to put in a good word for me, are you? Speak up for me in court?"

"No chance."

"So why should I bother talking to you?"

Thorne leaned back and folded his arms. "Listen, break into places, Noel, by all means. It's your job, after all. Break in and trash them a bit if you have to, while you're looking for the decent stuff, the gear that's going to score you the best deal. I can understand that, I really can.

"Not just the posh places, either. Don't just do the rich bastards who you might, *might* have a legitimate reason to enjoy turning over. No, why not rob from your own? Dump on your doorstep. Do the ordinary working idiots who live in your own neighborhood, on the putrid estate that you've already done your best to make that little bit worse than it would have been anyway, by pissing in the lift and leaving dirty needles all over what passes for a playground. Smash your neighbor's door in and see how high a black-and-white TV can get you. Or some cheap jewelry. Fuck it, any *good* stuff, the widescreens and the DVDs, will have been rented anyway, so who cares? Stupid fuckers aren't insured, that's not your fault, is it . . . ?"

"Jesus, have you finished?"

"Do it and feel nothing. See something and take it, because all that matters is what you might be able to get for it. Feel fuck all . . ."

"You're wasting your—"

"*Feel fuck all.* Then see how you feel when one day one of your mates needs some cash and puts his foot through your mother's window. Size-nine Nikes tramping around your mum's living room and going through her drawers. And maybe your mate's a little bit wired, a little bit over the edge, and maybe your mother's lying there in bed at the time—"

"It's because you're a copper."

Thorne stopped, took a breath, and waited.

"That's why I took a shit on your bed, all right?"

It made sense. Thorne wasn't so poor a detective that he hadn't considered the possibility that his flat had been targeted. That was the problem with Neighborhood Watch. You didn't always know which neighbors were watching . . .

"How did you know?" Thorne asked.

"I didn't, not before I got in there. There was a photo that had fallen down behind one of your speakers. You in your fucking uniform . . ."

Mullen leaned back and folded his arms as Thorne had done. He looked at him as he might look at a stereo or a VCR, evaluating it, working out whether it was worth taking.

"Your hair was darker then," Mullen said. "And you weren't such a fat cunt."

Thorne nodded. He remembered the photo, had wondered where it had gone. It wasn't a picture he was hugely fond of, but still, Mullen's response when he'd seen it a few weeks earlier had been a bit harsh.

"So you take one look at an old photo and decide to use my bed as a crapper, that about right?"

Mullen grinned, starting to enjoy himself. His teeth were browning where they met the gums. "Yeah, more or less . . ."

"You cocky little strip of piss . . ."

Thorne's movement, and the scrape of his chair across the floor, caused Mullen to jerk back and stiffen, momentarily defensive. He appeared to recover his confidence just as quickly.

"Look, it was nothing personal."

"And it won't be personal when I come round there, knock you over, and shit in your mouth, fair enough? I'm a copper and you're a burglar. Right, Noel? Clearly there's certain things we *have* to do . . ."

Mullen's expression was closer to pity than boredom. "You're not going to do anything."

Other than strike a few poses to try to make himself feel better, there was nothing that Thorne *could* do. He wondered if the old man he'd seen sitting opposite Darren Ellis had felt as useless.

"Are you sorry, Noel?"

"Am I what?"

"Sorry. Are you sorry?"

"Yeah. I'm sorry I got fucking caught."

Thorne's smile was genuine. A certain warped faith had been restored by Mullen's honesty. Perhaps, faced with a few years' hard time, he would learn a trick or two, learn how to turn it on in the same way that Darren Ellis had. For now, there was something heartening about Mullen's answer. Something reassuring about the fact that he really and truly didn't give a damn.

There was a moment when Thorne almost liked him.

The moment passed, and for a minute and more, Thorne stared into Mullen's unexcited eyes until the boy jumped up, moved quickly across the room, and began banging on the door.

Stone took the call, held the receiver out toward Holland. "For you . . ."

As Holland walked across their small office, Stone put his hand over the receiver. "She sounds sexy as well."

Holland said nothing and took the phone. He'd pretty much learned to put up with Stone's arrogance, but he still got impatient with the smirks and the shrugs and the knowing looks that actually knew fuck all.

Mind you, these days he got impatient with a lot of things.

"DC Holland."

"This is Joanne Lesser . . ."

"Oh, hello, Joanne." Holland looked up to see Stone rolling his eyes and mouthing her name. Holland casually stuck up a finger.

"No luck on the actual files yet," she said. "I did leave a message yesterday. About some of them being moved?"

"Okay. I didn't see that, but—"

"Don't worry, I'm still working on it. I found out something else, though."

"Right . . ." Holland picked up a pen, began to doodle as he listened.

"A colleague on the team here reckons that the old index cards, from years back, are all piled up down in our cellar. I'll try and dig them out, presuming they haven't all gone rotten . . ."

"Do you think the cards for Mark and Sarah Foley will be down there?"

"That's why I rang. I don't see why not. There's probably not much information, they're just small cards, you know? The proper files are probably six inches thick . . ."

"What's on them?" Holland glanced up to see Stone staring across at him, interested.

"Usually just the basic stuff," Lesser said. "Case number, DOBs, placement dates, and names of carers . . ."

Holland stopped doodling, wrote down *names & dates*. "That sounds great, Joanne. Really helpful . . ."

"I'll call you when I've got the information then, shall I?"

"Can you e-mail it? Probably safer . . ."

When he thanked her again for her trouble, he could almost *hear* the blushing.

"Sounded good," Stone said after Holland had hung up.

"Reckons she can get us a list of all the kids' foster parents," Holland explained. "The dates they were placed in care . . ."

Stone looked thoughtful. "Is she going to carry on looking for the full files?"

"Probably no stopping her, but I reckon these names and dates are as much as we're going to need."

"Let me know when you get them," Stone said. "I'll give you a hand on it."

Holland leaned back, stretched. "Shouldn't be much to do. I think I can manage it on my own . . ."

"Please yourself." Stone looked back to his computer screen, began to type.

Holland knew that it had been a fairly petty moment of self-assertion. More so, considering that he didn't really consider it to be a worthwhile line of inquiry in the first place. Thorne had got a bee in his bonnet about it, so Holland would do what needed doing, but he couldn't help thinking that they were almost certainly wasting their time.

He didn't see how knowing where Mark and Sarah Foley had been twenty-five years ago was going to help them find out where they were now.

Thorne stepped out of the tube station onto Kentish Town Road. He turned for home, walking down in the direction of Camden, and the police station in which he'd encountered Noel Mullen nearly twelve hours before.

He thought about what the boy had said . . .

I'm sorry I got fucking caught.

. . . and wondered if he'd ever make the killer of Remfry, Welch, Southern, and Charlie Dodd sorry. He had a feeling that if he *did* catch him, it would be just about the only thing the killer *would* be sorry about.

Thorne was vacillating, standing on the pavement outside the Bengal Lancer, when his phone beeped. He listened to the message, then pressed the button to call Eve straight back.

The apology wasn't the first thing he said, but it was pretty close.

"I'm sorry . . ."

"For what?"

"Lots of things. Not calling, for starters."

"I know you've been busy."

The owner of the restaurant, a man who knew Thorne very well, saw him through the window. He started waving, beckoning him inside. Thorne waved back, mouthing and pointing at the phone.

"Where are you?" Eve asked.

"Just heading home, trying to decide what to do about dinner."

"Stressful day?"

Maybe she'd heard it in his voice. He laughed. "I'm thinking about chucking it all in, becoming a florist."

"Bloom and Thorne sounds good . . ."

"Actually, no, I don't think I could stand the early mornings."

"You lazy bastard . . ."

And the sights, the sounds, the *smells* of Thorne's dream came straight back to him. He shivered, though it was warm enough to be walking around with his jacket thrown across his arm . . .

"Tom?"

"Sorry . . ." He blinked the pictures away. "You said something about Saturday. In your message . . ."

"I know you're probably working late."

"No, I'm not, for once. I'm signed out for most of the day. Unless something comes up." *An urgent meeting, a new lead, another body.* "So, should be fine . . ."

"It's not a big deal, but it's Denise's birthday, so her and me and Ben are going to be in the pub Saturday night. That's it, really. Just come along if you fancy it."

"What, a double date?"

"No. I just thought you might prefer it. No pressure . . ."

"Pressure?"

"Well, you have been sort of . . . blowing hot and cold . . ."

"Sorry . . ."

There was a pause. Thorne caught sight of the owner again, throwing up his hands. He heard Eve move the receiver from one ear to the other.

"Look, I'm sorry, too," she said. "I didn't want to get into this on the phone. Let's just have a drink on Saturday. Take it from there."

"That sounds good. I'll have something to show you as well."

Thorne enjoyed listening to the laugh that he hadn't heard in a while. He pictured the gap in the teeth. "Cut out the dirty talk," she said. "And go and get something to eat . . ."

A few minutes later, ten minutes since he'd first arrived outside the restaurant, and Thorne was still trying to decide what to do. There was stuff in the fridge he could eat. *Should* eat . . .

He pushed open the door, the smell of the Indian food just too good to resist. His friend, the owner, had already opened a bottle of Kingfisher.

TWENTY-ONE

"Who are you rooting for this afternoon then, Dave?"

Holland looked up from his desk to see DS Sam Karim beaming down at him. "Sorry . . . ?"

"The Charity Shield. Who d'you want to win it?"

Holland nodded. The traditional game on the eve of the season proper. Last year's FA Cup winners versus the Premiership champions.

"Whichever team isn't Manchester United," Holland said.

"Suit yourself, mate, we'll still win it easily. I fancy us for the league again as well."

"I don't understand, Sam. You're from Hounslow, aren't you?"

Karim wandered away, still smiling. "You're just jealous . . ."

Holland picked up the phone again and dialed. He didn't actually care one way or the other about football. Virtually everything he knew or understood about the game had been encapsulated in that fifteen-second conversation.

The line was still engaged. He hung up and looked back at his notes. Since Joanne Lesser had e-mailed the information across the day before, Holland had been working through the list of names pretty solidly. He was getting there, but it had been frustrating. Despite his bravado with Andy Stone, simply getting hold of people was sometimes tricky, even if the people themselves had no reason whatsoever to make it difficult.

The Foley children had spent the six months after the death of their parents in short-term foster care. Then, in January 1977, they'd begun the first of half a dozen long-term placements. There were still two sets of foster parents Holland had yet to speak to, but from the conversations he'd already had, a pattern had emerged. In almost every instance, the children had appeared to settle quite quickly, but had gradually become sullen and disruptive, especially in families where there were existing children. Those Holland spoke to admitted that it had been difficult, but also thought that it was understandable, considering what the children had been through. Mark and Sarah were basically nice kids, but had withdrawn, spending more and more time alone, trying to shut out everybody around them . . .

It was all interesting enough, but Holland was still not convinced that any of it would prove to be of any use. He had not yet spoken to the most recent set of foster parents, and that might at least turn up *something* they could work with. Brigstocke was entertaining the idea of getting photos of the Foley children, digitally aging them, and circulating the resulting images. It seemed a decent enough idea. The Nobles, who had cared for the children up to the beginning of 1984, were due back from Majorca later that day, and were likely to have the most recent pictures . . .

Holland reached for the phone. The number for the Lloyds, the third set of foster parents, was still busy. The instant he put the phone down, it began to ring.

It was Thorne.

"Fancy a drink tonight?" he said.

"Why not?" As soon as the words came out of his

mouth, Holland knew *exactly* why not, as he felt instantly guilty. He knew, on a Saturday night especially, he should talk to Sophie first. He also knew very well that she would smile and say she didn't mind. "Where are we going?"

"Bar in Hackney," Thorne said.

Holland could picture himself picking up his jacket and turning for the door, catching a glimpse as the film of tears formed in a moment across Sophie's eyes. He could already hear the bang of the door as he pulled it shut behind him, and feel each heavy step down toward the street like a low punch.

"What time?" Holland said.

"About half eight. Why don't I pick you up?"

"Eh? Kentish Town to the Elephant and then back up to Hackney? That's miles out of your way . . ."

"I don't mind."

"I'll just get the tube up to Bethnal Green and walk."

"No, it's fine, really . . ."

"What's this bar called? I'll meet you there."

Thorne's tone of voice told him that there was little point in arguing. "I'll be round at eight-thirty, Dave . . ."

Thorne had rung the bell, then walked back to strike the appropriate pose. By the time Holland emerged from his flat, Thorne was leaning on the car, grinning, like some sixties motor-show model gone very much to seed.

"Right," Holland said. "So the insurance money came through, then?"

"Not yet, but it *will*. I borrowed a bit from the bank." Holland stood, hands in pockets, looking extremely unsure. "It's a BMW," Thorne added, just in case Holland was in any doubt.

"It's a very *old* BMW . . ."

"It's a classic. This is a three-liter CSi. These are vintage cars, mate."

"It's yellow."

"It's *pulsar* yellow."

"Pardon me." Holland began a slow walk around the car. To Thorne, he looked like he was examining a freshly discovered corpse.

Thorne pointed in through the car window. "It's got leather seats . . ."

Holland was at the back of the car. He looked at the registration plate. "*P?* When's that . . . ?"

"There's a CD player mounted in the boot. Holds ten CDs . . ."

"What year is it?"

Thorne knew there was no way to make it sound good. "Nineteen seventy-five . . ."

Holland laughed. "Christ, it's almost as old as I am."

"There's only fifty-eight thousand miles on it . . ."

"You've gone mental. Did you have it checked for rust?"

"Yeah, I had a look. Seems fine . . ."

"Underneath, I mean. Did you get it jacked up?"

"It was restored four years ago and the bloke told me it's only done ten thousand miles since the engine was rebuilt."

"How much did you pay for it?"

"The clutch is virtually brand-new . . . or it might be the gearbox. One of them's new, anyway . . ."

"Five grand?" Thorne said nothing. "More? Bloody hell, there's no way you'll get anywhere near that for the Mondeo . . ."

"It's a present, all right? I've got fuck all else to spend money on."

"You don't know anything about old cars. You could have got something nearly new for the same money, something nice like that hire car you had. This'll cost you a fortune in the long run . . ."

"It's gorgeous, though, don't you think?" Thorne took

a tissue from his pocket and began polishing the badge on the car's bonnet.

Holland shrugged, opened the car door. "Doesn't matter when you're sitting on the hard shoulder, does it?"

Thorne stomped sulkily round to the driver's side of the car. "I've a good mind to make you *walk* to fucking Hackney now. Miserable bastard . . ."

"I'm just trying to be practical. What happens when the big end goes on the way to a murder scene?"

Thorne dropped down into the leather seat, turned to Holland, who was sinking into his. "Next time, I'll ask Trevor Jesmond if he fancies a drink . . ."

An hour later, Thorne's mood had improved significantly. Once the introductions had been made, Eve and the others had rushed straight out to look at the car and everyone agreed that it was gorgeous. It didn't stop Holland from looking for an ally a little later on while the girls were getting a round in.

"Come on, Ben, wouldn't you have gone for something a bit newer?"

"Sorry, I think it's great," Jameson said. "I've got a BMW myself . . ."

Thorne held his bottle up in salute, threw Holland a sarcastic smile. "See?"

"Tom says you make films."

"Corporate videos, mostly."

"Well, you must be doing pretty well. BMW . . ."

"It's okay, but I'm trying to get something of my own off the ground. Something I've written . . ."

Holland nodded. "That's hard, I suppose?"

"It's just a question of money. I need to do a bit more top-end work for Sony or Deutsche Bank and make a few less crappy training videos."

"What are you doing at the moment?" Thorne said.

Jameson took a swig from a bottle of Budvar. "Oh, it's riveting stuff right now. An ongoing local authority gig and some adverts for QVC."

Thorne grabbed some crisps from an open bag in front of him. "Oh, so they're your fault, are they?"

"Sorry," Jameson said, smiling, holding up his hands.

Holland smirked at Thorne. "I didn't have you down as a fan of the shopping channel."

"I have cable TV for the football, obviously." Thorne shoved the crisps into his mouth, wiped his fingers. "But when I've got nothing better to do late at night, I like to watch some failed actor with an orange face try and sell me cleaning equipment, yes."

The three sat in silence for a while. Thorne looked out of the window and across to where he'd parked the car. Holland sipped his pint, nodded his head to the low-level Coldplay track, while Jameson looked eagerly across to where Denise and Eve were standing at the bar.

The car was safe and still looking good. Thorne turned back and stared around. It was a newish but already quietly trendy gastro-pub. Eve had said there was a decent restaurant in a room out the back, but Thorne was happy enough where they were, with Belgian lager on draft and olives in bowls on the bar. They sat in a corner, around a scarred, refectory-type table in an assortment of chairs. Thorne had bagged a battered but comfortable leather armchair, and was doing his best to keep a similar one next to him free for Eve.

Though the place was popular, the bar itself was not crowded. Most people seemed eager to take advantage of the warm night and had gathered around the few tables on the pavement outside. The bar wasn't air-conditioned, but fans were spinning around overhead and the beer—as much as Thorne was allowing himself to drink—was cold.

The car was partly responsible for his mood, but Thorne was feeling as genuinely relaxed as he had for quite some while.

Eve and Denise came back with more beers and a bottle of wine and gently took the piss out of Holland, Thorne, and Jameson, for no better reason than that they were blokes. The men, for all their protestations and denials, enjoyed every minute of it, Thorne especially relishing the sort of attention he hadn't enjoyed for a very long time.

They talked about football and television and house prices. And inevitably, work.

"Come on, then, Dave," Denise said. "Tell us about this nutter you're after, the one who was on Eve's answering machine . . ."

Eve tried to interrupt. "Den . . ." She turned to Thorne. "Sorry . . ."

Thorne shrugged, not caring. "It's fine."

"Well, yes, he's a nutter," Holland said. "And yes, we're after him. *Still* after him."

"He sounds twisted," Jameson said. "Fascinating, though . . ."

Denise leaned forward toward Holland. "You know there's people like that around, 'course you do. When you've got a connection with one of them, though, however tenuous, it's freaky."

"Don't worry," Holland said. "You're not his type."

"I know. He hunts men, doesn't he? Men who've hurt women . . ."

There was a short but noticeably uncomfortable silence, which Denise broke as if it had never happened.

"People are always going to be fascinated by this sort of stuff, though, aren't they? It's a bit ghoulish, I suppose, but it's a damn sight more interesting than computers . . ."

Thorne took this as the cue to retell, for Holland's

benefit, his joke about what a PC "going down" meant in their line of work. The others laughed graciously, and Denise and Ben carried on chatting to Holland about the job. Whether they liked him or were just trying to make sure he didn't feel like a third wheel, it gave Thorne the chance to talk to Eve.

He bumped his chair up close to hers and leaned across.

"This was a good idea," he said.

"You weren't sure, though, were you?" She nodded toward Holland. "So you brought reinforcements along . . ."

"Are you pissed off?"

"I was an hour ago, yes. It's fine, though."

Thorne reached for his drink. "I just wanted to show him the car . . ."

Eve gave him a long look. It was clear that she didn't quite believe him. "So, apart from your case getting a bit more complicated, what happened between the night you came round for dinner and now?" Thorne glanced down, swilled the beer around in his glass, said nothing. "I thought you were really keen. You said as much."

"I was . . ."

"Even that night when you walked me back after we'd been in the pub you were a bit weird. Ever since you went to that wedding, in fact . . ."

Thorne bent his head and lowered his voice. "Look, I just go a bit mental when it looks like things might get serious. I don't know what I want, and I start to get—"

"Serious? We haven't even slept together yet . . ."

"That's exactly what I mean. It looked like we were going to. You know, it was in the cards, so maybe I just started backing away a bit."

"All that crap about the new bed . . ."

"I suppose so."

Eve turned to look at him. She waited a second or two

until he raised his head and met her stare. "So, what do you want now, Tom?"

A smile spread slowly across Thorne's face. He leaned over, his arm dropping down into the well of Eve's chair and slipping behind her waist. "I want to go to a hotel . . ."

For a moment Eve looked shocked, but then she began to smile, too. "What, tonight?"

"Why not? Shop's shut tomorrow, isn't it? I've got a nice car outside . . ."

Eve looked across to where Denise and Jameson were still deep in conversation with Holland. "God, it's a fantastic idea, but it's a bit awkward. It's Den's birthday . . ."

"Pretend it's mine."

"I don't know, I can't just leave."

"She won't mind."

Eve grabbed Thorne's hand and squeezed. "Let me see what I can do . . ."

An hour later, as they hovered outside, saying good-byes, Eve took Thorne's arm and spun him around. "I don't think tonight's a good idea."

"Did you have a word with Denise?" He looked across to where Eve's flatmate was kissing Holland on both cheeks. Behind them, Jameson stood waiting, hands thrust into his pockets. Denise caught Thorne's eye and gave him an odd smile . . .

"Not that I'm exactly in any fit state," Eve said. "I'd already had a bottle of red wine before you propositioned me . . ."

Thorne grinned. "Trust me, the drunker you are, the better it'll seem."

"What about next weekend? We could check into a nice hotel on the coast for a couple of nights." She looked up at him and nodded slowly. It must have been clear from his expression. "Right, I know . . ."

"Sorry. Until this case is over, I can't commit to anything like . . . Shit, a whole weekend away . . . it just isn't going to happen."

"It was a stupid idea . . ."

"It was a *great* idea. Let's go out one night next week. Saturday, or before . . ."

"Next Saturday's good."

"Right . . ." They took a few steps along the pavement, away from the bar. "Come on, it's still not too late. I'll swing for a really nice hotel, honestly. West End somewhere, full English breakfast . . ."

She put her hands around his neck and pulled him toward her. She whispered it in his ear before she kissed him softly on the cheek. "Saturday . . ."

As they separated, Thorne glanced across at the others standing by the bar entrance, and saw a look of something like disgust pass across Ben Jameson's face. Turning, Thorne saw that Jameson was watching Keith come hurrying toward the group, cradling a plastic bag.

Unable to hear quite what was said, Thorne watched as Keith delved into the bag and handed Denise something wrapped in red paper. Denise tore the package open and seemed delighted with what looked like a small, decorative box. She threw her arms around Keith's neck, then turned to show the present to Holland and Jameson.

Keith turned, red-faced, and looked across at where Eve was still standing, hand in hand with Thorne. She waved and started to walk toward him. Holland sauntered the other way, toward Thorne, smiling at Eve as they passed. He seemed a little startled when Thorne dropped a hand onto his shoulder.

"I'll run you home, Dave."

Holland looked confused. He glanced over his shoulder, watched Eve join her friends. "It's fine, really, I can get a cab . . ."

"There's no need."

Thorne drove down Whitechapel Road, heading south toward Tower Bridge. He took it slowly, still getting used to the steering and the clutch but also enjoying it, wanting the journey to last. They were listening to Merle Haggard as they moved slowly into the one-way system around Aldgate.

"What was going on back there, then?" Holland said.

"Keith works in Eve's shop sometimes. I think he's a bit—"

"No, I mean bringing me along on your night out, like a spare prick at a wedding."

Thorne checked the rearview mirror. "I wanted to show you the car." He didn't believe it himself, any more than when he'd told Eve the same thing earlier.

"Things all right with you and Eve?"

Thorne hesitated. Discussions like this one was shaping up to be weren't common between them, and where it might be going was impossible to predict. If Holland hadn't had a few too many, he'd probably be saying nothing. Even socially, the difference in their ranks was rarely forgotten. The unspoken acceptance of the need to keep a certain distance was usually knocking about somewhere, moderating.

Tonight, they were just two friends driving back from a bar, and Thorne decided to go with it.

"I've been fucking her around to be honest, Dave."

"What?"

"No, not like that. We haven't even . . ."

"Oh . . ."

"It's a long story, but basically she thinks I'm messing

her around, and I am. One minute I'm up for it, the next I'm relieved when it isn't happening."

For ten seconds or so before he spoke, Holland appeared to think about what Thorne had said. "What's all that about, then?"

"I don't know . . ."

The truth was that Thorne *didn't* know, and if *he* was confused, then he could only wonder at what the hell might have been going through Eve's mind. The whole relationship felt somehow teenage. The ups and downs, the mixed messages . . .

There was nothing teenage, nothing confusing, about the short film that began to run suddenly in Thorne's head. He watched himself and Eve in the lift that carried them up toward their nice hotel room. They were all over each other, their mouths hungrily exploring necks and shoulders and their hands probing the areas beneath buckles and straps.

Thorne gripped the wheel tighter, hearing the gulps for breath that came when the kissing stopped, and the moans when it began again. The bell as the lift door opened, and the rustle of Eve's legs moving beneath her skirt as they all but ran toward their room.

He saw himself push the card into the door, watched as the two of them stepped through and fumbled, giggling, for the light switch.

There was a body on their bed. Prostrate and bleeding. The blue necklace, cheap and dreadful, biting deep into the neck . . .

Thorne hit the brakes hard, squealing to a stop at a red light. Holland held his hand out, braced himself against the dashboard.

"Sorry," Thorne said. "Still getting the measure of it . . ."

They said nothing for a while, until the Tower of London loomed, spotlit ahead of them, and they moved slowly past it onto the bridge.

Thorne nudged Holland's arm and nodded upriver. "It's fucking great, isn't it?"

He loved crossing the Thames at night, never tiring of the spectacular views up and down the black river after dark. South to north across Waterloo Bridge was his favorite—to the left, the London Eye, and the dome of St. Paul's away in the City to the east—but crossing virtually any bridge, in any direction, at this time was usually enough to lift Thorne's spirits. Tonight, Butler's Wharf squatted to their left, while down below to the right of them, HMS *Belfast* seemed set in sullied amber, the river around it colored by the lights that ran along each bank.

Foul and fucked up and shitty as the place could be, it was a journey like this that Thorne would urge on anyone thinking about moving out of London . . .

"What about you and Sophie?" Thorne said. "All geared up for it?"

Holland turned, smiling, but looking like he might throw up. "I'm shitting myself, if you really want to know."

"Fair enough, it's a scary business. I've not had one, but—"

"It's not just the baby. It's what the baby's going to mean."

"Workwise, you mean?"

"It just feels like I'm being swept along, you know? Like I'm not in control of what I'm doing anymore." Thorne shook his head, opened his mouth to say something, but Holland plowed on, growing louder and more animated as he spoke. "Sophie says it's up to me what happens afterward, but she's going to stay at home with the baby and I'll be the only one earning . . ."

"She'd rather you were doing something else?"

"Yeah, but she was like that *before* she was pregnant. I mean, she'd be delighted if I got out of the job, no question, but there's no pressure. I'm worried that *I* might be the one to start thinking I should find something else. Something a bit better paid, you know?"

"Something safer?"

Holland turned and looked at Thorne hard. "Right." He turned away again, stared out of the window at the flaking billboards and car showrooms on the New Kent Road, moving past at almost exactly thirty miles per hour.

"I'm worried that I'll resent the baby," Holland said. His head fell sideways against the window. "For the choices it might force me to make . . ."

Thorne said nothing. He pressed a button on the sound system's control panel, searching through the CD until he found the track he was looking for. When the song began, he nudged up the volume. "You should listen to this," he said.

"What is it?"

"It's called 'Mama Tried.' It's about a man in prison . . ."

"That's what they're all about, isn't it?"

"It's really about growing up and accepting responsibility. It's about making the right choices . . ."

For a minute, Holland listened, or pretended to. By then they were coming up to the roundabout at the Elephant & Castle, his street just a little way beyond it. He shook his head suddenly and laughed.

"Growing up? *I'm* not the one with the midlife-crisis car . . ."

Thorne was starving by the time he got in. He stuck three pieces of bread under the grill while the video was rewinding. He'd managed to go the whole day without hearing the result of the match and was looking forward to watching it.

Half an hour into a fairly dull game, and Thorne was wondering why he'd made the effort . . .

It had been more than a decade since Tottenhan Hotspur had been involved in a Charity Shield, but Thorne and his father had been to the last few. They'd seen the goalless draw against Arsenal in '91, and the consecutive games in '81 and '82, after Cup Final wins on the bounce.

The first big game he'd ever gone to had been the Charity Shield in 1967. The trip to Wembley, an extra seventh-birthday present after Spurs had beaten Chelsea 2–1 and won the FA Cup. Thorne could still remember the roar, and his amazement at the sight of all that green, as his old man had led him up the steps toward their seats. He always loved that first sight of the grass, all the years they went to matches together after that, emerging into the noise and the light as they climbed up into the stand at White Hart Lane.

He wondered if his father had watched today's game. He'd doubtless have an opinion on it if he had.

Thorne made the call, and listened to twenty minutes of jokes without punch lines.

TWENTY-TWO

Carol Chamberlain put down the newspaper when Thorne came back to the table with the coffees.

"It's not great," she said.

Thorne glanced at the latest lurid headline, spooned the froth from his coffee. "It's not my problem."

Despite the best efforts of Trevor Jesmond and those above him, the media had got hold of the story a fortnight or so earlier, after the Southern killing. It hadn't quite been the tabloid frenzy that Brigstocke had predicted, but it was pretty basic stuff. One paper had printed pictures of zippered rapist masks with red crosses through them, underneath the headline THREE DOWN. Another had gathered testimony from half a dozen rape victims and run it alongside quotes like "Give This Man a Medal" and "The Only Good Rapist Is a Dead One" . . .

Monday morning's batch of stories involved complaints from those campaigning for the rights and integration of ex-prisoners. There were demands that more be done to catch the killer, accusations that the Met was dragging its feet. Only the night before, Thorne had watched a heated debate on *London Live* between representatives of rape-crisis organizations, their counterparts from prisoners'-rights pressure groups, and senior police officers. The assistant commissioner, flanked by a scary female commander and a sweating Trevor Jesmond, had reminded one lobby that the murder victims had themselves been raped, while assuring the other that everything possible was being done.

Thorne had turned the program off around the time Jesmond began to look like a rabbit caught in the headlights, blathering about two wrongs not making a right . . .

"Your superiors might decide to *make* it your problem," Chamberlain said.

Thorne smiled. "Is that what you used to do?"

"Of course. I did 'Passing the Buck' seminars at Hendon . . ."

They were sitting at a table in the shade, outside the small vegetarian café in the middle of Highgate Woods. It was all a bit organic and right-on for Thorne's taste, but Carol had wanted to eat outside somewhere and it had seemed as good a place as any.

The fancy bread was hideously overpriced, but it was all on expenses . . .

Carol Chamberlain's cold case had been taken away from her as soon as it had become hot again. She'd had no choice in the matter and was already working hard on something else. Still, Thorne knew how much they owed her and considered it the least he could do to keep her up to speed. More than that, he actually enjoyed their discussions, finding Chamberlain to be an incredibly useful sounding board. They'd met up or talked on the phone a few times now, since she'd first barged into his office. They gossiped and bitched and bounced ideas around . . .

"At least they haven't made the connection with the Foley killing," she said. "They don't know about Mark and Sarah yet . . ."

Thorne reached across for the paper and flipped it over. He scanned the football stories on the back page. "It's only a matter of time."

"It could be good, of course."

"How?"

"It might be the way to find them."

"Or frighten them away for good . . ."

Once coffee was finished and pudding decided against, Chamberlain stood and began piling up their plates. "Let's take the long way back to the cars." She rubbed her stomach. "Walk some of this off . . ."

"She was asking for you, Dave . . ."

Having fetched him from his office and pointed to the woman in question, Karim left Holland in the doorway of the Incident Room. Stone appeared silently at Holland's shoulder, and they stared across at where Joanne Lesser sat in a chair by the window.

"Mmm," Stone groaned. "Soul food . . ."

Holland nodded, turned to him. "Racist *and* sexist in two words. That's bloody good going even for you, Andy . . ."

"Fuck off."

"Christ, you're on good form, mate . . ."

"Seriously, she's very tasty, though. You're a lucky bastard." Holland looked at him. "Well, she's obviously up for it. First she's on the phone, now she's come in to see you personally . . ."

Holland led the way across the Incident Room, Lesser standing eagerly as he and Stone approached. He was sure that what Stone had been suggesting was only in his own, sexually skewed imagination. Still, for more than just the obvious reasons, he hoped that Joanne Lesser had something important to say.

Five minutes later, they sat, the three points of a small triangle, in Holland and Stone's office. Plastic cups of tea on the edges of desks . . .

"The dates have been bothering me," Lesser said.

"The dates of the foster placements?" Holland began sheafing through the notes on his lap.

"It's slightly different now, but back then we'd have ceased to monitor a placement once the child had turned sixteen. From then on, they were no longer deemed to be the responsibility of social services . . ."

"Right." Holland was still searching.

"I double-checked the information on the index cards—you know, the information that I sent to you—and it doesn't quite make sense."

"What doesn't?" Stone said.

"The last recorded monitoring date was February 1984. That would have been a home visit, most probably. At least a phone call . . ."

Holland had found the page he was looking for. He ran his finger down the list, stopped at the date Lesser had mentioned. "Mr. and Mrs. Noble." The Nobles should have been back from their holidays by now. He'd left a message, but they hadn't got back to him . . .

Lesser leaned forward on her chair, looking from Stone to Holland as she spoke. "I checked the children's dates of birth, just to be on the safe side, but there's still a problem."

Holland looked at the dates. He turned the page, looking for something else, and when he'd found it, he saw the anomaly. "They weren't old enough," he said.

Lesser nodded, the blush beginning around her throat. Holland could almost have blushed himself. This was something he should have seen, *would* have seen if he'd been giving it the proper attention. He'd been half-arsed, hadn't considered it important enough. He should have let Stone give him a hand when it had been offered. Now Stone was the one sitting there, probably enjoying every minute of it, as simple, *evident* facts were spelled out for Holland by a member of the public . . .

"Nineteen eighty-four?" Stone said. "So, the kids would have been . . ."

"Fifteen and thirteen," Lesser said. "Mark was almost sixteen, fair enough. If it had just been him I wouldn't have been concerned, but the little girl was nowhere near old enough for monitoring to stop. You can see why I thought it might be important . . ."

"What are the reasons you might stop monitoring a case?" Holland said.

"There's only two that I can think of. If a family moves away it would be handed over to a different area, or even a completely different county."

"I reckon that's it," Holland said. He began turning pages again until he found the current address for the Nobles. "Romford far enough?"

Lesser nodded. "Doesn't come under us."

"Does it say how long they've been living there, though?" Stone asked.

"No, I'll have to check. Last record in any local school is 1984, so there's every chance that's when they moved." He turned back to Lesser. "What's the other reason, Joanne? You said one reason was moving . . ."

"Adoption." Holland and Stone both looked back at her blankly. "Again, things are a bit more rigorous now, but then, once the adoption order had been signed, that was it. Not our responsibility anymore."

"I get the feeling you've already checked this . . ."

She shrugged. "I know someone in Adoption, so I gave her a ring. Their records are a bit more organized than ours. Have you got a pen?"

Holland couldn't help smiling. He stretched across and grabbed a pen from his desk. "Go ahead . . ."

"Irene and Roger Noble formally adopted Mark and Sarah Foley on February twelfth, 1984. They may well have moved shortly after that, but that was certainly the last contact the children had with Essex social services . . ."

Holland scribbled down the information. From everything they knew, it seemed that it was the last contact Mark and Sarah Foley had had with anybody.

They walked slowly around the edge of the cricket field toward the children's playground; moving along the path of shadow cast by a line of overhanging oaks and birches. Deep into the school holidays, there were plenty of people around. The temperature was starting to drop as the sky clouded over, but here and there were glimpses of a dark blue, like bruises fading on puffy flesh.

"Mark Foley still sounds like a good bet to me."

"Yeah, I think so, too," Thorne said. "Just wish I could cash it in."

"It'll happen. He can't stay hidden forever."

"I've still got a problem with motive, though."

Chamberlain threw Thorne a look of theatrical surprise. "I thought you were the type who didn't care about *why* . . ."

"Ultimately, it's not my job, is it? But if it's going to help me catch him . . ."

"Go on . . ."

"I can see the motive for killing Alan Franklin . . ."

"It's about as good as it gets. Franklin caused everything, might just as well have killed his parents. Took him long enough to get revenge, though."

"I think I can understand the waiting," Thorne said.

Chamberlain grinned. "Maybe he's just lazy."

Thorne thought he was pretty well qualified to give an opinion on that one. "I don't think so . . ."

They came slowly to a halt.

"He was growing up," Thorne said. "Letting his body grow strong, letting the hatred grow stronger. Then he waits until Franklin's old, until he feels safe, before he puts an end to it in that car park."

"Only that isn't an end to it . . ."

"No, it isn't. It should have been, though, shouldn't it? Mark settles it, gets clean away with it, gets on with his life."

"Whatever *that* is . . ."

"So why the hell does he pop up again now? Why these others? Why kill Remfry, Welch, and Southern?"

"Maybe he enjoys it."

"I'm damn sure he's enjoying it *now,* but that's not why he started. Not why he started again, I mean. Something else happened . . ."

"The rape element is crucial, though, you've always said that. Maybe he was raped himself."

"Maybe." Thorne felt like they were going over old ground. They'd considered this back when they thought the killer might have been an ex-prisoner, looking to settle an old score. It was possible, certainly, but it felt stale to him, and unhelpful.

Chamberlain jumped at a sudden, sharp *crack* from behind them. Half a dozen boys were messing about in the cricket nets, and for a minute or two, the pair of them stood and watched. When she finally spoke, Chamberlain had to lean in close to make herself heard over the noise the kids were making.

"Something I remember from a poem at school," she said. Thorne kept his eye on the action, inclining his head toward her to listen. 'Childhood is the kingdom where nobody dies . . . '"

"What's that from?" Thorne asked as they began walking again.

"One of those anthologies we had to read. I don't know . . ."

As they reached their cars, parked on the main road, Chamberlain stopped and put a hand on Thorne's arm. "It's good, knocking ideas around like this, Tom, it's useful. But don't forget that if the answer's there, if it's *anywhere,* it's in the details. It's in the facts that make up the pattern of a case."

Thorne nodded, opening the door of the BMW. He knew that there were answers. He knew, too, that he already had them somewhere, misfiled and, thus far, irretrievable. Lost among the tens of thousands of facts, relevant or otherwise, to the case. The ever-expanding headful of shit that he carried around with him all the time: names and places and dates and snippets of statements; words and numbers and small gestures; access codes and times of death; the look on a relative's face; the scuff mark on a hotel guest's shoe; the weight of a dead man's liver . . .

Thorne knew that the answer was buried in there somewhere and it bothered him. Something else bothered him and he thought twice before mentioning it.

"What you were saying about patterns . . ."

"What?"

"The second and third victims. He changed the pattern of killing between Welch and Southern."

"Of course he did. Because he presumed that once you'd connected the killings, you'd contact the prisons and warn them. He had to do the next one differently."

"What if he *knew,* rather than presumed?" Thorne said. "What if he knew because he's close to the investigation? We always talked about him having access of some kind. Then other stuff came along and the idea got blurred. What if I was wrong to dismiss the idea that the killer's one of us . . . ?"

When Thorne got back to Becke House, he was directed straight to Brigstocke's office. Holland was telling Brigstocke and Kitson about what Joanne Lesser had said, and his subsequent phone conversation with Mrs. Irene

Noble. Thorne made Holland backpedal, asked him to
go over Lesser's visit again until he was up to speed.

"It's interesting that the dates of the adoption and the
move look to be so close together," Brigstocke said.

"It gets a lot more interesting. When I finally got hold
of Irene Noble, told her I wanted to talk about Mark and
Sarah Foley, the first thing she did was to ask me if we'd
found them."

Thorne looked across at Brigstocke. "How would she
know we were looking?"

"No, sir, that's not what she meant," Holland said.
He flipped over a page in his notebook, read from it.
" 'Have you finally found them?' That's what she actually said. She's talking about twenty years ago." Holland
looked up and across at Thorne. "She claims that the
kids disappeared back in 1984 . . ."

"Just after the Nobles adopted them," Thorne said.

"Right." Brigstocke got up, walked around his desk.
"And around the time they moved away from Colchester."

Holland stuck his notebook away and leaned back
against a chair. "Now it gets even better. Mrs. Noble
reckons that there was an official investigation at the
time. The children were reported as missing, she says.
The police spent weeks looking for them . . ."

"You've checked?" Brigstocke asked.

"It's rubbish. I went back to 1983, just in case she was
getting the dates confused, and there's bugger all. No
records of any search, no records of missing persons reports. There was nothing national, nothing local. It
never happened . . ."

"What impression did you get when you spoke to
her?" Thorne asked.

"She sounded like she meant it. She was upset . . ."

"Turning it on, d'you reckon?"

"No, I don't think so. Sounded genuine enough . . ."

"Where's the husband?"

"Roger Noble died in 1990. Heart attack . . ."

Thorne thought about this for a second or two, then turned to Brigstocke. "Well, I reckon we'd better have a word with *her,* then." Brigstocke nodded. "Where is she, Dave?"

"She lives in Romford, but she's coming into town tomorrow. Likes to do her shopping in the West End, she says . . ."

Thorne pulled a face. "Oh, *does* she . . . ?"

"I've arranged to meet her at ten-thirty."

Brigstocke took off his glasses, pulled a crumpled tissue from his trouser pocket, and wiped the sweat from the frames. "Well done, Dave. You'd better go over all this with DS Karim as soon as you can. He'll need to reassign, issue fresh actions . . ."

"Sir . . ." Holland opened the door and stepped out.

"Yvonne, can you get across this as well? We might have a bit more luck finding Mark Foley and his sister, now we know that they changed their names . . ."

Kitson, who had said nothing, nodded and took a step toward the door.

"This is looking good, you know?" Brigstocke said. "Be great to give the detective chief superintendent some positive news . . ."

Thorne couldn't help himself. "Tell him I thought he looked smashing on the telly the other night . . ."

Brigstocke smiled in spite of himself. "Right, a pint later to celebrate?"

"Fuck all to celebrate," Thorne said. "I'll be there anyway, though . . ."

"Yvonne?"

Kitson shook her head. "Too much to do." She turned and stepped through the door, barking back at Brigstocke as she walked away toward the Incident Room, "Got to change a million and one data searches from 'Foley' to 'Noble' . . ."

Brigstocke looked over at Thorne. "What's got up *her* arse?"

"Don't ask me . . ."

"Maybe you should have a word . . ."

Thorne's mobile rang. He glanced at the screen and saw who was calling. He told Brigstocke he'd check back with him later and stepped out into the corridor, pulling the door closed behind him.

"Are we still on for Saturday?" Eve said.

"I hope so."

"Right. Dinner somewhere and back to your place."

"Sounds good. Fuck, you know what I still haven't done?"

"Who cares? You've got a sofa, haven't you?"

He had work to do, professionally and for his other, more personal project. Not that he considered the killing to be personal, not in terms of the self.

No, not really, and not to *him* anyway.

What he did to those animals in those hotel rooms wasn't actually about him, or for him. He'd always denied that, when it had come up, and he would continue to deny it. He was happy to do it, more than happy to put the line around their necks and pull, but if it had only been about him, it wouldn't be happening.

He was just a weapon . . .

Strangely, he felt that he put more of himself into his day job. More of him had passed into what he did, by the time he'd finished working on something, than it had watching any of those fuckers plead, then die. True, paying the mortgage meant being responsible to people, and what he did, even when he did it well, was rarely of any benefit to him personally, but he always felt part of it afterward. The work usually had his fingerprints on it somewhere.

He laughed at that and carried on working. His job was hotting up suddenly: stuff was coming in and he was really earning his money. He had less time now to get the other things organized, but actually there was very little that had to be done, and certainly no need to panic. It was all pretty much sorted.

Bar a few *t*'s to cross and the odd *i* to dot, the final killing had been arranged.

TWENTY-THREE

Thorne looked unconvinced. "I've never interviewed anybody in the same place I buy my pants."

"There's a first time for everything," Holland said.

They carried the coffees across to where Irene Noble was sitting waiting for them, flanked already—though the place had been open only half an hour or so—by large Marks & Spencer shopping bags. The café was a relatively new addition to the large store on Oxford Street, wedged into a corner of the ladies' clothing section and half-filled with shoppers who'd obviously made as early a start as Irene Noble.

As Thorne squeezed behind the table next to Holland, he glanced around at the dozen or so women getting their breath, ready to start again. Scattered around were one or two bored-looking men, grateful for the chance to sit down and not be asked their opinion for a few minutes.

Irene Noble took a small plastic container of sweeteners from her bag. She pressed the top, dropped a tiny tablet into her latte, and raised her eyebrows at Dave Holland. "They probably think I'm your mother," she said.

She was pretty well preserved for a woman who had to be sixty or so, though Thorne thought that she was trying a bit too hard. The hair was a little too blond and brittle, the fire-engine-red lipstick applied a touch too thickly. To Thorne, it seemed that this stage was probably the one that came right before giving up altogether. Before mentioning your age to strangers, and always wearing an overcoat, and not giving a damn anymore . . .

"Tell us about Mark and Sarah, Mrs. Noble."

She thought for a moment, smiling briefly before taking a sip of coffee. "Roger used to joke about it and say that we lost them in the move. You know, like a tea chest going missing." She saw the reaction on Thorne's face and shook her head. "It wasn't a nasty joke, it was affectionate. That was just his way. Something to make me laugh if I was crying, you understand? I did a lot of crying after it happened . . ."

"This was just after you adopted the children?" Holland said.

"The beginning of 1984. We'd had them four years or so by then. We had a few problems, 'course we did, but then things got on an even keel."

It was clear to Thorne that her voice was affected somewhat. A "telephone" voice. Thorne remembered that his mother had used to do the same thing. Airs and graces for the benefit of doctors, teachers, policemen . . .

"There were problems before, weren't there?" Holland said. "With the previous sets of foster parents."

"Right, and they gave up on the children straightaway. It was only Roger and I who stuck with it. We knew that it was just something we had to get through. They were very disturbed children and, God only knows, they had every right to be."

"What sort of problems?" Thorne said.

She paused for a few seconds before answering. "Behavioral problems. Adjusting, you know? Roger and I thought we'd got it under control. Obviously we were wrong." She reached for a teaspoon and stared down into her coffee cup as she stirred. "Behavioral." She said the word again, as if it were a medical term. Thorne glanced sideways at Holland, who gave him a small shrug in return.

"So you decided to adopt them?" Holland asked. Mrs. Noble nodded. "How did the kids feel about that?"

She looked at Holland as though he'd asked a very silly question. "They'd lost their real parents and been let down by every set of foster parents they'd had since. They were delighted that we were going to be a real family, and so were we. Roger and I had always wanted children. We might have missed out on nappies with those two, but we had plenty of sleepless nights, I can tell you . . ."

"I can believe it," Thorne said.

"And plenty after they disappeared. Plenty . . ."

"How did they disappear?"

She pushed her cup to one side, laid one liver-spotted hand across the other. "We moved on the Saturday morning and it was the usual chaos, you know? Boxes everywhere and removal men sliding about because there was snow on the ground. We told the kids they could sort their own stuff out, so they just got on with it. Shut themselves away upstairs . . ."

"Fighting over who was going to get the biggest room, I suppose?"

She looked quickly up at Thorne. "No. We'd sorted out their bedrooms early on, before we moved . . ."

"What happened?" Thorne said.

"They needed to have their own space, you under-stand?"

"What happened, Mrs. Noble?"

"Nobody heard them go, nobody saw a thing. They crept out like ghosts . . ."

"When did anybody find out they'd gone?"

"We were all over the place, you can imagine, trying

to get everything together. Trying to find the tea bags and the bloody kettle or what have you." She began to pick at a fingernail. "It was around dinnertime, I think. Can't remember exactly. It was after dark . . ."

"So what did you think?"

"We didn't really think anything at first. They always went out a lot. They were very independent, always off somewhere together. Mark always looked after Sarah, though. He always took care of his sister."

Thorne glanced sideways at Holland. "When were the police called?" Holland asked.

"The next morning. Obviously we knew there was something wrong when they hadn't come back. When their beds hadn't been slept in . . ."

Thorne leaned forward. He took one of the fancy Italian biscuits that came with the coffee and broke it in half, asking the question casually. "Who called the police?"

There was no hesitation. "Roger. Well, actually, he went down to the station himself. He thought things might get handled faster if he went there personally, and he was right. He said they got straight on it. Two of them came to the house while I was out searching in the park and round the local streets."

"Roger told you they came round?"

She nodded. "They had a look in the kids' bedrooms, you know? Asked all the normal questions. Took some photos away with them . . ."

Thorne looked at Holland. A reminder about getting photos of Mark and Sarah for Brigstocke's digital aging plan. Holland picked up on it, nodded, and made a note. Thorne popped the rest of the biscuit into his mouth, chewed for a few seconds before speaking again.

"Did the police presume the children had run away right from the start?"

"Well, that was the problem, wasn't it? Everything was in boxes, all over the show. It was hard to work out straightaway if they'd taken anything with them . . ."

"Eventually, though," Thorne said. "That was what they must have thought."

"Yes, after a day or two I worked out which clothes were missing. There was some money gone as well, but it took me a while to realize. I thought maybe I'd mislaid it somewhere in all the moving. Once the police knew about the children, about what they'd been through, Roger said they started treating it as a runaway thing more than anything else . . ."

"What did they do?"

"Very thorough, they were. Up and down the country. Appeals for information, searches at all the stations, that sort of thing. Roger got updates from them all the time. They were taking it very seriously, Roger said, for the first week or two, anyway."

"Roger said . . ."

"That's right. He went down and nagged them every day. Twice a day, sometimes, demanding to know what they were doing."

"For the first week or two, you said. After that . . . ?"

"Well, they told Roger, a chief inspector actually, told Roger that he was sure the children were safe. They were certain that if, you know, any harm *had* come to Mark or Sarah, they would have found out. I suppose they meant found a body . . ."

Thorne saw that the skin below Irene Noble's fingernail had torn and begun to bleed slightly where she'd been picking at it. He watched as she pressed a napkin to her tongue and dabbed at the pinpricks of blood. When she spoke again, it struck him that the telephone voice had gone, and that the Essex accent was coming through strongly. Whether she was unable to keep it up for long or had simply ceased bothering, it was impossible to tell.

"Never having had any of my own," she said, "I can't say for sure if I felt anything less because Mark and Sarah weren't mine, weren't my flesh and blood. D'you understand what I'm getting at?" Thorne nodded. "After the police told Roger they thought the children were safe, it wasn't so bad, you know? We weren't so scared. We just missed them. We got used to missing them eventually . . ."

"Did you ever see a police officer?" Thorne said. "In all the time they were looking for Mark and Sarah, did you yourself ever speak to a police officer?"

Thorne had been expecting a pause, perhaps a paling, but instead he got a smile. After a few seconds it wilted a little, and she seemed suddenly sad. Then, as she spoke, her face filled with an affectionate remembrance . . .

"Roger wanted to shield me from any of it. He did everything, handled it all. Perhaps it was his way of dealing with what had happened, throwing himself into it like he did, taking the responsibility, but I knew he was trying to protect me. He dealt with all the official side of things. The strain of it, of everything that happened, and that school business on top of it, drove my husband to an early grave."

Thorne blinked, took a breath or two. A suspicion, a *sense*, began to distill into something more potent. "What school business was that?" he asked.

"Roger worked over at St. Joseph's. It was the school where Mark and Sarah would have gone." She said it casually, like the children had done no more than fail an entrance exam. "It was just part-time, casual work, but he did all the bits and pieces that needed doing around the place. One day this man comes round, one of the parents, hammering on the door. Says his son's been involved in some kind of incident and mentioned Roger's name. Utter rubbish, of course, the man was on something, I think, but it really upset Roger. This lunatic wouldn't leave it and went to the headmaster. The school was keen to keep it low-key, which was right, *obviously,* since it was so stupid, but Roger wanted to do the right thing. He left quietly in the end, rather than upset the children. That was typical of him. It was scandalous, disgraceful that anybody could even *suggest* . . . There were always kids round here after school and on the holidays. Always kids in our house . . ."

"Roger liked children . . ."

She looked up, her face softening, grateful for Thorne's insight. For his understanding. "That's right. He would never have admitted it, but I think, deep down, he was always trying to make up for not having Mark and Sarah anymore. Being around other kids had been his own way of coping with what happened. Later on, after that unpleasantness, everything started to get on top of him. His heart just packed up in the end . . ."

"What was *your* way of coping, Irene?" Thorne said.

"I just prayed the kids were safe," she said. "That wherever Mark and Sarah went after they left us, they were out of harm's way . . ."

It was that sentence which stayed with Thorne, which he thought about as they struggled out of the West End through traffic, inching around Marble Arch, car and passengers overheating more than slightly.

"It was very convenient for Roger Noble," Holland said. "The kids going missing when they were between schools. They vanish from all education records . . ."

"It was certainly handy," Thorne said.

"They *did* go missing, didn't they? I'm just thinking out loud . . ."

Thorne shook his head. "Noble was responsible for them going, which is why he never reported it, but I don't think it was worse than that. If he killed them, who the hell are we looking for?"

"What are we going to do?" Holland asked. "Shouldn't we report it? That fucker could have abused loads of other kids."

"There's no point. He's long dead. He can't hurt any more kids now."

"What about *her*? Do you think she knew?"

Thorne thought about what Irene Noble had said. About praying the kids were out of harm's way. He shook his head. If she *had* known, she surely could not have said that and kept a straight face.

In the Grafton Arms, spitting distance from his flat, Thorne shared several pints and half a dozen games of pool with Phil Hendricks. The beer seemed to have little effect, and he lost five games out of the six.

"I'm not enjoying thrashing you as much as I normally would," Hendricks said. "You're so obviously preoccupied with all this other shit." Thorne, leaning back against the bar, said nothing. He watched as Hendricks potted the last couple of balls before putting the black down without any difficulty. "What about if we start putting money on it? That might focus your thoughts a bit more . . ."

"Let's leave it," Thorne said. "I'll finish this pint, and I'm off home . . ."

Hendricks took his Guinness from the top of the cigarette machine and walked across to join Thorne at the bar. "I still don't really see it," he said. "How could they not know? How could they not know *something* . . . ?"

Thorne shook his head, his glass at his lips. Among other things, they had been talking about Irene Noble and Sheila Franklin. About two women of more or less the same age, married to men whom they loved dearly, and whom, now that they were widows, they remembered with tenderness and affection. Two men whose memories lived on, fondly preserved as precious things. Two men beloved . . .

One a rapist and the other a child molester.

Thorne swallowed. "Maybe it's an age thing. You know, a different generation."

"That's crap," Hendricks said. "What about my mum and dad?" Thorne had met them once, they ran a guest-house in Salford. "My old man couldn't so much as fart without my mum knowing about it . . ."

Thorne nodded. It was a fair point. "Same with mine . . ."

"She knew what he was *thinking*, never mind doing."

Hendricks reached into the top pocket of his denim jacket, took a Silk Cut from a packet of ten. Thorne was irritated, in the way that only an ex-smoker *could* be. Irritated by the fact that his friend could smoke one or two, then put the pack away for a week or more, until he fancied another one as a bit of a treat. Smoke, and enjoy it, and not need another one. A packet of *ten*, for crying out loud . . .

"Are they going to be told?" Hendricks asked. "Those women? Is someone going to break the bad news about their dead hubbies?"

"No point yet. If we get a result they'll find out soon enough . . ."

Hendricks nodded and lit his cigarette. The curls of blue smoke drifted across to where a man and a woman were now playing pool. It hung in the light above the table.

"Maybe we only *think* we know what was going on with our parents," Thorne said. "Maybe we only know as much or as little as they did."

"I suppose . . ."

"There's an old country song called 'Behind Closed Doors' . . ."

"Bloody hell, here we go . . ."

"It's true, though, isn't it? So much family stuff is mythology. Shit that just gets handed down, and you never know for sure what really happened and what's made up. Nobody ever thinks to sit you down and pass it on. The truth of it. Before you know it, your history becomes hearsay." Thorne took a drink. He knew that at some point, he should have talked to his father. Found out more about his parents and *their* parents. He knew that there wasn't much point now . . .

"Fuck me," Hendricks said. "All that's in one song?"

"You are *such* an arsehole . . ."

They stepped away from the bar to make room for a group of lads, finished their drinks standing by the door.

"Where does all this leave you with Mark Foley?" Hendricks said.

"He's still our prime suspect."

"Whoever he might be . . ."

"Right, and *wherever*. But he's not making my life very easy."

"He'll slip up. We'll nail him when he does . . ."

"I'm not talking about catching him." Thorne was finding it hard to think about his murderer without picturing him as a fifteen-year-old child. He saw a boy protecting his sister, spiriting her away from a place where one, or perhaps both, of them was being abused. "I'm still trying to decide exactly what he *is*." Thorne turned to look at Hendricks. "This whole thing's all arse-about-face, d'you know that, Phil? Mark Foley or Noble or whoever the fuck he is now is a killer *and* he's a victim."

Hendricks shrugged. "So?"

"So, there's a part of him that part of *me* doesn't really want to catch . . ."

Thorne walked Hendricks back toward the tube. Hendricks asked Thorne about Eve, joked when he heard about their hot date on Saturday, and moaned about his own eventful but ultimately bleak love life.

Thorne wasn't paying an awful lot of attention. He was tired, imagining himself floating gently down on to his hillside, the bracken waving a welcome as he drew nearer to it. Jane Foley was suddenly there beside him, drifting to earth, and though he could not see her face clearly, he imagined the pain etched across it, for herself and for her children.

Thorne knew that when he and Jane Foley hit the ground, their bodies would travel right through the bracken and beyond. He knew that the hillside would collapse beneath their weight and that they would sink down deep through earth and water and the rotten wood of old coffins. Down through powdery bone and farther, into the blackness where there was no sound and the soil was packed tight around them.

TWENTY-FOUR

The telephone voice was even more pronounced on Irene Noble's answering-machine message. Holland waited for the beep, then spoke. "This is Detective Constable Holland from the Serious Crime Group. Yesterday, when myself and DI Thorne interviewed you, we forgot to ask about photographs of the children. We'd appreciate it if you might be able to lend us some pictures, which we will of course return whenever we finish with them. So, if you could get back to me as soon as possible on any of those numbers on the card we left you, I'd be very grateful. Many thanks . . ."

Holland put down the phone and looked up. From behind his desk on the other side of the office, Andy Stone was staring across at him.

"Photos of the Foley children?" Stone said.

"The DCI's still keen on getting them on the computer, aging them up."

Stone shook his head. "Waste of time. Never looks anything like the kids when they eventually turn up."

"If she's got photos from just before the children ran away, they'll be fifteen and thirteen. They can't have changed too much."

"You'd be amazed, mate. Have you never bumped into someone you haven't seen for a few years and not recognized them? That's after a few years . . ."

Holland thought about it and admitted that he had. He also knew, from the twin murder case he'd worked on with Thorne the year before, that if people wanted to change the way they looked, it wasn't actually that hard. Still, he reckoned that if the technology was there, there was no harm in using it.

Stone remained unconvinced. "It's a pretty basic software program that digitally ages the photographs. At the end of the day, it's all guesswork and a lot of assumptions. How can you know if someone's hair's going to fall out, or if they're going to put on loads of weight or whatever?"

"I've seen some that looked pretty close," Holland said.

Stone shrugged, went back to what he was doing. "Do we know she's got any photos at all?" he said, without looking up.

"Not for certain, no. Be a bit strange if she didn't, though. She was very fond of them . . ."

"You going to get somebody to go and pick them up?" Stone asked. "Or shoot over there yourself?"

"Hadn't really thought about it. I'll see what she says when she gets back to me, see when's a good time. You want to come along?"

"No . . ."

"She's single, but probably a bit old, even for you . . ."

"I'll give that one a miss, I think."

"Suit yourself." Holland noted down the time he'd made the call. Wednesday the seventh, 10:40 A.M. He'd give Irene Noble until the end of the day and call again. When Stone next started to speak, Holland looked across. Stone was leaning back in his chair, staring into space through narrowed eyes.

"*Very* fond of them? I think you're being a bit bloody generous . . ."

"I think she was more than very fond of them," Holland said. "But yes, she was also naive. Call it stupid, if you like . . ."

Stone snapped his gaze toward Holland. "If love is blind, she must have been fucking besotted . . ."

Whoever thought that computers would do away with paperwork was sadly mistaken. There was as much paper piled up on desks as there ever had been. The only difference was that now, most of it was printed out by computer . . .

Thorne sat and read through the stories of four murders.

Those same scraps of information that clogged his brain had also been recorded somewhere on paper. On laser-printed sheets of A4, on faded and curling reams of fax paper, on Post-it notes and preprinted memo sheets torn from a pad. The entire case was laid out like this before him. Ream after dog-eared ream, piled in stubby blocks of yellow and white and buff. Banded by elastic or bound with laminate sheets or stapled and stuffed into cardboard folders . . .

Thorne went over every piece of paper, of the jigsaw. Looking for the answer he knew to be there. Sifting through the shit, like a squawking gull flapping around a vast dump. Beady black eye searching for that morsel of interest . . .

Hearing the trace of that Yorkshire accent in Carol Chamberlain's voice. The good sense in every flat vowel of it.

If it's anywhere, it's in the details.

Opposite him, Yvonne Kitson sat typing, her face all but obscured by a paper mountain range of her own. She was still working on the Foley/Noble search, sorting through tens of thousands of addresses and car registrations and National Insurance numbers, as well as dealing with, collecting and collating, the information that was still coming in on the Southern killing.

Thorne looked across at her. He toyed with lobbing a ball of paper over to get her attention. He flicked briefly through the piles on his desk, looking for something he could screw up, then thought better of it . . .

"Apart from anything else," Thorne said, "murderers aren't doing the rain forests a whole lot of good."

Kitson looked up and across at him. "Sorry?"

He picked up a sheaf of postmortem reports and waved them. She nodded her understanding.

"How's it going, Yvonne?"

"We won't have any more luck finding him as Noble than we did as Foley. He was only Mark *Noble* for five minutes, anyway . . ."

"Which he'd have hated. That man's name . . ."

"Too bloody right. If I was him I'd've changed my name, or at least stopped using *that* one, as soon as I got the hell out of there."

Thorne could find nothing in what Kitson had said to argue with. He'd have gone to Brigstocke straightaway, suggested they concentrate their resources somewhere else. But he didn't have the faintest idea where . . .

"Let's just plow through it," he said.

The whole adoption/abuse/runaway lead was shaping up to be another one of those that came to nothing horribly quickly. It was hard enough trying to work out what might have happened to someone who'd run away from home six months before. To piece together the theoretical movements of a pair of teenagers who'd vanished from a house in Romford nearly twenty years earlier was almost certainly impossible.

They had little choice but to try, and while Holland, Stone, and the rest of the team did what they could,

Thorne was going back over everything they already had. Sure that they already had enough.

By lunchtime, he'd found nothing, and felt as though he'd read about every murder that had ever taken place. He'd watched the hands of the pathologist rooting about in every chest cavity and down into the cold, wet depths of every gut. He'd listened to the less than helpful words of everybody who'd so much as stood at the same bus stop as one of the victims.

He'd had a bellyful . . .

"What's on your sandwiches today, then?"

Kitson shook her head without looking up from her computer screen. "Didn't have time today. The kids were playing up, and everything got a bit . . ." The rest of the sentence hung there until Thorne spoke.

"You can't keep all the balls in the air all the time, Yvonne. You're allowed to drop one occasionally, you know." Kitson glanced up, gave him a thin smile. "Is everything all right, Yvonne?"

"Has somebody said something?" It came a little too quickly.

"No. You've just seemed a bit . . . out of it."

Kitson's smile thickened until she looked, to Thorne, much more like herself. Much more the type he could lob a ball of paper at.

"I'm just tired," she said.

This next killing had to be the last one, at least for a while. It made a pretty picture, and it also made bloody good sense. Afterward, the police investigation was bound to be stepped up, and the risk of getting caught, just statistically, would increase.

If he were to be caught, to be tried for his crimes, the next killing would be a very bad one to get done for. He would certainly be crucified with little argument. Now, though, with just the others under his belt, it would be something of a different matter. Standing trial for the murders of Remfry and Welch and Southern, he would fancy his chances . . .

If the papers were excited about the manhunt, they would be wetting themselves over a court case. The tabloids would back him, he was sure of it. He could probably even persuade one or other of them to shell out for his defense, pay to hire a top lawyer. He had decided already that should it ever come to it, he would speak in his own defense, would stand up and tell them exactly what he'd done and why. He was pretty confident that only a very brave judge would put him away for too long after that.

There would be an outcry from certain sections for sure, from the misguided and the bleeding hearts. From those who believed he should pay his debt to society, in the same way that those fine, upstanding citizens he'd killed had once done.

That would be all right with him. Let the silly bastards protest. Let them take the words *perversion* and *justice* and put them together like they owned them, even though they hadn't got the least fucking idea what either of them could really mean.

Perversion and justice. The degradation and the dashed hope. The hideous comedy that had started everything . . .

It was all a fantasy, of course, unless the police came knocking on his door in the next couple of days. After that, after the final killing, nothing he could say would save him. The loyalties of the gutter press would switch very bloody quickly, along with everybody else's, once the final victim had been discovered.

Rapists were one thing, but this was, after all, very much another.

* * *

Thorne was in the corner of the Major Incident Room feeding coins into the coffee machine when Karim approached him.

"Miss Bloom on line three, sir . . ."

Momentarily confused, Thorne reached for his back pocket, understanding when he found it empty. His mobile was on his desk in the office. Eve would have tried that first and then, having got no reply, would have called the office number . . .

Thorne crossed to a desk and picked up the phone. He held it to his chest until Karim had wandered far enough away.

"It's me. What's up?"

"Nothing serious. Keith's let me down, so I just need to change the time a bit on Saturday. I told him I was going out and he said that he'd lock up for me. Now he turns round and says that *he* needs to leave early as well, so I'm a bit stuffed . . ."

"It doesn't matter. Get over when you can."

"I know, I just wanted to get to your place early, drop some stuff off before we go out to eat."

"Sounds interesting . . ."

"It'll probably be nearer seven now, by the time I've sorted out the shop and put my face on."

"I can't see myself getting home a lot sooner than that anyway . . ."

"Sorry to screw our arrangements around, but it's not my fault. Keith's usually pretty reliable. Tom . . . ?"

Eve's voice had faded away. Thorne was no longer listening.

Our arrangements . . .

Zoom in close and hold.

The certainty of it came as swiftly, and snapped into place as tightly, as a ligature. Like the blue blur of the line as it whips past the face and down, only becoming clear when it begins to bite, Thorne knew in a second *exactly* what it was that he'd missed. What had lain shadowed and just out of reach. Now he saw it, brightly lit . . .

Something he'd read and something he hadn't . . .

They'd found all Jane Foley's letters to Remfry, the ones sent to him in prison and the couple that had been sent to his home address after his release. Nothing indicated that there were any letters missing, and why would there be?

Something *had* been missing, though.

Thorne had read those letters a dozen times, probably more, and nowhere had Jane Foley discussed the plans for her meeting with Douglas Remfry. The rendezvous itself was never talked about specifically. Not the time or the date. Not even the name of the hotel . . .

So how the hell had anything been arranged?

Something Thorne *could* remember reading had been written by Dave Holland. His report on that first visit to collect Remfry's stuff, the day he went over there with Andy Stone and pulled those letters out from under Remfry's bed. Mary Remfry had been keen to stress her son's success with women. She'd made a point of mentioning the women that were sniffing around after Dougie had been released. The women that were calling up . . .

Remfry, Welch, and Southern had not just walked into those hotels thinking they were going to meet Jane Foley. They'd *known* they were going to meet her.

They'd spoken to her.

TWENTY-FIVE

"Not just spoken on the phone either," Holland said. "I'm not sure about the others, but I think Southern might have *met* her."

They were gathered in Brigstocke's office, prior to a hastily arranged team briefing. Eighteen hectic hours since Thorne had put it together. Since he'd worked out that there *was* a her . . .

"Go on, Dave," Brigstocke said.

"I interviewed Southern's ex-girlfriend . . ."

Thorne remembered reading the statement. "Right. They split up not long before he was killed, didn't they?"

"That's just it. She said that the main reason she dumped him was that she'd heard about some other woman, thought he'd been two-timing her. Somebody told her that Southern had been bragging about it in the pub. Telling his mates he'd picked up this fantastic bit of stuff. Actually . . ."

"What?"

"I need to look at the statement, but I think Southern supposedly told his mates that she had more or less picked *him* up."

Thorne looked past Holland, down to Brigstocke's desk, at the series of black-and-white photographs laid out in two lines across it. "Jane Foley," he said.

"Who *is* she, really?" Kitson said.

"Could be anybody," Thorne said. "We can't discount any possibility. A model he hired or a hooker. The killer could have used her for the pictures, paid her to make the calls to Remfry and Welch. Given her a bit extra to pick up Howard Southern . . ."

Brigstocke was gathering his notes together. He didn't believe what Thorne was suggesting any more than Thorne himself did. "No, it's Sarah. The sister. Got to be . . ."

"Using her mother's name," Thorne said.

"This is all about the mother," Holland said. "It's all about Jane."

Thorne moved toward the desk, correcting Holland as he passed him. "It's all about a *family* . . ."

"Which means nothing's straightforward," Brigstocke said. "Which means it's a damn sight more fucked up and impossible to fathom than we can even begin to imagine."

Thorne was thinking out loud as much as anything. "I'm beginning to imagine it," he said. "Families can do damage."

"Are we about done?" Kitson asked suddenly. She moved toward the door without waiting for an answer. "I've got a couple of things to do before the briefing starts."

"I think so. Everybody clear?" Brigstocke looked at his watch and then at Thorne. The face of the watch was a whole lot easier to read. "Right, we'll start in five minutes, then . . ."

The "missed-call" message had been scribbled on a memo sheet and left on Holland's desk. He screwed the paper up into his fist as he began to dial the number.

"Mrs. Noble? This is Detective Constable Holland. Thanks very much for getting back to me." He'd meant to chase her up at the end of the day yesterday, but after

Thorne's moment of revelation, things had gone haywire . . .

"I'm afraid I didn't get your message until quite late," she said. "And I didn't know whether or not to call you at home."

"It would have been fine," Holland said. He probably wouldn't have heard the phone anyway over the sound of the argument he'd been having with Sophie.

"I will get these photos back, won't I?"

"Definitely. We'll take care of them, I promise."

"You'll need to give me a little bit of time to put my hands on them. They're in the cellar, I think. Actually, it might be the loft, but I'll find them . . ."

Holland looked over his shoulder. The Incident Room was filling up. There were doubtless still a dozen or more smokers outside somewhere, getting their last lungfuls of nicotine for an hour or two, but most available seats and areas of bare desktop were already taken.

"So what do you think? A day or two?"

"Oh yes, I should think so. I've picked up such a lot of old rubbish over the years, mind you . . ."

"Once you've got the photos, when can we come and pick them up?"

"I beg your pardon?"

Holland asked the question again, raising his voice above the growing level of hubbub around him.

"Any time you like," she answered. "I'm not going anywhere."

Thorne was alone in Brigstocke's office. There were only five minutes until the briefing was due to begin. Brigstocke, who would kick things off, was already in the Incident Room. After he'd said his piece, it would be down to Thorne.

He stood before the gallery of pictures on Brigstocke's desk. A series of images carefully designed to tempt and tease. To offer while at the same time giving absolutely nothing away . . .

Thorne could not be sure if the woman in the photographs was Sarah Foley. It didn't really matter. She was there and yet she was absent. In most of the shots she was kneeling, her head bowed, or else artfully shadowed. Thorne picked each picture up in turn, studied it, waited in vain for it to tell him something that it had managed, thus far, to keep to itself.

Aside from the powerful, disconcerting message the photos sent to his groin, Thorne saw nothing new.

Even physically, though the promise of submission was constant, little was revealed. In some of the photos the woman looked to have dark hair, while in others it seemed more fair. In two of them the hair definitely looked blond, but it could easily have been a wig. The body itself appeared to change, depending on how it was posed and lit. It was alternately lissome and muscular, its position making it impossible to accurately judge the height or even the build of the woman to whom it belonged.

Sarah Foley, if it *was* her, had not been captured.

Thorne looked at his watch. Another minute and he'd need to get out there. His job was to rev them up, to give the team enough to carry it into the home straight.

The next few days they'd work their arses off, and none more so than him. They'd be going back, as always, checking what they had in light of the new lead, but all the time there was forward momentum. He could already sense it, the hunger that increases when it smells the meal, a collective ticking in the blood. The investigation was picking up speed quickly, starting to race. From this point on, Thorne would make bloody sure nothing else got away from him.

Still, barring an actual arrest, by the weekend he'd be ready for a break. Saturday night with Eve and Sunday with his old man. He allowed himself a smile. If everything went well on Saturday night, he'd probably be making something of a late start the following morning.

Thorne was guessing that by knocking-off time on Saturday, he'd *need* something to divert him. There were other parts of him, *better* parts, that needed exercising, and he wasn't just talking about sex. It would be good to feel the fizz of it with Eve, the flush and the promise of it. The scary thrill and the wonderful release. He was also looking forward to spending a few hours with his father. He needed to feel that lurch, that welling up of whatever it was his old man could suck into Thorne's chest without trying . . .

Karim appeared in the doorway, gave him a look.

"On my way, Sam," Thorne said.

He would speak with real passion to the officers who were waiting for him. He wanted to catch this killer more than ever now, and he wanted to spread that desire around like a disease. He wanted to engineer that heady feeling of desperation and confidence that could sometimes make things happen all by itself.

But he would take care to hold the other feeling inside, the one that had begun to come and go, and cause something to jump and scuttle behind his ribs . . .

Yes, they were moving quickly. They were suddenly tearing along, they were up for it. But Thorne couldn't help but feel as if something was moving, equally fast and with just as much determination, toward *them*. There was going to be a collision, but he didn't know when or from which direction.

He wouldn't see it coming.

Thorne gathered up the photos from the desk, slipped them into a folder, and walked toward the Incident Room.

TWENTY-SIX

They spoke to each other slowly, in whispers.

"Did I wake you?"

"What time is it?"

"Late. Go back to sleep . . ."

"It's okay . . ."

"I'm sorry."

"Were you dreaming about it again?"

"Every bloody night at the moment. Jesus . . ."

"You never used to have dreams before, did you? I had them all the time, always did, but never you . . ."

"Well, I'm having them now. With a vengeance."

"That's an appropriate word."

"Will they stop, do you think? Afterward?"

"What?"

"The dreams. Will they stop once it's all over?"

"We'll know soon enough . . ."

"I'm nervous about this one."

"No need to be."

"We're less in control of it than with the others. You know? With them we knew what to expect, we knew everything that might happen. That was the advantage of the hotels, they were predictable . . ."

"It'll be fine . . ."

"You're right, 'course it will, I know. I wake up like this and I'm still thinking about the stuff in the dream and my head's all fucked up."

"Is that the only reason you're nervous? Something going wrong?"

"What else would it be?"

"That's all right, then."

"You'd better be there on time, though . . ."

"Don't be silly . . ."

"You'd better fucking be there, all right? Think about the traffic."

"I never have any problems with the traffic, and I've *always* been there."

"I know you have. Sorry . . ."

"What about Thorne?"

"Thorne won't be a problem."

"Good . . ."

"I'm so tired. I have to try and get back to sleep now."

He reached for her, slid an arm across her belly.

"Come here and I'll help you . . ."

TWENTY-SEVEN

Not a very long time before, on a freezing night when weather and loneliness had seemed meant for each other, Thorne had dialed a number he had copied from a postcard in a news agent's window. He'd driven over to a basement flat in Tufnell Park, handed over a few notes, and watched a fat, pink hand bring him off. He'd heard the woman's less than convincing groans and entreaties, the jangle of the charm bracelet that bounced on her wrist as she worked. He'd heard his own breath, and the low, desperate grunt as he finished.

Then he'd driven home and gone to bed, where he'd done it again himself for twenty-five pounds less . . .

Now Thorne moved around his office, willing away the last knockings of a muggy Saturday and remembering his hands-on adventure in vice with even less pleasure than he'd felt at the time. It was a measure of how low he had felt then. Of how much he was looking forward to his evening with Eve Bloom.

He would leave Becke House feeling as positive as he had in a long time. Things had moved quickly. The few days since the woman—who might or might not be Sarah Foley—had elbowed her way to the right part of Thorne's brain and to the forefront of his investigation had yielded encouraging results.

They'd reinterviewed Howard Southern's ex-girlfriend, confirmed her story about the other woman, and quickly managed to turn up several characters claiming to have seen Southern with a woman in the days leading up to his murder. Descriptions were predictably vague and contradictory, "slim" and "fair-haired" being the only adjectives that turned up more than once. A barmaid told how she'd seen the woman drag Southern away into a dark corner, where she was "all over him, but like she wanted him all to herself." A computer-generated portrait had been produced, but it was flatter and even more anonymous than such things normally were. The woman was no more there—on fly-ers and posters and front pages—than she was in the photos she had sent the men who were to be killed.

Still, it was progress . . .

Another line of inquiry involved the possibility that the woman did more than just woo the victims and lure them to their deaths. Though Thorne himself was dubious, it had at least to be considered that she had been present when they were killed.

They had gone back to the hotels in Slough and Roe-hampton, to the shelter in Paddington, and asked questions. Nothing exciting had turned up when CCTV footage was looked at again, but that was hardly surprising. If Mark Foley had known where the cameras were, then so would she. A woman who'd been working on reception at the Greenwood Hotel on the night Ian Welch was killed *did* remember seeing a blond woman hanging around. She'd thought the woman must have been with the party in the bar, but didn't see her talking to anyone. The receptionist thought she was "funny looking" . . .

Thorne was not sure *what* role the woman had played. He wondered exactly what they would charge her with when they did find her. "Conspiracy to commit" was probably favorite. Yes, she might have turned up at the hotels, might even have answered the hotel-room doors to the victims, while Mark Foley stood hidden, tightening the length of washing line around his fingers . . .

Beyond that . . . ?

If this woman *was* Sarah Foley, Thorne could not imagine her watching. He could not imagine her brother *being* watched as he brutally raped another man . . .

It was dark, unnatural thoughts such as this one that Thorne determined, at least for a night, to dismiss from his mind as he moved through the Incident Room, saying his good-byes.

The doors opened as he reached the lift. Without breaking stride, Thorne walked in and turned to press the button. After a few seconds he watched the room, the desks, the *case* disappear before his eyes as the doors closed . . .

Thorne stepped from the lift and headed toward the car park, all the time thinking about what he was going to wear later on. He reckoned he'd have about half an hour after he got home before Eve was due. Maybe a bit more, if the traffic was as light as it should be.

The BMW cruised up to the barrier, then, fifteen seconds later, moved under it and out onto the road. A Carter Family compilation was selected, and the volume turned up. He wondered what music he should put on later. Would Eve run screaming from the place as soon as she knew about the country stuff?

He was such an idiot. Why had he messed around? Why the fuck had he even *subconsciously* been putting this off?

Thorne was still ludicrously excited by the car, by the shape and the feel and the sound of it. He put his foot down, enjoying the noise of the engine, smiling for several reasons as he accelerated toward the North Circular and home.

Picking up speed . . .

* * *

Holland drove across Lambeth Bridge, no more than ten minutes from home. He remembered crossing the river farther east, on Saturday night exactly a week before. Blind drunk and talking nonsense in Thorne's new car.

He thought about the look on Sophie's face when she'd found him later on the bathroom floor. He'd raised his head from the cool porcelain of the toilet and seen nothing he felt comfortable with. What he'd seen on her face was worry, carved in deep, and with the strange clarity that only alcohol can bring, Holland knew that it wasn't for him. For the first time, he saw that she was concerned for herself, and for the baby she was carrying. Concerned that in choosing *him* as the father of her child, she'd fucked up big-time . . .

The hangover had worn off a damn sight faster than the guilt.

Holland decided that he'd do his bit to make tonight a good one. He'd stop off and pick up a nice bottle of wine for them to have with dinner, to finish off afterward, spread out in front of the TV. Sophie still enjoyed the odd glass of wine. It was supposed to be good for her, though before the pregnancy, she would certainly not have stopped at just the one glass. She'd have happily put away a bottle, while Holland watched as her cheeks began to flush, and waited, never knowing whether she'd become mushy or nasty. Either was fine by him. She'd make fun of him and start to tease, or else she'd wrap herself around him and talk about the future, and either way they'd usually end up making love.

Before the pregnancy . . .

There was a row of shops just past the Imperial War Museum: a Turkish grocer's, a paper shop, and a small supermarket. As Holland pulled over to the curb, he began to ache with the realization that it was getting hard to remember what things were like before Sophie became pregnant.

The good things, anyway.

It never took him very long to get ready.

He didn't dress up in anything special. There were no pointless rituals, no periods of intense mental preparation, none of that rubbish. He thought about what he was doing, of course he did. He was sensible, he went over it all, but that took no more time than it did to pack his bag.

There wasn't very much to carry. Nothing that wouldn't fit into a small rucksack. Previously, with the ones in the hotel rooms, he'd taken something bigger, a bag he could stuff the sheets and bedclothes into. That wouldn't be necessary this time.

The gloves, the hood, the weapons . . .

He'd already sharpened the knife, then used it to cut off a length from the reel of washing line. He coiled it up and stuffed it into a pocket at the front of the black leather backpack.

It was funny, the things people carried around with them in bags. Who knew what secrets, what glimpses into people's lives, might come tumbling out if you could empty their backpacks and briefcases, their plastic sports bags and canvas holdalls? For sure, you'd need to sift through a mountain of files and folders, of newspapers and sandwiches in plastic wrap, before you found anything of interest. A ransom note or a blackmail demand. Perhaps the odd dirty mag or pair of handcuffs. Then, if you were lucky, you might find the one bag in ten thousand or a thousand or less that contained a gun or a bloodstained hammer or a severed finger . . .

You'd almost certainly be surprised if it was a woman's handbag.

He smiled as the last thing went in, and he fastened the strap. Anybody rooting through the bag he was packing would probably just be very embarrassed.

Thorne stood staring at himself in the full-length mirror on the back of his wardrobe door. He was trying to decide whether to stick with the plain white shirt or go back to the blue denim when the doorbell made his mind up for him.

On the way to the door, he nudged the volume of the music down just a little. He'd decided, after much soul-searching, that George Jones would suit any mood that might be required. He had some of the quirky fifties songs lined up for now, but was ready to bring out the Billy Sherill stuff from two decades later when the time came. There was surely no more romantic song ever recorded than "He Stopped Loving Her Today" . . .

Eve marched into the center of the room, cast a quick eye over the place, then over Thorne. "You look very summery," she said.

She was wearing a simple brown cotton dress that buttoned up the front. "So do you," Thorne said. He looked down at his white shirt. "I thought about wearing a tie . . ."

She took a step toward him. "God, we're not going anywhere posh, are we?"

"No . . ."

"Good. I like the shirt open-necked anyway . . ."

They kissed, their hands growing busier with every few seconds that passed. As Thorne's fingers engaged with the second button on her dress, Eve broke off and stepped away, smiling. "Now, I don't necessarily think that wild gymnastic shagging on a full stomach is a good idea," she said. "But I could eat *something,* and I'd definitely like a drink . . ."

Thorne laughed. "Right, is it a bit warm to eat curry?"

"Curry's good anytime."

"There's a fantastic Indian round the corner."

"Sounds perfect."

"Or there's any number of great places in Islington or Camden. Loads of nice restaurants in Crouch End. You haven't been in my new car yet . . ."

Eve walked across to the window, fastening her buttons. "Let's go local. It won't be fair if only one of us has had a drink."

"No argument from me. Let me grab a jacket . . ."

"Don't bother, we're not going anywhere just yet."

"No?"

Eve turned from the window, raising her hands to adjust the clips in her hair. Her breasts pushed against the front of her dress, and Thorne could see the redness where she'd shaved under her arms. "I've got something in the van," she said. "I'll need a hand bringing it in."

It wasn't until Holland looked at the clock on the dash that he realized it had been ten minutes since he'd pulled up outside the flat.

It was just after seven o'clock.

Ten minutes and more of sitting, clutching the plastic bag with the wine inside it, unable to get out of the car.

It was a few minutes after that, when Holland stared, confused for a moment at the small dark patches appearing on his trousers, and realized that he was crying. He lifted his head and squeezed his eyes shut, the next breath a sigh that caught in his throat and became a sob.

Then a series of them, like punches to the heart.

For want of anything else, he wrapped his forearms around the bag, the wine bottle between his face and the steering wheel as his head dropped slowly forward. He felt the pressure of the bottle through the bag, cold against his cheek, and then, within a few minutes, the bag began to grow warm and slippery with tears, each desperate gasp between sobs sucking the clammy plastic into his mouth . . .

Like the puking wretch he'd been seven days before, Holland could do nothing but let it come and wait for it to finish.

He cried for himself, and for Sophie, and for the child that would be theirs in five weeks. He wept, guilty and sorry and stupid and scared. The tears whose sting was sharpest, though, that were squeezed out faster and bigger than most, were those he shed in anger at the spineless, selfish bastard he knew he had become.

When it was over, Holland lifted his sticky face up just enough to slide a sleeve across it, like a child. He sat, sniffing and staring up at the flat. Before, a general confusion and some pathetic, nameless fear had been twin hands pressing him down into his seat, preventing him from going inside. Now, although there was nothing vague about the shame he was feeling, like a welt across his gut, it was equally effective.

He couldn't go inside, not yet.

Holland looked down at his briefcase in the passenger footwell. He knew that even if he took work upstairs, tried to get straight into it, the first smile from Sophie would be enough to set him off again.

Maybe he could just drive around . . .

He reached down and grabbed the case, rummaged inside until he found the sheet of paper he was looking for. He cleared his throat as he took out his phone and dialed the number. Even so, when it was answered, the first word or two he spoke sounded choked and heavy.

"Mrs. Noble, it's Dave Holland here again. I know it's an odd time, but I was wondering if now might be a good time to pop over and pick up those photos . . . ?"

TWENTY-EIGHT

Holland made it to Romford in a notch under forty minutes, and stepped out of the car to find Irene Noble waiting on her doorstep. She marched down the path toward him. "You did that pretty quickly. It usually comes down to the traffic in the Blackwall Tunnel. This is probably the best time, actually . . ."

She was wearing a cream trouser suit and full makeup. Holland saw her glance toward the houses on either side. He guessed that she was hoping to see the twitch of a net curtain, a sign that one of the neighbors might be watching the young man walking toward her door.

"It was fairly easy," Holland said. "There wasn't much traffic at all . . ."

He followed her inside, where he was enthusiastically greeted by a small off-white dog. Its fur was matted and smelly, but Holland tried his best to make a fuss of it as it yapped and licked and scrabbled at his shins.

Mrs. Noble shooed the dog into the kitchen. "Candy's getting old now," she said. "Actually, she was Roger's dog, once upon a time. She was still only a puppy when he passed away."

Holland smiled sympathetically as they stepped through into the living room. A blue three-piece suite sat on a carpet of pink and purple swirls, and a glass-topped coffee table stood square on to the fireplace. A squashed corduroy cushion, covered in tufts of white dog hair, was the only thing in the room that didn't look spotless.

Holland took a step toward a beechwood cabinet that ran along the back wall. Its doors were mirrored, and its top covered in framed photographs of children.

Mrs. Noble walked across and picked up a picture. "Mark and Sarah aren't here," she said. "I couldn't bear looking at them and not knowing. I put them away once I felt sure they weren't coming back. Put them away and bloody well forgot where." She must have seen concern pass across Holland's face and reached out a hand to touch his arm. "Don't worry, you haven't had a wasted journey. I finally found pictures of them tucked away inside our old wedding album . . ."

Holland nodded his understanding. She turned the photo she was holding so that he could see the picture. "David's a stockbroker, doing really well." She put the frame back and began pointing to others. "Susan's a nurse up at the Royal Free, Gary went into the army and now he's training to become a printer, Claire's about to have her third baby . . ."

"There's a lot of them," Holland said.

"We fostered long-term mostly, which was the way I wanted it. I couldn't stand to see them go, you know, just when they were starting to belong. Still, we had more than twenty kids, before and after Mark and Sarah. I know what *most* of them are doing . . ."

She smiled sadly, not needing to say any more. Holland smiled back, thinking of those twenty other kids, and the man who was once their foster father, and wondering . . .

"I didn't know whether you'd have eaten," she said. "So after you phoned I took a lasagne out of the freezer. It won't be five minutes . . ."

"Oh, right . . ."

"I presume you can have a drink?"

In spite of what he'd previously thought of her, Holland was suddenly filled with something like affection for this woman. He thought about all the children she'd lost in one way or another, and her simple belief in a man whose heart was too full of darkness to go on beating any longer. He felt comfortable . . .

"Let's both have a drink," he said. "I've got a nice bottle of wine in the car."

"You have to let me pay you for the mattress," Thorne said.

"It's fine, really. You can get dinner . . ."

"How much was it?"

"It's a late birthday present," Eve said. "To replace the first one." She smiled. "I don't remember seeing the plant anywhere at the flat, so I presume you've managed to kill it."

"Oh, right. I was going to tell you about that," Thorne said.

A waiter brought over their wine, and at the same time the manager came across to the table and laid down a platter of poppadoms. "On the house," he said. He put a hand on Thorne's shoulder and winked at Eve. "One of my very best customers," he said. "But tonight is the first time he has been here with a young lady . . ."

When the manager had moved away, Eve poured herself and Thorne a large glass of wine each. "I'm not sure how to take that," she said. "Does he mean that you normally come here with young *men*?"

Thorne nodded, guiltily. "That was another thing I was going to tell you . . ."

She laughed. "So you come in here on your own a lot, then?"

"Not a *lot*." He nodded toward the manager. "He's talking about the number of takeaways . . ."

"I've got this image of you now, sitting in here on your own like Billy No-Mates, eating chicken tikka massala . . ."

"Hang on." Thorne tried to look hurt. "I do have one or two friends."

Eve chopped the pile of poppadoms into pieces. She picked up a big bit, ladled onions and chutney onto it. "Tell me about them. What do they do?"

Thorne shrugged. "They're all connected to work in one way or another, I suppose." He reached for a piece of poppadom, took a bite. "Phil's a pathologist . . ."

She nodded, like it meant something.

"What?" Thorne said.

"You never really switch off, do you?"

"Actually, me and Phil talk about football most of the time . . ."

"Seriously."

Thorne took a gulp of wine, feeling it swill the bits from the surface of his teeth, thinking about what Eve was saying. "I don't believe that anybody ever leaves what they do behind completely," he said. "We all talk shop, don't we? Everyone gets . . . reminded of things." She stared back at him, rubbing the rim of her wineglass across her chin. "Come on, if you're out somewhere and you see some amazing display of flowers . . ."

"Flowers aren't bodies, are they?"

Thorne was disturbed to feel himself growing slightly irritated. He fought to keep it out of his voice as he picked up the bottle and topped up both their glasses. "Well, some people might say that they're dying from the moment they're picked."

Eve nodded slowly. "Everything's dying," she said. "What's the bloody point of anything at all? We may as well just ask the waiter to put ground glass in the biryani."

Thorne looked at her, saw her eyes widen and the corners of her mouth begin to twitch. They began to laugh at almost the same moment.

"I never know when you're winding me up," he said.

She slid her hand across the table, took hold of his. "Can you leave it behind just for a while, Tom?" she said. "Tonight I want you to switch off . . ."

"Kids are a bloody handful," Irene Noble said. "They change things beyond all recognition." She stared across at Holland. "But you'll still be glad you did it . . ."

Holland had supposed that if they talked at all, they might well talk about kids. He never imagined that they might end up talking about *his*.

"I just feel so guilty," he said. "For resenting what might happen to me. For even *thinking* about walking away from it."

"You'll feel stuff that's a whole lot stranger and more painful than that. You'll feel like you would die for them and the next minute you'd happily murder them. You'll worry about where they are and then you'll wish you could have a second to yourself. Every emotion is unconditional . . ."

"You're talking about afterward, when the baby's there. What about feeling like this *now*?"

"It's normal. It's not just the woman's emotions that get messed around with. Mind you, *you* can't use hormones as an excuse . . ."

Holland laughed, the two glasses of wine he'd put away helping him to feel relaxed. An hour or so earlier, he'd felt far less sure of himself. He'd thought, when they'd started to eat and he'd suddenly begun pouring it all out, that there might be more waterworks on the way, but Irene had helped him stay calm, convinced him that everything would work out for the best . . .

"I'll take these out." She stood up, lifting the tray from the empty seat on the sofa next to her.

Holland passed over his empty plate. "Thanks, that was great." He was talking about more than just a lasagne that had been cold in the middle.

He sat back down and listened as she pottered around in the kitchen. He could hear her talking softly to the dog, loading the dishes into the dishwasher.

It had been a conversation that Holland would never have had with his mother. Irene Noble, give or take a year or two, was the same age as his mother—a woman who'd been buying baby clothes for the last six months. A woman who refused to admit that anything could go wrong *ever*, and remained blissfully unaware that things were less than hunky-dory between her eldest son and his pregnant girlfriend.

Irene came back in brandishing choc-ices. "I always keep a stock of these in the freezer. Bloody marvelous in this weather . . ."

For a minute they said nothing. They sat and ate their ice creams, and listened to the noise of the dog's claws skittering across the linoleum as she scrabbled about in the kitchen.

As Irene Noble started to speak, pulling her feet up onto the sofa like a teenager, Holland watched her face shift and settle until every one of her years was clearly visible on it.

"Whatever problems you have, I hope you work them out together, all three of you. But they won't be in the same league as some of the things that kids have brought with them through my front door. You pass them on, you know. Hand them down, like baldness or diabetes or the color of your eyes . . ."

"You're talking about Mark and Sarah . . ."

"The other day I was very harsh about the two sets of carers who had the children before we did. About their inability to cope. The truth is that we weren't really coping any better than they had."

"You adopted them."

"I think it was our last effort at making them feel part of something bigger. Two parents and two children. We wanted them to come out of themselves, to engage with the rest of the world a bit more."

"It's understandable, though," Holland said. "That they'd be tight-knit. That the two of them would be very close, after what happened." He looked away from her, down to the floor, thinking, *And what was still happening . . .*

"They were *too* close," she said. "That was the problem. When they disappeared, Sarah was pregnant, and the baby she was carrying was Mark's."

TWENTY-NINE

They walked slowly back down Kentish Town Road toward Thorne's flat. At not much after nine o'clock, it was just starting to darken but was still warm enough to walk without a jacket. The road was as busy and noisy as ever. Cars moved past them constantly; those that could had their tops down; most had sidelights on.

Despite what Eve had said earlier, they had both tucked a fair amount of food away, though Thorne put the feeling in his stomach down to something else entirely. Before they'd left the flat, Eve had helped him make the bed, laying a clean white sheet across the new mattress she'd brought with her. Thorne knew very well that when they got back there, she was going to help him unmake it again.

There were some things in his life that he counted as certainties: there was always another body somewhere; you could never get rid of blood completely; people who killed without motive tended to do it again. But *this* was the sort of promise that Thorne hadn't been on for a very long time . . .

Eve grabbed his hand suddenly and raised it up, bringing their bare forearms together. "You'd look a lot better with a decent tan," she said.

"Is that an invitation?"

"When was the last time you had a proper holiday?"

Even after thinking about it for a minute, Thorne

couldn't provide anything as specific as a year. Lack of time was not so much the problem as lack of inclination and anybody to go away with. "It's been a while," he said.

"Are you a lying-on-the-beach kind of guy, or do you prefer to do stuff?"

"Both, really. Or neither. I think lying on the beach gets a bit boring, but probably not *quite* as boring as walking round a museum . . ."

"Not easily pleased, are you?"

"Sorry . . ."

"All right, where would you like to go, if you could go anywhere?"

"I've always fancied Nashville."

She nodded. "Right. The country-and-western thing . . ."

"Another one of my dark secrets . . ."

"I quite liked it."

"Really?"

"You're not going to get kinky later on, though, are you? Dress up in leather chaps? Bring out the bullwhip and spurs . . . ?"

They turned right onto Prince of Wales Road, the sound of live jazz coming from the Pizza Express on the corner. Thorne wondered if a pizza might not have been a better idea. The combination of curry and humidity meant that beads of perspiration were popping all over him.

They were still hand in hand and Thorne could feel the moisture between their palms. He wasn't sure whether it was her sweat or his own.

The bike weaved effortlessly through the traffic. Occasionally, where it got really heavy, or the road narrowed, he would have to sit and wait. Idling in line among the bike messengers and trainee cabbies on mopeds. Soon enough, there would be a gap and he would be away, the backpack bouncing against his back as he drove across sleeping policemen and holes in the road . . .

He pulled up at traffic lights and checked his watch. He was probably going to get there a bit early, but it wouldn't matter. He would park up, stroll off somewhere, and wait. Keeping out of sight, until it was time.

Next to him, a big Kawasaki revved up, ready for the green light. A girl in cutoff jeans rode on the back, squeezing her boyfriend tighter with each growl he twisted from the engine. On amber, the Jap bike was gone, and he watched it go, easing his own machine slowly away from the lights.

Picking up no more speed than was necessary . . .

He had plenty of time, and the last thing he wanted was to be pulled over.

It wasn't so much a question of the ticket or the points on his license. He was so excited, so full of what he was about to do, that were some copper to pull him over and ask where he was going, he might just have to tell him.

Holland looked at his watch and was shocked to see that he'd been there for an hour and a half.

"I need to be getting back," he said. "Could I have those photographs?"

Irene Noble climbed a little wearily from the sofa, slipped her shoes back on. "I'll go and fetch them . . ."

While he was waiting, Holland sat, going over their conversation and marveling at the capacity people had for self-deception. Irene Noble was far from being a stupid woman. He found it hard to understand why, even though she claimed that they, and previous carers, had caught the children in bed together, she had so readily presumed that Sarah Foley had been made pregnant by her brother. Had no other explanation occurred to her?

He heard her coming down the stairs, shouting to him.

"It doesn't seem five minutes since these were taken."

Probably no other explanation she could live with . . .

She walked into the room holding out a small bundle of photos, half a dozen Polaroids and a couple of slightly bigger standard prints. Holland took them from her. She stepped back and perched on the arm of the sofa, pointing to the pictures as he began to look through them.

"Those are the two I had in frames on the sideboard. They're the ones that were taken at school the year before they disappeared. The others are from a birthday party we had for Sarah. Her eleventh, it would have been. Roger had just bought this instant camera . . ."

From the moment he'd looked down at the first photograph, Holland had stopped hearing anything but the sound of his own breathing. A girl in a blue-patterned dress, her hair tied back, smiling as though at something only she found funny. Holland lifted the picture of Sarah up, revealing its companion, the portrait of her brother.

"Jesus," he said.

Irene stood up. "What's the matter?"

Holland flicked through the other photos to make sure, stopping at one in particular and staring at it, elated and terrified. He couldn't hear as Irene Noble continued to ask him what was wrong, didn't see her moving across the room toward him.

Sarah Foley sat at the table, the knife in her hand poised above a cake, the girls either side of her looking far more excited than she did. Just visible in the top right of the picture, Mark stood in the corner of the room. His fingers were curled around the edge of the door, as if he were preparing to throw it open and run through it, or else push away from it, launching himself toward the camera and whoever lay beyond it.

Her face was thinner then, and his perhaps a little

fuller. The eyes were wider and the skin smoother, but that was understandable. These were the faces of children, which had yet to weather, but Holland was familiar with their expressions.

He was looking at pictures of people he recognized.

THIRTY

Thorne lay in bed, listening hard, trying to ascertain exactly what might be happening from the sounds he could hear coming from the bathroom . . .

For the want of anything more original to say, he'd offered Eve a coffee as soon as they'd got back to the flat, hoping she'd turn it down and delighted when she did. She'd gone to the toilet then, and he'd moved around the flat, opening windows, grinning at himself in the mirror like a schoolboy as he passed the mantelpiece on the way to the stereo. With the first few bars of "Good Year for the Roses" filling the room, Thorne had turned to find her standing only inches away . . .

They'd half danced, half stumbled through to the bedroom, and collapsed onto the new mattress. The laughter gave way quickly to more passionate noises as their hands and mouths went to work on each other, the wine and the wait making their movements hungrier, more desperate than they'd been earlier, before they'd left for the restaurant . . .

Then suddenly Eve had stopped and begun to laugh again. She'd pushed herself off the bed, grinned, and announced that she needed another visit to the bathroom. As soon as she'd closed the door behind her, Thorne had stripped quickly and slid beneath the duvet, grateful to have avoided that awkward moment when the love handles were revealed, but feeling, all the same, that a certain spontaneity had gone . . .

Now he could hear nothing through the wall between bedroom and bathroom. As he thought about it, the impetus might have been lost, but no more so than it would have been when the moment came for him to fiddle clumsily around with a condom. He thought about the packet he'd bought the day before, from the machine in the toilets at the Royal Oak. It lay nestled in the drawer of his bedside cabinet, alongside the athlete's foot cream and indigestion tablets.

He decided that it might save time and trouble if he took a condom out of the packet and laid it ready. As he reached across to open the drawer, a thought struck him. Perhaps she was in the bathroom, fiddling clumsily around with a diaphragm . . .

Thorne heard water running. He sat up a little higher in bed, leaned his head back against the wall, and turned his ear to it.

She was probably brushing her teeth . . .

He wondered whether he should slip out of bed, put on his dressing gown, and join her. How would it feel if her teeth were clean while his mouth still tasted of curry? Would it seem strange, the two of them spitting into the sink together before they'd so much as felt each other up?

The door opened, and Eve walked back in. She stopped next to the bed and looked down at him. Her clothes were straightened and smooth, as though it were already the following morning and she had come to kiss him good-bye. She looked sexier than anything he could remember, looked as if she found *him* more attractive than ever, and yet, for a second, Thorne wondered if she was about to turn and leave.

Before he could say anything, she laid her handbag

gently down by the side of the bed, took a step back, and began to undress.

The home number was engaged, so Holland tried Thorne's mobile. The phone sat on a table in a tiny alcove beneath the stairs, where Holland fought for space with coats, umbrellas, and plastic bags filled with boots and shoes.

Irene Noble hovered behind him. "Who are you calling? Are you allowed to tell me?"

"Detective Inspector Thorne. You met him the other day . . ."

"Oh yes. Perhaps he's got a mobile."

"I'm trying it now . . ." Holland turned away, suddenly uncomfortable with her so close. In his hurry to make the call, to pass on what he'd discovered, it hadn't occurred to him that he should really be doing it privately. He'd been relaxed, enjoying himself. Now he was on duty again, and he knew there were things he had to tell Thorne that Irene Noble shouldn't hear. "I'm sorry, but you'll have to . . ."

Holland heard Thorne's voice telling him how sorry he was that he couldn't talk to him, asking him to leave a message. Holland pressed a button to end the call. This was a message that he wanted to deliver personally.

Still clutching the photographs of Mark and Sarah Foley, Holland was out of there in less than a minute.

He thanked Irene Noble as he backed away down the path toward his car, all the time wondering if there was a quicker way back toward North London, telling himself that there was no need to go mad, that their suspects had no way of knowing they'd been identified and would not be going anywhere.

The last thing Holland told Irene Noble, shouting through his open window just before he pulled away, was that he'd take good care of her photos. In truth, he didn't know when she was likely to see them again. Holland would show them to Thorne. He would show them to Brigstocke. They would use them to secure a warrant . . .

Holland could not know for sure how it would proceed from there, what the timeline would be, how much would be passed on to the media. Every case ended differently. Still, there was a chance, if they wanted to stem the flow of damaging publicity, and made the arrests over the weekend, that the next time Irene Noble saw the pictures would be on the front pages of the papers on Monday morning.

"You're gorgeous," Thorne said, staring down, wanting her. "I can't believe it's taken so bloody long to get here."

"Whose fault is that?"

"Mine, I know."

"Glad you're here now, though?"

"God, yeah." Thorne grinned. "I'm thinking about what would have happened if I hadn't answered the phone in that hotel room, when we found the first body. You might have called an hour later. It could easily have been somebody else who answered that phone . . ."

She shrugged. "Then it could very easily have been somebody else who was here now."

Her body felt warm and smooth against his. He was sure, rusty and as inept a reader of signs as he was, that he saw desire in her eyes. Yet a minute before, when he'd placed a hand for the first time against the naked flesh of her breast, he'd felt a tension. There was a reserve suddenly, which seemed slightly at odds with what Thorne had been led to expect. She'd made the first move, cracked those dirty jokes about the bed, about being up for it. Now, at the last moment, she was revealing herself to be not quite as forward as she pretended to be.

Thorne felt a barrier go up. Fragile and perhaps only a touch away from collapse, and unbearably sexy . . .

She wanted him to do the work, to be a man. It was as though she longed to submit to him, to herself, but needed a little help. Thorne was massively excited. He could sense what might be waiting if she allowed herself to go over the edge. More than anything, he wanted to nudge her toward it . . .

"You're *so* gorgeous," he said, and dropped his mouth down onto hers.

As if on cue, Thorne could hear a song beginning in the other room. This was the one he'd thought would be so perfect. The story of a man whose love for a woman ended only on the day they carried him out of his front door in a box. Thorne let the familiar richness of George Jones's voice roll over him as he ran his hands across Eve's body.

He was dimly aware of another familiar sound. The bedroom door creaked open, hissing as it moved across the carpet. It was a noise that often disturbed him in the early hours, and one that, tonight of all nights, he could well do without.

Thorne stopped what he was doing and smiled at Eve, waiting to feel the unwelcome weight of the cat landing on the end of the bed . . .

Holland took the Romford Road as far as Forest Gate, then cut over toward Wanstead Flats. This was not an area of London he knew well. With one hand on the steering wheel and the other holding open the *A-Z*, he was making up his route as he went.

He'd called Sophie as soon as he'd left Irene Noble's house, to explain why he hadn't come home. He'd told her that something important had come up, grateful that it was no longer a lie. She had told him that she was tired, that she would be getting an early night, but he could hear in her voice that she was less than thrilled. He managed to tell her that he loved her before she put the phone down.

Holland tried phoning Thorne's home number. It was still engaged. He dialed the mobile again, hung up as soon as he heard Thorne's recorded message . . .

He was doing fifty on the long, straight road that cut across Hackney Marshes. It was another area in this strange part of the city that was green enough on the page of the *A-Z*, but seemed grim and far from welcoming after dark. He'd feel happier once he picked up the A107 at Clapton. He could see it at the bottom of the page, only a fingernail away from where he was now. Then it was pretty much a straight line up through Stamford Hill and on to the Seven Sisters Road. Ten minutes more, past Finsbury Park and across the Holloway Road, and he would be at Thorne's place.

Once again, he thought about doing the simple thing and calling Brigstocke. It was probably the *correct* thing to do, but his first loyalty, as always, was to Thorne. He recalled an American cop show he and Sophie had watched one evening: *NYPD Blue* maybe, or *Homicide*. An officer had talked about giving his partner a "heads-up" on something, when really he should have taken the matter higher. Thorne wasn't his partner, of course, but it was still more or less how Holland felt.

Thorne would be grateful for a heads-up on this one . . .

Surer now of his bearings, Holland laid the *A-Z* down on the passenger seat and dialed Thorne's flat again. He listened to the monotonous beep of the engaged signal, wondering why he wasn't hearing the usual, irritating "call-waiting" message.

Holland had a good idea whom Thorne would be talking to. He remembered a night in the Royal Oak when Thorne had been talking about himself and his father, and their "forty-five-minute conversations about fuck all." Tonight it was likely to be fuck all *and* a Spurs win in the opening game of the season. Holland could picture Thorne sitting there listening, a can of supermarket lager on the go, desperately trying to get his old man off the line so that they could both settle down and watch the goals on TV.

Two–one against Chelsea at Stamford Bridge. Thorne should at least be in a good mood.

Holland reached across and retrieved the photographs from beneath the *A-Z*. He wondered what sort of mood Thorne would be in, twenty minutes or so from now, after he'd taken a look at *them* . . .

Thorne froze, in confusion as much as anything, when he turned and saw the man taking off his crash helmet.

"How the fuck did *you* get in?" Thorne said. For a few dizzy and bewildering seconds, all he could think of was that this was some sort of jealous-boyfriend situation he'd unwittingly got caught up in, and that he was about to get involved in a very embarrassing fistfight. It was the look on the man's face, as much as the knife he was pulling from his rucksack, that told Thorne something altogether different was happening.

Thorne turned to Eve, whipping his head around fast, and straight into the knife that *she* held, pointed toward him. The blade sliced a clean line across his chin, the point sinking itself half an inch or so into the soft flesh beneath his jaw.

He cried out, threw himself sideways, and began to bleed on to the pillow.

The man took a step toward the bed.

One small part of Thorne's brain continued to function rationally, to formulate a thought. *The knife was in her bag.* The rest of it began to give shape to something dark, to a fear he'd felt before only as something fleeting and skittish, but that was now borne inside him, heavy and hooked beneath his breastbone. He pictured it, alive and feeding in his chest. He felt its strong, thin fingers wrapped around his ribs, hanging from them, pulling him down.

Thorne lifted his head up and pressed a hand to the gash across his chin. He tried not to let the terror sound in his voice when he spoke.

"Mark and Sarah . . ."

At the mention of his real name, a shadow fell across the man's face. "Move away from my sister, now."

Thorne shuffled across the mattress, oddly uncomfortable with his nakedness. He watched the woman step, nude and smiling, from the other side of the bed and gather up her clothes.

"Eve, this is so stupid . . ."

Ben Jameson's eyes moved quickly, from his sister's body back to Thorne. "Get onto the fucking floor . . ."

THIRTY-ONE

While they were preparing him, Thorne tried to take the growing fear, the blood, the pain and keep them somewhere separate. Somewhere he could store them up, stoke them into a rage he might be able to use. The rest of his brain was focusing, coming up with answers, putting it together. Adrenaline causing the engine to race . . .

The two of them worked together quickly and efficiently. Before Thorne could even think about how he might move against them, against the two knives, it became an impossibility. Eve slipped the belt from Thorne's chinos, wrapped it around his wrists until it hurt. Ben manipulated his body, pushing the head down toward the carpet, hoiking up the knees, spreading the calves. They operated as a team, movement and stillness in sync, one busy while the other held a knife close. Thorne was never more than a few inches away from a blade. Any move, other than those he was instructed to make, was out of the question.

Now his body mirrored those he'd seen before. Distorted and discolored. In hotel rooms and in dreams . . .

Thorne lay naked, facedown on the floor, knees pulled up beneath him and hindquarters raised. His head and hands pointed toward the bedroom door. Blood from the knife wound soaked into the carpet and grew sticky beneath his cheek.

"It didn't matter in the rest of the room," Thorne said. "In those hotels, traces just got lost among everybody else's. But you had to get rid of the *bedding,* didn't you, Eve? That would have been clean, that would just have had traces of you and the victim . . ."

Though Thorne couldn't see it, Eve smiled. "Once I got them into bed, they were helpless. Same as you."

"I never raped anybody, Eve . . ."

"It's a bit late, don't you think?" Jameson said. "To be slotting pieces into your little puzzle? It's rather fucking pointless, considering where you are."

"Who wants to die ignorant?"

"You can't do much about that," Jameson said, "*however* many answers you get . . ."

"Is this the pet project you talked about? These killings? The thing of your own you wanted to get off the ground . . ."

Jameson laughed. "That's quite funny. Be a damn sight more interesting than local authority training videos, that's for sure. There you go, there's one more piece of your puzzle. One more thing to make you a bit less ignorant . . ."

Thorne was already trying to work it out. "It's how you got into the Register, isn't it? Not sure where the connection is. Social services?"

Eve provided the answer. "The National Probation Directorate. Specifically the Sex Offenders and Corrections Unit . . ."

"*Towards a National Information Strategy* isn't *Citizen Kane,*" Jameson said. "But they were more than happy for me to do all the research I needed and their security *was* very sloppy. They were somewhat lax about unattended computers, access to databases, that sort of thing. Mind you, that *was* exactly why they wanted the video made in the first place . . ."

It suddenly struck Thorne that Jameson had probably

been on the list that was compiled of contact numbers for Charlie Dodd. A video production company would not have seemed suspicious, bearing in mind the nature of Dodd's business. Never having known it, Thorne would not have recognized the name of Jameson's company anyway. It didn't matter a great deal now . . .

"That was fortunate for you," Thorne said.

"We all need a bit of luck now and again," Eve said. "Some of us more than others . . ."

Thorne lifted his face from the carpet, feeling fibers and tiny pieces of grit sticking to the dried blood on his chin. He took the weight on his forehead and looked back through the gap underneath his arm. Jameson was delving into the rucksack he'd placed on the end of the bed. Eve stood by his side, her eyes never leaving Thorne.

"We should get this done," she said.

Thorne saw a flash of blue as Jameson pulled out the length of washing line, then one of black, which he presumed was the hood. He felt the fear that was the creature in his chest grow heavier. He closed his eyes and saw it climbing, using the slats of his rib cage like a ladder, heaving itself upward little by little.

As was so often the way, it was the last part of the journey that was proving the most frustrating. It had taken ages to get across the Holloway Road at the Nag's Head and up to Tufnell Park. Now the ridiculous number of traffic lights and pedestrian crossings on the Kentish Town Road was providing a last-minute annoyance.

Holland thought about calling again. He decided that even if Thorne was off the phone or had turned the mobile back on, he was more or less there now anyway, so there wasn't much point . . .

Holland drove down the inside lane, swerving back out right when he came up against a bus and deftly cutting off a black cab in the process. At the next set of lights the taxi came up *his* inside and the driver wound down his window to give him an earful. Holland held up his warrant card, told the fat cabbie to fuck off, and watched, smiling, as he did.

When the lights changed, Holland swung into Prince of Wales Road. Thorne's street was the third on the right. He slowed to a stop, glancing down at the photos while he was waiting for a break in the traffic.

When one finally came, he turned, wondering if they'd even allow Thorne to be there when they made the arrests.

"It *is* the most fantastic story, though," Jameson said. "Maybe I should write it, change all the names, of course, to protect the innocent . . ."

"Whoever *they* are," Thorne said.

"It would be in three parts. Three *acts,* if you like, same as any classic screenplay . . ."

"You live and learn."

"Not for much longer."

The black thing inside Thorne climbed another rib . . .

"For the first part we have to go back in time. Flared trousers and shit hair and a piece of scum who probably has both. A man who drags a woman into a storeroom and rapes her."

"Your mother . . ."

Thorne felt the vibrations as feet moved quickly across the carpet toward him, then the pain of a heel pressing down onto the side of his face. "Let him tell it," Eve said.

"The rapist, thanks largely to the police, is found not guilty. The woman suffers a breakdown. Her husband goes mad." Jameson emptied the facts from his mouth like he was spitting out dirt. "He kills her and then him-self and their bodies are discovered by their two young children, who are subsequently taken into foster care. It's a dramatic start, don't you reckon?"

"That's why I'm here, isn't it?" Thorne said. The shoe came back down across the side of his face and ear. Jameson said something he couldn't make out and the foot was lifted. Thorne turned his head and saw Eve moving back across the room toward her brother. " 'Thanks largely to the police,' that's what you said. So, I have to die because of the way some fuckwit handled a rape case nearly thirty years ago." He received no answer. "Yes? Is that about right?"

"There's no point bleating about life being unfair," Eve said. "We're the last people you'll get any sympathy from there . . ."

"I understand why. I just want to know why *me?*"

"Because you answered the phone."

And Thorne saw that it really was that simple. The message left by the killer on Eve Bloom's answering machine had always bothered him, and finally he understood why. It had been "left" so that Eve had an excuse to call the hotel—a call to a murder scene that would be answered by a police officer. The wreaths had been ordered after the subsequent killings purely to make it look like part of a pattern.

They had selected their rapists with care. Their final victim, Thorne himself, had been chosen completely at random. He remembered what he'd said to Eve, what she'd said to him, twenty minutes earlier in bed:

It could easily have been somebody else who answered that phone . . .

Then it could very easily have been somebody else who was here now.

He could still see the look on her face as she'd said it. He imagined the look on his father's as he received the news of Thorne's death.

"I've got a great title as well," Jameson said. "For this

sordid little horror story. What do you think of 'Out of the Frying Pan into the Fire'?"

"We know about Roger Noble . . ."

"Oh, you do?" For the first time, though Jameson did not raise his voice, Thorne could hear emotion behind it, white-hot and lethal. "You might know what he did, but you can't know how it felt."

"Bad enough so that you had to leave."

"Well done . . ."

"To protect your sister . . ."

"Noble didn't want to hurt me," Eve said. "He wanted to hurt my baby."

"He made you pregnant?"

Jameson laughed. "We're back to ignorance. We should have a little bell to ring, or a buzzer, for when you get it wrong or say something stupid. Noble liked *boys*. The baby was mine."

"Ours," Eve said. "So we left when they tried to make me get rid of it."

Thorne realized that it had been shame he'd heard in Irene Noble's voice when she'd stared into her Marks & Spencer coffee and talked about "behavioral" problems. It had probably been her idea to move in the first place, to get the abortion performed in a different area, to avoid the scandal . . .

"What happened to the child?" Thorne asked.

Jameson answered matter-of-factly. "We lost it. Who knows, when all this is over, we might try again."

For perhaps half a minute, nobody spoke. Thorne lay in agony, a breeze from somewhere passing across his bare skin. The feeling had gone from his hands, and the thumping of his heart was lifting his chest clear off the carpet.

When all this is over . . .

He imagined the look that was passing between the two people who planned to kill him. He pictured something tender, an expression of the love between a man and a woman, who talked about having a baby together once he had been raped and strangled to death.

Thorne moaned in pain as he twisted his head across to the other side. "I'm guessing that the final part of this story involves the murders," he said. "Remfry and Welch and Dodd and Southern. Me as the symbolic climax. It's the middle bit that's still a mystery, after you disappeared. What happened between Franklin and the men in prison? Why did you start killing again?"

"Lightning struck twice," Eve said.

Then the doorbell rang . . .

Thorne tensed and raised his head, but their speed, their *commitment,* was overpowering. In a heartbeat they were on him, a knife pressed into each side of his throat, cutting off the breath he'd need before he had a chance to cry out . . .

Hendricks picked up almost immediately.

"Listen," Holland said, "I'm outside DI Thorne's place and I can't get any reply, but his phone's engaged . . ."

"He probably left it off the hook, while he's busy giving Eliza Doolittle a good seeing to."

Holland felt ice at his neck. "Sorry?"

"He had a hot date with his sexy florist. I'm not surprised he doesn't want to answer the door . . ."

"Oh, Jesus . . ."

"What is it?"

Holland told Hendricks about the pictures, about Mark and Sarah Foley. Hendricks announced that he was coming straight over. The panic Holland heard in the pathologist's voice stemmed the rising tide of it he felt in himself.

Then, looking across the road, he saw the motorbike . . .

"Dave . . . ?"

Holland felt the engine that was ticking over within him moving up a gear. "Listen, Phil, before you leave, get on the phone. Call Brigstocke and fill him in. Get some backup round here now. And an ambulance . . ."

"What are you going to do?"

Holland was walking along the pavement, away from Thorne's place. He was thinking about the alleyway that he remembered running along the side of a house three or four doors up. "I'm not sure . . ."

He was seeing a face through a crash helmet. Seeing the face of a killer, smiling at the lie within the truth.

I've got a BMW myself . . .

Smiling, because BMW makes bikes as well as cars . . .

THIRTY-TWO

"Why don't you just get out now while you still can?" Thorne said. "You'll spend the rest of your lives in prison. You'll never see each other again . . ."

Jameson sounded unconcerned. "Don't get worked up. Whoever that was at your door, they've gone."

Thorne twisted his head, aimed his voice toward Eve. "People know you were coming over here, for fuck's sake. There'll be fibers, bits of skin everywhere. In the bed . . ."

"Of course there will," Eve said. "I'm your girlfriend. Which is why *I'll* be the one calling the police."

Thorne was stunned, but he saw immediately that they would get away with it. It was very simple. With Thorne dead, Jameson would kiss his sister good-bye for a while and slip away. On his way out, he would kick in the door that she'd previously left open for him, make sure there were signs of a forced entry.

Then she would dial 999 . . .

He had no doubt that Eve would play the part of the traumatized witness and, later, the grieving girlfriend perfectly. He knew all too well how good she was, how convincingly she would pick up the pieces of her life. He could see the officers falling a little bit in love with her as they took her shocking statement.

The idea that they would not be made to pay for his death caused a surge of fury to rush through Thorne. He did not need it, but he felt a jolt of added determination to cling on fiercely to every second.

"Tell me about the lightning, Eve."

She said nothing, but Jameson took the bait. "Franklin was always going to pay for what he did. It just took me a while to get round to it . . ."

Jameson had moved to stand between Thorne and the door. Eve had crossed back to the bed. He presumed that Jameson was still holding the hood, and the washing line, but he could not be certain. Thorne guessed that Roger Noble had been fortunate, dropping dead when he did. Something in Jameson's voice suggested that, had he still been alive, Jameson would have "got round" to him as well . . .

"So why not leave it there?" Thorne asked.

"We did," Eve said. "Carried on with the lives we'd made, that we'd *re*made, for ourselves, until I had one too many slow dances at a party. Until some piece of shit thought that 'no' meant 'yes' and followed me home . . ."

Facedown on the carpet, Thorne knew full well the expression on her face. He'd seen it before, the night they'd walked across London Fields and he'd told her about the case. Told her things she already knew far better than he did . . .

Just think of this bloke as cutting reoffending rates . . .

"It would be stupid to ask if you reported the rape to the police," Thorne said.

Jameson took a step toward him, his black boots moving into Thorne's field of vision. "Very fucking stupid. We dealt with that one ourselves . . ."

Thorne remembered the *other* case Holland and Stone had pulled off CRIMINT. A man found raped and strangled in the boot of a car. The ligature had been removed, but Thorne could now be pretty certain that it had been washing line.

He'd solved another murder in the last few moments before his own . . .

"Which all brings us bang up-to-date," Jameson said.

To me, Thorne thought. He knew he was the last in a line of dead men, connected by the strongest, strangest thread of all. The family tie that refused to break, even when it had become twisted beyond all recognition.

"You kill the man you blame for the death of your mother and father, and for your abuse at the hands of the foster parent who replaces them. You kill the man who attacked your sister. You develop a taste for it—"

"Not a taste for *killing*, no."

"My mistake. A taste for some perverted idea of justice . . ."

"Listen to yourself . . ."

"Tell me you don't enjoy it . . ."

Eve's voice was flat, barely above a whisper. "I want to do this now," she said.

Thorne could feel her walking toward him. At the same time Jameson moved quickly, one step bringing him next to Thorne, another lifting a boot up and across Thorne's back, until he was straddling him.

Thorne knew what was coming, but refused to submit to it. He reacted instinctively, thrusting his legs backward and pushing his groin down toward the carpet. Hands grabbed his legs, clawed at his thighs as they struggled to lift them, fought to bring his rear end upright, to make it accessible . . .

Pain and numbness had left the top half of Thorne's body as good as useless. It was no more than a dead thing, with only the dark mass that clung to his ribs still flourishing. Swinging inside him, wet and weighty, clattering off the wall of his chest as he kicked and thrashed.

"Stop it," Jameson said.

Thorne cried out, the terror suddenly far greater than the rage. His voice sounded high and weak, and was quickly replaced by the deafening roar and squeal of agony as Jameson's gloved fist pounded into the side of his head, again and again, until Thorne could do nothing but let go, and be still, and wait for it to stop.

Seconds stretched and passed, and though Thorne had lost track of who was where, he was aware of movement, of arms and legs, of pressure . . .

He was aware of Eve's voice as the scream in his head died down a little, and he heard her saying, "Hold him."

He was aware that he had started to cry, and was grateful that he hadn't lost control of bladder or bowels.

Thorne raised his head an inch off the floor. The wetness slipped beneath his chin and into the gash, stinging. "One thing," he said, looking for Jameson, his voice somewhere between a gasp and a rattle, "just for my own satisfaction. Are you going to rape me before or after I'm dead? We never *could* work that out . . ."

Jameson was sitting across the top of Thorne's back. He leaned down close to his ear. "Ding, ding. Stupid again. *I've* never raped anyone . . ."

Thorne felt his head being lifted up by the hair and twisted around. He quickly forgot about the searing pain in his neck and shoulders when he saw what Eve was holding. It was dull, and dark, and thick as his fist. A warped simulation of a sex organ, designed only for the pleasure of one who sought to invade and to injure.

A weapon, pure and simple.

"No need to bother with the condom, this time," Eve said.

Thorne thought about the traces found at the first postmortem. The natural assumption that the victim had been penetrated by flesh and blood. That the rapist wore a condom. That the rapist was a man . . .

In wholly different circumstances, Thorne might even have laughed, but he knew very well what the thing Eve held in her hand would do, condom or not, when she rammed it into him . . .

"To answer your question, though," Jameson said, "we find that doing both things at the same time works pretty well for us."

Holland thought he heard a cry as he dropped down onto the kitchen floor. He froze, listening. There was music playing in the living room. Thorne's usual country crap. From somewhere, there was a series of dull thuds, and then silence.

He moved slowly and quietly through into the living room, in much the same way as the burglar who'd come in through the same window six weeks earlier. From the table on the far side of the room a red light caught his eye, flashing from the handset that had been taken off the hook. Thorne's mobile was next to it. Holland didn't need to go any closer to know that it had been switched off . . .

The song faded out, and in the gap before the next one started, Holland heard the low murmur of voices. He turned toward the sound as the music began again.

They were in the bedroom. Jameson, and the girl, and . . .

Though he couldn't make out what was being said, relief flooded through him as he recognized one of the voices as Thorne's.

The relief turned into something that tasted bitter in his mouth as Holland realized that he needed to act quickly, that he would have no idea what to expect on the other side of the bedroom door. He thought about Sophie as he stood, rooted to the spot, looking around the room for something he might use as a weapon.

Thorne felt the pain shoot through his neck and shoulders as Jameson shifted his weight. He watched a hand pass in front of his face. The washing line was looped around the fingers . . .

"Strange how a man's mind works," Jameson said. "Even close to death, they were all far more afraid of what was happening at the back end than the front . . ."

Thorne winced as Eve's hand pressed down onto the small of his back. He tensed and sucked in a breath at the touch of cold plastic brushing against his thigh.

"On that scale of one to ten," she said, "how keen are you *now*?"

Thorne clenched, and drove his pelvis down toward the floor, but he was unable to flatten himself. He felt only the gentle resistance of the pillows that had been placed beneath him, raising his backside just enough, however much he tried to move away . . .

Jameson grabbed a handful of Thorne's hair, lifted up his head. "Some advice, for what it's worth." Thorne grunted, shook his head. "It's best not to fight the line when you feel it round your neck . . ."

Thorne channeled every last ounce of strength he had left into his neck, driving his head back down toward the floor.

He could feel his hair being torn away by the roots . . .

He could feel the thick tip of the phallus pushing at the crack of his buttocks . . .

He pushed his face toward the carpet, knowing that Jameson just needed enough room, enough space to get the hood on. The line would quickly follow and then it would all be over . . .

"Take it or leave it," Jameson said. "Seriously, though, if you let me get on with it and let the line do its job, you'll be unconscious long before she's finished . . ."

Thorne screamed, and at the same moment, Jameson stopped pulling and smashed Thorne's head forward onto the floor. Thorne lay still, momentarily stunned, for the few seconds that Jameson needed to slip the hood over his head.

Even as he writhed and jerked, Thorne felt a bizarre calm, which grew deeper as the ligature tightened around his neck. He felt the fear inside him shrivel to nothing. He saw faces burst and scatter as flashes of light. He drifted through a black space so thick that he knew it had more to do with death than darkness.

The crash of the door and the shouting are like distant sound effects that echo and grow suddenly deafening as the pressure around his neck is released . . .

Thorne sucked air into his lungs and reared up, snarling and snapping his head back into something, feeling it give and soften. The weight fell or was lifted from him, and he pitched forward, rolling over onto his back. He lifted his hands, numbed by the belt, and began scrabbling with dead fingers to remove the hood.

A scream, and then a crack, and the piercing squeal of castors as the bed moves at speed across the floor . . .

He stared up at the ceiling, heard grunts of effort and pain, and the crash of bodies impacting with something solid. Dropping his head to the side, Thorne saw Jameson and Holland in a heap by the wardrobe. He saw the wardrobe door swing slowly open and, in the mirror on the back, he saw Eve coming at him.

Spinning quickly from the reflection to the real thing. . . .

With her knife raised, she launched herself, or stumbled or fell, toward him, and Thorne could do little but turn his face away and kick up hard at her. As she opened her mouth, grimacing with the effort or with the hatred, Thorne's foot crashed into the underside of her jaw, knocking her head back and sending a thick string of blood arcing high above them both. The last drops were still raining down long moments after she'd fallen to the floor like a side of meat . . .

Thorne climbed gingerly to his feet and moved slowly across to where Holland was standing, doubled over and white-faced, panting. Jameson lay moaning on the floor, one arm bent awkwardly behind him and the other stretched toward a knife that he was never going to reach. He looked up, his expression impossible to read through the pulpy red mess that Thorne's head had made of his face.

A bottle of wine lay on its side, half rolled beneath the wardrobe. Thorne nudged it out with his foot as Holland began untying the belt around his wrists.

"It was all I could find," Holland said between gulps of air. "I think I broke the fucker's arm with it . . ."

Hands free, Thorne turned and walked back to where Eve was sprawled near the bedroom door. She still had the knife in her hand, but barely noticed as Thorne took it away from her. She was busy scanning the blood-stained carpet for half of her tongue, bitten off as cleanly as her father's had been, when he'd dropped from a banister all those years before.

Thorne sank down to the floor, leaned back against the bed. He felt the pain start to return. In his head, in his arms, everywhere.

From the other room he could hear George Jones singing like nothing had happened.

He stared at himself in the mirror on the back of the wardrobe door. Naked and covered in blood, he looked like some kind of ravening savage. He watched himself slowly move a hand to cover his genitals.

"I phoned Hendricks," Holland said. "There's backup on the way."

Thorne nodded. "That's good. That's very good, Dave. Pass me my fucking underpants first, though, would you . . . ?"

Part Four

The Kingdom Where Nobody Dies

THIRTY-THREE

Yvonne Kitson rang him on his way to St. Albans.

"Tom, how are you doing?"

"I'm good. What about you?"

"I'm fine. Listen . . ."

Thorne knew very well that Kitson was far from fine. Her husband had taken the kids after discovering her affair with a senior officer and now her career looked likely to fall apart as comprehensively as her family. It had been her husband who had made the call to her superiors, told them exactly what his wife had been up to, and with whom . . .

"Listen," she said, "I thought you'd like to know straightaway. We've got a provisional date for the trial."

It had been six weeks since the arrests of Eve Bloom and Ben Jameson. Since Thorne had been led from his own flat, a hand on his arm and a blanket around his shoulders, like so many victims he'd watched in the past, shuffling toward police cars and ambulances, saucer-eyed and colorless.

Now they would need to go through it all again. The case was already being put together, but now, with a date set, the pace would really pick up. The documentation had to be disclosed to the Crown Prosecution Service and the witnesses properly prepared. Everything had to be carefully gathered and shaped so that professionals could take it into a courtroom and use it to get a conviction.

Thorne of course would be spared the donkey work. His moment would come later, in the witness box.

Not that Thorne had ever *stopped* going through it . . .

In stark contrast to real life, Eve Bloom was always disturbingly honest in the Restorative Justice Conferences Thorne imagined with her daily. Of course there had never been the slightest interest in him sexually. If she'd wanted to, she could easily have slept with him at her place. What *wouldn't* have been so easy with a flatmate around was what she and her brother had been planning to do all along.

That she hadn't had the opportunity to do it sooner, to get Thorne where she wanted him at *his* place, was down to a seventeen-year-old smackhead who'd burgled Thorne's flat and, without knowing it, saved his life.

It was down to something else, too, of course . . .

Thorne had called it laziness. A fear of things going further. A reluctance to move a relationship along. Could it really have been something else altogether? Some indefinable instinct for self-preservation? Whatever it was, Thorne was grateful for it. He hoped, God forbid it should ever be needed, that he would recognize it next time around . . .

Thorne ended the call with Kitson and turned *Nixon* back up. He'd given Lambchop another chance and was pleased that he had. Their sound, somehow lush and stripped down at the same time, was hypnotic. He listened to the singer's strange whisperings and thought about the trial. He thought about wounds opening and scars healing, about others whose lives had been nudged, or knocked or smashed forever out of kilter . . .

Sheila Franklin and Irene Noble and Peter Foley . . .

Denise Hollins, who'd lived with one murderer and shared her bed with another. Thorne had stayed in touch with her, but their conversations were rarely easy. She could not even start to put together the intricate jigsaw of her shattered life, when so many of the tiny pieces had yet to be found.

Dave Holland, father of a three-day-old baby. Thorne was sure he would do his best to make the history of his own brand-new family a simple one . . .

Thorne's exit was coming up and he tried to focus on some of the more mundane elements of the court case.

He indicated and moved across to the inside lane, thinking about shaving off the beard he'd grown to cover the scar, and about getting his suit dry-cleaned. Thinking about reminding Phil Hendricks to take all his earrings out before giving evidence . . .

Thorne's father had the bits of two or three different radios spread out on the table in front of him. Every so often he'd slam a piece down or swear loudly in frustration. Then he'd look across at Thorne, sitting on the sofa, and grin like a child who's been caught misbehaving.

Thorne was looking at a picture of his father from maybe thirty years before. The majority of the old photo albums were faded and falling apart; none had been taken out of the sideboard since his mother had died. She had been the photographer, the one who always remembered to take along the Instamatic, who bought the albums from Boots and spent evenings pasting in the pictures . . .

Thorne looked from the photo to the real thing, from the young man to the old. His father looked up at him. Thorne noticed, as he always did, the hair that, like his own, was grayer on one side than the other.

"Do you want some tea?" his father said.

Thorne understood the code. "I'll make you some in a minute . . ."

He turned a stiff, faded page and stared at a picture of a young couple, their arms around a child of six or seven. The three of them sat, squinting against the sunlight, a deep green sea of bracken rising up behind them.

Thorne smiled at the can of beer in his father's hand, at the expression on his mother's face having talked some hapless passerby into taking the picture. He stared down at the boy, mugging happily at the camera. The brown eyes round and bright, the shadows yet to fall across his face.

Long before anybody died.

**DON'T MISS THE NEXT THRILLER
FROM
MARK BILLINGHAM**

THE BURNING GIRL

Available soon in hardcover from
William Morrow

Prologue

FEBRUARY

the price of
being human

Later, Carol Chamberlain would convince herself that she had actually been dreaming about Jessica Clarke when she got the first call. That the noise of the phone ringing had dragged her awake; away from the sound and the smell of it. The fuzzy picture of a girl running, the colors climbing up her back, exploding and flying at her neck like scarves of gold and crimson.

Whether the dream was imagined or not, she'd begun to see it all again the moment she'd put down the phone. Sitting on the edge of the bed, shivering; Jack, who had stirred only momentarily, dead to the world behind her.

She saw it all.

The colors were as bright, and the sound as clear and crisp as it had been that morning twenty years before. She was certain of it. Though Carol had not been there, had not seen any of it with her own eyes, she had spoken to everyone, *everyone* who had. Now she believed that when she ran over it in her mind, when she imagined it, she was seeing it all exactly as it had happened . . .

The sound—of the man's feet on the grass as he climbed the slope, of his tuneless humming—was drowned out by the noise from the playground. Beneath the high-pitched peaks of shouts and screams was a low throb of chatter and gossip, a wave of conversation that rolled across the playground and away down the hillside, toward the main road.

The man listened to it as he got nearer, unable to make out anything clearly. It would almost certainly be talk about boys and music. Who was in and who was out. He could hear another sound, too: the buzz of a lawnmower from the far side of the school where a team of gardeners was working. They wore green boiler-suits, and so did he. His was only missing the embroidered council logo.

Hands in his pockets, cap pulled down low on his head, he walked around the perimeter of the playground to where the girl and a bunch of her friends were gathered. A few of them were leaning back on the metal, cross-hatched fence, bouncing gently against it, relaxed.

The man removed the secateurs from his belt and squatted, inches away from the girls on the other side of the fence. With one hand, he began snipping at the weeds that sprouted around the base of a concrete fence post. With the other, he reached into his pocket for the can of lighter fluid.

It had always been the smell, more than anything, that had worried him. He'd made sure the can was full and there was not the faintest hiss or gurgle as he squeezed, as the jet of fluid shot from the plastic nozzle through the gap in the fence. His concern was that some hint of it, a whiff as it soaked into the material of the blue, knee-length skirt, might drift up on the breeze and alert the girl or one of her friends.

He needn't have worried. By the time he'd laid the can down on the grass and reached for the lighter, he'd used half the fuel at least, and the girls had been too busy chattering to notice anything. It surprised him that for fifteen seconds or more the girl's skirt smoldered quietly before finally catching. He was also surprised by the fact that she wasn't the one who screamed first . . .

Jessica had only one ear on Ali's story about the party she'd been to and Manda's tale of the latest tiff with her boyfriend. She was still thinking about the stupid row with her mum that had gone on the whole weekend, and the talking-to she'd been given by her father before he'd left for work that morning. When Ali pulled a face and the others laughed, Jessica joined in without really appreciating the joke.

It felt like a small tug at first, and then a tickle, and she leaned forward to smooth down the back of her skirt. She saw Manda's face change then, watched her mouth widen, but she never heard the sound that came out of it. Jessica was already feeling the agony lick at the tops of her legs as she lurched away from the fence and started to run . . .

Long distant from it now, Carol Chamberlain imagined the panic and the pain—as shocked as she always was at the unbearable events unfolding in her mind's eye.

Horribly quickly. Dreadfully slowly . . .

An hour before dawn, it was dark inside the bedroom, but the searing light of something unnatural blazed behind her eyes. With hindsight, with *knowledge*, she was everywhere, able to see and hear it all.

She saw girls' mouths gape like those of old women, their eyes big and glassy as their feet carried them away from the flames. Away from their friend.

She saw Jessica carve a ragged path across the playground, her arms flailing. She heard the screams, the thump of shoes against asphalt, the sizzle as the hair caught. She watched what she knew to be a child move like a thrown firework, skittering across a pavement. Slowing down, fizzing . . .

And she saw the face of a man, of *Rooker*, as he turned and jogged away down the slope. His legs moving faster and faster. Almost, but not quite, falling as he careered down the hill toward his car.

Carol Chamberlain turned and stared at the phone. She thought about the anonymous call she had received twenty minutes earlier. The simple message from a man who could not possibly have been Gordon Rooker.

"I burned her . . ."

ONE

The train was stationary, somewhere between Golders Green and Hampstead, when the woman stepped into the carriage.

Just gone seven on a Monday night. The passengers a pretty fair cross-section of Londoners heading home late, or into the West End to make a night of it. Suits and *Evening Standard*s. The office two-piece and a dog-eared thriller. All human life, in replica football kits and Oxfam chic and Ciro Citterio casuals. Heads bouncing against windows and lolling in sleep, or nodding in time to Coldplay or Craig David or DJ Shadow.

For no good reason other than it was on the Northern Line, the train lurched forward suddenly, then stopped again a few seconds later. People looked at the feet of those opposite, or read the adverts above their heads. The silence, save for the tinny basslines bleeding from headphones, exaggerated the lack of connection.

At one end of the carriage, two black boys sat together. One looked fifteen or sixteen but was probably younger. He wore a red bandanna, an oversized American football jersey and baggy jeans. He was laden with rings and necklaces. Next to him was a much smaller boy, his younger brother perhaps, dressed almost identically.

To the man sitting opposite them, the clothes, the jewelry, the *attitude* seemed ridiculous on a child whose expensive trainers didn't even reach the floor. The man was stocky, in his early forties, and wore a battered brown leather jacket. He looked away when the bigger boy caught him staring, and ran a hand through hair that was grayer on one side than the other. It looked, to Tom Thorne, as if the two boys had blown their pocket money in a shop called "Mr. Tiny Gangsta."

Within a second or two of the woman coming through the door, the atmosphere in the carriage had changed. From buttoned-up to fully locked-down. English, *in extremis* . . .

Thorne looked at her just long enough to take in the headscarf and the thick, dark eyebrows and the baby cradled beneath one arm. Then he looked away. He didn't quite duck behind a newspaper, like many of those around him, but he was ashamed to admit to himself that this was only because he didn't have one.

Thorne stared at his shoes, but was aware of the hand that was thrust out as the woman stood over him. He could see the polystyrene cup, the top of it picked at, or perhaps chewed away. He could hear the woman speak softly in a language he didn't understand and didn't need to.

She shook the cup in front of his face and Thorne heard nothing rattle.

Then it became a routine: the cup held out, the question asked, the plea ignored and on to the next. Thorne looked up as she moved away down the carriage, feeling an ache building in his gut as he stared at the curve of her back beneath a dark cardigan, the stillness of the arm that supported her baby. He turned away as the ache sharpened into a stab of sorrow for her, and for himself.

He turned in time to watch the older boy lean across to his brother. Sucking his teeth before he spoke. A hiss, like cats in a bag.

"I really hate them people . . ."

Thorne was still depressed twenty minutes later when he walked out of the tube station on to Kentish Town

Road. He wasn't feeling much better by the time he kicked the door of his flat shut behind him. But his mood would not stay black for long.

From the living room, a voice was suddenly raised, sullen and wounded, above the noise of the television: "What bloody time d'you call this?"

Thorne dropped his bag, took four steps down the hall and turned to see Phil Hendricks stretched out on the sofa. The pathologist was taller, skinnier and, at thirty-three, ten years younger than Thorne. He was wearing black, as always—jeans and a V-neck sweater—with the usual assortment of rings, spikes and studs through most of the available space on and around his face. There were other piercings elsewhere, but Thorne wanted to know as little about those as possible.

Hendricks pointed the remote and flicked off the television. "Dinner will be utterly ruined." He was normally about as camp as an armored car, so the jokey attempt at being queeny in his flat Mancunian accent made Thorne smile all the more.

"Right," Thorne said. "Like you can even boil an egg."

"Well, it *would* have been ruined."

"What are we having, anyway?"

Hendricks swung his feet down to the floor and rubbed a hand back and forth across his closely shaved skull. "Menu's next to the phone." He waved a hand toward the small table in the corner. "I'm having the usual, plus an extra mushroom bhaji."

Thorne shrugged off his jacket and carried it back out into the hall. He came back in, bent to turn down the radiator, carried a dirty mug through to the kitchen. He picked up Hendricks' biker boots from in front of the sofa and carried *them* out into the hall.

Then he picked up the phone and called the Bengal Lancer . . .

Hendricks had been sleeping on Thorne's sofa bed since just after Christmas, when the collection of mushrooms growing in his own place had reached monstrous proportions. The builders and damp-proofers were supposed to be there for less than a week, but as with all such estimates the reality hadn't quite matched up. Thorne was still unsure why Hendricks hadn't just moved in with his current boyfriend, Brendan—he still spent a couple of nights a week there as it was. Thorne's best guess was that, with a relationship as on and off as theirs, even a temporary move would have been somewhat risky.

He and Hendricks were a little cramped in Thorne's small flat, but Thorne had to admit that he enjoyed the company. They discussed, fully and frankly, the relative merits of Spurs and Arsenal. They argued about Thorne's consuming love of country music. They bickered about Thorne's sudden and uncharacteristic passion for tidiness.

While they were waiting for the curry to arrive, Thorne put on a Lucinda Williams album. He and Hendricks argued about it for a while, and then they began to talk about other things . . .

"Mickey Clayton died as a result of gunshot wounds to the head," Hendricks said.

Thorne peered across at him over the top of his beer can. "I'm guessing that wasn't one of your trickier ones. What with most of his head plastered all over the walls when we found him."

Hendricks pulled a face. "The full report should be on your desk tomorrow afternoon."

"Thanks, Phil." He enjoyed taking the piss, but, aside from being just about his closest friend, Hendricks was the best pathologist Thorne had ever worked with. Contrary to appearances, and despite the sarcasm and the off-color jokes, there was no one better at understanding the dead. Hendricks listened as they whispered their secrets, translating them from the mysterious language of the slab.

"Did you get the bullet?" Thorne asked. The killer had used a nine-millimeter weapon; what was left of the bullets had been found near the previous victims, or still inside what was left of their skulls . . .

"You won't need a match to tell you it's the same killer."

"The X?" It had been obvious when the body had been discovered the previous morning. The nylon shirt hoiked up to the back of the neck, the blood-trails running from two deep, diagonal cuts—left shoulder to right hip and vice versa.

"Still not sure about the blade, though. I thought it might be a Stanley knife, but I reckon it could be a machete, something like that."

Thorne nodded. A machete was the weapon of choice with a number of gangland enforcers. "Yardies or Yakuza, maybe . . ."

"Well, whoever's paying him, he's enjoying the work. He shoots them pretty quickly afterward, so I can't be a hundred percent sure, but I think he does his bit of creative carving while they're still alive."

The man responsible for the death of Mickey Clayton, and three men before him in the previous six weeks, was like no contract killer Thorne had ever come across or heard about. To these shadowy figures—men who were willing to kill for anything upward of a few thousand pounds—anonymity was everything. This one was different. He liked to leave his mark. "X marks the spot," Thorne said.

"Or X as in 'crossed out.'" Hendricks drained his can. "So, what about you? Good day at the office, dear?"

Thorne grunted as he stood up. He took Hendricks' empty can and went through to the kitchen to get them both fresh ones. Staring aimlessly into the fridge, Thorne tried in vain to remember his last good day at the office . . .

His team—of which Hendricks was the civilian member—at the Serious Crime Group (West) had been seconded to help out the Projects Team at SO7—the Serious and Organized Crime Unit. It had quickly become apparent that *organized* was one thing this particular operation was not. The resources of SO7 were stretched paper thin—or at least that was their story. There *was* a major turf war between two old family firms south of the river, and an escalation in a series of ongoing disputes among Triad gangs that had seen three shootings in one week and a pitched battle on Gerrard Street. All the same, Thorne suspected that he and his team were basically there to cover other people's arses.

There was nothing in it for him. If arrests were ever made, the credit would go elsewhere, and anyway, there was precious little satisfaction in chasing down those responsible for getting rid of pondlife like Mickey Clayton.

The series of fatal "X" shootings—of which Clayton's was the fourth—was a major assault on the operations of one of north London's biggest gangland families, but the simple fact was that the Projects Team hadn't the first idea who was doing the assaulting. All the obvious rivals had been approached and discounted. All the usual underground sources had been paid and pumped for information, none of which had proved useful. It became clear that a major new operation had established itself and was keen to make a splash. Thorne and his team were on board to find out who they were. Who was paying a contract killer, quickly dubbed the X-Man, to hurt the Ryan family?

"He's making life hard for himself, though, isn't he?" Thorne started talking from the kitchen and continued as he brought the beers into the living room. "This X thing, this signature or whatever it is, it limits what he can do, where he can do it. He can't just ride up on a motorbike or wait for them outside a pub. He needs a bit of time and space."

Hendricks took a can. "He obviously puts a lot of effort into his work. Plans it. I bet he's bloody expensive."

Thorne thought Hendricks was probably right. "It's still cheap though, isn't it? When you think about it. To kill someone, I mean. Twenty, twenty-five grand's about top whack. That's a damn sight less than the people putting out the contracts pay for their Jeeps and top-of-the-range Mercs."

"What d'you reckon I can get for a couple of hundred quid?" Hendricks asked. "There's this mortuary assistant at Westminster who's getting on my tits."

Thorne thought about it for a second. "Chinese burn?"

The laugh was the first decent one that Thorne could remember sharing with anyone for a few days . . .

"How can it be the Yardies?" Hendricks said when he'd stopped giggling. "Or Yakuza? We know our hitman's not black or Japanese . . ."

A witness claimed to have seen the killer leaving the scene of the third murder and had given a vague description of a white male in his thirties. The witness, Marcus Moloney, was an "associate" of the Ryan family, and not what you'd call an upright citizen, but he seemed pretty sure about what he'd seen.

"It's not that simple," Thorne said. "It might have been, ten years ago, when people stuck to their own, but now they don't care so much and the freelancers just go where the work is. The Triads use Yardies. Yardies work with the Russians. They nicked a gang of Yakuza last year for recruiting outside schools. They were as good as giving out application forms; signing up Greek lads, Asians, Turks, whoever."

Hendricks smiled. "It's nice to see that they're all equal-opportunities employers . . ."

Thorne grunted, and the two of them settled back into saying nothing for a few minutes. Thorne closed his eyes and picked at the goatee he'd grown toward the end of the previous year. The beard created the illusion of a jawline and covered up the scar from a knife wound.

The puckered line that ran diagonally across Thorne's chin was the only visible reminder of a night six months before when he'd both begged for his life and prayed for death to come quickly. There were other scars, easier to disguise, but far more troublesome. Thorne would reach into his gut in the darkness and finger them until they re-opened into wounds. He could imagine the scab forming then, blood black across the tender flesh. The crust that would itch and crumble beneath his fingernails, exquisite and agonizing, for him to poke and pick at . . .

Lucinda Williams sang softly about an all-consuming lust, her voice sweet and saw-toothed at the same time, rising like smoke above a single acoustic guitar.

Thorne and Hendricks both started slightly when the phone rang.

"Tom?" A woman's voice.

Thorne sank back into his armchair with the phone. He shouted across to Hendricks deliberately loud enough for the caller to hear, "Oh Christ, it's that mad old woman who keeps phoning me up . . ."

Hendricks grinned and shouted back, "Tell her I can smell the cat food from here!"

"Come on then, Carol," Thorne said. "Tell me what's been happening in glamorous Worthing. Any 'cat stuck up tree' incidents or Zimmer-frame pile-ups I should know about?"

The woman on the other end of the line was in no mood for the usual banter. "I need to talk to you, Tom. I need you to listen . . ."

So, Thorne listened. The curry arrived and went cold, but he didn't even think about it. He could tell as soon as she started to talk that something was seriously wrong.

In all the time he'd known Carol Chamberlain, Thorne had never heard her cry before.